# The Fool's Path

# The Fool's Path

NANCY J. ATTWELL

B

BOWMAN'S PRESS, LLC

2005

Published by Bowman's Press, LLC
PO Box 3836
Ithaca, NY 14852

Text is composed in Adobe Minion and Goudy Text.

FIRST EDITION

ISBN 1-933142-12-X    cloth
ISBN 1-933142-13-8    paper

LCCN: 2004112496

Printed in the United States of America

0  9  8  7  6  5  4  3  2  1

*To Anne Marie,*

*who said I could do it;*

*and*

*to Joanna Marie,*

*who gave me the reason.*

## Acknowledgements

I COULD NOT POSSIBLY NAME all the friends and family members who have supported and encouraged me as I've worked on *The Fool's Path*. To all of you who continued to ask, "How's that book coming along?" I thank you. Now, it's time to start asking me for the sequel!

In the writing/publishing world, I would like to thank the late Elizabeth Bowne (teacher), Carolyn Swayze (agent), Chris Pollock (writing partner), Jo Jackson (editor), Phil Wilson (designer), and authors Don McQuinn, Loranne Brown, Jeanne Mackin, and (soon-to-be-published) Susan Stone. (Check out their books!) My special thanks goes to Rosemary Daniell and all the women of Zona Rosa — a writers' workshop *extraordinaire*. (Check out Rosemary's new book, too.)

In the reading/critiquing world, I thank Anne Balys (retreat provider), Lynn Turnquist (chocolate caterer), Donna Zoller, Gudy Stevenson, Lynn Adams, Bekie Jackson, Douglas Land, Kirsten Zerbini, and Lucy Barcelo.

In the zany world of my home life, I thank my children, Michael, Daniel, Joanna, Stephen, Elizabeth, and Rose, for learning early that a sword is a wonderful gift. To my parents, Bert and Joyce, I also say thanks, for a lifetime of love and support.

And most of all, I thank my husband, Peter. For everything.

# The Fool's Path

A TALE FROM THE

Lothemian Legacy

# Chapter 1

EBASTIAN WAKENED to the whispered sound of a footstep beside his bed an instant before he felt the deadly chill of steel against his neck. For the briefest moment he felt no fear; surely this was one of Raynar's midnight jests. But the voice at his ear, familiar though it was, did not belong to his friend.

"Hold still, fool, as you value your life."

Westfeld's captain! The shiver of alarm which shook Sebastian brought him to full alertness. He could see the knight now, shadowed in the dim light thrown from the torches in the corridor, but could not yet tell how many others had invaded his chamber. Two, at least, judging by the oaths and groans coming from Raynar's pallet.

"You traitorous wretch," Sebastian said, forcing his words through clenched teeth. "My father will have your head for this."

"So, the pup looks to his sire for protection. Then you are twice a fool, Sebastian. Why do you think the duke summoned you to Eaglesheid, if not for this?"

"You lie." The accusation exploded from deep within, yet on the heel of that declaration came doubt. Had he not learned long ago that there were no certainties when dealing with the lord of Westfeld? Perhaps the duke had ordered this attack. But why?

Sebastian shook the implications of that thought from his mind, for this was not the time to dwell on the vagaries of the duke's temperament. Unless his ears deceived him, Raynar also had been accosted, which meant no help would be coming from that quarter. He must bend his wits to some other means of escape.

"I grant it is possible," he amended, "for despite your arrogance, you have not the stomach to act on your own." Under shield of conversation, Sebastian tensed his muscles. "But has the duke—my father—also ordered you to slit my throat?"

"Nay—"

"Then remove that blade. Now!" As he spoke, Sebastian rolled sideways off the bed, then crouched in ready defense. With equal speed his attacker pulled back the knife before it drew blood, but in the next motion slid his sword from his scabbard and pressed it to Sebastian's bare chest. Sebastian uncurled his back and stood tall, yet the blade held steady.

"The duke did not order me to slit your throat," the captain continued as though nothing had interrupted their conversation. "But neither did he forbid it. Would he condemn me for such a deed? Or would he instead ply me with reward? All men know that your four straight limbs are an affront to his own crippled ones. Every time he sees your long bones striding across his hall, he curses your birth. If your face did not so nearly mirror his own, he would have disavowed you long ago."

"I thought it was the fatted calf which was to be killed, not the returning son." Sebastian waited, hoping to see some hint that the captain recognized the absurdity of this situation, but when he saw no answering light in the man's eyes he steeled his will for the coming confrontation. "Beware, lest you forget that very birth you mock. Whether I hold my father's favor or not, I am heir to this accursed duchy and will one day be your lord."

"If you should live so long." The knight turned the sword and drew it upward, sliding it across the skin of Sebastian's chest until it reached the edge of his jaw, forcing his chin to an awkward angle. He held the point there for a long moment, then dropped it down to rest just beneath Sebastian's heart. "I will accomplish what I have been sent to do, never fear."

"Which is?"

A feral grin bared the captain's teeth. "To throw Raynar into the dungeon, of course."

At this unexpected answer, Sebastian jerked his eyes toward the pallet on the opposite side of the room. Two soldiers were tugging Raynar to his feet, twisting his arm so tightly that his shoulder arched high and his fingers splayed across his back. The blade of a misericorde was pressed against his throat.

The sight of Raynar's face, so grayed with pain that his squared chin seemed chiseled of stone, shocked Sebastian more than all else. "Have you gone mad? Raynar has done nothing to deserve such ill-usage, and you know it well."

"Do you think to sway me with such logic?"

"If you harm him, I swear, you will answer to me."

"You cannot brazen your way out of this with useless threats. Admit your defeat."

"I am no longer an impotent lad to be bullied at your will."

"You're wasting your breath." With a quick wave of his hand, the captain signaled to his men that they were to push Raynar toward the door. "If you value your own life, Sebastian, do not interfere."

"By all the saints," Sebastian roared, giving in to his anger at last. "Will you take him naked?"

The knight answered with a bold laugh. "If you stop your shouting and let us take him in peace, then he will receive every possible comfort. It's up to you."

"I will not agree to such a—"

"But you must, my friend." It was Raynar who interrupted, his voice rich with indifference though his arm was still pinioned behind his back. "I appreciate your willingness to be gutted by that sword for my sake. Even so, would it not be more to the point—if you will pardon my feeble attempt at humor—to seek audience with your father and learn the reason he is offering me the hospitality of his dungeon?"

Sebastian glanced heavenward. Must he now fight Raynar, too? "My father has neither the right nor the reason to abuse you so roundly," he said, more curtly than he intended.

"You forget that we are in the aerie of the Eagle now. Though I may not like it, he may treat me as he wills."

"Will you jest even as he devours you?"

"Assuredly. If I still have my tongue. But as long as there is a sword at my back I intend to meekly follow wherever the good captain leads." Raynar paused, then continued with more intensity. "Think, Sebastian! At this moment it is not my life on the balance, but yours. And I would rather not be forced to step over your body when I leave this room."

There was no denying Raynar's simple logic.

"Very well, then." Sebastian turned and glared at his father's captain. "Do as you have said, but listen well to my warning. I am Sir Raynar's liege and I will not suffer him to be harmed."

"You would do well to listen to Raynar's words. We are in the Eagle's aerie, and if he orders Raynar's head delivered on a trencher, I will gladly obey. So pray, Sebastian, that he does not."

Once Raynar had been pushed out into the passageway—fully clothed and carrying his bedroll beneath his arm—the door to the chamber slammed shut and Sebastian was left alone. Groaning aloud, he let fly a volley of sharpened curses aimed directly at his own stupidity. He should have known that his father had not sent for him out of any fond desire for his company. Why had he been blinded by the warm welcome and pleased by the goblets upraised in his honor? Had not twenty-eight years of experience taught him that Westfeld cared for nothing beyond his ceaseless need for revenge?

Grabbing up his tunic, he pulled it over his head with such ferocity that it stung his ear; but after he had thrust his arms into the holes and tugged the linen down to cover his hips, he paused. Was not this headlong rush exactly what his father expected? Surely some part of his plan was to place his son at a disadvantage in their coming confrontation. Tousled and hurried and reckless with anger, Sebastian would be no match for the calm superiority of the duke of Westfeld. Without a doubt, even now Duke Frederick was seated in his chair, eagerly awaiting the moment his son burst into his bedchamber spouting curses like an idiot.

Let the duke wait, then. And let him wonder if he had misjudged his son.

Sebastian crossed to the roughly-hewn oak chest which lodged his belongings. His fingers delved beneath the well-worn tunics and chausses to the more finely-wrought fabrics below. Each piece of clothing he would wear tonight would serve a purpose. Armor over linen, silk over iron, leather over silk, gold around the leather. The eagle of Westfeld around his neck, to proclaim his birthright. The chevrons of Terlinden etched into his buckler, to recall the powerful baron who had trained him and given him his sword. And most important of all, the lion of Lothemia pinned to his breast, to remind his father that he stood high in the favor of the king.

Though the night was still dark when Sebastian entered his father's chamber, Duke Frederick of Westfeld was fully robed and seated in the chair beside his bed. His black beard carried threads of gray, yet implied no weakness. Indeed, the flickering light from the candles emphasized the angular lines of his face while casting shadows of height and strength. His good right leg was thrust forward and the fingers of his right hand were curled over the wooden arm to prominently display his signet ring emblazoned with the twin-headed eagle of Westfeld.

Willing himself to patience, Sebastian strode across the carpeted floor until he stood a spear's length from his father. "Why did you order Raynar's arrest?"

"It served my purpose."

"Which is?"

Westfeld's answering smile was as thin and frosty as his hair. "To bring you here. I desire words with you. Words which will not wait until morn."

Sebastian stared at his father in disbelief. "Are you telling me that you ordered a midnight attack by the man who has always treated me more like a cur than your son, simply because you wished me to come to your chamber?"

"I did."

"Whyever did you not just send for me?"

The duke shrugged as though it were of no importance. "I wished to be certain you would come."

"I came to Eaglesheid at your bidding without tarrying even a day, though Terlinden urged me not to make such haste. Why would I refuse to come these few steps further to your chamber? I am your son." After a slight hesitation, he added, "And I am ever ready to obey your wishes."

"It pleases me to hear that." Westfeld relaxed against the wooden back of his chair and waved his hand in a gesture that simulated apology. "Perhaps, I have been overzealous in my actions."

Wary of a costly misstep, Sebastian gave the expected reply. "Tell me what it is you wish, my lord, and it shall be done."

In response, his father stood and began to circle the room in his slow, rolling gait. When finally he stopped at the foot of the bed and caressed its silken hangings, his dark eyes were glistening with anticipation. "I have received word that my enemy has at last left the safety of his own borders and is traveling north."

"Branold?" Sebastian's head began to ache. "After all these years? Take care, my lord. He is no longer a powerless younger son, but duke of Gildren in his own right. And connected by marriage to half the houses of Lothemia."

"*His own right?* By his own wrongs, you mean! To inherit that duchy, three older brothers had first to die. How Branold must have gloated as each one fell from the tree until his was the only remaining branch. First he stole a wife and then a ducal crown." Shaking his fist, Westfeld's face contorted until it seemed more twisted than his limbs. "And while Branold was out thieving and murdering his way to power, good King Stefan sat on his throne and did nothing."

"No one, but you, believes Gildren responsible for the fate of his brothers."

"Am I not the one with reason to know the villainous heart behind his beguiling smile? Mark well my words. No matter how long it takes, I will see Branold humbled." Having finished his outburst, the duke relaxed. Once again his eyes grew bright with pleasure. "It is my good fortune that Branold has never understood the depth of my desire for his destruction. Some ten days ago he left his duchy escorted by only a small company, and sped north. My spies followed as he passed through Terlinden's lands until he at last crossed the river into Bestilden. It is perfect! Twice before I have sent men to capture him and twice before I have failed. But this time he will be mine."

"And why are you so confident of victory this time?" Sebastian asked, though he feared he knew the answer.

"Because this time I am sending a knight who is renowned for his feats of arms throughout the kingdom of Lothemia and beyond. A knight with a mesnie so well-trained that he carries away the greatest prizes at every tournament he enters. A knight who can not only gain free passage into the lands of Terlinden to set an ambush, but is so well-known there that he will surely hear news of Branold, while Branold will hear no rumor of *his* coming. I am sending you, Sebastian. And that is why I will not fail."

"I'll not do it," Sebastian answered without hesitation.

"You dare to refuse me?"

"I am not oath-bound to you, my lord. The land I hold, I hold from the king. I give you my filial obedience but it does not extend to this. To take a duke of the realm into captivity without warning or reason is—"

"Without reason?" Duke Frederick shouted. "The man abducted my betrothed as she traveled to her wedding beneath the protection of my banner. Have you forgotten?"

"I have not." He had been only ten, but the violent rage which had been unleashed when the duke had learned he had been cuckolded was something Sebastian would never forget. Even at that young age, his horror that his father would lift his sword to strike down the messenger of the ill-tidings had been tinged with relief that the bride had been spared a life of certain misery. "Nor have I forgotten your oath of revenge. But nearly two decades have passed. And what is more, not only has the Lady Judith long since died, but Gildren has taken a second wife and you have remarried— thrice!"

"If you think the passage of years will dim the need of a man for vengeance, you are a fool."

"I think a man is a fool who has need of such vengeance." Sebastian watched his father flush at the insult then deliberately softened the impact of his words. "Do you not think, my lord, that the Lady Judith brought

Gildren his own punishment? She bore him but two daughters and then died, leaving her mother in his care. And that wretched old woman is rumored to be cursed by God. You should be grateful that he took the lady and saved you from such a fate."

"That may be the justice of God, and it may be fitting, but nonetheless I will have my own. And you," he pointed his finger at Sebastian while impaling him with the sharpness of his gaze, "shall be my instrument for that revenge."

"And if I refuse?"

"Then your friend, Raynar, will remain in Eaglesheid's dungeon."

The duke had sprung his trap at last and caught Sebastian in its teeth. Now he must writhe as he sought some means of escape. From painful experience, he knew that even should he succeed, some vital part of him would be left behind.

"This has nothing to do with Raynar." He kept his voice low, as though bargaining for some bauble at the fair.

"You speak truly. I was grieved to order his arrest. He is an amusing companion with a quick and witty tongue. It does seem a shame that he must endure the cellars for a matter in which he is innocent." The tilt of Westfeld's head indicated he had not finished as he paused to resettle himself in his chair. He leaned forward and grinned. "But I will have my prisoner. And if you will not bring me Gildren, who is guilty, then I will take Raynar, who is not."

"Have you sunk so low that you would punish a guest who has done you no harm?"

Duke Frederick shook his head and sighed as though he could not believe his son's lack of insight. "You mistake me. I thought I made myself plain. You are my target, Sebastian. I know well the agonies of conscience that tear everlastingly at your heart, and I know that you will suffer twice over for every discomfort Raynar endures."

"Then why not just imprison me and be done with it?"

"But what would I gain? I still would not have my revenge. And you, with your monkish sensibilities, would be smugly proud of your sufferings. No, Sebastian. You must make the choice. Will you hold to your honor as a knight; and let your companion-in-arms rot away in an airless stinking cell? Or will you succumb to pity for a friend; and betray your chivalrous oaths? I repeat my words. You must make the choice. And then you must live with the consequences."

Not willing that his father should see his face, Sebastian swung around and crossed to the window. What manner of man would demand such a sacrifice of honor from his only son and heir, for no greater purpose than to salve his wounded pride? And what would Westfeld gain should Sebastian be successful in his attack upon Gildren? Land? Spoils of war? A woman for his bed? Nothing. Nothing save revenge, and the scorn of all the knights of Christendom.

He planted his hands on the stone sill and leaned forward. Overhead, the stars glistened, a shimmering blanket that eased the darkness of the night. Carried on the cool night air came the pungent tang of the river and the hollowed sound of the barges bumping against the wooden pier. He closed his eyes. Beyond these walls, beyond the duchy of Westfeld, lay freedom. A world where his father's wishes did not hold sway. But he could never ride away. Not if it meant leaving Raynar behind. They had been friends too many years. Sent together when they were still lads to be fostered in Terlinden's household, they had won their spurs and set out to make their names. Together they had learned of wine and war and women. Together they had cursed and bled and triumphed. And together they had forged a friendship so strong that nothing, and no one, could tear it apart. Sebastian would sooner lose his own life than allow Raynar to be treated in so cruel a manner. He had no choice. The duke would win. He'd have his prisoner and his revenge. Sebastian would do as his father demanded—but first he must wrest some small victory from the talons of the Eagle.

"I yield." He spun around to face his father. "I will do it. I will bring Branold of Gildren to you. With one condition."

"And what is that?"

"You must first free Raynar to come with me."

Westfeld gaped, as though he thought Sebastian were the lunatic. "Do you think me senile that I cannot see the folly in that?"

"Without Raynar I will not succeed."

"Phah! There is none to equal you. The stories of your prowess are legion."

"Since when did you start believing in tales told to children? Whatever skill I have, it is because in every battle I have ever fought, Raynar has been at my side. He *is* my right hand." Holding his father's gaze, Sebastian slowly crossed the room until he was so close that he towered over the duke. "Why would you order me into battle, then cripple me before I go?" He pointed down at his father's twisted leg. "Is this your ultimate retribution against my sound limbs? Or is it something more? Do you fear victory? Is that why your enemy has always eluded capture? If you gain your revenge, will you lose your reason to hate?"

"You speak nonsense." Duke Frederick was taut with anger.

"Do I? Then prove it. Release Raynar to me. And though my word should suffice, I will give whatever pledge you ask in assurance that I will bring Branold of Gildren here, to be your prisoner."

Duke Frederick did not answer immediately. His eyes narrowed and his knotted fingers drummed out the rhythms of his thoughts. When their pace grew faster and then abruptly ceased, Sebastian knew his father had reached his decision.

"So be it." With his voice as sharp as a blade, the duke cut deep. "You shall swear by your own life that you will bring Branold here to Eaglesheid. But if you fail me, it is your blood I will demand. Mark me well, Sebastian. If you fail, it is you who will pay the price."

Sebastian stared at his father, searching for some small sign that he had not truly meant his words; the duke, unflinching, met his gaze.

Intense loneliness washed over him. This man was so devoid of paternal feeling that he would prefer to be barren of offspring than to turn aside even one step from his long-chosen path. Further argument would serve no purpose. Nodding his agreement Sebastian turned to leave the room, but even then, he hesitated, pausing on the threshold, waiting. The silence stretched on, until at last the loneliness vanished, to be replaced by a coldness so deep he doubted it could ever thaw.

Without looking back, Sebastian left Westfeld behind.

# Chapter 2

SEBASTIAN LAUGHED ALOUD, a clear, joyous sound that res-
onated across the courtyard, blended with the muffled notes of
the lutes, and was then joined in turn by the echoing laughter of
the sentries on the royal ramparts of Breden.

"Are you ready, my friend?" He grinned as he poked Raynar's huge belly,
sinking his fingers deep into the feather-filled cushion tucked beneath the
voluminous gown. "Are you firmly seated on that donkey?"

Raynar adjusted the smaller bolster that padded his chest, then tucked
the last few strands of hair beneath the laced edging of his wimple. His eyes
were dancing, but he sighed as though he were sorely aggrieved. "However
did the Lady Mary endure the journey to Bethlehem in such an awkward
condition? I shall be fortunate not to tumble from the back of this ass before we walk through that doorway. Since you were the one who thought to
stir again the warmth of the king's affection by approaching in such guise,
why am I the one to suffer this discomfort? Why are *you* not sitting atop
this beast?"

Sebastian laughed again. "You won the toss, did you not? And it is well
t'was you and not I, for my knees would be doubled beneath my chin.
Besides, you look such a lovely maid. Who could resist those brown eyes of
yours, so wide and round, just like a mooning calf."

"Thank you, my Lord Joseph." Raynar drew the edge of his headpiece across his face and fluttered his lashes. "But not too virginal, I hope?"

The young guard standing erect at the hall entrance made a valorous attempt to restrain his mirth, but when Raynar winked, he nearly choked on his laughter as he called out, "Welcome to Breden, my lords. Or rather...my lord and my lady."

"Make haste, my good man." Sebastian patted the Saracen robe he wore over his own tunic. "I am dressed for the desert but it is cold here in the yard."

Though his words were light, apprehension now clenched his belly. Nearly two years had passed since he had laid his ambush and so completely surprised Gildren that the battle had been over in minutes. While Gildren's men had been stripped of their weapons then released to fly home with the news of their lord's capture, the duke, himself, had been swiftly carried off to Eaglesheid. Of course, the matter had not ended there. Gildren's nephew, Gregory of Marre, had soon arrived with a small army and pitched camp on the plain surrounding Eaglesheid. But this attempt at rescue had been foiled when Westfeld sent word that if one spear were launched against the walls, he would bring the prisoner onto the ramparts and lop off his head. Gregory had withdrawn, and since that day the impasse had remained unbroken: Gildren's supporters harangued the king; the king entreated and commanded Westfeld; and Westfeld perched on his ducal chair—and laughed.

Guilt-ridden for the part he had played in Gildren's downfall, Sebastian had not dared to approach the king; not even when news of the untimely death of the king's only son had arrived these three months past. Would the king welcome his return now? Or would he be sent scuttling from court in disgrace?

The guard pushed down on the latch, swung open the great wooden door which led to the king's hall, and signaled to the trumpeter. A few moments later a series of shrill notes sliced through the din. As curious eyes turned to the doorway, Sebastian led the donkey forward.

With perfect timing, just before the babble began once more, Raynar pitched his voice high and false. "I have traveled far and am weary. Is there no room at this inn?"

An applause of uproarious laughter rang out, filling the hall to the rafters. "That is Sebastian," called out someone. "Surely the fair Mary can be none other than Raynar."

At that, Raynar, who was sitting begowned, beveiled, and titanically pregnant on the back of the donkey, dismounted and hoisted his skirt to reveal a hosed and well-muscled leg. A cry went up, "Raynar! Sebastian!" which soon became a chant as the two penitents were escorted through the cheering crowd to the dais where Lothemia's king and queen sat on a pair of gilded thrones.

"So you come at last, Sebastian." King Stefan indicated they should both draw near. "I wondered when you would gather your courage and come stand before me again. I doubted you would spend the rest of your life skulking behind the walls of Eaglesheid with your shame."

Sebastian dipped his head. "I am here now, sire. I am ever your humble servant."

"I trust no more of my barons will disappear into your father's aerie?"

"Upon my honor, sire."

"And why do you choose this moment to approach me? What is your desire?"

"To take my place at your side once more as a counselor and a friend."

"Then I command you to seek a way to end this foolishness."

"You know that Westfeld pays little heed to my words."

"Then you must find the right words! Even the toughest dragon has a vulnerable underbelly—a point of weakness." The king's eyes glinted hard, then softened as he sighed, "I am tired, Sebastian. I desire an end to this matter. Perhaps the recent death of my son has addled my mind, but I cannot bear to watch a good man waste his years away. Find a way to release Branold without bloodshed. I command this as your king and liege; but I ask it as your friend."

Relieved, Sebastian bowed his acquiescence.

"And now you…Raynar?" Turning from Sebastian, King Stefan raised his brow at the muscular maiden standing before him, then pointed at Raynar's rounded belly. "I see you have abandoned your chastity since last we met. As your king, I demand a penance from you."

"A penance, sire?" Gripping the sides of his gown, Raynar gave an exaggerated curtsey. "Surely I have instead earned a reward this Christmas eve? A bale of hay for my donkey, perhaps? And another for my bed? Hay, I mean, of course."

At last the king smiled. "Well said. Your reward will be to sit in my presence and amuse me awhile." But the moment he had spoken, the smile disappeared and he took the queen's hand into his own. "Few men have wit enough to make me laugh these days. Though I grieved deeply last summer when I sent my daughter, Elisabeth, in marriage to King Maximilian of Albenar, that parting was a sliver compared to the dagger which now has been thrust into my heart. I cannot bear that my son is dead, yet I still live."

Sebastian's own worries seemed suddenly light compared to the depth of pain he saw in this man's eyes. "Your sorrow is well-placed, sire," he said, as he sought a way to soothe Stefan's grief. "The prince was a worthy knight and a worthy son. His passing is indeed lamented."

Knowing well that Raynar's company would uplift the king more than his own, Sebastian soon discarded his costume and began to work his way across the hall towards the warmth of the hearth; but the cavernous room was crowded, especially near the burning Yule log, and soon he gave up and paused to look around. Boughs of cedar, woven together with precious threading, depended from the rafters and draped from the lintels. Circlets of ivy and holly, dotted with ruby-red berries, covered the tapestried walls; sprigs of mistletoe and bay adorned the tables. But most impressive of all was the paradise tree, an enormous evergreen with apples hanging from its branches, that towered over all else in the center of the hall.

Without a doubt, the king had prepared a Yuletide celebration to surpass all those that had gone before. Sebastian lifted his shoulders and breathed deeply. It was good to know that Stefan had not lost the political keenness that had always served him well. Though the man might mourn in private, the king must never forget that he had lost more than a son: He had lost his only heir. Unless he regally displayed his strength for all his realm to see, the wolves would soon begin to circle around the weakened remnants of his dynasty.

Again Sebastian shrugged, this time to dismiss all such thoughts from his mind. Why should he concern himself with matters of state today? The minstrels singing in the gallery had the right of it—it was Yuletide—time for music, and wine, and love!

A squire, dressed in the crimson and blue livery of Lothemia, stood by a cask of beer. He was ladling as quickly as goblets of horn, or pewter, or leather, could be brought to him. Beside him, another man was working the spigot of a wine butt with equal dexterity.

Sebastian quaffed the remaining mouthful in his goblet and moved toward the butler, but had taken little more than a step when he was distracted by someone calling his name. He turned and grinned. With her colorful gown billowing about her, and the trailer of her headpiece shaking as she vigorously waved her hand, Lady Bertha looked rather more like a jousting pavilion than a duchess.

"Come here, you young rapscallion," she shouted out her command. "You are needed over here."

"My lady," he said, as he kissed her proffered hand then bent down and affectionately dropped a kiss on each of her cheeks. "I am pleased to see you. Are you alone? Or is my lord of Terlinden in your company?"

"Surely you know that I go nowhere without Gebbard."

Sebastian laughed in agreement. "I do. And he returns the favor, my lady. There is no more uxorious man in the world."

"How do you fare, Sebastian? It is nigh on two years since we saw you last. Does your father, the duke, treat you well?"

"Well enough," Sebastian answered, still smiling, though with effort now.

She peered at him closely. "And his prisoner? How does Gildren fare?"

All mirth fled. "He is well. And as content as a man may be who can see freedom from his window daily, yet can never reach out and grasp it."

"And what is the intent of your father in this matter?"

"My lady, you err if you think that Westfeld shares his purposes with me."

"Then whyever do you linger there?" Her eyes peeked out from her flesh like moons faintly glimmering in the folds of the dusk. "Why do not you and Raynar mount up your horses and ride far away from Eaglesheid?"

Sebastian hesitated, then answered her honestly, for this woman had been as a mother to him during the many years he had fostered at Terlinden and there was no need to dissemble. "My greatest desire is to shake the dust of Eaglesheid from my boots. I wish nothing more of Westfeld. Neither the duchy nor the duke. Yet I cannot forget that I am the one who brought Branold to Eaglesheid and thus am responsible for his fate. Quite simply, I do not wish to see him die. I hope that my presence there might delay that evil day, though I have no doubt that it will come."

"And will you then raise your sword in his defense?"

"I know not." Sebastian faced her directly. "Truly, I know not the answer to that question, though it is one I have asked myself many times; but I greatly fear that Westfeld asks the same question, and accordingly, may one day order Branold to his death simply to put me to the test."

"So, if a way could be found to free Gildren without a bloodletting, you would be willing to lend your aid?"

A light sparked within Sebastian's eyes, an eager flame that brightened their dark depths. "Not only am I willing, but I have received the king's command to do the task. Do you know a way he may be freed?"

"I have an idea but it is only a seed in my mind. I intend to water it and see if it will grow. But come, Sebastian, that is not why I called you. There is a game of musical round-about beginning here and your lap is needed. I tried to persuade Sir Bevis to join, but he claims his old bones will no longer bend. You cannot have any such excuse."

"My knees are yours to command, my lady, for they are as easily bent as the virtue of a maid." He then raised his brows in mock gravity. "And speaking of maidens, are you also joining the game?"

"Incorrigible." She poked his chest and pushed him back toward the whirling circle of players. "If you do not watch your tongue, I'll sit on your lap myself, and then see just how much bending you will do, whether it be of knees or virginal virtues."

Lady Bertha had not set him to an onerous task. Far from it. Every few minutes the vielle would cease its raspy tune, and another girl, giddy with laughter, would throw herself onto his lap while squealing with delight.

With each round, the circle of kneeling knights grew smaller and the frauleins grew more abandoned in their attempts to remain in the game by claiming a seat. Twice, Sebastian lost his balance and was thrown backward onto the rushes, landing with his partner in a wanton heap.

The clapping and the cheering grew louder, until he alone was left with two maids dancing around and around him, swirling in time to the music. The musician teased the audience by winding out his tune until it seemed he would never stop and then, suddenly, dropped his bow.

Once more, Sebastian was toppled over by the buxom fraulein who threw herself into his arms. But in the same instant that he embraced the curves of the maid who claimed the victory, his eyes met those of the other—and he fell.

The paradise tree, its red fruit dangling from golden threads, framed her where she stood. She was the fairest creature he had ever seen. Sweet. Delicious. Her arched brows marked eyes that were heavily-rimmed with lashes. Her cheeks were high, yet soft. Her hair, as rich in color as a polished cherry-wood trestle tumbled across her shoulders. And her lips begged for kissing.

"Well done, Sir Knight." The ripples of her laughter cascaded around her.

It was impossible for him to speak. He was sprawled lengthwise on the rushes, firmly weighted-down by the victor who had her arms entwined around his neck and was boldly claiming her prize by covering his mouth with kisses. With as much enthusiasm as he could muster, Sebastian returned a kiss, loosened the clinging arms, and lifted the girl to her feet.

But the entrancing nymph had disappeared.

Scanning the crowd, he could see no sign of her, not even a swirling trace of her holly-hued velvet. Intent on his search, he started forward but was again interrupted by Lady Bertha.

"Why so downcast, Sebastian?"

"You mistake me," he protested. "I am searching for someone. Have you seen the girl who nearly caught me in the game? The small one, with curls the color of honey?"

The duchess plucked a sprig of the evergreen tree and, stretching high, tucked it behind Sebastian's ear. "I'm not so certain that Katrina didn't catch you after all. Your face is nearly as scarlet as that embroidery on the edge of your tunic."

"Do you know her?" Sebastian swiveled around to look full at the duchess. "A little."

"Who is she?" Sebastian knew he sounded like a squire in the throes of calf-love, but he did not care.

"I give you fair warning that you'll not be pleased." Lady Bertha's voice was stern, but it was belied by the look of anticipation that illumined the creases of her face. "She is Katrina. Of Gildren."

A cold wave of shock rolled over Sebastian, and he shivered. "She is Branold's daughter?" His question sounded to his own ears like a distant echo drifting across a void.

She fluttered her fingers in front of his face as she crooned with delight. "You really have fallen into the abyss of love. I was certain the fraulein would appeal to you, yet still I supposed I should have to nudge you over the edge."

"Do you jest with me, or do you speak with certainty? Is she in truth of Gildren?" He held his breath, hoping to hear that Lady Bertha had been engaged in some mummery of her own.

But she shook her head in denial. "She is Gildren's daughter, no doubt. The eldest of his two by that very Judith who ought to have been your father's bride. I have already spoken with the child at length. She is charming. And innocent. She would make a perfect wife. Indeed, I have been thinking that I should arrange a betrothal between the fraulein ... and Derick. Do you think, Sebastian, that Gildren could be persuaded to approve such a match between his daughter and my eldest son?"

Sebastian's emotions had been buffeted with such bruising rapidity that he could barely comprehend this added information. To have fallen so suddenly beneath the spell of a total stranger, only to learn that she was the daughter of the man to whom he owed the greatest debt in this world, was burden enough. And now, moments later, he was being asked to consider the merits of her marriage to another!

He stared down at Lady Bertha as he tried to focus his scattered thoughts onto her question. "My lady, whyever would he not agree to such a match? Not only would his daughter be wed to the future duke of Terlinden but he, himself, would have a powerful new ally who sits on the border of Westfeld—his enemy and jailer. All that, plus the dower lands which would enrichen his purse! Such an arrangement could only be to Gildren's advantage."

"And what would your father do when he heard of such an alliance?"

"His fury would blister the walls of Eaglesheid."

"But would he attempt to prevent the betrothal?"

"Assuredly. If he could see the means to do it."

She inclined her head. "And might he not be so desperate to find that way, that he would urge his own son to steal the fraulein from Derick?"

Sebastian's lips tightened. "I have had enough of abductions, my lady. I would not do it, whatever the reason."

"I do not mean an abduction," she scolded. "The days when a man could woo and win a woman by throwing her over his saddle have passed."

"Then I do not understand your meaning."

She leaned forward and lowered her voice. "By providing your father with the means to strip Gildren of all matrimonial gain."

"I don't see how—"

"Gildren's freedom in exchange for your marriage to his daughter. A simple exchange. Think of the humiliation for Gildren to have to abandon a brilliant alliance, gaining nothing beyond his own life. What is more, once married, Katrina would no longer be an asset of Gildren but, instead, would be a weapon in the hands of Westfeld." She placed her hand on Sebastian's arm to calm his agitation. "You and I may not agree with such reasoning, but I am persuaded that is how your father would view the matter. Or, could be so led. And if he thought that you go unwillingly to the marriage, his eagerness for the union would only increase."

"Are you saying," Sebastian answered after a long silence, "that you do not truly wish your son to marry Fraulein Katrina? That you only offer Derick as bait to force my father to negotiate my own marriage to her? And thus to spring Gildren from his trap?"

"That is precisely what I am saying."

"But why? Why would you do such a thing? What reason do you have to desire that Branold have his freedom?"

"Sebastian," she said. "You ate at my board for nearly a dozen years. You trained with my sons and played at love with my daughters. It is not Gildren I would free, for his fate means little to me. It is you."

He looked over her head to the majestic pine that reached to more than half the height of the hall. But its strength was a chimera, for the mighty trunk had been shorn from its roots. Already the branches were turning brittle and the needles were beginning to fall. It was destined for the fire.

Gently, he took Lady Bertha's hand into his own. "My lady, I owe Branold of Gildren a great debt. Yet now we speak of matters that could send him to his death. Do you not realize that were one whispered word to reach the ears of Westfeld linking my name with that of Gildren's daughter, then he would immediately have Gildren put to the sword? Nothing would please my father more than to wound so many with one well-aimed stroke."

"Then you had best make certain that no word does reach his ear. But do you not understand that fate has given you a chance to make amends to Gildren and to heal the wound in your own soul? I tell you truly, Sebastian, that you are a fool if you turn aside now. If you fail, what will be lost? Nothing will have changed. You already know that Gildren's head sits very lightly on his shoulders. But if you win—if you can beat your father in the game to which he has been making all the rules—then Gildren will have his freedom. And you? You, Sebastian, will have the fair Katrina for your bed."

# Chapter 3

LEANOR SAT ON HER BED in the half-dark, more alone and more afraid than ever before in her sixteen years. Reason told her to rise and light the torch in the rack beside the door, but instinct was stronger. Wrapping her arms around her legs, burying her face in her knees, she remained still, and listened.

"Open the door, fraulein, " a deep voice commanded. "It's Wolfram. I have your sister."

Katrina! Willing herself to a calmness she did not feel, Eleanor flew across the room, slid the lock from its sheath, and flung open the door. Then she gasped, for Wolfram the One-Eared was holding Katrina limp and unconscious in his arms.

"What has happened to her?" she cried out, but before he could answer she grabbed his sleeve and pulled him into the room. "Lay her down. But be careful!"

Hovering at his side while he knelt and laid Katrina onto the narrow bed, Eleanor held her questions until her sister was settled; then, she turned to Wolfram with a fierceness which would brook no delay. "What has my lady done to her?"

"She has been beaten. But, praise be to the saints, one of the lads ran to fetch me. The boy knew I would not let your stepmother mistreat the

Lady Judith's daughter. I came as quickly as I could; but, alas, not quickly enough."

"Bring me light." Keeping her eyes on her sister while he kindled the torch, Eleanor prepared herself. Even so, she groaned in dismay. A half-dozen lashes had been laid across Katrina's back. The wounds were not deep, but dark blood soaked the remnants of her gown. With great care, Eleanor peeled away the strips of cloth, breathing a prayer of thankfulness that her sister had lost all consciousness.

"These will heal," she said, after peering at the wounds; but her voice shook and she clutched her hands together to stop their trembling. Katrina, eldest daughter of Branold of Gildren, had been pampered all her life as thoroughly as any gyrfalcon. Even Duchess Isabel, their stepmother, who had ruled alone during these two years of her husband's captivity, had never denied her anything. Yet now Katrina's fair skin was scored with raw and bleeding flesh.

"Why has she done this?"

Wolfram turned to Eleanor with some surprise. "But you were there in the solar when this began, were you not?"

"I saw nothing which helps me understand!" She jumped to her feet and began to pace the room. "We were making thread and chatting as usual about matters of no importance, when Katrina pushed aside her spindle and stopped working. Then, without any warning, Isabel suddenly erupted into such a rage you would think the very walls would collapse beneath her fury. Shrieking like a demon forced to swallow sacred bread, she grabbed Katrina by her hair and lifted her from the stool."

"There must have been more," he pressed.

"I tell you, there was nothing. No words passed between them at all." Eleanor stopped mid-step, and blushed. "At least none that I can repeat. Then the guard came running in with John at his heels and I frantically tried to get them to pull Isabel away from her because she was shaking and shaking her, but when she screeched at them to take me to my room to be dealt with later, the guard actually lifted me over his shoulder and carried me from the room." Eleanor clutched Wolfram's arm. "I have chased my thoughts around and around but I cannot understand. What has angered her so?"

"I know not, but I have never trusted that interloper. She is a viper brought by your own father to dwell within his household."

Eleanor shook her head in vehement disagreement. Unlike Wolfram, she had respected Isabel ever since her arrival at Ravensberg four years before, a young bride scant years older than Katrina and Eleanor themselves. It seemed to her that Isabel had met a difficult challenge with spirit and grudging grace—until today. Today, something had gone terribly awry.

"There must be a reason," she insisted. "But until we know what it is, how can we know when next her fury may explode?"

Wolfram pursed his lips and frowned as he looked down at Katrina. Her right arm was propped on the pillow but her left hung limply to the floor. With great tenderness he lifted her fingers and placed them beside her brow; then he touched the right side of his own head where his ear ought to have been. "I fought for your father on that long-ago day when he took your mother for his bride, saving her from marriage to that black-bearded ogre of Westfeld. I would have given more than my ear for the Lady Judith. I would have given my life. Trust me now, fraulein, I will allow no one to harm you or your sister again."

"But how? You hold little power here."

"I'll send for your cousin, Gregory."

Though the words were spoken with assurance, Eleanor knew they had cost him dear. Wolfram's loyalties were absolute and undivided. Any man who admired the duke's second wife was a traitor to the memory of the first. And Gregory of Marre was one of the myriad of men who admired Isabel very much.

"Thank you," Eleanor said. "It is well-thought. In Papa's absence, our cousin is the only one who holds authority above Isabel. Bid him come straight away."

"I will send a messenger at first light tomorrow."

"Now you must go, Sir Wolfram, for Katrina needs my care. Send a girl with some fresh water and a poultice of comfrey and thyme."

"Yes, mistress." Wolfram crossed to the door, turned, and gave a slight bow. "Have no fear, fraulein. I'll not let you be harmed."

While she waited, Eleanor dragged from the corner the ancient chest that once had belonged to their mother, and placed it at the side of the bed as a stool. She brushed her hand softly across Katrina's brow, then frowned: Katrina's humors were moist and warm. Was that usual? She did not know: Never before had she treated wounds from a lash. How could she make her sister more comfortable? The brass key which hung like a locket around Katrina's neck appeared heavy against her pale skin, and for a moment Eleanor considered removing it; but she could not bear to see Katrina stripped of something so precious while she lay unawares.

Wishing to do something to ease her sister's suffering, she unloosed the riband which bound Katrina's hair, freeing her curls—the thick and lustrous curls that their father called his greatest treasure—combing and smoothing them with her fingers; then she twisted the hair into a large loop and tied it, binding it high so it would not brush against her wounds. When the water and the healing herbs finally arrived, she moistened strips of linen and placed them loosely across Katrina's back.

Thus the hours passed as Eleanor tended her sister, stroking her brow, singing softly, changing the cool cloths, until sometime during the night Katrina drifted into a deep, but natural, sleep. Exhausted, Eleanor crawled into her own bed, and slept.

Dawn had barely broken on the following day when Eleanor moved down the stairwell and through the kitchens, her chamber pot tucked within the crook of her arm. As she stepped out into the cool of the morning, she was greeted by a burst of yellow—jonquils she had planted years before—and by the low cooing of doves. Moving beyond the walled garden, she instinctively sidestepped the piles of dung and made her way to the cesspit behind the coop. There, with an absent-minded flick of her wrist, she dumped the contents of her pot and rinsed it clean. While she used the grasses at hand to dry the rim, her mind whirled.

There was no denying that Isabel and Katrina heartily disliked one another. The two women were of a similar size—both so small that Eleanor felt gangly and awkward in their presence—but there all similarities ceased. Katrina had a dusky, earthy beauty that reminded one of the luscious ripeness of a peach at summer's end. Isabel, on the other hand, was as vivid as a spring day, her bright auburn hair a flame against her pale skin.

Yet despite their jealousies, neither had been overtly hostile. Isabel, glowing like a fire when stirred by a breeze, would blaze and draw attention to herself, while Katrina would flush and retreat into silence. Never had they exchanged sharp words. Never had there been an outburst. And never had Isabel raised her hand against Katrina. What could have happened to cause Lady Isabel to erupt into such an uncontrolled rage?

"Elly, don't ye think that there pot be clean enough now?"

Eleanor gasped and spun around. "Greta, I'm so scared," she cried out, when she saw the old washerwoman.

"Now Elly," the woman soothed. "There's no need t' be afeared fer yer own skin. You ain't hidin' no baby in yer belly, are you?"

"Of course not! Have you taken leave of your senses?"

"You don't know, then. About yer sister. That's what my ladyship be all riled up about. Katie be havin' a baby. I daresay yer stepmother don't like that much. She be the one wantin' a baby. A son be what she wants and what she can't have whilst yer poor father be gone." Greta continued chattering, giving Eleanor time to compose herself. "Poor Lady Is'bel. She must be chokin' on her own gizzard thinkin' about the duke's grandson runnin' around Ravensberg, be he a bastard or not. How come you din't know, when you sleep right beside her? I knowed somethin' was wrong. I wash yer linens and rags and I knowed. Then I looked at her and I saw. I hoped Lady Is'bel wouldn'a see, but I don't bide much with bindin' a woman's middle. I'se seen some misshapen babies born when that trick's bin tried."

"I've been such a fool. I should have known. I should have helped her."

"Well, she be yer elder. She shouldn'a expect you t'—"

"Older, yes," Eleanor interrupted. "But definitely not wiser. You know well that Katrina is ruled by her heart."

"Ye're right, Elly. Looks like her heart led her t' trouble this time."

"Who's the baby's father?"

"Well, I was sorter hopin' you might have some thought as t' that." Greta glanced sideways up at Eleanor, but when Eleanor shook her head, she continued, "That be the problem. That be what yer stepmother be wantin' t' find out. That be why she took on so. Who knows? P'raps even yer father would've tried t' beat the truth out of her. He may be a dotin' father, but he has his honor t' think about."

"He would never lay a hand on her!"

"Ye're right, I think. But many a father's done elsewise, so's I heared, and that be what I know."

Eleanor bowed her head, enshrouding herself beneath her silken hair. After a moment of stillness, she lifted her face to her old friend. "I must find some way to protect her from Lady Isabel's wrath."

There was a look of approval in Greta's eyes. "Be Katie all right?"

"She was awake when I left, and in some pain. All the more because she has never suffered such an indignity before. But the lash did not cut deeply. If it does not go putrid, she will be fine." Eleanor brushed off her hands and bent to retrieve her pot. "It is time I return to Katrina. She will be wanting me."

To Eleanor's great surprise, her sister had already arisen. Dressed in a loose shift, Katrina was leaning against the stone sill of the window with her shoulders curled forward as though the very weight of them was too much to bear. She turned when Eleanor entered, but did not respond to her startled greeting.

"I must leave Ravensberg," she said, simply, as she traced her fingers over the curve of her belly.

"Surely you don't mean that?" Eleanor asked, in astonishment.

"I do mean it." Katrina's eyes, dark and desperate, brimmed with tears. "I am with child, Eleanor."

"I know," Eleanor quickly reassured her. "Greta just told me."

"Then help me to leave."

Frustrated that she could not gather her sister into her arms for fear of causing her pain, Eleanor set down the pot and swiftly crossed the room. "Do not speak of such a thing," she said.

"I must. Oh, Eleanor, how can I make you understand? I am so afraid that I will give in and tell the duchess the name of my lover—"

"As you should."

"—and then she will kill my child."

"She would not!" Eleanor stepped back a pace, shocked at such an accusation. "Isabel is not a murderer."

"How can you defend her?" Katrina choked on a sob. "She is not one of us! She is the outsider in our midst."

"She is Papa's wife, and should not have to fight so hard for respect."

"Why are you so determined to take her part?" As tears streamed down her cheeks, Katrina turned so that her scored back now confronted Eleanor. "Look at these wounds! Are they not real? Do they not show you what Isabel is truly like?"

A wave of nausea swept over her at the sight of the moisture seeping through Katrina's shift. "They are real." Eleanor's voice softened with apology.

"Then you must help me to leave Ravensberg."

"Truly, there is no need. Wolfram is here to protect you now, and what is more, he has sent for Gregory. You know well that our cousin would never allow you, or your child, to suffer harm."

"I'm not so certain," Katrina said, as she slowly shook her head. "If he learned the name of my baby's father, he would be furious. I know not what he would do."

"Who is this villain who has misused you so foully?"

Katrina raised her hand as though in defense. "Do not ask me to betray him, Eleanor, for I'll not do it. You will not learn his name from me." The tears still remained, but they now glistened like dewdrops in her eyes. "One day soon he will come for me, riding through the gates of Ravensberg with his trumpet blowing and his banner waving, and then all will be well. But until that day I shall keep my secret. Until then, no one shall know his name."

"This is no fantasy, Katrina. This is not a tale that the minnesingers tell around the midwinter fire. That babe you carry is as real as those strokes across your back. How can you defend such a man?"

"Because he is good and true. Believe me, Eleanor, I would wish such a man for you, someday."

Eleanor was tempted to retort that she had no desire to have a man who would so casually bed her and leave her to deal with the consequences, but knowing that such blunt honesty would only make matters worse, she said, instead, "If you will not tell me who he is, at least tell me where it is you met him. He cannot be of Gildren." Surely, there could not be a man in Ravensberg who would lay a hand on the duke's own daughter!

Katrina stood in silence, her brow puckered and her mouth drawn in a pout of concentration. She sniffled, and with the back of her hand brushed away the tears, leaving a streak shining on her cheek. "All right, I will tell you," she said. "Else you will glare at every man you pass, wondering if he is the one. I met him at the king's Christmas court; so you need have no fear that he will ever cross your path here at Ravensberg."

"Who is he?" Eleanor cried out in frustration.

But at that, Katrina threw herself onto the bed and began to sob. Her shoulders shook violently and the wounds on her back began to bleed afresh. Appalled, Eleanor sat down beside her and stroked her hair with trembling fingers.

"I'm sorry, Katrina. I won't ask again. Please don't cry. Please don't cry, Katie. I will help you, somehow. I will help you. Don't cry. I will help you."

"To leave?"

As tears rolled down Eleanor's own cheeks, she hastily wiped them away. "I promise you I'll find a way. Hush, Katie, hush. Please don't cry."

After hearing those words, Katrina closed her eyes and relaxed; and only a few moments later lay asleep.

With a great sigh, Eleanor stood. Who was this man who had such a hold on Katrina's affections that she would refuse to divulge his name, even to those who desired nothing more than her safety and happiness? Whoever he was, she hoped he would someday suffer as her sister was suffering now! She truly hoped that he would live to know such fear for the life of a child, and the loneliness of holding a secret deep within.

In the meantime, perhaps Katrina was right. Perhaps, she should leave Ravensberg for a time. What could be the harm? Very gently Eleanor laid her own coverlet across Katrina's back; then straightening her shoulders in an unconscious gesture of determination, she left the chamber to search out Wolfram.

When she returned, her sister was kneeling beside the bed, one hand tracing the pattern of nails on their mother's old chest, the other fingering the key which hung from the golden chain around her neck.

"You are just in time," was Katrina's greeting. "Shall we open this together? Just like when we were children?"

Eleanor smiled as she set down the tray. "I have brought some food but it can wait." As she knelt, they shared a conspiratorial grin; then Katrina drew the chain over her head and handed it to Eleanor, who fitted the key into the brass-embossed lock.

"One, two, three—" They counted in unison as she turned the key, then together they lifted the lid. The sweet familiar scent of cedar wafted out, and their smiles widened as they touched the sumptuous fabric.

"Do you remember the night Mama wore this gown?" Eleanor asked, her voice full of awe.

Katrina nodded as she lifted the ruby-colored velvet to her cheek. "When she came in that door, she was wearing so many jewels that everything about her seemed to be shining. But it was her eyes that were the brightest, glowing like dancing stars. She was so happy." A fervor entered Katrina's voice. "I want to have love like Mama had. I will have that love! I would rather die then settle for anything less."

Eleanor's smile dimmed. "There was a cost; never forget that. Papa would not now be languishing behind Eaglesheid's walls if he had not abducted another man's bride."

"Do you think he cares? Do you think he would regret such a small thing as his freedom after so many years of happiness?"

"I know I would. If not on my own behalf, then for the pain I caused others."

"You think too much," Katrina scoffed. "If someone tried to carry you off, you would probably box his ears and send him away. You will die a shriveled old woman, miserable down to her very bones. But not me. I will have that kind of love. Without it, I think I would go mad!" For a fleeting moment there was a look of such intensity on Katrina's face that she looked half-mad already. Then it was gone.

"You are talking foolishness. You—" Eleanor started to argue but stopped mid-sentence. "I am sorry. Instead of comforting you, here I am quarreling. You need this food to regain your strength."

"You cannot deceive me with your talk of food. There's something else on your mind."

Eleanor had begun to reach for the tray, but pulled back her hand. "You know me all too well. There is something else. I have spoken with Sir Wolfram. He also believes you to be in danger as long as you stay here."

"I told you so."

Ignoring this childish remark, Eleanor took Katrina's hands into her own. "We have talked together at length. It was my thought that you could go to Grandmama Sophie's chamber to await Gregory's arrival, but Wolfram insists that the old keep is the first place Isabel will look." She frowned down at their entwined fingers. "He is probably right. The second possibility is that you go north, to our uncle of Bestilden. Despite all that happened in the past, surely Mama's brother would take you into his protection. But that is such a long and dangerous journey that it would be fool-hardy to attempt it unless the need were absolute. It is Wolfram's advice that you go to a place of shelter in the forest to await further news."

Katrina, her face as pale as moonlight, nodded, but did not speak.

"I wish he could be the one to travel with you, but he is too noticeable. A man with only one ear would be marked wherever he went. If Isabel were to search for you—and Wolfram is certain she will—then his presence would lay a trail much too easily followed. So, I have asked John to go with you."

"John? But he's not a knight! How can John be my hero?"

Eleanor sighed. How could she make Katrina see that this was no game; that in real life babies were born fatherless, romantic heroes turned out to be skinny boys with too many teeth, and dragons were not slain at a lady's command.

"No, he is no knight. He is only a fuller's son who runs and fetches at command. But he is hardworking and strong, and I am convinced he will protect you with his life. You cannot travel as Fraulein Katrina of Ravensberg—not if you truly wish to disappear from our stepmother's view. You will need to set aside your fine silks and your pretty combs and wear the linens of an ordinary peasant.

"There is an old hunting lodge in the forest, not more than a league distant. Though it is well-hidden, both John and Wolfram were with Papa some years ago when their party rested there, and they are each certain they could find it again. That is where John will take you until it is safe for your return. Wolfram will be the messenger, and will bring all that you need for comfort, as he may. But in the end, if your worst fears are true and there is no safety here at Ravensberg, then John will take you north.

"Think on this, Katie. It will not be easy. You must travel some distance hidden in a cart, then walk through the forest taking only what John can carry. There will be little more than the simplest of furnishings, for the lodge is but a small and temporary shelter. Are you very certain that this is what you would do?"

Without speaking, Katrina tossed the gown aside, raised herself to her knees, and began searching through the chest, carelessly spilling its contents onto the floor until she found what she sought.

Eleanor's brow furrowed with puzzlement. "Mama's dancing slippers," she said, wondering what absurdity was in Katrina's mind now.

Katrina handed one to her sister. "Isn't it beautiful?"

Eleanor took the satin slipper and, lovingly, placed her hand within the exquisite shoe. "I had forgotten how beautiful this is—how unique." It was true. Five craftsmen, each a master in his field, had combined their skills to create this gift that Branold had given to his beloved wife: the tanner to soften the leather, the leathersmith to form the shoes which had fitted Judith's feet as comfortably as her own skin, the dressmaker to add with invisible stitches a satin dressing, the embroiderer to decorate the toes with a brilliant bouquet of flowers, and the jeweler to provide the amber, rubies and emeralds that formed the center of each little flower.

"These slippers mean Mama to me," Katrina said. "I will carry one in a pouch around my waist, hidden beneath my shift. I will have the jewels to use if ever I have the need. But you must keep the other here. That way, Mama will be with us both until we are together again." Eyes glinting with resolution, Katrina held Eleanor's gaze. "I will go with John tomorrow. I must."

Tears welled in Eleanor's own eyes as she nodded. "I love you, Katie."

"I love you, too. You are more dear to me, Eleanor, than you can ever know. Be careful and watch out for Isabel. I cannot bear that you should be hurt."

Eleanor leaned forward and rested her head on Katrina's brow. "Take care of yourself—and your child. I will light a candle every day for your safe return."

The following morning, as she stood looking out of one of the upper windows, Eleanor was the only person who took particular notice of a hay-wagon that exited through the open gateway. Very quickly, it moved down the hill on which Ravensberg was built and vanished from sight. For a moment, she considered climbing the battlement wall so that she would have a clear view of the road where it ran straight across the farmland before it struck into the forest. No. She must not. She must do nothing today to draw attention to her actions. For a moment longer she stood, feeling the cool breeze as it gently touched her face, then she returned to her chamber alone.

# Chapter 4

John felt utterly defeated. The plan which had sounded so good behind sheltering walls—ride in a cart, trek in the forest, stay in a hunter's cot, meet with the one-eared knight—all had failed. Nothing had been as it should. The jolting of the wagon had irritated the fraulein's wounds so much that by the time the carter had stopped and they crawled from beneath the pile of hay, her sores had begun to fester. The poor girl had tried to walk, but soon was so overcome by pain that they were forced to cease their search for shelter.

By morning it had been clear that Mistress Katrina was very ill. She shivered and cried, and though John covered her with the blanket, he could do no more. Never had he felt so helpless. For many hours he had sat at her side, watching her, waiting for her to come to her senses and tell him what to do. Finally, in desperation, he had left her and continued his search.

When at last he had found it beneath an arch of bracken, his hopes were completely destroyed. The cot was falling upon itself in decay. And it stank. A woman's corpse lay within, not long-dead, but already rotting in the heat. Unmanfully, he'd retched at the sight; then swallowing his fear along with his pride, had hurried back to his mistress, hoping to find her awake and well. But she was neither. Burning with the fever of delirium, she was raving at the very trees above her head.

And he was the one to blame. He had not been man enough to defy the duchess when she was beating her stepdaughter. And now the fraulein would die.

The day passed. And the long night. But the morning light brought no relief. Barely had the sun appeared when the sky darkened and rain poured down. Mistress Katrina shivered, racked with chills so violent that her teeth clattered. Her eyes were wild. She moaned and cried, and sometimes screamed in her agony.

The rain stopped near midday. John spent the passing hours trying to puzzle out what to do, but the process left him muddled and confused. His thoughts turned around and around in his head and he could make no sense of them.

Seeking some order, he at last picked up a twig. "The first thing I can do, is nothing at all. We can sit here until we die. Then we can frighten another traveler as I was frightened yesterday by that corpse." He grimaced as he laid the twig at his side.

"Another thing I can do ..." He took a second stick into his hand. "Go back to Ravensberg. It's her home." Wolfram had insisted that the life of his mistress was in danger. But was it true? Would the duchess actually murder her stepdaughter? Then he remembered Lady Isabel's face, distorted with rage. "He's right," John said aloud. "I can't take her back."

After laying that twig alongside the other, he reached for a third. "I can return to the road, but go away from Ravensberg." He frowned as he paused. "But Wolfram said the duchess will search for us." As the image of mailed knights kicking up the dust of the road entered his mind, he shuddered. John snapped in half the stick he was fingering, hurling one piece away and placing the other in the line on the ground.

"Another choice," he stated, as he laid a fourth sprig down. "We can leave the road and travel into the forest." He closed his eyes a moment before he continued. "But this I fear the most. The forest is deep and goes on forever. It could be a trap we never leave." As he pictured a rabbit caught in a snare he lifted his hand in frustration and abruptly swept the four sticks away.

The day was passing and he could delay no longer. With a great sigh, John made his decision. Gently, he laid his mistress down and prepared himself for their journey. When all was ready, he knelt and touched her burning brow. "Mistress, I'm going to take you someplace safe. I'll not let Lady Isabel find you." There was no response. He lifted her into his arms then headed west, into the forest, leaving the road behind.

Using the sun to guide him, whenever he chanced to see it through the leaves, John continued to struggle westward. Hours later, his efforts were finally rewarded when he stepped out from the forest into the midst of a flock of sheep in a large clearing. Across the lea stood a village of more than a dozen huts, each a rectangular block of wattle and daub, thickly-roofed with thatch.

He could see a few women and children kneeling in the dirt, weeding between the young sprouts of wheat, but he ignored them. His eyes were drawn across the field to a doorway, where a woman stood, holding an infant in her arms.

"A mother with a babe," he murmured. "Surely her man could use some help."

Still bearing Mistress Katrina in his arms, John wove his way through the grazing flock, towards the woman. When a second child crawled through the doorway and sat on the ground at the woman's feet, his hopes grew.

She did not move as he approached, and not until he stopped a pace in front of her did she speak. "Well?" Her voice was aggressive. "What be ye wantin'?"

"No harm, I promise you. We're travelers. My...my..." John clamped his mouth shut and flushed.

"Yer what?" demanded the woman. She glowered at John with an angry expression that matched the wild, tangled mass of her hair.

"Er...my wife...is ill. She needs shelter and warmth and food."

The peasant gave a harsh laugh. "And ye be thinkin' I might give her them?"

"I'd pay you. Not in coin," he rushed on before she could interrupt. "In work. Surely, your man could use help? I owe my time to no man. I am free."

Her interest was plainly evident in the relaxing of her stance. "Mayhap that changes things. I've no husband. He died jus' afore th' plantin.'"

"Would you look after her?"

"Aye. If ye'll work the fields. Bring her in then." The woman stepped aside and indicated to John to enter the hut. "My name be Meg."

"And I am John."

"And yer wife?"

"Ka…" John clamped his mouth shut and worked his thoughts as quickly as he could. "Kate. She's called Kate."

It took several moments for John's eyes to adjust to the darkness within the cot. When he could see, he looked around with approval and relief. Contrary to her physical appearance, Meg was a good housekeeper. To the left, enclosed by a fencing made from brambles and swept clean of its filth, was a pen for the animals. In the center stood a stone fire pit on which a pot of soup was bubbling. And to the right lay a rudely-made table and an orderly stack of woven pallets.

"Here." Meg crossed the room and unfurled a pallet with a shake of her wrist. "Lay yer Kate down. What be the matter with her?"

John did not respond immediately, but carried his mistress to the mat and laid her on her side. "She's with child." He pointed to her belly. "But worse, she's been lashed and suffers from a fever."

"Lashed!" Meg's quick hands lifted the shift over Katrina's head, while John turned away in embarrassment. "Who did this ter her?"

Shame burned John deeper than a brand. In God's eyes he was a man like Wolfram, was he not? Yet, unlike Wolfram, he had stood aside and allowed his mistress to be so cruelly hurt. Did he not then own the blame?

"The fault's mine that she now suffers so," he answered.

"Men," Meg said in disgust. "Ye beat yer wives then blame them when they dies. I say it be fittin' if ye break yer own back doin' the plantin'. There be a sack of peas at th' door. Now go ter work."

John sighed with relief when he heard the villagers arriving home from the fields of their overlord, for he was tired and could now lay down his tool.

Little more than a week had passed since he and Mistress Katrina had arrived looking for shelter, but already his days had fallen into an inescapable pattern. He would rise with the sun and tend the animals while Meg prepared the meal of black bean bread and water. Then, leaving his mistress in Meg's care, he would hasten to the fields and spend the remainder of the day weeding, mowing, or trying to break through the soil with his wooden hoe. He had felt the frustration of encountering rocks that needed to be patiently dug out with his dinner knife, and he had felt the exhilaration of looking over a patch of earth, freshly turned and mixed with dung. When the day was over, he would stand erect and stretch, feeling hot pains across his shoulders and down his back. He would then hurry to Meg's hut, always hoping to find that his mistress's fever had released her from its fiery bonds.

Now, as John eased his body upright, he shielded his eyes against the setting sun. The villagers were directly in his line of vision as they lumbered down the gentle slope toward their homes. They all looked as tired as he felt. As he watched, John was stirred by affection for these new friends of his. Not once had they questioned his presence in their village. It was true that on the evening of his arrival he had been greeted with hooded looks, but when he had taken his place amongst them, working in the fields, they had made him welcome.

After one last stretch, John scooped up his tools and hastened from the field, eager to see how his mistress fared. It worried him that she was taking so long to regain her health. Her fever, although no longer engulfing her, still lingered, and she seemed to move in and out of a dream world all her own. He prayed often that her strength would return, fearing that if she were to be delivered of a child in such a weakened state, she would not survive.

He had almost reached the doorway to Meg's house when his stride was interrupted by a man who approached from his left. "Sir?" The man spoke with hesitation.

John stopped and turned. "Aye?" It was one of the peasants who had spent the day working in his lord's field. He stood before John, silent, looking at the ground.

"Aye?" John said again, prodding the man to speak.

But the man would not be hurried. He lifted his head and focused his eye on some object above the doorway behind John's back. When he spoke at last, his eyes didn't shift, but his foot swept back and forth tracing an arc in the dirt. " 'ere was some strangers t'day." The words were spoken with effort. "They come on 'orses. They be askin' things."

John's stomach felt as though the air had been punched out of it. "What questions?" The man's drawl was maddening.

" 'ad we seen a girl." Again there was a long pause. "A girl with a swollen belly. 'n a man who answers t' John."

"And what did you tell them?"

"Ain't seen anyone."

"Thank you." There was no point in denying that he was the one they sought. "Did they leave you alone then?"

"Aye. 'r fingers was crossed ahind 'r backs. Don't want no demons t'git us fer th' lie."

"Thank you, friend." John touched the frightened man lightly on his shoulder. Then he turned and stooped to enter the hut, his mind full of his fear.

The first thing he saw was Mistress Katrina, sitting up and leaning against the post which supported the northern wall. Realizing that she was lucid, John tried to compose his features and hoped that in the smoky darkness she had not seen his face. Without speaking, he crossed in a single stride to the fire where he served himself a bowl of the almost meatless stew. Settling himself into a comfortable crouch more than an arm's length from his mistress, he began to eat. With great care he picked out the few chunks and balanced them on his knee to enjoy at the last, then tipped the bowl to his mouth and drank the broth.

Meg's chin tilted. "Don't ye jus' beat all. Here, ye come, ev'ry day, worried half t' death 'bout yer wife and then t'day, when she is sittin' and eatin' and lookin' like t' be better, ye give her nary a glance."

John stopped chewing the piece of meat in his mouth and looked up. He read the look of exasperation on Meg's face, then turned and saw anger discolor Mistress Katrina's. With his tongue, he shoved the meat into his cheek where it bulged and constricted his speech. "Ka … Ka …" He coughed into his hand, muffling the word. "I'm glad to see you better. Truly I am. It's a miracle." He coughed again in a hopeless attempt to cover his discomfort. "What else can I say?"

"Plenty!" answered Meg, then added with a touch of humor, "P'raps ye're wantin' to be alone?" Scooping up her two babies she left, after saying, "Make hay now, John. I ain't goin' to do this ev'ry day, am I?"

Though John was certain Meg expected him to step forward and gather Mistress Katrina into his arms, in fact he did the opposite. He immediately backed up and pressed himself against the wooden beam, while continuing to chew the recalcitrant piece of meat which still remained in his mouth.

"Mistress," he said, after swallowing the morsel with difficulty. "I'm glad to see you better."

"Did you dare to tell them I was your wife?"

He clenched his fists across his chest and stared down at them. "I'm sorry, mistress. I feared to tell them I was your servant. I knew not what they've heard, even here."

A look of consternation flitted across her face, then she suddenly brightened. "I see. It will do very well, then, until my own true husband comes to rescue me."

No one had told him that the fraulein was married! "But I thought … mistress … I thought …" He could not find the words to finish his sentence without giving insult.

"It can do no harm to tell you now. I am well and truly wed. We spoke our vows before God, and an old priest."

"If I'd known, I would've … I mean I should've … I'll take you to your husband. He can protect you and his child." John had remembered the riders, with fear.

"I wish it could be," she sighed. "But the time has not yet come."

"But mistress—"

"No, John. You must call me Kate. Is that not the name you told your friend? I like the sound of that."

"Mistress—" He stopped as she raised her eyebrows at him, then corrected himself. "Kate. Let me take you to your husband."

"He told me to wait for him, and wait I shall."

"Does he know of—" He choked on his words as he waved his hand in the direction of her belly.

"No." She tilted her head, as though the effort to shake it was too much.

"Then we must tell him."

"You know nothing! I promised to keep the secret of our marriage, and I'll not fail him." Katrina paused before she added, more quietly, "You must listen to me. It is my father's life at risk. If I force my husband to recognize me too soon, then my father will die."

This was so confusing that John began to wonder if her wits had been addled by the fever. "But what does your father have to do with this?"

Meg burst through the doorway, carrying one child and dragging the other. Taking deep gulping breaths, she tried to speak, but it was several moments before either John or Katrina could understand what she was trying to say. Her words tumbled out—there were armed men nearby searching every hut.

"Mistress, you must hide!" John scanned the room, his eyes darting from corner to corner.

"Ye be the one they seek?" Meg asked in an angry whisper. "Ye can't stay here. Go! Get out!" Outside, the sound of confusion increased. To the shouting was added the shrieking of children and the high wail of a woman's fear.

"What is happening?" Katrina seemed strangely unconcerned.

"They are Lady Isabel's men."

Now she paled and shuddered, and in her panic tried to struggle to her feet. "Help me, John! I feel so weak."

It was too late. A figure loomed in the doorway, filling it with darkness. All within remained still, save the toddler who let out a cry of fear and crawled to his mother. Meg scooped the child up and held him close while John reached for the dinner knife that hung on his belt. He knew the knife was too small to be of any use against the steel of a sword, but he was not going to let Mistress Katrina be taken without a fight.

"Wolfram." Katrina breathed his name in relief and fell back to her seat. John, however, kept his weapon poised in the palm of his hand and did not take his eyes from the knight. Ignoring him, Wolfram stepped into the room and knelt before his mistress.

"Fraulein Katrina! Thank God I am that one who has found you. Lady Isabel has sent men everywhere, searching for you, with orders to return you to the castle."

Shrinking back in fear, Katrina cried out, "But she wishes me dead. You're not going to take me back, are you, Wolfram?"

"Never!"

"She wishes me dead," Katrina repeated, as though it were a litany.

Wolfram swung around to John. "Can you do nothing right, knave? Why is she here? If one of the villagers betrays her presence I will have to fight my own companions." He eyed the small knife in John's hand. "Are you willing to fight?"

"No one will take her without killing me first."

Wolfram nodded and started to speak, but Katrina interrupted. "She would like to see me dead!" There was such a note of breathless excitement in her voice that the others all turned to her. "Don't you see? If she believes that I am dead then she will cease searching for me and I will be able to wait safely for my child's birth. You must return to Ravensberg and convince the duchess that I have died."

"But ... but that is impossible." Wolfram stammered in his astonishment.

"What is impossible is that I abide here in constant fear. But if she believes me dead, then she will cease the search and I will be free to regain my strength in peace."

"How could I possibly persuade my men to believe such a tale?" He waved toward the door and the shouting sounds of confusion not far beyond. "Am I to just walk out of here saying that you have died and we must call off the search and go home? It is impossible. I have no proof. No token. No corpse."

"I've a corpse," John said without thought. Now all turned to him in amazement. "That is ... what I mean is that I know where a body lies."

"This is absurd. It would look nothing like Mistress Katrina."

John regretted his speech, but his mind raced. Could that body serve the purpose? It had been more than a week since he had seen it. The weather had been hot and the stench would surely be worse. With a little more certainty, he said, "I know where a body lies. I can lead you to it. A man would need a stout stomach to get too close. It could serve."

"Then it is settled." This time, Katrina's words were a command.

Wolfram paused only a moment before he nodded in acquiescence. "Agreed. The duchess will never rest until you are found and your child destroyed."

The noises outside were dangerously near. Wolfram crossed to the door. "Fare thee well, mistress," he whispered. "Have no fear. They will not take you."

Then, grabbing John, he gave him a shove that propelled him through the doorway, nearly knocking down a soldier just bending to enter. Ignoring the man, he bellowed to Meg behind him. "And you, too, woman. Come out of there with your brats before I skewer them both."

As the other knights hurried to join him, Wolfram shouted, "I have found the renegade manservant." He grabbed John by his shirt and tossed him hard, then landed a kick that rolled him even farther away. John now lay several feet from Meg's door. Drawing his sword, Wolfram straddled him. "Where is the fraulein? Where is Mistress Katrina, you knave?"

"She's dead," John sobbed.

"You lie," Wolfram roared.

"Nay, sir, I do not. I tell the truth. I swear it!"

"If this be true, why did you not immediately return to Ravensberg with the news?"

"Please, don't hurt me. I swear I meant her no harm. I only brought the mistress away at her own command. She fell ill with a fever and I couldn't save her. I was afraid. I didn't know what to do, so I left her where she lay, and I hid."

"I think you lie. Have you proof of her death?" snarled Wolfram.

John cast his eyes from side to side as though seeking some means of escape, then whispered, "Aye, sir. I can show you where her body lies."

"How far?"

He frowned as he tried to figure how long he could delay the search. "One day, or more. If I can find it ... her."

"You will find her or you will feel the twist of steel in your belly."

It was nearly full dark, so the soldiers made camp in the clearing. Bound wrist and ankles, John was forced to lie on the ground without comfort of bedroll or blanket. Even so, he slept deeply until he was awakened by a kick in his side. His bonds were released but he was given no food. The sun was barely spreading its light over the field when they set off, leaving the village behind.

John led the men on a day long trek through the forest, hoping to confuse his captors' sense of direction without losing his own. Not a thought was spared for his comfort and his stomach rumbled with hunger. Finally, coming to a stream, he bent to drink but was landed a kick that sent him flying full face into the water.

"Let him drink," Wolfram interceded, then glaring down at John demanded, "How much farther, knave? I begin to think you lead us in circles."

Cupping his hands, John drank deeply, then stood. "Sir. We are nearly there."

Wolfram's eyes seemed drawn momentarily to something he saw beyond John in the thicket, but quickly he returned them to his prisoner. "We had better find this place soon or you will feel the blade at your throat."

Only a short while later John pointed to the dilapidated building that was slowly becoming one with the wood around it. "That is where I took her when she was ill. And that is where she died. And unless the wolves have devoured her, she lies there still."

"Lead on," one of the men ordered, raising his sword.

"Sir, I cannot!" John fell to his knees and began to retch.

Wolfram motioned to his companion to enter the hovel. Covering his nose, the man bent his head and ducked inside, but returned almost immediately, pale and clenching his teeth.

"She is there?" Wolfram asked.

The man nodded, unable yet to control his stomach enough to speak.

"Then she is indeed dead." In a voice filled with revulsion, Wolfram added, "I, for one, am not going to move that stinking corpse, be she the duke's daughter or not. We'll torch the cot." He hesitated, as though in confusion. "Do you think this is the news Lady Isabel wishes to hear?"

One just shrugged, but the other whined, "We were not responsible for her death. We only discovered her body."

"Are we agreed, then, that we shall return to Ravensberg and tell Lady Isabel the fraulein has been found?"

"Aye. But let us also tell her we have avenged her death." The first knight stared at John. "We can take back the heart of this knave as proof."

John did not move. This was no more than he deserved. Though frightened, he was determined to meet his death as he should, knowing that his mistress now was safe.

"I think . . ." said Wolfram, drawing his words out, as though they were some exquisite form of torture. "That is a pleasure I shall reserve for myself. I have a private score to settle with this man. Make a pyre of this old cot for our mistress. We'll burn it well, before we ride on." Wolfram raised his sword to touch John's neck as he continued to speak to his comrades. "I will join you, soon, with the bloody prize."

Neither of the men argued. As they scrambled to find their flint, Wolfram backed John into the wood with the point of his sword. When they had gone a short furlong he hissed, "Stay here and begin screaming." He raised his arm and John flinched, but Wolfram charged past him and disappeared beneath the trees.

Crouched on his knees, John let out several terror-stricken shrieks, then waited in wide-eyed silence. Soon Wolfram was back, holding in his hand a bloody piece of meat.

"There was a young stag caught in the bush by the water's edge. I simply borrowed his heart. Return now to Mistress Katrina and protect her well. But I warn you, knave, that if harm befalls her, I will seek you to the ends of the earth to do the same to you as I have done to this buck." He indicated the heart in his hand. "I will return to you soon, bringing such things as you will need for her comfort. Do not come to Ravensberg until you are bid. And do not desert your mistress."

"Sir. I'll care for her well. I love her life better than my own."

"That I have seen already. If it were otherwise, the stag would yet have his heart." Then Wolfram turned and strode off, toward the curling trail of smoke.

John remained on his knees for a long, long time before he rose and began the journey back to the village where his mistress waited.

# Chapter 5

ISABEL WAS DRAWN IRRESISTIBLY to the battlements. With her cloak wrapped around her, more in a gesture of self-defense than to offer any protection from the elements, she had stood day-after-day, watching for the return of her messengers. She was desperate for news. Desperate to hear that Katrina had been found, safe and well.

The girl had been missing for nearly two weeks! Where could she have gone that she so completely eluded the searchers? And how could she possibly survive? Katrina was incredibly vulnerable. The foolish child had not one iota of wit. Indeed, she had never needed it. Every person at Ravensberg had stumbled over his feet to please the girl, asking for nothing in return except the brilliance of one of her smiles.

Isabel looked down at her own feet and frowned, for she recognized the jealousy in her last thought; it was a jealousy she was determined to expunge before it led her into even greater folly. Shame flooded her at the memory of that terrible afternoon. The familial peace had been shattered when she had suddenly been confronted with the knowledge that Katrina bore a child. In that moment, all of her own heartache and loneliness seemed so unbearable that she had released the monstrous anger that had been coiled within her like a poisonous snake. Beyond rational thought, she had grabbed up her whip and actually beaten her own stepdaughter, not even stopping when the blood began to flow. If Wolfram had not arrived just when he did, how much darker would her deed have been? How could she ever hope to atone for such a sin?

Still clutching her cloak, Isabel turned and walked to the next embrasure. This opening more directly faced the mountains, and by squinting into the morning sunlight she was able to see up into their forested slopes. Again she stood, silent and still, willing someone to appear from beneath the trees. Where was Branold's daughter? And the babe she carried within?

"Riders approach, my lady."

Isabel spun around. "Is it the searchers?" she asked the guard.

"No, duchess. It's a large party, bearing the arms of Marre."

"Oh, thank God! It is Gregory then."

"Of that I am certain, my lady."

"Welcome to Ravensberg, Gregory." Isabel held out both hands to her husband's nephew. "You cannot know how pleased I am to see you."

He clasped her fingers within his gloves. "She is not yet found?"

"No."

"I blame myself—"

"Do not take this upon yourself," she interrupted. "That is more than chivalry demands. You were not even here."

"But that is the very reason I bear the fault," he said, as he stripped off his gauntlets. "My uncle charged me with the care of all that was his until his return, and most particularly with the care of his wife and daughters. If I had been here as I ought, then none of this would have happened."

"You speak nonsense. You have not been spending your time in idleness. You have responsibilities to Marre as well. Branold never intended you to abandon your duties to his sister—your mother—to take up his cause. You hold no blame in this matter. There is only one to blame, and that is myself. I have no doubt that I am the cause of Katrina's flight."

"Say no more." Gregory took Isabel's shoulders and shook her gently, glancing around as he did to make certain their words were spoken in privacy. "I know more than you may imagine for Wolfram sent me a missive. That man is a pompous fool, and a dangerous one. He hates you, my lady. Beware of Wolfram."

"His hatred is neither here nor there." She shrugged off his warning. "What did he tell you of Katrina?"

"That she has played the harlot. If he hoped to gain my sympathy by telling me of my cousin's tender condition, he was mistaken. The foolish girl will not only bring shame upon us all, but will hinder her father's cause as well. No one could allow such behavior to go unpunished."

"She is still young, and someone has used her foully."

"Then let her return and tell us who it is who has debauched her so that he may be properly punished."

"She keeps her honor in her own way."

"I have no patience for her behavior. She is Gildren's daughter but has given her loyalty elsewhere."

"You don't know that. You do not even know if she gave herself freely."

"You defend her so soundly. Tell me, then, why you beat her?"

"Because I did not stop to think but allowed my rage to consume me. She is a child still. When she is found, let her be in peace. She will have a great enough burden to bear as it is, for her secret will not keep."

Gregory relaxed a little, but still his face was grim. "She has seventeen years and has proved herself a woman."

"Not Katrina," Isabel insisted. "When she has threescore years she will still be a child—and you know well what I mean."

Gregory's shoulders drooped. "You are right. When my cousin returns, she will be safe from my hands."

Isabel smiled at his reluctant acquiescence, then said with certainty, "She would have been safe anyway. You would never have touched her. You adore Katrina."

"But that is precisely what makes her betrayal so much the worse—" His last word was cut short, for the sentry in the watchtower above the gate cried out.

"Riders approaching!"

Gregory dashed over to the nearest stair leading to the battlements. Holding her skirt high as she raced across the cobbles, Isabel followed.

"Is it Katrina?" she called out.

"Three knights and none else," he answered in dismay.

The trio were still some distance away, on the plain which footed the hill, but they were riding fast and would surely reach the gates before many minutes had passed. Turning to the guard who stood on the stones below, Isabel ordered, tersely, hoping she was not making a mistake, "Send for Fraulein Eleanor."

Wolfram could feel the blood from the deer's heart seeping through his pouch and dampening the cloth of his surcoat. He was glad to have this reminder of his encounter with Katrina and her manservant, for it helped him to hold onto his anger as he rode. He would never forgive Lady Isabel for forcing Katrina into such dreadful circumstances, and he vowed that he would find some way to take his revenge.

Their journey was nearly over. He and his two companions were climbing the hill on which Ravensberg stood and would soon be riding through its open gates. Their arrival had obviously been marked; there was a scurry of activity on the battlements and he could see many people hurrying closer for a view. What could be better? Let all the household see how joyfully Lady Isabel received the news of her stepdaughter's death. Let the duchess publicly condemn herself as the murderer he had always known her to be.

She was there in the yard, and he could tell by the expectant look on her face that she eagerly awaited the news he brought. Releasing his horse to the groom, Wolfram strode forward, seeing nothing but Lady Isabel.

He neither knelt, nor bowed, nor lowered his head, nor even removed his helmet.

"My lady," he said, his voice rich with disdain. "I have brought news that will surely gladden your heart." Staring into her eyes, he saw the light of hope kindled. Good. Soon her downfall would be complete, for she was fool enough not to disguise her elation.

A smile of anticipation curled his lips. "Fraulein Katrina is dead."

At his moment of triumph, a scream pulled his attention from the duchess's face. Whirling around, he saw Eleanor midway across the yard, standing stock-still, her fair skin now blanched white; and then she sank to the ground. He started to move toward her but was stopped by a strong arm against his chest. For the first time since his arrival, he noticed Gregory's presence at Lady Isabel's side.

"How dare you bring such dire news to us in such cruel fashion?" Gregory's huge hands encircled Wolfram's neck. Blackness engulfed Wolfram, and a pulsing agony. Isabel's voice floated in the distance, as though deep under water—"Gregory! Cease!"—Gregory dropped his hands and Wolfram fell.

His own hands now clutched his neck as he gasped for air. For a moment he was so overcome by the nausea and pain that he did not hear the conversation above him, but when he was hauled to his feet, then forced to kneel, his consciousness returned.

"Varlet! Apologize to your mistress or suffer the consequences." Gregory's voice was close in his ear, but it was accompanied by angry murmurs nearby.

"I will not." His throat burned and the words sounded strained and harsh, but were audible just the same. "I'm not the one who is disloyal. Look in my pouch. There's John's heart to prove it. He has paid with his life for his failure to protect his mistress."

"It was never John's loyalty which was in question."

"Nor mine."

"Not until this moment. Retract your words, Wolfram, and beg your lady's forgiveness, as you value your own life."

Wolfram gritted his teeth. He heartily regretted that his accusation had been overheard by Eleanor, for he had intended to go to her swiftly to reassure her of her sister's well-being. But there was no way on this side of heaven that he would apologize to the duke's strumpet.

"I say that the Lady Isabel wished for the fraulein's death, and did all she could to achieve it. I am willing to defend the truth of my words in single combat. It is the duke's honor I fight to protect."

"Swine!" Gregory spat at Wolfram's face. "You are no friend to the duke if you would malign his chosen wife. It is me you will fight, for in his absence I will defend the honor of my lord and his lady."

Wolfram felt the spittle drip down his cheek but did not wipe it away. "I have no quarrel with you," he said, suddenly aware of how far matters had gone. "Nor with my lord the duke. I am loyal to the death to Lord Branold."

"Then retract your words for all to hear."

Wolfram hesitated. Were they all blind? Was he the only one to see how dangerous Lady Isabel truly was? If so, then he must accept this challenge and prove that he was right before all the world.

Pulling himself up tall, Wolfram lifted his hand and wiped his face. "I will not. I say that Fraulein Katrina is dead. My men will attest to that. And I say also that it is as the Lady Isabel wishes."

"Then to protect the honor of my lord and uncle, and the honor of his lady and his house, I challenge you to single combat this very afternoon."

"It is too soon," Wolfram objected, for he knew he must speak with Eleanor.

Gregory did not relent. "There will be no delay. The house of Gildren must mourn its daughter. If I win today, Sir Wolfram, you must offer public apology and leave the duchy."

"Agreed. But if I am the winner, Sir Gregory, you must return the duchess to her father's home."

"So be it." Gregory spun around and, taking the hussy's arm, began to walk away, but turned again to fling a final taunt over his shoulder. "Go pack your belongings, Wolfram. I'll see you into exile the moment this contest is over."

There were no lists at the ready, so it was agreed that the open meadow at the base of the hill would serve for the trial. A master was appointed and the two contestant knights withdrew to their lodgings to prepare themselves for combat.

Standing beneath the canopy that protected her from the heat of the sun, Isabel waited. She knew she should be frightened, for in truth, she was the one on trial today. The victor of the forthcoming battle would declare her guilt or innocence for all to hear. But this mattered not. All she could think about was the magnitude of her failure, and the suffering she had brought to Branold by causing his daughter's death.

The thought was unbearable. Branold was her own hero. Like a Tristan or a Parzival, he had ridden into her life four years before and, sweeping aside all protestations from her father, had carried her off to safety. Had he understood how great her need for rescue had been? She thought he did. Always he had treated her with gentleness and humor, and not once, no matter the provocation, had he raised either his voice or his hand against her.

Calls and shouts announced the arrival of the contestants, but Isabel restrained her curiosity and did not turn to watch their approach. Not until they reached the field and strode confidently into her view, did she at last see the two knights.

She spared only a quick glance for Wolfram—though that was long enough to see the look of haughty disdain on his face—for it was Gregory's fate alone that concerned her. As he approached, his helm tucked within the circle of his arm, Isabel at last felt fear. What if Gregory were killed today? It should not happen, for the joust was not a blood-sport, but such accidents did occur. Was not Katrina's death enough? How would Branold ever survive a second such blow?

Isabel felt her will falter. As Gregory knelt before her she nearly ordered him to withdraw himself from the conflict. Her hesitation must have shown for Gregory gently reprimanded her.

"My lady, it is Gildren's honor I fight to redeem today. Though my uncle be stripped of all he holds dear, let those who love him at least take care to leave him his honor."

Properly chastised, Isabel did not argue. Instead, she tore the laced cuff from her sleeve and handed it to her champion. "I do thank you, Gregory, on behalf of my lord husband. Place this token on your helm, and may God grant you the victory so that justice may prevail."

He smiled in approval as he took the cuff.

"Take care, Gregory," she whispered, so that only he could hear. "I would rather leave Ravensberg myself than have your death on my hands, too."

"If I defeat your accuser in fair battle today, then you will know the truth—that you bear no guilt in this matter."

"So be it," Isabel answered and kissed his cheek.

The shrill blast of the clarion was almost magical, for in the next moment all motion was held in suspense. Roused to action in the same instant, both knights echoed back a savage battle cry.

Isabel watched only Gregory. Lowering his lance and couching it against his body, he dug his spurs into the side of his horse and began his run toward Wolfram. At first, his mount moved slowly, but with each new stride, the powerful muscles in its shanks rippled and its speed increased until the dirt was flying beneath the horse's hoofs and the earth was drumming its passage.

Tensing, Isabel trained her eye to Gregory's shield for she knew it to be his only defense. For one heart-stopping moment she thought he had misjudged his timing, had left his chest exposed to his opponent's lance; and she clenched her fists in anguish. Then she saw his ruse. At the last second before the blows met, he turned his horse and took the powerful buffet directly in the center of his shield.

Wolfram had no time to respond, nor to correct his balance. His lance splintered into a dozen pieces and he was cast sideways with such force that he was thrown from his saddle.

Gregory leapt from his horse. He did not crowd Wolfram with his approach, but stood back, allowing him time to recover his breath and vision. Not until the fallen man began to move did Gregory press closer. From his belt he drew his misericorde and thrust the knife towards Wolfram's neck.

"No!" Isabel cried, as she lifted her skirts and ran across the field. But as she neared, she saw she had misjudged her husband's nephew. Gregory was not doing murder. He was slicing through the leather thongs of Wolfram's battered helmet to give him more room to breathe.

The black centers in Wolfram's eyes were like shadowed moons. He raised his hand to touch the back of his head, but dropped it when he saw Isabel.

"You have been defeated in fair battle," Gregory said. "Now keep your word."

"I'll keep it," Wolfram answered as he struggled to stand. He tottered on his feet, but managed to stay erect. "Withdraw words, m'lady. It's—" He stopped and a look of terror passed over his face. In a moment it had gone, but panic now entered his voice and he blinked rapidly, as though struggling to see through a haze. A ribbon of blood flowed down the back of his neck. "El'nor! Mus' see El'nor!"

With a frenzied force, he wrestled the hands that held him. "Katrina!" he cried out with complete clarity. "She—" But his head curled into his chest and he slowly sank to the ground.

With a grunt of surprise, Gregory touched the wound on the back of Wolfram's head; then with disgust, he dropped the lifeless body.

"Take him away," he ordered. "His passing is nothing, but it is time to mourn. The daughter of our lord is dead."

# Chapter 6

SUNLIGHT SPARKLED ON THE WATERS of the outer moat as the party of knights, gaily caparisoned and holding aloft their colorful pennants, set spur to their chargers and departed through Eaglesheid's massive gates. Scarcely a heartbeat passed before iron-shod hooves hit the wooden planks of the drawbridge, causing a hollowed explosion of sound. Deep-throated shouts of exultation arose from the riders and were echoed back as cheers from the spectators on the wall.

In the midst of the company rode Sebastian, attempting unsuccessfully to mask his elation with a look of disinterested boredom. As the wind rushed past his ears, his blood seemed to hammer in rhythm with the pounding of his horse's hooves, beating a pulse of ecstasy. After five long months, he was at last riding to Ravensberg to claim Katrina as his bride. Within a fortnight they would stand together at the church door and say their vows. And another fortnight hence, on the very day Sebastian returned with his wife to Eaglesheid, Duke Branold would be free.

Hidden within a pocket sewn inside his surcoat, lay a document containing the nuptial agreement that had been signed by the two feuding patriarchs. As Sebastian softly fingered the parchment through his clothing, a surge of pride rushed through him. He had played a brilliant game over these months. With great subtlety, never revealing his personal interest in the matter, he had led his father to the belief that it would be a greater form of victory to cheat Branold of his alliance with Terlinden than to hold him captive behind his walls. Westfeld had been tricked into releasing his prisoner.

Catching himself about to laugh aloud for the sheer joy of it, Sebastian clamped his mouth shut and ground his teeth into a tightlipped smirk. Raynar knew him too well to believe that he would feel so lighthearted over taking a stranger to wife. Although it grieved Sebastian to keep such a weighty secret from his friend, he knew he must. No word must be spoken of his clandestine marriage to Katrina, five months before, lest, somehow, word of it reach Westfeld's ears.

Raynar chuckled as he called out to Sebastian without slowing the pace of his horse. "I think this wedding to Branold's daughter pleases you, my friend. There is a rare glint in your eyes."

"It does please me," Sebastian shouted in return. "If I must take a wife, then why not Katrina of Gildren, who is nearly as famed for her beauty as was her mother, Judith?" A bubble of joy rose within him, not in contemplation of the future, but in remembrance of the past.

—It had been Twelfth Night, the last night of the king's Christmas court. The great hall at Breden had been ablaze with light and alive with riotous celebration; but Sebastian and Katrina had not been amongst the revelers. Alone in the chapel, with only the aging priest at their side, they had faced each other and said their vows.

Removing from his own finger the golden ring with the twin-headed eagle of Westfeld, Sebastian had slipped it successively over three of Katrina's fingers. "In the name of the Father, the Son, and the Holy Ghost, I take you, Katrina of Gildren to be my wife." He had not left the ring on her hand. Holding it before him like a talisman, he had continued, "With this ring, I thee wed, and with this gold I thee honor. I make my pledge that soon I will endow thee as I ought, then place this ring where it belongs and where it shall remain. The eagle will nest with the raven, and thus we will bring an end to my father's blood-oath."

The priest, stepping between them, had placed his wizened fingers on each of their shoulders. "I know full well why you wed in secret, my lord.

And though I fear you have been persuaded by a woman's tears, I do not deny your right to marry as you ..." A fit of coughing had interrupted him momentarily ... "as you will. If you truly wish the deed to be done so that it cannot be broken, you must consummate your marriage here, this night. The ..." Again he coughed. "I beg your pardon, my lord. What I am trying to say is that the spoken word means little until the body has added its *amen*."

To Sebastian's astonishment, the old man had then grasped their elbows and propelled them to the open door of his own small cell.

"I will watch and pray here, and set you a call before the next hour is rung."

After setting the candle in its sconce and slipping the bolt into place, Sebastian had turned to faced his wife. She was flushed, but the warmth of her color and the questioning look in her eyes only added to her beauty. Yet still he had not moved; and it was she who had broken the spell. With as much grace as a practiced seductress, she had removed the cap from her head releasing her hair from its confinement. Unbound—and as curly as newly-sheared lambs' wool—it tumbled in wild abandon to her waist. Sebastian could scarcely breathe. Slowly, he had reached out and taken a silken lock into his hand.

Was that the moment he had completely given her his heart? Perhaps. Gone were all thoughts of kings and prisoners, or of oaths and debts. All that remained was a throbbing, pounding love, and a determination to cherish her for the rest of his life.

"Katrina, my love, I am so very sorry. Your wedding day should have been celebrated with a feast to end all feasts. Your gown should have been the most exquisite. Your father should have given his blessing as he laid your hand in mine. Even a peasant bride would expect more than you have had this day. And yet," he caressed her cheek, trailing his finger across her lips, "I am certain there has been no other path for us to follow. Now that we are truly wed nothing can keep us apart. We are no longer two, but one. I pledge you my life, my heart, my soul. When we depart, I will return to Eaglesheid and attempt to bring peace between our families."

Her laugh was more like a child than the woman of the moment before. "I desire no blessings on our marriage as long as I have you. In such a manner did my mother marry my father ... it is the way of all true love." And then she had lifted her hands and untied the ribands on her gown. Once loosened, it slid from her shoulders, but the fullness of her breasts had prevented it from falling to the floor—

Sebastian shifted uncomfortably on his horse. If he let his memories linger there, in that small chamber at Breden, this would be an exceedingly long and tortuous ride. Deliberately, he turned his thoughts from that fleeting hour he had spent with his bride to the mundane details of his present journey.

Thirty leagues, south and east, lay between Eaglesheid and the mountain fortress of Ravensberg. Even so, it would not be an arduous trek: The difficulty lay in feeding and quartering his men, for his company was large. Nearly a score of knights and their squires rode with him, while twice that number followed, forming an escort for the baggage train bearing gifts for Lady Isabel.

The days passed peacefully. No rivals were encountered on the road, no brigands disturbed them, and no monks offered them inordinate quantities of local beer. The men rode easily, for a knight is as comfortable on his horse as a priest is on his knees. Overhead, the June sun shone warm. The countryside was alive with the freshness of spring. Although most of the land was forested, they often passed large fields that had been cleared for farming, and the soil that showed beneath the young plants was rich and dark. Abbeys dotted the countryside, for the fertile farmland was an enticement to men of all estates. Castles also loomed up frequently, guardians of the wealth of the soil. An ancient road lay beneath, testimony that this land had always been prized for its bounty.

On their second day out from Eaglesheid, their pace had slowed and they rode at an easy trot. Raynar turned to the young standard-bearer on his far side. "Look closely, my boy," he said as he pointed into the distance. "Those are the Alps."

The boy's eyes widened. "But it's just clouds, isn't it, Sir Raynar?"

"Nay, lad," Raynar chuckled. "It's the mountains. I like to think of them as Amazons. Proud and haughty in their nakedness, yet waiting through the ages for someone to come and melt their ice. We should be able to see them better by evening, if the sky remains clear. Did you know those peaks are always covered with snow?"

"Even on the hottest summer day?" he asked in disbelief, looking across to Sebastian, who nodded in confirmation. "But how is that possible, Sir Raynar?"

"Well, I once heard it was to punish a selfish man."

The lad grinned. "Tell me. Please?"

"Now you've done it," Sebastian groaned. "We'll not have another moment's peace today." But he cocked his ears to listen to the story as eagerly as the boy.

Raynar tossed a look of disgust at Sebastian then gave all his attention to the lad. "Once there was a baron who lived in a large castle right on the side of the alp. He was blessed with many good things, for the mountain was fertile and he had much wealth. He also had a beautiful wife who gave him three daughters, and a son for an heir.

"But the baron grew more and more morose with each passing day. From his castle perched high on the mountain, he could see far, far into the distance, onto other mountains which he did not own.

"Now one day, he heard that the ruler of those lands had an only child, a beautiful daughter. The evil baron, deciding that he would marry the girl, killed his faithful wife. But it was to no purpose for the fraulein refused to marry him and no one could make her say her vows.

"The baron stormed on his mountaintop for many passing days. He swore he would have the land for his own, or no one would.

"And then he had a cunning idea. He would send his son to woo the girl, and when the lad returned with his bride-to-be the baron would marry her himself. And that is what he did. When the girl saw the handsome knight, she nearly swooned with love for him and eagerly agreed to marry him. But the lad could not bear to deceive her for he was fainting with love himself, so they pledged their troth and never returned to the mountain.

"But when the baron heard the news, he flew into a rage and roared and cursed in his anger and vowed to revenge his son's treachery. So doing, he mounted his horse and set out on a long journey, north and ever north, to the land where there is always snow and never night or day. There he came to the castle of the Snow Queen. One look at her would have frozen his heart, if it were not frozen already, for she was more cold than she was beautiful. And she was very, very beautiful.

"And he brought the Snow Queen back to his mountain and bade her make herself at home, knowing full well what she would do. She blew her icy breath in a blast that froze the mountain tops so solidly that they could not melt for a thousand years. But then she did what he had not expected. She turned and blew her icy breath on him.

"And if you were to go to that very spot, you could see him still, frozen solid in the ice which he had brought to his own mountain."

The lad's eyes were shining with wonder. "Is it true?"

"Let me teach you an important lesson, my boy. The truth, once spoken, becomes the tale; and in the same manner, tales become the truth."

Sebastian interrupted with a laugh. "And if you believe a single word that passes Sir Raynar's lips, then you are a fool."

"A fool, Sebastian?" Raynar raised his brow in mock seriousness. "To what greater honor could a man aspire?"

"Then, Raynar, I will leave you to your lessons." Sebastian reached out and patted his friend affectionately on his shoulder. "You teach them so very well!"

On the fourth day of their journey, the sun had already passed its zenith when the fortress of Ravensberg first came into sight. At the urging of their guide, the party had ridden to the top of a hill on which perched an ancient abbey. It was not the beer, welcome as it was, that motivated their detour, but the view. Beneath them, the forested land leveled then stretched out onto an open plain which then again, in turn, met the mountain foothills. There in the distance, visible only as a discoloration on the hillside, lay Ravensberg, their destination.

"Will we get there before nightfall?" One of the knights asked the question in everyone's mind.

"Aye. We should do that. If all goes well," their guide answered.

Sebastian eased his horse forward. Leaning over the neck of his mount, his finger traced the path of a river that lay in the valley. "Is the water deep?"

"Aye. It can be. Look there, my lord." The guide pointed. "See the path that runs down the hill and then cuts into the forest?"

"I see it."

"And look beyond the river. Do you see the faint outline of it again, just beyond the bend in the river?"

Sebastian shaded his eyes. "Yes."

"It is known as the fool's path, my lord. Many a man has tried to reach the far riverbank by following this trail. But they do not meet. It is an illusion. There is a different road which must be taken if one wishes to cross to the other side."

"I presume, old man, that you know where the correct path lies?" It was Raynar who spoke, transmitting in his voice their impatience.

"I know the ford, Sir Raynar. The water runs quickly over the rocks, yet I have never known it to be impassable, even in the spring. By the grace of God, we should reach Ravensberg before the curfew bell rings." With those words the guide eased his horse forward and led the party down the hill and into the forest.

Sebastian was just beginning to despair of reaching their destination before nightfall when they broke out of the trees and onto the open farmland. Across the plain, the castle was clearly visible. Urging their mounts to a gallop, the men sped forward and the distance rapidly narrowed. The sound of a trumpet arose from within the walls, and as if in answer, they dug their heels into their horse's sides, eager to reach the end of their journey.

But unexpectedly, from out of the gates halfway up the hill, rode a half-dozen men, followed by a handful more on foot with bows slung across their backs. Though the knights were not dressed for battle, their swords were drawn and at the ready. More telling, behind them the gates were pulled shut and additional archers took defensive positions on the walls.

Sebastian reacted with the speed of a natural leader. With one slashing motion of his arm, he signaled his companions to halt. Without taking his eyes from the approaching band, he waved his hand in the direction of the standard-bearer.

"It's our banner. They think we are enemies. Wait here, all of you. Under no circumstances are any of you to come forward or act in a threatening manner. If I am struck down, you must turn immediately and ride away. Hear me! We are here for a wedding, not a war." The words had been spoken quickly, for the attacking knights had nearly reached level ground, but the urgency in his voice was understood by all.

"Nay, Sebastian," shouted Raynar, as Sebastian dismounted.

Sebastian gave him a fierce look. "Sir Raynar, remember your oath of obedience." Then, he ran forward, holding his sword above his head. When he had gone some twenty paces he stopped and threw his weapon with an exaggerated, sideward motion, tossing it high and slow, so that no one would miss the action. All eyes watched it fall, far out of his reach. There was no doubting his meaning. He wished for a parley.

Standing still, Sebastian watched and waited as a half-dozen bows were lifted, fitted with arrows, and pointed at his heart. Silently he cursed himself for his folly. He had been so eager to see Katrina again that he had forgotten to take even the simplest of precautions. How could he have been so foolish as to forget to send an emissary to warn Lady Isabel of his imminent arrival? If he were killed, then Lord Branold would also die, and even Katrina's life would be placed in danger.

It seemed an age before the foremost rider dismounted, handed his sword to another, and began to move forward. Recognizing Gildren's nephew, Gregory of Marre, Sebastian strode to meet him.

As they spoke, Sebastian was acutely aware of his surroundings. On the one side, directly beneath the castle walls, a small party of archers stood poised, their bowstrings as taut as the muscles on their faces. On the other, a larger body of knights, garbed in their mail, waited. Though no weapons were drawn, their gloved fingers were wrapped tightly around the hilts of their swords. Over them all, the turrets of the castle threw long talons of darkness, for the sun had nearly disappeared behind the hills.

When he and Gregory had reached agreement they stretched out their arms and firmly clasped each others hand. The stillness broken, postures on both sides relaxed; and a shout of joy was raised by Sebastian's troops who were relieved that their peaceful mission had not turned into a bloodletting.

Raynar dismounted and strode forward. "Sebastian, you are a fool! You should not have taken such a risk."

"You are right." Sebastian grinned broadly in his relief. "I was a fool—not to have planned our approach more carefully. But if it was my stupidity that led us into trouble in the first place, then it is only fitting that it is my folly that leads us out."

"If they had killed you, then there would have been open war."

"Not if you obeyed my orders."

"Every inch of my body was alert and my eyeballs were looking in different directions. At the same time, I watched both you and those bastards who were aiming their arrows at your heart. If you had been harmed, I would have reacted instantly for your revenge."

Sebastian stood still. When he spoke there was a hardness in his voice. "I am your liege. It is your duty to obey me."

"No." Raynar shook his head, and said softly, "You were my friend before you were my liege-lord. I would never desert you—even at the king's command."

Sebastian tried to feel anger but he could not. He clasped Raynar to him and held him close for a moment. "Thank you. Perhaps I knew you would not obey me. Perhaps I counted on it. Come. Let us enter Ravensberg with Sir Gregory." He pointed to the knight who stood a short distance away, watching them. "Come, Raynar. I am ready to meet my bride!"

# Chapter 7

RAYNAR HAD NEVER SEEN SEBASTIAN in such an irrepressible mood. He laughed. He teased. He had a merry word for everyone. As he moved through Ravensberg's hall, he left a trail of excitement in his wake. The maids blushed at his compliments and the youths gazed at him in open admiration. Even the older servitors, frowning at first as they recollected that this man was the son of the hated Duke Frederick, began to nod their heads and cluck their tongues in approval. Raynar shook his own head in amazement, marveling that the same events that had left himself exhausted, had somehow intoxicated his friend.

The parchment with the treaty had been delivered to Lady Isabel. There was nothing now to do but wait. Holding a goblet of thick red wine, Raynar flopped onto a three-legged stool and leaned against the wall. When a page approached Sebastian and led him away to an audience with the duchess, Raynar only acknowledged his departure with a weak salute. The hum of voices and the beat of footsteps hurrying back and forth between the tables and the kitchens combined to tempt him to sleep. His eyelids drooped and his goblet began to tip precariously to one side.

"I bid you welcome, Sir Raynar."

The wine nearly spilt when he awoke from his doze with a start. It was his battle-trained instincts that saved the rushes from a dousing.

Before him stood a young woman with a sad, grave face. Raynar rose to his feet and bowed deeply, with a dexterity that proved he'd had much practice for not a drop of the ruby liquid was lost. "At your service, fraulein."

She laughed, in acceptance of the comic role he had chosen to play, but it was a joyless sound with no accompanying humor in her eyes. There would be no sport here, of that he was certain. He should dismiss her from his interest without wasting any time. Yet, incredibly, he was intrigued. What was it about her? She was nearly as tall as himself, yet graceful. Her skin was fair; her eyes gray-blue; her hair the color of ripened wheat. But—there was something more. Some deep inner stillness drew Raynar to her, as a thirsty hart is drawn to a pool.

Holding out her hand, she introduced herself. "I am Eleanor. Lord Branold's daughter."

Deftly, he transferred his goblet to his left hand and raised her fingers to his lips. "I should have known. If you had given me but a moment longer, I am certain I would have guessed."

"But why?"

"You are very like him. He carries the appearance of his ancestors so strongly that I occasionally have imagined him with furs around his shoulders standing in the prow of his long ship."

Her eyes leapt to life, no longer dull, but as focused as a blade of steel. "You have seen him?"

"Frequently. I have just come from Eaglesheid. Since you are not Katrina, his eldest, you must be the younger of the two." He leaned forward in his eagerness to tell of the purpose of their embassy. "I bring news which will give you cheer. Your father will soon be free."

She ducked her head, but not before he saw a trickle of tears wash away the sharpness of her gaze. "But it is too late!"

Raynar frowned at her in bewilderment.

"I am very sorry." Eleanor sniffled, then squared her shoulders and wiped her eyes with the corner of her shawl. "Of course, I am happy. How could I not rejoice at such news? Please forgive me. I desired to welcome you to Ravensberg, not to christen you with salt water."

"I am welcomed." With his free hand, Raynar drew her onto the stool then settled himself cross-legged on the floor. "Speak with me a moment, if you will. Your words confuse me. Why is it too late for your father to return home?" As he asked the question he raised his goblet to his lips.

"Because..." Her shoulders drooped. "Because my sister, Katrina, is dead. We received the news but four days past."

The wine finally landed on the front of Raynar's tunic as he sputtered in his surprise. "But it isn't possible! She is to marry Sebastian."

"I hardly think she will be able to!" she said, with incredible fierceness. "She is dead. I am sorry that your plans are ruined, but there is nothing left for any of us except pain and regret. If only—" She stopped suddenly and clamped her mouth shut.

But Raynar would not be denied. "If only what?" he pressed.

She sighed. "There are so many regrets. But there's one that keeps ringing in my head. If only she had not gone to Breden last Yuletide, then none of this would have happened."

"She was at Breden?" Raynar clenched his goblet so that his fingers wouldn't shake. "At the king's Christmas court?"

Sensing his tension, she frowned at him, but did not speak.

"But I was there! Tell me, fraulein. What did your sister look like? Was she very much like you?"

Eleanor shook her head. "Nothing at all like me. She was petite, and delicate, and very beautiful. Her eyes were like yours, brown as nuts, and she had the longest lashes you have ever seen. But it was her hair people truly noticed. When it was loose, it hung to her waist in an amazing mass of curls, but even twisted up, there was none that could compare. Do you remember her?"

He shook his head. "I am sorry. There were so many people there." But with sudden certainty he knew Sebastian remembered Katrina very well. Was that the reason Sebastian had so eagerly pursued this marriage?

The knowledge that this was true hit Raynar like an unexpected blow from a lance. How had Sebastian been able to hide his feelings so well? And why? The two of them had always shared everything: food, plans, plunder, and dreams. He felt a twinge of resentment but it was quickly supplanted by pity. The fraulein was dead. The truce was broken. Sebastian had come for a wedding, but he would be mourning instead.

Forcing his thoughts away from Sebastian, Raynar focused on the girl before him. She was like a willow in winter, bending beneath the burden of her pain. "How did she die, Fraulein Eleanor?" he asked, as gently as he could. "You said you had word of her death. Was she not here at Ravensberg?"

"No." Eleanor looked down and began to run her fingers through the fringed edge of her shawl. "It is a strange story. She had not been well since she returned from Breden, but beyond that, there was nothing. She must have had a touch of delirium, for she packed a sack with a few belongings and left the castle early one morning, a fortnight ago." Eleanor glanced up, then returned her gaze to her hands. "Why she left and how she evaded the searchers, we know not. Of course, Lady Isabel sent out men to find her, but when they did it was too late. She had already died from her fever. And I—"

"Mistress?" A page broke into their conversation.

Slowly, as though readjusting her thoughts, Eleanor turned to the lad. "Yes?"

"The duchess bids you to her antechamber. And you also, Sir Raynar."

"Thank you. We shall come straight away."

They stood and walked together. "Let us speak of this no more," she said, then emphasized her desire to change the nature of their discussion by sweeping her hand to encompass the hall. "What do you think of our castle, Sir Raynar?"

He looked about and began to stammer a response, for in truth the hall was old and left much to be desired. How could he answer without giving insult?

"Would it help you choose your answer, if I told you that Lady Isabel calls it a relic, fit only for men who are themselves old relics. When first she arrived she was appalled by the smells and the dampness and the lack of light."

Relieved that he need not give false praise, Raynar relaxed. "Then, not wishing to disparage the opinion of a lady, I will say only that it is a confining space."

"But as for myself, I find it cozy."

"Then I will say that it is a very comfortable place to visit."

Eleanor chuckled, a low but genuine sound. "The ramparts are crumbling."

"It is appealing in its history."

"The well has been known to dry up."

"It is … ahh … dry?"

She smiled and Raynar felt a thrill of pleasure.

"You win nothing for that answer. Now this room," she stopped and pointed at the closed door which they approached, "is Lady Isabel's pride. My stepmother hired a master mason from Rome to design a place where she could sit in privacy."

He nodded as she knocked.

It was Lady Isabel who threw open the door. "Welcome, Sir Raynar. Your fame precedes you. We are delighted to have you here at Ravensberg, and trust you may be persuaded to entertain us with a tale this evening in our hall."

Raynar spared a quick glance for Sebastian, who was standing motionless and silent on the far side of the room, then returned his attention to his hostess. As he bowed and kissed her hand he marveled at her brilliant beauty. "Thank you for your kindness, my lady. And now that I have beheld you, I can understand why it is that Lord Branold pines to return to his home." Then he cursed himself for his stupidity. Where was his golden tongue now, when he needed it so desperately? What an inept fool he was to speak of Gildren's return, just when all hope of it had been destroyed.

Yet no distress marred Isabel's face; indeed she radiated happiness. "Sir Raynar. Eleanor." She included them both in her gesture. "We are to have a celebration. I have sent for goblets and some fresh wine—ah, here we are. Come, Sir Sebastian, and join us." Without hurrying her movements or her announcement, the duchess poured generous portions into each chalice and served the wine to her guests.

Confused, Raynar tried to anticipate her announcement. Why was Lady Isabel bursting with excitement? Sebastian's rigid face certainly held no answers.

Holding her cup aloft, Lady Isabel turned toward Sebastian. "I propose a toast to my new son."

Raynar choked, and for the second time that evening spilt wine on his garment. But when he glanced askance at Eleanor, he saw that she was looking beyond him to Sebastian, her face soft and shy.

"How can you possibly be surprised, Sir Raynar?" Lady Isabel asked. "Was this not the purpose of your journey?"

"Yes, my lady. But I ..." Before he further embarrassed himself by stating that he did not understand how a marriage could take place when the bride was dead, realization struck him—and with it a sense of loss. Making a show of wiping the wine from his shirt, he turned to Lady Isabel. The broad grin he wore proved he was a man of good humor, even when the jest was on himself.

"Indeed you are right, my lady. But I had forgotten the terms of the contract. Now that the younger daughter is the elder, of course she will make the agreed marriage. Allow me to congratulate you, Lady Isabel, and to offer you my condolences on the recent death of your stepdaughter."

The line of Sebastian's mouth tightened. Taking this as evidence that his conjectures were correct, Raynar determined to free him from this situation.

"Fraulein Eleanor, you will make a most beautiful bride." Bending over her hand he gave it a gentle kiss. "I can heartily recommend your bridegroom to you, having known him for the greater part of his life."

Then he raised his cup. "My lady, allow me to offer a toast."

"Certainly." Isabel sounded pleased.

"To Lord Branold, the absent host. May he soon take his rightful place again."

"Thank you, Sir Raynar. You are very kind."

"When is the marriage to occur?"

"The day after the arrival of your baggage carts." Isabel turned to her stepdaughter and indicated the parchment which lay on the nearby table. "According to the terms of this contract, your father will be released the moment you arrive at Eaglesheid as the wife of Sir Sebastian."

Tears glistened in Eleanor's eyes, and when she nodded her understanding, Raynar seized the opportunity to redirect the conversation. "My lady, though I am loath to admit to any weakness, I cannot deny that the smells of food being prepared have unmanned me. Is this some torture designed to break the will of lusty knights? If so, then I must admit to its success."

Isabel laughed, a clear sweet sound. "Indeed, sir, that pleases me to hear. I command you to come to the board and amuse me. Surely, that will not be an onerous task for you?"

"Nay, my fair lady, it will be a pleasure."

Eleanor blushed as she looked at Sebastian. "My lord? Will you join me at the board?"

Finally, Sebastian looked at her and spoke. One word. "Yes." Then he held out his arm and escorted her into the hall.

Eleanor could not allow that day to end without sharing her happiness with her beloved grandmother. Poor Lady Sophie—who lived the life of a recluse in the castle keep—had suffered grievously since Katrina's death. With little to intrude upon her solitude and distract her attention, she had been unrelievedly immersed in her own private sorrow.

"Is that you, child?" The distorted tones of Sophie's voice called out to Eleanor, even before she entered the tower room.

"Of course it is, Grandmama," she laughed.

"But you sound so strange—Eleanor!" The spindle sailed out of the dowager's hand and landed in the cushion of carded wool at her feet. "What has happened, child? You are glowing like an angel. Even with the candles burning, I can see that."

Eleanor flew across the room and knelt at Lady Sophie's feet. Taking the blue-veined hands into her own, she looked up, past the grotesque features of her grandmother's face, into the loving depths of her eyes.

"I have met tonight the man I am to marry."

"Ah. And I do not need to ask if he pleases you."

"If I could choose any man in Christendom to be my husband, it would be he."

"So sure!" her grandmother exclaimed. "Even I did not fall for my Bestilden so quickly." She paused. "How strange it is. I always thought it was your sister who would throw her candle at the moon. She was so like my Judith ..." Her voice trailed off, and for a moment she appeared to withdraw within herself, then she jerked her head upward and touched Eleanor's cheek with her finger.

"So, who is this man who stole your sturdy heart? Is he some heathenish princeling with wild roguish ways, or a vain Frankish rooster?"

Eleanor laughed as she kissed Lady Sophie's hand. "Neither. And before you disappear into your dreams, let me tell you the rest of the news. Papa is coming home!"

The dowager's breath caught in her throat and she stared at Eleanor with wonder. "Branold," she whispered. "I did not think I would live to see the day. Tell me, child. And be quick."

"Westfeld and Gildren have agreed to an alliance of marriage. Gildren's freedom in exchange for his daughter. I am to marry his son, Sebastian."

"The man who stole your heart?"

"Yes." Eleanor smiled.

"Who is not a barbarian like his father?"

"Not a barbarian at all."

"Tall?"

"Tall. With dark hair that curls around his ears, and dark eyes that pucker at the corners in the most appealing way."

"Ah! So you fell for a peacock, not a rooster."

Eleanor shook her head, as though she were seriously considering the question. "I have seen comely men before, yet have never lost my heart."

"Now don't give me any defense. My Bestilden was the handsomest man I ever met—or so it seemed to me—though not everyone would agree, not at all. But never mind that. Tell me, child, does this Sebastian admire you as well?"

Eleanor looked down at the floor and frowned. "In truth, he has paid me scant attention. He has been polite, but..." She was silent for a moment, then raised her head and met her grandmother's eyes. "I do not think he could describe my looks. I doubt he even knows the color of my hair, though he fed me from his plate all through the supper."

"Then let us see what we can do to capture his attention," Sophie said as she retrieved her spindle and the skein of wool, and set them aside. "My

Bestilden always said that putting the plumage on was almost as much fun as taking it off again. Come, child, we'll see what we can find in these old chests for you." She pointed to one of the larger coffers. "There. Open that one first."

Kneeling, Eleanor obeyed her grandmother. When she raised the lid, exposing the cloth which had been hidden from sight for years, she gasped aloud in delight. "These are beautiful, Grandmama. Such wondrous fabrics. These were not made here in Gildren."

Sophie caressed the exquisite materials. "Oh, what memories these bring back, child. You cannot imagine what a delightful place this world was when I was young. There were always pleasures—hunts or tournaments or grand feasts. Everyone was attracted to our court—actors, troubadours, jugglers, and of course all the young knights on their quests for glory.

"In those days, people really knew how to live. Even the weather was better." Her eyes glowed with her memories. "The winters were really winter. Cold and crisp. We would wrap ourselves in deliciously warm fox fur and ride the hunt across the frozen ground with our icy breath trailing behind. There is nothing in all the world to make one feel so alive—"

Sophie stopped suddenly, her enthusiasm gone. "What wouldn't I give to feel alive again."

With a heavy sigh, she returned her attention to the clothing in the chest. "You are right about this cloth. Your grandfather was a great and powerful man, and whenever he traveled he would search it out and bring it back, for he knew how much I loved it. The Flemish and Florentine merchants knew to save him their best. Look at these." As she spoke she began pulling the gowns from the chest. "Velvets and linens from Brussels, lace from Brugge, satins from Florence, silks from Constantinople. Nothing but the finest for Sophie, Duchess of Bestilden.

"But look at me now." She pointed to her face, disfigured by the pox. "What would my dear Besti say if he saw me now?"

"If he loved you as much as you claim, Grandmama, he would have grieved for your pain and continued to love you still."

"Perhaps," Lady Sophie looked doubtful. "I know it is what your father would have done were it Judith who had survived, but I am not certain about my Bestilden. Yet I could not blame him, for in truth, I cannot accept myself. If I could, then there would be no reason for me to hide here away from the world."

Her hand dropped into her lap and her eyes searched the face of her granddaughter with sorrow. "I blame myself for Katrina's death. If I had not relinquished my authority to Isabel, perhaps Katrina would be alive today."

Eleanor stood and walked a pace toward the window. The shutters were open and the moonlight flowed into the room. "There are too many people blaming themselves for Katrina's death. You, me, Gregory... even Isabel."

Lady Sophie immediately tensed, but said nothing.

"I went to the duchess after Wolfram died. Before that I had been so numbed by my sorrow that I could not leave my bed. But when I heard of Wolfram's death, I was so overcome that I went to her chamber to confront her."

Eleanor closed her eyes as she remembered the scene. Isabel had been pacing the room—wild-eyed in her distress. 'I love your father,' she had cried. 'All I ever wanted was to bear his children and make him happy. Yet I have ruined all. I would give anything, even my life, if it would bring Katrina home!' And Eleanor had calmed her, and together they had promised that the secret of Katrina's child would be kept. For Isabel. For Eleanor. For Branold. But most of all, for Katrina. To let her memory rest in peace.

"She was distraught by Katrina's death," Eleanor said now. "And we pledged each other our support."

"I never thought I should live to see so much sorrow." Sophie shook her head as she stroked the gown on her lap. "The Fates have mocked me for the pleasures of my youth. To take your mother who wanted to live, and leave me who wanted to die, was a cruel jest indeed.

"But we have forgotten our task," she said, as she reached for the circlet of keys at her waist. "What has happened has happened and can't be changed. Our task now, is to unlock all the chests until we find the clothes which will make your Sebastian forget all else."

But try as they might, they could not find one gown which could be made to serve Eleanor, for she was a good six fingers taller than any of her feminine ancestors. Holding up one of the prettiest, a delicately embroidered silk shift, Eleanor chuckled, "It's no use, Grandmama. This would fit Katrina, but it certainly will not fit me." The sound died in her throat and she whispered, "If Katrina were still alive, this would be for her wedding that we are preparing. It is as though all these things are waiting here for her."

"Katrina is dead, child. Mourn for her, but do not mourn your own fate." She looked startled. "A good lesson for myself, I should say. Now, I am going to shut all of these up where they can lie for another decade. Who knows? Perhaps there is someone else all these clothes await."

# Chapter 8

T HAT FIRST MORNING after their arrival at Ravensberg, Sebastian roused Raynar so early that the two of them were at the gate almost before the dawn. Making no attempt to bridle his impatience, Sebastian curtly ordered the porter to raise the portcullis. The man obeyed, but grumbled about foreigners as he bent his strength to the pulley.

As he waited, Sebastian said nothing. He did not need to. The scowl that furrowed his face expressed his impatience better than any words. Even his horse, sensing his frustration, tossed its head and danced sideways in agitation. Gripping the reins, Sebastian mastered the passions which threatened to break loose. In contrast, Raynar sat at ease on his mount, one hand loosely holding the reins and the other an apple he had pilfered from the storeroom. Yet when the iron teeth were at last raised, they both burst into motion at the same instant. In a flash they passed the porter: Sebastian, with his jaw clenched and his body pressed forward, and Raynar, who with uncanny accuracy tossed a coin and an apple core to the irate man.

The two knights rode hard. Quickly they crossed the plain that fronted the castle and its hill, then barely slowing their pace, plunged into the forest. Here, they tested their equestrian skills to the limit, careering through a dangerous course of rotting logs, dried creek-beds, and low-hanging branches. Every nerve and sense had to be used at its keenest level. No longer was Raynar lackadaisical nor Sebastian tensely overwrought. Nothing existed except themselves and their chosen opponent, the forest.

Without any warning, they broke out of the trees and were riding down a street—in reality a narrow path—which divided the two halves of a tiny village. Still they continued their wild, headlong gallop. Chickens shrieked and frantically flapped out of harm's way. One skinny piglet, too young even to recognize the sounds of danger, was crushed beneath the hooves of Raynar's horse. Its squeal of terror was silenced almost at the moment it began.

Past the huts, heading again toward the trees which stood at the outer edge of the clearing, they continued their reckless race. Newly planted corn and young plants of onions and beans, just beginning to appear from beneath the soil, all were scattered beneath the onslaught of the eight ironclad hooves. Just as they were about to leave the field and reenter the wood, there was again movement in their pathway. This time it was a toddler, struggling to stand and balance on his feet.

Letting out a cry that could be either curse or warning, Raynar pulled ferociously on his reins. His horse stopped its forward motion but its forelegs rose upward and wildly pawed the air, searching for solid ground. In the same moment, Sebastian slowed his own horse, slid off its back, and in one perfectly-timed motion rolled himself and the tiny boy out of danger's path.

As Sebastian sat in the dirt, clutching the child, the light around him dimmed. He heard nothing, felt nothing, saw nothing. How long he sat there, he knew not. It was Raynar's voice, distant at first, then louder and more insistent, that finally drew him back to the world. Blinking away the haze that still covered his eyes, Sebastian turned to his friend, realizing in the same instant that his arms were empty.

"Have you lost your mind?" Raynar rounded on him in fury. "You could have been crushed! Just like that piglet back there."

Ignoring Raynar for a moment, Sebastian sought the source of the high-pitched wail that suddenly sounded as clear to him as a trumpet's blast on a winter's night. The child, who looked scarcely old enough to walk, was lurching on stubby legs toward the distant huts, arms outstretched as he sought to hold his balance. Sebastian sighed with relief, casting up a prayer of thankfulness that the lad had suffered no permanent harm.

He pointed at the little boy as he turned back to Raynar. "And what about that child? Should I have left him to be crushed?"

"You have no right to endanger your life to save a peasant's brat."

"Doubtless the lad's mother would have been happy with the exchange."

"You speak such foolishness. She is a nothing. Her child is a nothing."

"Listen to yourself! Do you truly think that I am greater in God's eyes, because I wear a sword and a polished buckle? I knew the risk, Raynar, and I deemed it worth the effort."

But Raynar's anger was not assuaged. "Are you so anxious to avoid this wedding that you would kill yourself instead?"

Sebastian stiffened. Without deigning to answer, he remounted his horse and set off across the field, but this time at a more sedate pace. Raynar followed him in silence for many minutes, then at last he drew alongside.

"Forget the child. I do not acknowledge that you are right; except to admit that if you thought as I do on these matters, then I would have no reason to admire you. But as for the other—about your marriage—it is time for us to talk." Raynar waited, half-expecting Sebastian to set spur and ride away; but when he continued to walk at the same pace, Raynar persevered. "I was slow to see how matters lay, but I now understand, at least in part. You met Fraulein Katrina at Breden, determined to marry her, and with Terlinden's help manipulated your father to that end. It was Katrina you came to marry—not just Branold's daughter. When we arrived yesterday and learned of her death, you certainly could have found some honorable way to renege on the treaty's terms. Yet you did not. And that is what I cannot fathom."

Sebastian had stopped his horse while Raynar spoke, and now he turned it until their horses faced one another, neck to neck. Even then he did not speak for a long time.

"She did not even receive a Christian burial," he finally said, as he stared at the dust on his arm. "Her ashes were left to blow away in the wind. I loved her, Raynar. It is as simple as that. And yet she was the daughter of the man whose life I have nearly destroyed. All this night long I have searched my soul, holding a torch to every dusty corner, seeking every hidden deceit. And this I've come to know. Neither my love, nor even my lust, bore weight against the debt I owed to Gildren. If I had not truly believed that marriage to Katrina could buy Branold his freedom, I would have ridden away from Breden, never to see her again. But she is dead, and unless I marry her sister it all is for naught! So, I will marry Eleanor."

As he spoke those last words Sebastian shuddered, for he had not told all. Indeed, the very worst had been left unspoken. Not even to Raynar could Sebastian reveal the secret of his marriage to Katrina, for Church law forbade a man to marry the sister of his wife.

To hide his agitation, Sebastian leaned forward and stroked the neck of his horse. When he sat up again, he shook his head and sighed. "How my father would laugh to see me now! Though years have passed since that night at Eaglesheid, I still am struggling to escape his trap. Every time I pry open its teeth, it slams shut again, catching another vulnerable part." Then he shrugged, as though to make light of his own words. "I suppose it's rather comical after all. The hand that should be reaching down to help me out of the mire is the very one that first pushed me in."

"Well, if that's the kind of amusement you enjoy, I wish you had told me years ago." Raynar raised his brow with a wry grin. "I have put forth much effort to make you laugh with feats of wit…and witless feats. Next time, I'll just shove you into a swamp."

"Go ahead, throw me in. Just make certain you pull me out again." Sebastian smiled, then returned to the discussion at hand. "Every part of me cries out against this alliance. Though I will follow the path before me, Raynar I swear to you that I'll not be bound. I desire no more betrayal, or loss."

"And Eleanor?" Raynar asked, as they began their return to Ravensberg. "Do you not think of her in this matter?"

"Of course I do. Though she's as unappealing as an unlit fire, I would wish her no ill. But surely she has no expectations of me. She knows I do not marry her for love. I arrived with a treaty, not simpering odes." They traveled some distance in silence before Sebastian asked, "Have you never thought to marry?"

"You know I love my horse too well. Show me a road to travel and give me a story to tell. That's all I've ever wanted."

"Has there never been anyone to tempt you otherwise?"

"There was one...once. But it served no purpose."

"Would she not have you?"

"I'll never know. By the time I met her, it was too late. She was already spoken for. It seems we are both doomed to be unlucky in love. You know, Sebastian, that I wish you happiness with all my heart."

The men reached out, bridging the distance between their horses, clasping one another's shoulders, and communicating with their eyes the depth of their friendship.

During the next few days, preparations for the marriage celebration moved forward with astonishing swiftness. As agreed, the nuptials were to be performed on the morning following the arrival of the carts from Eaglesheid. Raynar expressed his surprise that Sebastian was willing to proceed with such swiftness, but Sebastian dismissed his question. "It is the same when you prepare for battle—the hours beforehand seem interminable. There is no benefit to delay. None at all. I want to get this over with, then live out my life such as I may."

Although Sebastian and Raynar had little enough to do, that was not true of the residents of Ravensberg. From sunrise to sunset and even beyond, the womenfolk labored. Fingers flew as they stitched the linen cloths and garments which would be packed into chests and sent with Eleanor to Eaglesheid. The older children were given silver to shine, stairways to scrub and corners to clear of cobwebs. The children who were too young for these tasks were set to watch the ones who were younger still. Townsfolk were hired to help the understaffed cooks in the kitchens or the squires who were busy repairing and polishing the armor and the metal-works. Bags of wheat were taken to the gristmill to be ground into flour. Lady Isabel had especially ordered that two sacks of white flour were to be prepared so that all the bread at the wedding feast would be of the purest quality. The butcher was commanded to have on hand two barley-fattened cows and a dozen suckling piglets that would be slaughtered at first light on the wedding morning.

When, on the sixth day after Sebastian's arrival, a shout went up that the baggage carts had been sighted, there was a rush of onlookers to peer over the battlements. There, with the sunlight glancing off the armor of the escorting knights, was the train, moving slowly across the field.

It took only minutes for the news to spread throughout the castle. For the first time in a week the work was set aside as everyone hurried into the yard. Before long, the carts reached the road at the foot of the hill and began the slow ascent to the castle. Sebastian and Raynar mounted their horses and rode forward to meet their party. Many other knights followed. The youngsters, who had been trying to peer over the inner walls while their mothers had been seeking to restrain them, quickly darted out through the open gateway. By the time the carts rolled under the lintel, they were surrounded by laughing, dancing children. The skittish war horses were immediately led away, but the larger, gentler ones which pulled the carts, stood where they were placed and ignored the bodies which pressed up against them.

Sebastian stepped forward and formally presented the contents of the wagons to Lady Isabel; then Raynar spread his arms and cried out, "Let us not leave these people in suspense any longer. Untie the ropes! My lady, come closer, so you may see. And you also Fraulein Eleanor. What is taking so long with those knots? Do not people here in the mountains know how to handle a rope? You need not be a sailor to have such a skill. Here lad, let me lift you up and you may pull back that canvas. There! That's more like it. Sebastian, where is your trumpet? I think a trumpet would serve well right now. Nobody has a trumpet? Well, a little improvisation never hurts." He raised his hands to his lips and with surprising clarity blew an elaborate flourish.

The canvas on the first cart was pulled back. Raynar pointed at the sacks with his right hand and shouted to the crowd, "Behold! And rejoice!"

Together, Sebastian and Raynar supervised the opening of the sacks, one by one. They were filled almost to overflowing with exotic foodstuffs: almonds, pecans, salt, ginger, figs, and raisins. The cook's eyes were not the only ones which widened as the contents were displayed for Lady Isabel's approval. Clapping their hands, the children began to dance around, squealing in their delight.

The second cart elicited even more excitement, for it held five large butts of wine. Each was marked with a different symbol, indicating the five different localities of Bordeaux, Bordelais, Rochelle, Cyprus and Crete. Sebastian called for four goblets, but when a servant turned to run toward the castle storerooms, Raynar forestalled him.

"We will drink in style. Open the first chest, there on the last cart," he pointed.

Hands flew to it but the lid would not open until one of the knights produced a small key that was hanging from his girdle. When the lid was finally raised, a gasp of amazement went up at the display of silver goblets and plates nestled in the straw. Raynar quickly drew out four goblets, ordered a knight to sit on the lid of the chest, and returned to Sebastian.

Holding one of the cups beneath the spigot of the nearest butt, Sebastian filled it nearly to the brim. Then, handing it carefully to Lady Isabel, he spoke in a loud voice for the many onlookers to hear. "My lady, drink your own wine in your own goblet, a special gift from my father, Frederick, duke of Westfeld, in token of his pledge to release your husband, Branold, duke of Gildren." There was no need to add the duke's comment that he hoped Lady Isabel would drink it and choke. "This wine is the best that is available in Christendom … if my father is to be believed."

"Thank you, Sir Sebastian. I have every reason to believe that your father is as good as his word." A cheer rose from the crowd and Lord Branold's name was chanted over and over. Turning to the steward who was standing nearby, taking a mental inventory of the contents of the three wagons, Isabel ordered that a cask of beer be brought up from the buttery. "We will have a celebration. Where are the musicians?" Her sparkling eyes searched through the crowd. One of the lutenists pushed himself forward and she called to him, "Hurry, Anselm. Run and fetch your instrument. This is a great day for us all. Your lord will be returning home!"

The cheer swelled louder and louder as her words were passed through the crowd. Eleanor's eyes danced, and she raised her goblet in a salute to her betrothed. Allowing his cup to touch hers lightly, Sebastian gave her a chilled smile, then turned toward the wagons to help supervise the unloading.

The following day dawned barely noticed, for it was dark, rainy and utterly dismal. It was late when Sebastian awoke, yet still he lay abed, desperately clinging to the sleep he had left behind. He had been dreaming of Katrina. She had been here, in Ravensberg, alive. He had been holding her, stroking her silky skin, breathing the scent of her glorious hair, lost in a rising passion which had mounted higher and higher and then abruptly, and frustratingly, disappeared into nothingness as he had awakened unfulfilled. The dream had left him desolate, aching for the woman he loved. Yet his despair only increased his determination: He would pay tribute to his love for Katrina by giving her the gift of her father's liberty.

The only man who could have prevented him from taking this dreadful step was dead, for the priest at Breden had died midwinter, killed by his tired lungs. Would God ever forgive him for what he was about to do? Or was God like his earthly father, only seeking the opportunity to make him suffer. And would he ever know?

An hour passed and still Sebastian was unable to summon the will to rise from his bed. Raynar chuckled when he entered the room. "You must be the only person who is not up and frantically busy. Come. Get dressed." He reached for the floor, scooped up Sebastian's crumpled tunic, and threw it at him. "We have time for a ride before you are needed today. The priest insists that you are to fast this morning, but I see no reason why a man needs an empty stomach to pledge his troth. Here—" A chunk of bread appeared out of his sleeve and flew at Sebastian. "I salvaged a morsel for you."

"Stop throwing things at me. That is all I need today—a madman raving at my bedside."

Raynar grinned wickedly. "I see you are in wonderful humor this morning, my lord."

"And what would you expect?" Sebastian grumbled as he sat up and began to dress. "This is not exactly the happiest day of my life."

Raynar's face shadowed, but he turned away and walked toward the small window through which the misty chill was swirling. For a moment he said nothing, as though he were intent on the sodden landscape. When finally he did speak, his voice was controlled, disinterested, slightly mocking.

"I know what you have told me, but if you wish, you can still escape this wedding. No one will wonder at us riding off together. And if we do not return…" He shrugged. "Well, it will be too late. I would rather enjoy the rage into which that would send the lovely Isabel. It's a pity I would not be here to see it."

"I wish more than anything that I could ride away, but it's not possible." Sebastian spoke with steely determination. "This wedding must take place."

"Sebastian."

Their eyes met, and Sebastian was surprised by the rare seriousness that he now saw on Raynar's face.

"I trust that when you marry the fraulein you intend to do right by her."

"Do you think I am suddenly going to begin mistreating women, just because I am married to one?"

"Of course not. I am sorry. It's just that—" Raynar broke off, but then continued with his usual humor. "Well, you have not had much practice at being married, have you?"

"You are right!" Sebastian's eyes flashed as he thrust his dagger into his girdle. "Not nearly enough!" Pushing past Raynar, he strode out of the room, but turned again as he crossed the threshold. "But by the saints," he shouted, "I've had much more than you!"

The wedding feast had been in progress for many hours. The quantity of food and the variety of delicacies and entertainments, although not unsurpassed, had certainly been impressive.

Seated with Eleanor at his sword-arm and his hostess at his left, Sebastian lifted his cup in satisfaction. He had finally achieved the goal toward which he had been moving ever since the chalice of wine had been placed in his hands by the priest during the nuptial communion—to become drunk enough that the inane jests, more than hinting at the pleasures he would find tonight in his marriage bed, seemed uproariously funny—to become drunk enough that the press of faces leering up the length of the table at him, became one unrecognizable cluster of well-wishing friends—to become drunk enough that he could no longer see the frown which lay hidden beneath Raynar's brilliant smile—and most of all, to become drunk enough that the rigid form of the girl sitting beside him faded into a blur of sensuality.

There was a flurry of activity followed by an outburst of riotous laughter and table-thumping. Like a ripple in a pool, the sound spread as the jest was repeated for those who had not heard the original.

"The juggler slipped..." A balding, bearded knight leaned forward, laughing and licking his lips salaciously. "One of his knives drew blood on his forearm. And then he said, 'I daresay that's not the only blood a blade will spill tonight!' " As the meaning of the jest struck home, everyone roared with approval; even Eleanor laughed, although her cheeks were shaded a touch of pink.

"A taper! A taper!" A voice called out, and soon drunken voices had taken up the chant and heavy hands were banging on the tables. "A taper!" It was time to light the bridal couple to bed.

In the soft candlelight, as they were escorted through the passageways to their bedchamber, Eleanor looked very young and vulnerable and Sebastian felt a tremor of sympathy—or was it merely lust? He shrugged. It mattered not. Either one would serve tonight.

The chamber was far too small to allow the entire party to participate in the disrobing. Some of the guests crowded into the doorway, straining to catch a glimpse of the couple, but most lingered in the corridor and the stairwell, still drinking and singing their vulgar melodies. Gregory was given the honor of removing Sebastian's sword belt, and then Raynar led the rest of the young men in stripping him as quickly as possible.

Sebastian could not see Eleanor, for she was surrounded by chattering women, but he could see that her disrobing was proceeding steadily. Each item of her clothing was held aloft amidst shouts of approval and bawdy catcalls from the onlookers. The priest was blessing the bed, sprinkling it with holy water, praying for numerous offspring. Raynar was clapping him on the shoulder. Isabel kissing his cheek. The women were tucking Eleanor into bed... and finally they were alone.

Yet now that the time had come to consummate this marriage, doubt arose within him, and a regret so strong that he felt himself lost in a void of uncertainty. Could he truly take this last, irrevocable step toward that place he did not wish to go? But thigh to thigh, arm to arm, Eleanor's silken body pressed against his. The blue mist of her eyes, so near upon his pillow, held a strangely mysterious depth. Even so, he did not move. Then, with a boldness he did not expect, Eleanor reached out her finger and touched his lips. "My husband," she said simply. Soft and timid, the words were yet filled with invitation.

And Sebastian drew her into his arms.

# Chapter 9

**S**IR RAYNAR? ARE YOU AWAKE? Sir Raynar?" The soft childish voice slowly penetrated through the mists of Raynar's sleep. With a groan, he kicked out at the deadweight resting on his greaves, then clutched his blanket against the chill of the early-morning air. As he pried open his eyes, his tongue—thick and furry and exceedingly bitter—formed an angry curse. Just in time his vision cleared enough for him to see the anxious face at his side. Raynar stifled his words with a sigh. This young unknown page was only the messenger. Doubtless Sebastian would insist that the poor child did not deserve to feel even the dulled edge of his wrath.

"What is it, lad?" Although he attempted to mix some warmth into the question, the result was something between a dry cough and the cawing of crow.

"I've been sent to fetch you."

Raynar glanced around. The remnants of the wedding feast that had lasted into the early hours of the morn, had not yet been cleared from the boards; and the bodies of the merrymakers so littered the floor that one could be forgiven for thinking that some strong enchantment had caused the revelers to fall into a sleep wherever they stood. He, himself, still had his fingers wrapped around the stem of an empty goblet.

"Who sent you?" Surely, not even such a reluctant bridegroom as Sebastian would be out of his bed so early on his post-nuptial morn!

"My mistress. Duchess Isabel."

Stranger and stranger. Why should the fair Isabel desire his company before the dawn had even broken? There was no harm in asking. Forewarned is forearmed. "And know you the reason, lad?"

The boy shook his head. "But I do know that the gatekeeper was summoned from his bed to admit a party of knights, not long past. Their leader is one of Terlinden's sons."

In an instant Raynar abandoned all lethargy. Although a renowned warrior and canny leader, Duke Gebbard had such a controlled temperament that on one occasion Lady Bertha had lamented that in all likelihood he would not even rouse himself to her defense until she had been thrown over her ravisher's shoulders and carried away. The image of the exceedingly round duchess being molested by anyone in such a manner, had been so hilarious that the entire hall had erupted into hoots of laughter—the duke and duchess included. So, what could possibly be so urgent that Terlinden would now send one of his own sons riding through the night?

The winding stairway to Isabel's chamber was narrow and dank. The stale air of the confined space, thick with the odor of human refuse rising from the privy built into the window ledge, nearly overpowered Raynar's lungs. Small wonder it was that the duchess had built the room behind the hall for her own use. The greater wonder was that she had not chosen to use that chamber now, with such an illustrious guest—for any son of Terlinden was also nephew to the king. The need for secrecy must be beyond even the need for comfort.

There were only five others in the circular chamber: Sebastian, Eleanor, Isabel, Gregory, and Sir Derick—Terlinden's eldest son. To hide his apprehension, Raynar let his gaze wander around the room, until he locked eyes with Sebastian. With a barely perceptible nod, Sebastian acknowledged that he, too, felt this fear. Derick was the very man whose pretended betrothal to Katrina had been used to tempt Westfeld to unclench the fist wrapped around his prisoner's neck. Had something in the plan now gone awry?

Derick's first words brought relief—if not comprehension.

"I bring you word from the king, of a tournament to be held at Breden two weeks hence. The heralds have already gone forth with the news." To this strange and unexpected greeting, none made comment, and after a moment's pause Derick continued. "For certes, you know I have not come with such urgency to speak only of frivolities; but before I speak further, I demand that each one of you be sworn to secrecy. Some of you I know well ..." He indicated to Raynar and Sebastian ... "and others not at all. But to all of you I say, if you cannot give me your word of honor to keep your silence, then leave this chamber now."

The effect as he slowly scanned the faces, resting his gaze in sharp intensity on each one, was of a hawk surveying his territory for intruders. When no one moved, he nodded. "Good. Then listen in peace while I speak. Someone has attempted to take the life of the king." Again his eyes swept over everyone, more piercing this time, as though he desired to see beyond the external to what lay within the heart. "I see outrage in you all, as well I might. I hope I see no deceit.

"The attempt failed, thanks only to my uncle's fondness for the hounds which always lie beneath the table at his feet. He fed but a morsel of his lamprey pie to one, who began immediately to suffer spasms and was dead ere long. It was a well-planned crime. As all men know, the natural poison in lampreys will occasionally kill, and had the king expired after indulging himself of that dish he loves so well, none would ever have been the wiser. There is no doubt it was poison. The dog had only one large mouthful—not enough to bring such harm in so swift a manner were it the lamprey alone. As it was, Uncle Stefan had already dribbled some juices into his own mouth, and suffered for it the rest of the day."

"Has the cook been questioned?" Sebastian asked.

"He has. And the servitors, too. They confess nothing and everything. They have cried their innocence and accused nearly every man in the kingdom. They know nothing."

"Does the king think, then, that this attack comes from within? Is it not likely that the threat comes from beyond the borders of Lothemia?"

"It is very possible." Derick rubbed his hand across his chin, brushing the stubble as he frowned in concentration. "There are other circumstances known to very few." He paused and looked again at each face around the room. "The king holds great concern for the future of his kingdom once he has gone. Now that his only son has died, it has been suggested that he set aside the queen and take a younger bride. The king still has years enough that he may hope to see another son grow to manhood."

Eleanor's sharp intake of breath drew Derick's attention to her.

"I know your thought. Perhaps the queen—sister to my own father—is behind this plot." He shook his head. "But it cannot be, for the queen is the very one who has brought forth this proposal. My aunt has offered to step aside, allowing the pope to annul their marriage for reasons of consanguinity. For certes, some relationship within the needed degree could be found to satisfy the requirements of the Church. But the king cherishes his wife and is loathe to part from her." Derick gave Eleanor a warm smile. "It was well-thought, my lady, but do not doubt the queen."

"Then whom does the king suspect?" This was Gregory, who had stepped forward. "Tell us, and we shall avenge this attempt at regicide!"

"Perhaps, you need not look very far." Derick cocked his head to one side. "There are whispers that my father, Terlinden, has the most to gain should the king now die. After all, if the king takes a new bride, then my father would no longer be his brother-by-law and would lose his position of influence. And what is more, I, myself, was there at the table that night. Perhaps, Gregory of Marre, I am the one you seek."

"There will always be such rumors," scoffed Raynar. "Doubtless the dog is also suspect. But is there not a more obvious place to look? The king's daughter, Elisabeth, would lose all chance of inheritance were the king to sire another son."

"Are you a seer, as well as a bard, Raynar? This is indeed the point. Elisabeth's husband, King Maximilian of Albenar, has always lusted after Lothemia; he would have good cause to prevent her father from begetting another son. But King Stefan knows that to name a female as heir is to cause a civil war. Who has forgotten how England bled after the first Henry chose his daughter as his successor. That must never happen here. The king will not leave the throne to Elisabeth.

"To that end—to protect not only his own life, but more importantly, the lifeblood of Lothemia—my uncle has established this ruse of a tournament so that all his barons and knights will be gathered at Breden. Then, in the cathedral before those many witnesses, he will declare his brother, Lothar, to be his chosen heir. Each man there will swear loyalty, or forfeit his lands. Until that deed is done, the king remains in the gravest danger. His life must be protected at all cost. For this reason he sends to those he may trust, commanding them to ride with all speed to stand at his side."

Derick turned to stand before the duchess. Her unruly hair, untied, floated around her face like a fiery cloud. The hooded flicker of Derick's eyes as they darted over her curves, revealed much of his inner thoughts. "Lady Isabel, though your husband is not here, he has always been the king's staunchest supporter. Do you now pledge his men to stand beside the king?"

Isabel lifted her chin and narrowed her gaze. "Though Duke Branold be not here, I am his wife, and it is his will that still rules at Ravensberg. His men will stand with the king."

Making no further comment, Derick turned next to Gregory. "Gregory of Marre, your father's loyalties are unknown for he keeps to himself in his mountain fortress. But you had your fosterage here at Ravensberg. I do not ask you as Marre's son, but as Gildren's nephew. Will you lead men of Ravensberg to stand beside the king?"

"My loyalty lies with the king and my obedience with Gildren. My sword and my men are at the Lady Isabel's command."

His face still stern, Derick nodded, and moved across to Sebastian.

"Sebastian of Westfeld, your father is the king's most untrustworthy baron. What proof can you give of your own loyalty to the king?"

Sebastian placed his hand on Eleanor's shoulder. "I have done as the king has commanded. I have married into the house of Gildren, and Branold will soon be free. No greater token of my loyalty can I give. My sword I pledge to the king. I will ride with you this day, with Raynar at my side."

Stepping back, Derick swept his hand in an arc, including the entire company in his gesture. "Although haste is needed, we will not ride today. We will provision ourselves for the journey, bearing in mind that the future is unknown and that we may be riding to battle. We will leave at first light tomorrow. Gather whatever men of Gildren and Westfeld you may, yet do not forget your vows of silence.

"And now, Lady Isabel, I would beg of you food and a bed, for myself and for my men. We have ridden through the night to reach the safety of your gates."

"Of course, Sir Derick." The duchess inclined her head, but before she left the room she turned swiftly to Sebastian. Inexplicably, her cheeks were flushed and her eyes bright with anger. "I would have some words with you, Sir Sebastian. Please await me in my antechamber. I will come as soon as I have seen to the comfort of my guests."

After rousing Westfeld's squires from their beds of straw in the stable, and listing their tasks for the day, Raynar strolled toward the hall in search of some food to break his fast. He was pleased when he encountered Eleanor near the chapel. Together, they continued to the hall.

"I have said my prayers, Sir Raynar," she teased. "Have you?"

"There is nothing I desire that is in God's hands to give me."

"So, you control your own destiny?"

"As much as any man. In truth, my needs are few."

"Are you so unselfish, then?"

He laughed. "Far from it. Indeed, I deny myself little. My desires may be few but I am a glutton when it comes to their fulfillment."

"I am too well-bred to ask what those desires might be, but I—"

They were standing in front of the door to Isabel's antechamber, and from within her upraised voice sounded clear. "I will not hear of it. You must go with Eleanor. You must—"

"I refuse to listen to you." Sebastian's deep voice shouted an interruption. "Do not speak of Eleanor again! I am weary of all this; weary of everything; weary of her."

Without any purpose other than to stop their vicious words before they caused Eleanor more pain, Raynar shoved open the door. Both Sebastian and Isabel were standing in the center of the small room, taut with fury.

"My lord!" Eleanor gasped.

Raynar pulled Eleanor into the room and firmly shut the door while encouraging her by laying his hand on the small of her back.

"My lord, what is the cause of this quarrel?" she demanded.

"I will tell you." Sebastian's eyes were blazing but it was his voice that scorched. "Your stepmother insists I must not ride with Derick tomorrow, but return with you at once to Eaglesheid. She is trying to force me, like some feeble-minded lad, to bend to her will. While the life of the king and the very security of the kingdom hang in the balance, she wants me to mount up and ride the other way."

"You disgust me," Isabel spat out the words. "You and your father both. You have bedded your bride and now I want my husband released."

"I was to marry your eldest daughter! By all the saints, that treaty is a millstone I have put around my own neck." His clenched fists struck the air as though it were some invisible enemy; then he shoved Raynar aside and fled the room.

Isabel slumped, and in that moment seemed incredibly vulnerable. With eyes wide and desperate, she appealed to Raynar. "I want my husband home. A contract is a contract. I have kept my part faithfully, without questions or accusations. Now it is time for Sebastian to keep his."

"Would it be so dreadful if he delayed until he returns from Breden?"

"When he returns?" Her agitation returned. "When will that be? One month? Two months? Six months hence? What if there is a battle and he is injured or killed? What if the king demands further services of him? There is always another battle. Another tourney. Another fight to fight. But I will have no more of it. If it were not for Sebastian, my husband would be here with me now. Sebastian owes me far more than he owes the king! How dare he try to delay even one day more?"

Raynar shook his head, frustrated by the impasse. "I will go and speak with him and try to persuade him. I think...I hope...he may be persuaded."

"Good. I will depend on you." All emotion left her voice. "I shall lay a feast tonight in his honor. Eleanor, be prepared to depart on the morrow. Now, excuse me." Eleanor and Raynar stepped back as she swept past them, leaving them alone.

"I must go and see to the packing," said Eleanor, with great weariness. "Please understand that I, myself, would not choose to bind Sebastian beyond his will, yet it is true that my father awaits his freedom."

"You are right, as is the duchess," Raynar acknowledged. "Yet it is also right that Sebastian should go to the king." He shook his head. "In all the years I have known him, I have never seen him this angry. In truth, I think it is himself he is battling. He has chosen his course, Eleanor. He may not like what he has chosen, but he will follow it."

"But that is what confuses me. He came here bearing the terms of the contract himself, yet he acts like a man who cannot quite believe how fate is dealing with him." She looked down at her hands. "I can reach only one conclusion."

"And that is?"

"I am totally repugnant to him."

Raynar tipped her chin upward so that he could see directly into her eyes. For a moment he said nothing as he watched the storm of emotions within their depths, like seething clouds in gray sky. Then gently he whispered, "If that is true, he would be a blind man, Eleanor. A blind man and a fool."

Streaks of red were already coloring the sky when Eleanor climbed the stair to the small chamber she and Katrina had shared for so many years. Already this day seemed endless, though the feasting had not yet begun. She had not seen Sebastian since their encounter that morning—neither had she allowed her thoughts to linger on his words. Yet the time had now come when she could no longer neglect her pain. He had married her and taken her to his bed. But he did not want her. He didn't want her body. He didn't want her companionship. And he certainly didn't want her love.

She had been watching from this very window when he had arrived at Ravensberg the previous week. The joy of living had been so evident in his every movement that her heart had quickened to see him. Now, today, he was bitter and angry, caught in a grief that seemed to overwhelm him. What had happened?

Eleanor fell onto her bed and stared out at the evening sky. Gentle sunbeams were streaming through the window, bringing with them the hazy June warmth. Gazing around the room she marveled at how quickly and completely the patterns of her life had been overturned. And then her eyes froze on the ornately carved trunk which contained her mother's clothes. Her forehead furrowed as she considered the ancient chest. It would be a simple matter to order the grooms to load it onto the cart, but how would Isabel react were she to see it there? It was true that she had generously given Eleanor clothing and linens, and even a precious loom to carry away with her, but did that mean she would allow this trunk to leave without knowing what it contained? And if Isabel were to order the lid to be opened, would she not covet the contents for herself?

Slipping to the floor, Eleanor knelt before the chest and ran her hands lovingly over the surface. In here lay precious memories of a time, long since past, when her mother's laughter had echoed through the passageways and her father's confident stride had rung on the cobblestones. Lace and velvets and the jeweled slippers—!

Memory struck, sending cold fingers to clutch at her heart. She bowed over with sudden pain and tears slid down her cheeks. Katrina was gone, and with her not only their mother's jeweled slipper but the very key to open this chest. How could she possibly bear this last cruel betrayal of fate? Was it not enough that her future appeared to stretch bleak and loveless before her? Must she also endure losing all the happiness of her past?

The tears flowed faster, but she wiped them away and stood, forcing herself erect. Head held up, breathing deeply, she paced back and forth. Back and forth. Not until her weeping had ceased and she had brought her thoughts within her control, did she turn again to look at the chest.

Again she knelt and touched the wood. Surely all was not lost. She would send this coffer and its beloved contents to Lady Sophie in her isolated tower. There, it would lie safe from Isabel's curious eyes. Someday she would return and force the lid, but until that time these remnants of her childhood would lie secure and undisturbed. Calm now, Eleanor sat on the floor and leaned her head against the chest. Her eyes drifted shut, and the peace of the evening flowed around her.

She was jolted fully awake by an idea so exciting that she leapt to her feet and began to pace once more. This time there was a spring to her step and her hands worked up and down as she concentrated on her thoughts. There was a way to give both Sebastian and Isabel what they so greatly desired! She was Sebastian's wife, was she not? Was that not all the contract required? There was no need for Sebastian to be in the company that escorted her to Eaglesheid. While she went north to join her father, surely he could go to fight for his king.

She would leave Ravensberg tomorrow. And she would leave without regrets. Her old life was finished; it was time to begin anew.

Would Sebastian ever want her for his wife? That was a question she could not answer. But one thing she knew. When he was ready—when he had fought his battles and was ready to come home—she would be at Eaglesheid, waiting for him with open arms.

# Chapter 10

I HAD THOUGHT THAT A PLACE called Eaglesheid would be perched on a mountaintop." Eleanor had pulled up her horse, and now gazed with some surprise across the flat expanse below. More than a week had passed since she had left her alpine home in the company of these men of Westfeld. And as they had ridden northward the beauty of the rolling land had been a continuous wonder; yet, somehow, she had expected mountain peaks to reappear. But Eaglesheid lay in the midst of a vast plain that stretched beyond sight, into the distance.

Shielding her eyes against the midday sun, she stared down at the castle which held not only her father, but her future. Built atop the bluff on the near side of the Rhilen—a swift-flowing river carrying the mountain waters north, then east—its massive walls were the only visible defense.

"What kind of an eagle builds its nest on an open plain?" she asked, in amazement.

"A wise one." The knight leading the expedition smiled and swept his hand in a gesture that included not only the fields and forests, but the peasants and oxen at work. "The soil here is rich and fertile with nary a stone. It is a prize worth defending more than any mountaintop. And the river is deep and easily navigated. The merchants who travel it bring wealth to the duke for they must pay a toll to pass by, or forfeit their goods."

"Duke Frederick is a pirate, then?"

"Nay." The smile became a chuckle. "He protects the merchants from pirates. None dare waylay a boat passing through the duchy under the duke's protection."

"Is that where the name comes from? Are the boats the duke's prey?"

Laughing now, the knight answered, "When you get an idea, my lady, you hold to it. But be reassured, for the origin of the name is much more commonplace. Do you see that ridge of hills, barely visible through the haze?" He pointed more southward than where they now stood. "The original keep was there. It was Frederick the Swarthy who was given the duchy for its defense against the northmen. His grandson, another Frederick, began the construction of the new castle at the river's side, and later the old keep was abandoned. It is used only as a watchtower now; but the eagle was carried to its new home."

"It is a beautiful land," she said, with genuine admiration as she scanned the entire valley. There was, indeed, a pastoral allure in the busy idleness of the scene with its gentle blending of hues: the rich loam of the fallow fields, the golds and greens of the young crops, the pinkish wool of the newly-shorn sheep, the verdant foliage of the forest, the sword-silver line of the river—

"Aye, my lady. It is."

The knight's answer pulled her out of her reverie. All pleasure was swept away in a rush of anxiety as she looked again upon Eaglesheid Castle. "I wish to ride ahead of the baggage carts. Surely we need not stay with them, now that we are so close to our journey's end?"

"You are eager to see your new home?"

"I am eager to see my father." Eleanor spoke the words dispassionately, which only emphasized their importance.

"We will ride at once, my lady."

Within the hour Eleanor stood before the arched entrance to Eaglesheid's hall. Panic clenched her entrails like a fiendish hand, and she wondered why she had been so foolish as to hurry this moment. Was it malice, alone, that had led Duke Frederick to order this reunion with her father to take place in the hall, beneath the public eye; or had the duke some diabolical foreknowledge of the grievous blow her father must soon endure? Making great show of arranging the trailing ends of her scarf, Eleanor gathered her strength and breathed a fervent prayer that she could give her father some warning that all was not well at Ravensberg, some warning of the bolt which was about to be loosed into his heart. Though she could not forestall his pain, she would wish to save his pride.

The double doors were thrown open, the trumpet winded its tune, and the porter called out, "Lady Eleanor of Westfeld!"

As though woven into an absurd tapestry, no one moved. Pages, esquires, and knights, all were staring at her with unfeigned curiosity. Her own gaze quickly slid past them, forward, up to the front of the hall. Seated in a high-backed chair at the center of the dais was Duke Frederick—none other could have that outrageous black beard!—and to his right, as though an honored guest, sat Branold, duke of Gildren, her father.

It was her father who broke the stillness. First, he clenched his fist and drew it to his chest, but a moment later leapt to his feet and strode across the hall. As he neared, Eleanor struggled to overcome the faintness which threatened to engulf her. Straightening her shoulders, she took a deep breath and met her father's bewildered eyes.

With pretense of ignoring the onlookers, Eleanor held out her arms to him, inviting him to clasp her close. When her cheek was pressed to his, she whispered, "Prepare yourself, Papa. I bear ill tidings."

She felt him stiffen and knew he had understood. His large hand cradled her head and he bent down to kiss her ear.

"Katrina? She is dead?"

Eleanor nodded, drew herself away, and peered up at him. Two years had passed since she had seen him last, but he was not much changed. His brow was slightly higher, and his hair, once fair like her own, was now streaked with gray. Yet, all in all, he did not appear ill-used.

It was his eyes which told his torment. Their blue depths were dulled, and their corners drooped in defeat. But a moment later, the duke blinked and drew himself to his full height; the flame of steel shone forth once more.

"Come, my daughter," he said, as tucked her arm within his own. "I have one last battle here to fight. Then I go home."

There was obvious curiosity on Duke Frederick's face, and a laughable condescension, but no hint of the ogre she had been expecting. Despite his beard, he bore a shadowed resemblance to Sebastian and for a moment she felt a stirring of affection. But then his gaze hardened, and she knew the similarity was only a facade. His jaundiced features bespoke a man poisoned by selfishness, a man committed to nothing beyond his own passions.

"My lord," she said, as she dropped a curtsey at his feet.

"Lady…Eleanor? Well met. But forgive my confusion for I had thought to welcome a Katrina to my home."

"My sister has died." Eleanor met Westfeld's gaze without wavering. "Thus I have married your son in her place. Gildren's eldest daughter, as the contract required."

"Died?" Frederick smirked as he swung around to face her father. "Well, well, Branold. This is news indeed."

Her father had bowed his head, but now he lifted his chin and shrugged. "I am sorry indeed, for there is no disputing that Katrina was a pretty child. But I am sorrier still that she has spoiled my revenge. She was sickly and weak, you see, and unlikely to bear any sons."

Frederick glared down at him. "So, you had thought to cheat me, had you? And pawn me off with a useless mare and deprive me of my victory? My condolences. It seems that your schemes have been defeated." He waved his hand at Eleanor. "This one looks healthy enough. I shall have grandsons from her. Mark well my words, Branold. Mark well my words!"

When all was dark and quiet, Eleanor slipped from her room and made her way through the passageways to her father's chamber. After glancing around to make certain she was alone, she knocked softly on the wooden door and entered.

He was slumped on his stool, curled forward with his arms pressed against his thighs and his chin tucked to his chest.

"Papa," Eleanor whispered, as she rushed forward and knelt at his knees. Wrapping his fingers in her hair, he bent his brow to her head, then sat in utter stillness. When the silence could no longer be endured, he groaned with a voice as raw as an open wound. "What happened? What happened to my Katie?"

Eleanor had been dreading this moment, and hesitated before she answered. Could she deny her father the truth? Did she really have that right? But poor misguided Katrina had already paid such a heavy price for her folly. She was dead. And with her the child. Nothing was left of her in this world, saving the memories of those who bore her love. Eleanor could not bear to see Katrina stripped of her father's untainted affection.

"No one knows, Papa, how she truly died."

His head jerked up and he stared at her in astonishment. "How can that be? What are you trying to tell me?"

Eleanor stood and crossed the room, turning her back to her father, giving herself time to order her thoughts. "She was pining with love for someone she met at the king's Christmas court. Though she kept her own council, I think her heart was breaking. If only she had told me!" Now Eleanor spun around and faced him with her own agony of self-doubt. "But she held her secret until it was too late!"

Clasping her fingers together, Eleanor calmed herself before she continued. "She was unwell in her misery. Perhaps even feverish. And ... she just wandered away ... and disappeared into the forest."

Her father flinched. "A lover? Did she go to meet a lover?" Yet through his pain shone the hope that still she lived.

"No." Eleanor blinked back her tears. "The duchess sent men out searching, yet even so, nearly a fortnight passed before we had news. It was Wolfram who found her. There is no doubting, Papa. He had seen her body himself."

"Then it is true." Her father slumped in defeat. "No man is more loyal than Wolfram."

Eleanor regretted having mentioned the knight, but it was too late now. "Papa." She recrossed the room and lightly touched his shoulder. "There is something else you must know."

He raised his eyes to meet her own—and she was shocked by the hollowed bleakness which lay within their depths.

"There is more?"

"Wolfram also is dead."

"Are there none left alive at Ravensberg?" The bitter words were flung out as he jumped to his feet and strode across the room, shaking his fists at an opponent he could not see. "Is there nothing but death around me?"

"There is none to blame for Wolfram's death, but himself!" Eleanor still felt the pain of Wolfram's betrayal. How could he have brought the news of Katrina's death in so heartless a manner? "He spoke to Lady Isabel with bruising cruelty, and when he would not retract his words, Gregory was forced to protect your honor in single combat. Wolfram was not meant to die—but he fell from his horse and struck his head."

"Another death," her father groaned. "Another stupid, useless death. You know what this means, do you not? It means that Westfeld has won his revenge. After all these years he has it at last, and in full measure too. This is the price I have paid for loving my Judith."

His anger drained away as quickly as it had arisen and he sank to the bed with a heavy moan. Feeling useless and forlorn, Eleanor sank to her knees at his side.

Lifting his head, he placed his fingers beneath her chin. "But Westfeld has not won everything for he has made one grave mistake. In his foolishness, he believes that he has stolen you and your children from me. But Duke Frederick knows nothing of men's hearts. He cannot take you from me. It is an impossible thing! Distance cannot dim our bonds. Your children will belong to me as surely as I still breathe, and I shall cherish them wherever I live.

"And as for Sebastian—Westfeld lost him years ago. It is I who will be richer for this marriage, for I will be gathering Sebastian into my family."

"But he is the one who brought you here, to this!"

"So I said myself, until I realized he was only serving me as I had served his father. How can I, who took my bride by the sword, condemn another for abducting me? That is one foolish path of recrimination I will not tread." Brushing her hair from her brow, he searched her face. He did not smile—for he could not—but she felt his love just the same. "Sebastian and I have spent much time together, and I feel a great affection for him. He could have ridden away from here two years ago, but he did not. Sometimes I believe he has been more a prisoner here than I. He will be a good husband to you."

"Thank you," she said, marveling that through his pain he had known she needed reassurance.

"But my own future feels bleak." Again he shook his head. "It will be a cold homecoming for me."

"Not so! Lady Isabel awaits you eagerly. She could not endure a delay of even one day, so impatient is she for your return."

"Isabel." He enunciated her name as though it were in a foreign tongue. "It is passing strange that it is to a more distant past my memories have taken me. My Judith, who has been gone these many years, has been more alive to me than my living, breathing wife."

"Isabel desperately wants children," Eleanor urged. "You could yet have sons to bear your name."

"Begin again? I know not if I can."

"Do not speak so! You have a new life ahead of you, even as have I."

Cupping her hands within his own, he pleaded. "Give me grandsons, Eleanor. Give me grandsons—and be happy."

During her first weeks at Eaglesheid, Duke Frederick completely ignored her presence. Eleanor did not know whether to feel relief or humiliation. Uncertain and confused, she lost her appetite and began to feel a lethargy creep over her.

One evening, as the pages brought the roasted partridge to the board, the greasy odors accosted her. She shuddered and clutched her stomach. Embarrassed at her weakness she willed her stomach to be calm, but when the roast pig arrived she was forced to flee. Gulping the fresh air outside she managed to control her nausea and returned to the table with reluctance. What would Westfeld say to such unseemly behavior? She felt certain he was only awaiting an opportunity to humble her more. Pale and silent, she sat through the remainder of the meal, eating nothing, only moving the food from place to place on her trencher.

"Lady Eleanor."

She turned to the duke, prepared to see censure on his face. Instead, he was beaming. "Do you desire to go to your chamber?"

"Yes, my lord," she answered, though still mistrusting his kindness.

"Then go now. Hannah, attend to your mistress."

Perplexed but relieved, Eleanor left the hall and soon lay sleeping in her bed.

Several days passed. Surprised at the weakness of her own body, Eleanor struggled against the exhaustion that constantly attended her, a lethargy so great that even her weaving could not hold her interest long. Knowing the duke's vindictive nature, she did not understand the kindness he showed her now, and she waited in apprehension for his wrath to fall. Finally it was Hannah who pointed out that, surely, her time would be better spent embroidering infant linens than making lengths of cloth. Stunned by this meekly-given revelation, Eleanor could not even speak. Then her heart leapt as she thought of Sebastian, and she began to laugh with joy.

# Chapter 11

**K**ATRINA LONGED FOR RAVENSBERG. When the season of planting had passed without word from Wolfram, and her infant had begun to dance in her womb, her certainty had turned to doubt. When the harvesters had gathered their sheaves, and her child had strained to be born, her doubt had turned to fear. When the grain had been threshed and carried to the mills, and the chill winds had blown, and the leaves had fallen from the trees, and the snow had begun to pile in drifts around the doorway, and her daughter had cried in red-faced distress at the roughness of the binding cloths, her fear had turned to anger and then to regret. Kate wanted to go home.

She could not deny that John did all he could to ensure that she and her tiny daughter, Ella, were comfortable, secure, and well-fed. The fire pit in the center of the cot never lacked wood and the soup pot never lacked meat. And as though his husbandry were not enough, John tried to wile away the long, empty hours of her isolation with varied entertainments. Chessmen had been crafted from a selection of stones, dice from hart-bones, and a small ball from the bladder of a piglet. At Yuletide, he had hung boughs of spruce in the doorway, brought fresh rushes for the floor, and somehow managed to ensnare a pheasant which, after hanging for days in the corner of the hut, had been stuffed with acorns, roasted, and served with an exaggerated flourish. But none of John's efforts had diminished her yearning for Ravensberg.

Strange as it seemed, it was not to Sebastian that her thoughts fled during her many lonely hours, but to Eleanor. Memories of their childhood together kept her company. As the days and weeks passed, she came to understand how much she had depended upon her sister, and how much she loved her. She could scarcely wait to see her again. And to proudly show her Ella, little Eleanor, her namesake.

Then one evening, when the air was still crisp and cold, John ducked into the doorway. "Kate!" he called out. "I've the best news."

Cradling the sleeping baby in her arms, she looked up in wonder. John was trembling with excitement! What could have happened? "What is it? Are the snows melting?" They had long ago agreed that once the paths were clear, John would return to Ravensberg to seek the answer to the riddle of Wolfram's neglect. "Will you soon be able to go?"

"It's better than that!" John squatted in front of Kate. The very fact that he did not reach out to stroke Ella's golden curls showed how intent he was on telling his story. "Today I met a stranger in the forest when I was gathering wood. I greeted him and we talked of this and that and then I asked him what news was in the world. He grinned at me as though he had a secret. Then he asked if I knew there's a new king? I told him I knew nothing of kings, old or new. So he puffed himself up and said that everyone was talking about it. The king—the old one—Stefan—turned purple while dancing. His eyes bulged and then he fell right over and died. So Lothar, his brother, now is king."

"Is this your good news?" Kate asked, in amazement. "That the king is dead?"

"Nay, Kate. Listen! There's more. I let him talk, you see, to set him at his ease. But then I asked how he knew these things, and he said the tale's being told in every market. 'Oh,' I said, 'that's just the towns. What about the castles?' I said that because I wanted to know if he had news of Ravensberg. And he did! He answered that he'd just come from Ravensberg—"

Kate inhaled sharply, but did not speak.

"—and has seen the duke for himself!"

"The duke?" She stared at him in bewilderment.

"Aye, Kate." John's eyes were shining. "That's what he said. And I thought to myself that it can't be. So I asked him what he meant by such a thing for I'm no knobscap and know well that the duke is not at Ravensberg but a prisoner in Eaglesheid. 'Nay,' he said. 'It used to be so, but a treaty was signed and Duke Branold has been home these many months.'"

A wild joy exploded within Kate, filling her with such lightness she felt she could almost fly. "Papa's back! Oh John, I cannot believe it!" In her glee she threw her arms around his neck, pressing Ella between them. The baby awoke and began to cry.

"Ella!" Kate began to dance around the room. "Your grandfather is back. We can go home! We can go home!"

"There's yet more." John's grin grew wider. "Ella will soon have a cousin."

"What?" Kate stopped whirling and stared at him. "What do you mean? How can that be?" Then she shrieked in delight. "Eleanor? Eleanor is having a baby?"

John nodded. "Her time must be near. He says they're watching the road from Eaglesheid, waiting for word of the birth."

Kate stopped dancing and frowned at John. This made no sense. Surely John had got this wrong. "Eaglesheid?" she asked. "Why Eaglesheid?"

"That's the amazing part." John continued to grin. "By the treaty which freed your father, your sister married Duke Frederick's son."

Kate's eyes widened, and then she blinked. "Which son?"

"He only has one. I know not his name."

"Sebastian," she whispered. Then she began to scream.

～

Kate was drowning in the waters of insanity—and she was glad. To descend into black oblivion and leave this burden of grief behind was all she desired. Gratefully, she relaxed and allowed herself to sink deeper and deeper into her misery, closer and closer to madness. Then a cry, distant and muffled reached her. Her will rejected it but her body could not. Milk began to flow from her breasts, and their tingling need tugged at a memory she had been pushing away. It was a memory of ... of ...

"Ella!" she gasped, and now frantic, struggled to reach the surface. When she sat up, suddenly, she was gasping for air. "Where is Ella?" she cried in big gulping breaths, then sobbed with relief when John placed her beloved baby in her arms. As Ella suckled, Kate rocked back and forth, tears streaming down her face.

Her daughter finished nursing and fell asleep, her pink cheek still nestled against Kate's breast. With great tenderness, Kate stroked Ella's hair, wrapping the downy-fine curls around her fingers. "John," she said, and looked up to meet his eyes. "I want you to take us to Eaglesheid."

Before he could speak—and she could see that his reply would be vehement—she lifted a finger to her lips and pointed at the sleeping baby.

"You now know my secret. Sebastian of Westfeld is the man I married. He is Ella's father. And yet he has also married Eleanor and sired a child on her! This must be some diabolical plan to wreak further vengeance on my father's house. This must have been his thought when first we met at Breden; and for this purpose alone, he wooed me to his bed. Yet, if I confront the fiend and accuse him of his vile treachery, then Eleanor must be forsaken and lose all. I will not allow that demon to destroy my sister as he destroyed me.

"So this I choose." She began again her rocking. "Katrina of Gildren is gone, as surely as if she has died. But as long as Ella needs me, I will be here for her—and it is Sebastian who will give me the strength to endure each day. That is why we must go to Eaglesheid. We'll not go to the castle, but to some village where we can dwell and work, and know that he lives near.

"I am feeling stronger already." She stilled herself and stared up at him. "You did not know, did you John, that love is useless folly for it strips us of all reason. Hatred is much better. I tell you truly—it is hate that gives one the strength to survive!"

# Chapter 12

PERSPIRATION WAS STREAMING down Kate's face. All morning she had been working hard in the bright midsummer sun, alone in this field, excepting four-year old Ella. She rested on her hoe and looked around for her daughter. Movement behind one of the thorny bushes caught her eye, and she smiled as she saw Ella playing in the dirt. In all likelihood she had found some fuzzy insect or rodent to befriend, for the child had an innate fondness for all living creatures.

Kate was tempted to lay down her tool, go sit beside her daughter, and let Ella's eager chatter soothe away her own weariness. Instead, she lifted her hoe and continued her work. There was no time to spare. The dirt in this field needed to be loosened and weeded if she and John were to have any chance of harvesting enough food to survive the coming winter. It was work she despised, but she had to do it. John had his own obligations to the duke to fulfill.

At the thought of John digging in Sebastian's fields, sweating and laboring to lay food on Sebastian's table, a surge of hatred flowed through her. And with it, she felt her energy renewed.

It had been four years ago, Ella's first summer, when she and John had arrived here. By a peasant's measure they had been wealthy then. They had a cart, a mule, a half-dozen hens, two pigs, several bags of grain and other varied goods for their household—all purchased by bartering one of the jewels from her mother's slipper. That had been a dangerous undertaking, and John had warned her that he had been successful by merest chance. Only in the direst need could they dare to use the jewels again.

It had also been four years ago that Kate had demanded from John his ultimate sacrifice. Not his life—his freedom. She had commanded him to go to the old duke, who had then still been alive, and give the oath of fealty in exchange for some acres and his protection. Certainly, John had argued. He had sworn and cried and said that if he were a better man he would slay her rather than allow her to reduce herself to such circumstances, an abomination of the natural order. He had offered to take her to her uncle of Bestilden. He had offered to take her to one of the charter towns. He had begged and pleaded, but in the end he had obeyed. He had gone to Duke Frederick, knelt before him, bowed his head, placed his hands within the grasp of his new lord, and sworn his oath. With trembling hands he had signed the X on the parchment which granted:

> To JOHN of Towne: 15 acres, freehold. He must provide four work-days every week, from the 2nd day of April to the 29th day of September, and provide six boon works at his lord's behest. He must also provide a cubit of kindling at Yuletide. He must also take his lord's goods to market in Brummel, as his lord desires. For this he will be paid the count of four work-days, 5 loaves, and 1 franc.

Since then, the days had been filled with ceaseless work. Kate had been forced to admit that she knew less about farming than the average peasant child. She was well-used to the sight of serfs working in the fields—tilling, planting, weeding, and harvesting—but she knew nothing of where the seed came from, how to plant it, how to protect it, and most of all, what to do with it once it was fully ripened and ready to harvest. Nothing could surpass the frustration she had felt one summer's afternoon as she had stood in the midst of the small patch of wheat that somehow had grown to maturity. With pride, she had picked one of the tasseled heads, inhaled its dusty odor, and brushed it across her cheek. "We shall have bread," she had thought. But then she had stared at the grain in horror. How were they going to have bread? How did this course, raw weed become the soft, nourishing flour that she needed?

If they had not arrived with their own store of goods they would not have survived that first winter. Each succeeding year their outlook became bleaker. Their mule had died. Their pigs had been slaughtered. One hen alone remained and their supplies were nearly gone.

Kate raised her head and gazed eastward across the fields toward Eaglesheid. It lay some miles distant, far beyond her sight, but still she knew it was there. She needed to feel its despised presence, acknowledge its terrible power over their lives, and then rage at Sebastian's cruelty. As the wind from Eaglesheid touched her cheeks, she turned, renewed, to her work.

So engrossed was she in her battle against the unyielding ground that she did not at first hear the horse that approached from behind. When she suddenly realized that someone was near, she spun around, keeping a firm grip on the handle of her hoe.

The knight reined in, and with obvious amusement asked, "Are you thinking of using that thing on me?"

Kate stared at him in silence. He was bronzed and hardened—at the peak of a man's strength. There was no sign of weakness nor tenderness in his brown eyes. And no sign of recognition either.

It was Sebastian.

Drawing on her store of venom, Kate filled herself with hate. He had risen in the world, for he had been duke of the vast lands of Westfeld for many months now; but he was still the same man who had deceived not only her, but also her sister. And worse than that, he had denied his daughter her birthright.

She could see he was startled by her hostility for his brows drew together in confusion. Nudging his horse, he moved forward and peered down at her. Yet Kate knew with a certainty that he would not know her. Katrina may not have died, but she had ceased to exist. The butterfly had metamorphosed into a creature of the earth. The smooth white skin had browned and cracked. The soft curls were knotted. The delicate bone line was gaunt. The shoulders were weary, the back was bent, the hands were callused. And as if these changes were not enough, over everything, in every crack and crevice, lay a layer of dirt deep enough to disguise a king as a beggar.

Even so, something in her appearance shook him, for he reached down and grabbed her wrist. "Who are you?" he demanded, as his eyes bored through her.

She knew she must not speak!

He thrust her hand away, then a glint of amusement returned to his voice. "Do you think, woman, that I desire such as you? Is that why you look at me so? Well, have no fear. Your virtue is safe from me." And with a laugh, he turned to leave.

Kate knew she should let him ride away, as once he had before, but the need to speak overwhelmed her. She lowered her tone and spoke in false accents. "You are a demon."

Sebastian swung back to her in astonishment. "What do you know of such things?"

Kate gritted her teeth as she fought for self-control. She must not spill the tears which rose within her. "I have lived in hell."

As Sebastian stared at her, his face paled and a look of absolute despair darkened his eyes. "Then we have much in common, you and I, for I have lived there too!" He was gone before she could answer, riding away, fast and hard.

Released, tears now flowed down her face. In that outpouring, all the bitterness Kate had cherished so long was washed away. With complete clarity she understood that the man she had just seen had suffered deeply. Was suffering still! She acknowledged now that it was not Sebastian who had harmed her, but some strange, twisted fate which had swept them both up and tossed them both aside. But as her hate dissolved, her strength waned too.

"Who was that man, mama? Did the man hurt you?"

Ella was tugging at her hand, her face filled with concern.

"No. He didn't hurt me."

"Then why're you crying?"

Kate knelt and gathered her daughter into her arms. "Because I have remembered something that happened a long time ago."

"Something bad?"

"No. Something good. Something very very good." At her own words she looked intently at Ella. Her child. Sebastian's child. She was so exquisite, with Kate's own slightness of build and delicate structure of bone. Her hair was as blond as Eleanor's, yet it had that particular bounty of curls that had been passed from mother to daughter for many generations, to Sophie and Judith and herself, and now to little Ella. Kate sighed. Her daughter's eyes, dark and thickly lashed, were the only inheritance she would ever receive from her father.

Kate kissed her forehead with a gentle sadness. "Come, Ella. We're going home."

Ella looked at her mother with amazement, for they never returned from the fields so early in the day. Kate shrugged, and started to walk toward their cot.

"Shall I bring the hoe, Mama?"

"It doesn't matter. If you like."

And then Kate said something that caused Ella to pick up the hoe and follow after her, silently, and in great bewilderment.

"I won't be needing it any more."

There was still a good portion of daylight left when John arrived home. With pleasure he saw Ella waiting for him, as she often did. Without speaking a word she slipped her hand into his and matched her pace to his long stride.

"Well, my princess. Did you have a good day today?"

"No," she answered. "Not s'good."

John laughed and hoisted her up into his arms. "What? Did you meet no creeping friends to keep you company?"

"I did, I did! And it was fun! But then a man came on a horse an' Mama cried."

John's mood changed at once. His voice was harsh with fear when he asked, "Did he hurt her?"

She shook her head. "He was so be-ootiful! But when he rode away on his big horse, we came home."

By now, John was running. As he came to the cottage he put Ella down so quickly that she fell and landed on the ground.

"Kate!" he cried out, frantic to hear her voice. "Kate! Are you all right?"

She was there in the hut. Just sitting on the mat, rocking slightly, plaiting her hair. In two strides he was across the room and kneeling before her. "Kate? Are you all right?" he repeated.

"Oh, yes." Her voice seemed breathless.

John reached out and took her hand into his. He rubbed her callused fingers, but it was his own hand that was trembling. He had sworn to protect his mistress, yet was forced to leave her alone and vulnerable, day after day. And today something had happened to make her cry!

He spoke softly, trying to hide the intensity of his fear. "Ella said a rider came by. Did he…bother you?"

"Oh, no! He wouldn't hurt me, you know."

"You're all right then?"

"Of course. Oh, John. I am so sorry. I forgot to make the supper. Would you mind doing it?"

"No. Of course not." Slowly he stood, and continued to gaze down at her. She was so quiet and peaceful as she sat there braiding—or was it unbraiding?—her hair. Yet it was her very calmness that filled him with dread.

He did not know why, for it seemed that she spoke the truth when she said she had not been harmed. Yet he knew, with an awful certainty, that she had been changed.

# Chapter 13

THE JINGLING OF THE BELLS on the horses's bridles accompanied the raucous carols sung by the riders in celebration of this perfect summer's day. Brimming with joy, Branold beamed down at the child nestled within the protection of his arms. Three-year-old Mariel, excited to be included in this outing, was babbling her delight in her sweet high-pitched voice. Grinning, Branold turned to his wife. Though Isabel was riding sedately at his side, a lilting smile belied her pleasure, while her eyes flashed such a brilliant green that they outshone the emeralds encircling her neck.

After traveling less than a league, the party halted. They were in a knoll midway up one of the steeper of the alpine foothills, recently cleared of both brush and sheep.

Branold laughed aloud as they were greeted by liveried servants. In the glistening sunlight stood a feast, ready to be served in an open-air hall. Dais, trestles, linens, chairs, musicians, jesters, and even the dogs, were all there beneath the trees.

"Isabel, you have completely surprised me." He held out his arm and led her to her seat.

"Do not let down your guard yet," she admonished him with a twinkle in her eye. "There are still more surprises to come."

She was right. Branold enjoyed the afternoon so heartily that he began to wish it were possible to always dine out-of-doors in the sunshine. The afternoon shadows were just beginning to cast a cooling shade when Isabel signaled with a nod to the porter. A small, nervous man was brought forward and presented to Branold.

"Do you remember our guest?"

Puzzled, Branold studied the man. He was neither knight, nor cleric, nor merchant, for he wore only a plain, belted tunic, yet the golden wristlet around his arm declared him no peasant either. Though there was something familiar about him, Branold could not connect him with any particular memory. Finally, admitting his shortfall, he shook his head. "I am sorry, Isabel. I do not."

Pleased, she smiled. "This is Master Antonelli. He is the master mason from Rome who designed the antechamber at Ravensberg."

"Ah, I remember now. Welcome, Master Antonelli to my ..." He waved his arms at the trees around him. "To my humble abode."

Smiling even more broadly, eyes alight, Isabel held out her hand to Branold. "It is no accident that Master Antonelli is here. Indeed, it is with his help that we have planned this entertainment."

"You desire another antechamber?"

"Yes, my husband and lord. And the castle to go with it! Master Antonelli, lay out your plans for the duke."

A trumpet was flourished and two small boys unrolled before Branold an untrimmed parchment. Branold stared at the markings on it a moment, tracing the lines with his eyes, then looked at Master Antonelli with amazement. "You have used a quill to draw a picture of a castle?"

"Aye, my lord." The master mason dipped his head. "It is not exactly as it should look. It will not be so flat. Yet this will help you see the vision which is in my head."

Branold concentrated on the drawing. It was spectacular! The center of the castle, the living quarters, had progressed far beyond the fortified keep of Branold's ancestors. Atop the hall stood two additional stories that could hold a warren of comfortable chambers. Several turrets, seemingly more for decoration than defense, rose skyward, lending an air of lightness to the structure. Yet, like the underbelly of the porcupine, this soft center was not unprotected. Three concentric rings of wall formed an impressive shield around the interior living quarters. And though the inner rings had small guardrooms, six round flanking towers defended the outer battlements.

"Does it not take your breath away?" Isabel asked.

Branold had meant to laugh, but he was too awed. Turning to Master Antonelli, he asked, "Is this possible to build?"

"Aye, my lord."

"Then you are a genius, my man."

Again the man ducked his head, although his cheeks glowed with pride. "It is the duchess who is the genius, my lord. This was her commission. I did only as she asked."

"And Branold," Isabel interrupted. "Right here, where we are sitting, is the very spot where the dais will lie in the great hall. Master Antonelli took great care that this cloth was laid in the exact place. Look around you. What better defense could we have than the mountain behind. Yet what beauty! Can you imagine the prestige which will come to Gildren when you build this?"

Still Branold hesitated. "This drawing is impressive. And I salute the man who can see to the construction of such a work. But it would take a lifetime to finish and I am not certain that the resources of Gildren should be poured into such an undertaking."

"It may be your sons who complete it but it will be your name that will be sung in the courts. But listen, Branold. There is more. Master Antonelli has planned that the castle be built in stages. The curtain wall, with the gatehouse, towers and barracks will be built first. Then the innermost part, including the hall and many of the private chambers. In ten years time, if all goes well, you should be able to invite the king to partake of your hospitality."

Bemused, Branold looked at his wife. "Isabel, can you give me one good reason, other than vanity, that I should build this castle?"

He was surprised at his wife's laugh of glee. "I knew you were going to ask that. You have worried that Ravensberg does not have enough water to with-stand a long siege. But look here," she pointed at an X within the innermost circle. "That, Branold, is a natural spring. What better reason could you have? A well that will never run dry."

"Master Antonelli," Branold said after the barest pause, "I acquiesce to my wife's intellect and to your talent. Build me your castle!"

# Chapter 14

ELEANOR STOOD AT THE HEAD of the drawbridge with her ladies, waving one last time to the departing riders. A dozen children dashed past her and ran up onto the battlements to shout out their farewells to the knights. Laughing at their attempts to see over the walls that reached high above their heads, she called out, "Freddy and Bran, be careful! You'll hurt Papa if you fall on his head."

"Me climb too." Judith leaned close and laid a damp kiss on her mother's cheek, but Eleanor ignored the bribe.

"No, Judi. You stay here with me."

The summer sun was warm. Eleanor's women, in no hurry to return indoors, continued to chatter in the courtyard. The ripples of their laughter should have lifted her spirits; instead, she felt awash in loneliness. She wished she could hear their words and share just a little in their camaraderie. Then, again, perhaps it was best she could not.

Eleanor knew well it was common jest that Westfeld's duke returned home only to christen one baby and conceive another. Though the cruel gibe hurt, she could not deny that it contained a great deal of truth. Sebastian's absences were both frequent and prolonged. With scarce warning, he and Raynar and all their men would ride in, to send Eaglesheid into a flutter of activity. Servants would scamper to light fires in every hearth;

squires to place fodder in every stall; and the cooks to double the quantity of food for the evening's board. A barrel of beer would be brought forth from the cellar, and a butt of wine, and the hall would resound with story and song. That day would pass. And another. And another. And then his barely-bridled impatience would break free, and the duke would order his men to prepare for immediate departure.

Eleanor nestled her face into the soft halo of Judith's curly locks, and inhaled the sweet scent of honey. How could Sebastian content himself with ruffling the hair of his children once or twice a year? How could a man who owned such a vast and beautiful domain treat it so carelessly? How could he not take seriously his responsibilities to the youths who had been entrusted into his care? And why would a man of his intellect, ability and position waste away his years as though he himself were still a frivolous youth?

Even so, it was not his negligence that irritated Eleanor most: it was the strange fact that this lethargy only overtook him here, at Eaglesheid. The tales she heard of his deeds spoke of a rare combination of courage and compassion, while she could see for herself that his men treated him with the honor only a worthy leader earned. King Lothar, also, respected his counsel, and her own father deemed him a most worthy son. What was the matter with her husband that he could not enjoy his own home?

Eleanor's arms were beginning to tire from Judith's weight. Handing the child to one of her women, she rubbed her hands across the small of her back and then smiled as she felt the babe within her kick in response. Sebastian had, even if unwittingly, given her much. Between the joys of watching her children grow and the stimulation of directing the affairs of the duchy, her cup was very full.

She turned to cross the yard to the walled herb-garden behind the kitchens, but her next thought made her stop and sigh. How wonderful it would be to have that cup not only full, but overflowing. One thing could do that for her. One thing. For Sebastian to look directly into her eyes and smile.

A loud and abrasive voice interrupted her reverie. "Milady!"

A woman approached, dragging behind her a young boy. She was no simple peasant—her clothes were too fine for someone who labored in the fields—yet there was a rudeness in the cloth which declared she was no lady either. Whatever her estate, her belligerent tone made it very clear that she intended some manner of confrontation.

Straightening her shoulders, Eleanor deliberately settled a serene look on her face. "Are you speaking to me?" she asked.

"Aye!" The word was full of aggression. "I would speak alone with you, milady."

"You may speak to me here. State your purpose."

"If you wish, milady." The woman peered around at the many people who were within hearing distance, and a look of satisfaction spread across her face. Roughly, she tugged the child to stand in front of her, then pinched the lobes of his ears between her fingers to prevent him from pulling away.

Eleanor glanced at the boy; then looked again. Her throat tightened as she tried to swallow. Undernourished and dirty though he was, he was enough like her son Frederick to be a brother, almost a twin. The greatest difference between the two lay in the coloring of their eyes. Frederick's eyes were blue, like her own, but this lad's were large and brown, and achingly familiar. There was no doubting why this woman had come.

"I brought my son to you so his father, the duke of Westfeld, can provide for him."

A rush of anger coursed through Eleanor like a river in flood. How dare Sebastian do this to her? Was it not enough that he humiliated her with his constant absence? Did he also have to shame her by allowing his bastard to be brought into her presence? It was outrageous! It should not be borne. No one could deny her the right to have the woman whipped for her presumption. And if Sebastian called foul, she would merely point out that if he did not want her taking matters into her own hand, then his own two hands best remain at Eaglesheid.

She opened her mouth to speak, but as she did, she looked down at the child. In a face blanched white with pain, the dark misery in his eyes held a forlorn entreaty. Her own hurt ebbed away. This boy was Sebastian's son. She loved her husband—imperfect though he may be. Hesitantly, she held out her hand and tilted the boy's chin so she could look directly into his eyes. Then she drew him forward, releasing him from the cruel grasp, turning him around so that he now faced his mother with her own hands on his shoulders.

"Anything that is my husband's is mine also." She spoke the words clearly, with a raised voice so that all would hear.

Confused, the woman held silence for a moment, then said with greater belligerence, "Give me some gold and I'll take him away and not bother you again."

Eleanor looked down at the boy she held. There were bruises on his arm, and she could feel him trembling at his mother's words.

"No," she said. "You will not take him away. He will be raised as a duke's son ought. I thank you for bringing him to me."

"No!" the woman shrieked. "You can't have him."

Eleanor stayed silent.

"If you want him, you must pay me for him!" she shouted, revealing the true reason for her anger.

Eleanor restrained her impulse to slap the hussy. "I will not *pay* you anything for him," she said. "Neither for ransom nor for purchase. Yet, I will more than generously *recompense* you for all you have spent on his care. I will see that you are given a bag of gold. But if you ever return to me again, you will heartily regret it."

"Agreed," she said, without any hesitation. "And I wish you joy of him. He is a bastard! Just like his father!"

Eleanor did not respond. Leaving the matter in the hands of Karl, her steward, she turned and walked away, taking the lad with her.

Without a word she led him through the hall and up the stairway to her own chamber where she stood him beside the loom, in front of the window, so that the light fell directly onto his face. Then she stepped back a pace to look at him more clearly.

Gone, for the moment, was her anger with Sebastian. She was remembering another ill-conceived child. Katrina's baby had been fatherless—and because of that lack both Katrina and the babe had died. She would not allow such tragedy to happen again. Whatever Sebastian's sin, she would make certain that his child was kept safe.

"So, it seems I have acquired a new son." Eleanor smiled lightly as she spoke.

A look of wonder lifted the anxiety from his face. "Aye, milady."

"Your mother … will you miss her?" Eleanor remembered well the nights she had soaked her bed with tears after the death of her own mother.

He did not hesitate with his answer. "No, milady."

"How old are you?"

"Six."

"I thought so." She grinned at him, though this time it was an effort. Did she dare to ask when his natal day was? Was it not better to assume that he had been born before her own son, Frederick? Better that, than to know for certain that Sebastian had gone directly from her marriage bed to another? No. She had to know the whole truth. Then she could face it, accept it, and live with it.

"My son, Frederick, is also six. I wonder which of you is the elder? Do you know what time of year you were born?"

"Near the May Day."

"So then, you are younger than Frederick." With practiced restraint, she did not show her hurt. "Just a little younger, though. I suppose it will seem strange for you to have an older brother. Tell me, lad, what is your name?"

"Sebastian."

So completely unprepared was she for that answer that all her defenses slipped, and she stared at him in consternation.

"It's my name," he said, clenching his fists as if in defense.

"I know." Her words now were rushed and unthinking. "But would you not like to change it? A new name for a new home?"

"Why should I?"

"Because that name hurts me."

Poor child. How could she be so selfish? His name was all that he had and he had as much right to it as anyone. "Never mind. You may keep your name. It doesn't really matter. Now come with me … Sebastian. Let me take you to the nursery that you will share with Frederick and Branold. Freddy is a little older than you and Bran a little younger." She lightly brushed the hair off his forehead with her fingertips, and then impulsively, she kissed him. "I hope you will be happy here."

He nodded, but did not speak.

Taking the boy by the hand, she led him to the room where her sons slept. When she opened the door, she interrupted a game of 'chase the frog around the room.'

"Boys, I have someone for you to meet."

Young Branold ran over to his mother and threw his arms around her skirts. Frederick stopped to scoop up his frenzied green pet before following his younger brother.

"Now stop!" She was laughing. "Settle down! I want you to meet Se—"

"Arthur!" interrupted the boy.

"Arthur." Her eyes beamed their pleasure at him, and he glowed in return.

"He was a famous king, milady," he said.

"He was indeed. And brave and honorable. Well boys, this is Arthur. And he is going to live here with us because he is your half-brother."

Frederick's brow suddenly furrowed with great puzzlement. He tilted his head to one side and then to the other as he stared at Arthur.

"What is the matter, Frederick?" Eleanor asked, hoping his answer would not give Arthur insult.

"But which half is missing, Mama? His front is all there—is it his back?"

Laughing aloud, she ruffled his hair and signaled to Arthur. "Turn around, Arthur, and let Freddy see this wonder."

He did as she bid, and soon all three were whirling around the room, Freddy and Bran watching Arthur in amazement. It would be good to leave them alone. Surely the boy would be much happier in the children's company than in her own.

"I will leave you boys to get acquainted, but I'll send Hannah with a platter of food and the porter with the bath."

While they were still laughing, she left the room; as she closed the door behind her, she heard Bran exclaim, "I knew we were going to have a new baby, but I didn't know he was going to be so big!"

# Chapter 15

"COME, ELEANOR." Sebastian held out his hand to her in a rare gesture of affection. "Let us go down to the gate together to greet Terlinden and his lady."

She smiled as she slid her fingers between his. Three years had passed since she had taken Arthur into her home—three years in which her life with Sebastian had carried on much as before. Yet, today was different. Today, as they awaited the arrival of their guests, her husband was brimming with an excitement that made her own spirits soar.

"You betray yourself, Eleanor."

"I do?"

He moistened his thumb with his tongue, then gently brushed her cheek. "It's a smudge of ash. You should let others do the work for you."

"But I enjoy it," she protested.

"I know you do." His eyes were warm with affection. "But you must consider the babe you carry. Take your ease, Eleanor; you have labor hard enough ahead of you. Enjoy these days now."

Eleanor nodded as she flushed with pleasure.

Again he reached out, this time to brush his finger across her brow—and then Eleanor gasped. The sleeve of his tunic had fallen back, to reveal a bright pink scar slashed across his forearm like a brand.

"Sebastian! You have been burnt! What happened?"

His hand dropped and all tenderness fled. "It is nothing, my lady. It is not your concern."

"Is not your well-being as much a concern to me, as mine is to you?"

"I will not discuss this. I was burnt; it has healed; that is the end of it." Then his voice softened once more. "Come, Eleanor. They are crossing the bridge. Let us not quarrel, today. This is a day for pleasure."

The days and nights which followed were filled with laughter. Gebbard and Bertha, the duke and duchess of Terlinden, gray-haired though they were did not hesitate to encourage their hosts to prepare extravagant entertainments for their enjoyment. Spectacular feasts were spiced with caroling, mummery, dancing, and contests of wit. Picnics leavened the hunts. Gold purses enlivened the tourneys.

Eleanor had never been so happy in her life.

"You should travel more, my dear," Lady Bertha said to Eleanor as they sat companionably under the shelter of a colorful pavilion, awaiting the return of the hunting party. Numerous esquires were busy, directing the servitors in the placement of the trestles and the laying of the linen cloths, while the ladies were wandering along the edge of the river, enjoying the warmth of the summer sun. Lady Bertha and Eleanor alone sat beneath the tenting. But not in idleness, for their hands were busy embroidering a large banner which lay loosely across their laps.

"Sebastian is a rogue to keep you at home while he tourneys all over Christendom."

Eleanor smiled and patted her rounded belly. "I would be quite a burden for him."

"Nonsense! That is only your fifth child. I gave birth to twelve, and only half in my own bed at Badenar. Sebastian would know how that was, for he used to travel with us. Indeed, he was my own page when Dagor was born. I remember those days well. By the saints, what a pair Sebastian and Raynar were when they fostered with us. I am surprised they are still breathing considering all the scrapes they used to get into. Still do, if half the rumors I hear are true."

"I am certain they are. Just watching the two of them together this past week has made me grin so much that my cheeks ache. It is for the sake of my face, you know, that I spend these quiet moments with you. And those boys of mine—Frederick and Arthur and Bran—all I can say is that it is a good thing that Raynar lets them tag along behind him, or they would be climbing in the rafters in their excitement."

Bertha looked up and cocked her brow. "I admit to some surprise, dear Eleanor, in this matter of Arthur. It is one thing for wives to tolerate the women—even my precious Gebbard would not deny his own desires—but their offspring are another thing altogether. To raise a bastard in your household is like suckling a viper in your nest. Find them when they are infants, I say, and get rid of them."

"Get rid of them?" Eleanor's stomach lurched at the implication.

"It is easy enough," Bertha said, with a shrug. "It is better for them; better for you; and definitely better for your trueborn sons."

"So, I am to deny a child the opportunity to bring me pleasure, on the chance that he may bring me pain?" She tempered her words against the violent images in her mind. What did Lady Bertha do? Drown them?

"Ah, well. I will say no more. I can see that you dote on your Arthur, and I truly hope you never have cause to regret your generosity. I do admit he is a charming lad." Lady Bertha peered down at her stitching for a moment, then added, "Of course, I like all boys. I daresay I should have been one myself, though I have never heard my Gebbard complain. I hold nothing against your two dear daughters, for they are sweet things, but give me boys any time. I am glad I had so many myself, not to mention all the others we have raised in our household. Still are! My Hugh is only eight years old, you know."

Eleanor dropped her needle into her lap and stared at her companion. "You have an eight-year old child?"

Lady Bertha laughed. "If you think you are confounded, imagine how I felt. He is fully six years younger than my Adele. Praise be, he was a boy. We are fostering many lads with him now, including Prince Stefan of Albenar, Elisabeth's son. You knew of course, that my lord is his great-uncle? That the dowager queen is Gebbard's sister?"

"I did," she said, as she resumed her embroidery. "What a tragedy that Elisabeth died when her baby was born. I wonder if she ever held him?"

"That is certainly true, but the greater tragedy is that the boy has been deprived of his birthright. By all rights, Stefan should be king."

Eleanor stopped mid-stitch and stared at Lady Bertha in surprise. "But that is not possible! His father, the king, still lives. And his half-brother, Conrad, is the heir!"

"You mistake me. It is not of Albenar I speak; as you say, he is only a second son in that kingdom." Lady Bertha dipped her needle into the silk. "Here, in Lothemia, it is a different matter. Stefan is the grandson and namesake of the old king. The only grandson, mind you. Though his claim be through the female line, does that make it any less?"

Eleanor was amazed at such logic. "No one has ever challenged Lothar's right to rule. Stefan was not even conceived when his grandfather died!"

"That may be. But there are some who would see the throne return to the old king's line."

Bending her head low, Eleanor stared at the picture on her cloth—a gyrfalcon plummeting to the ground. "And what of the three princes of Lothar's own loins?"

"Ah, that is a difficult matter. Three princelings, growing bigger every day. But enough of that, Eleanor, my dear. I shall not bother you with such talk. Tell me. Do you think your babe a boy or a girl?"

"I know not," answered Eleanor, more tersely than she intended. "I like my daughters as well as my sons."

Lady Bertha acknowledged the dart with a laugh. "And have those sons of yours begun their training?"

"No. Only in play."

"You should put your mind to the matter. My lord has already begun training Stefan and Hugh on the field, though of course they still use tipped swords. When Stefan comes to the throne, Hugh will be his right-hand man."

"Our boys will begin in good time," Eleanor said, as she pushed a skein of threading onto the floor and bent down to retrieve it. She dared not let the duchess see her face until she had a moment to compose herself. All joy in her companion's company fled. Lady Bertha's treasonous words now lay between them.

Whether Lady Bertha's revelations had been deliberate or not, Eleanor was now certain that sinister purpose had motivated this visit, and she waited for it to be revealed.

Raynar frowned with worry as he watched Eleanor. Something had changed within her these past two days. She still laughed at the jests with unfeigned delight and scolded the children—and himself—good-naturedly for their pranks, but he could sense that beneath her enthusiasm she was as taut as the string on a lyre.

Crossing the hall, he sat down on the bench at her side and leaned back against the wall. "How fare your plans for the weaving, Eleanor?" It was a good choice for the conversation. Her eyes were suddenly lit with pleasure.

"I have three looms already, and the women are learning to make some beautiful cloth. You haven't told Sebastian, have you?"

"No, I have not told him," he smiled. "Your secret is safe."

"Thank you. I truly would like to surprise him."

"And ..." Raynar raised his brow. "Make certain he does not forbid the plan?"

Eleanor blushed, her fair complexion now tinged rose. "You know me too well, and you are right. I do wish to make certain he does not forbid the plan, though that does not seem likely, does it? I have been gainsaid nothing these past years."

She did not speak for a moment but Raynar kept silent for he could see there was more she wished to say. The flush had disappeared and now her eyes were grayed with blusterous thoughts. Finally, she took a deep breath, and asked, "I have seen this past fortnight how it could have been, were Sebastian willing to call Eaglesheid his home. Why will he not stay?"

Raynar looked around. The hall was crowded with men and women, laughing and flirting and playing the games of dice. This was a perfect moment of privacy to speak with Eleanor of things she ought to know.

"Sebastian is one of the most stubborn men I have ever known: it is the stubbornness of a kind and faithful heart, willing to risk much, even his own life, for what he believes to be right. That makes him braver—yet more foolish—than other men."

"What do you mean? It sounds like a riddle."

"Often and often I have seen him risk his life to save another, when other men, myself included, would simply shrug their shoulders and walk away. More to the point, he has also held that stubbornness in love. I think I must tell you, Eleanor, that years ago he loved a girl. To his sorrow, she died before they could marry. Even after all these years, his loyalty is so strong that he refuses to abandon her memory. Yet, I daresay, that were I to ask him what she looked like or even what it was about her that he so admired, he would not be able to answer. All he knows is that he once loved her, and he is so faithful that he refuses to leave the memory behind." Raynar longed to trace the line of hair across her cheek; instead, he clenched his fists in his lap. "Does this hurt, to hear these things?"

Eleanor looked down at her own hands in silence, and then lifted her eyes to his. "It should. But it doesn't. I am relieved to understand. Of course, I have always known Sebastian did not marry me for love, although you know well that I would wish it were so." She tilted her chin higher. "If that cannot be, then it cannot be. So answer me truly. Is it me he avoids? Or his duchy?"

Raynar wondered that she knew him so little to think that he would speak the words which would crush her. With a deliberately caustic laugh, he answered a different truth. "Sebastian's father was a hard man who twisted and abused all that should have been between a father and a son, until Sebastian came to despise him and everything he stood for. Unfortunately, Sebastian has yet to learn that he, himself, is now Westfeld. It is himself, and not his father, he is hurting by his rejection of the duchy."

"But his own sons! Why would he not wish to be a better father than Duke Frederick was to him? He sees them so rarely, and pays them scant attention when he does."

"I'm sorry." Raynar shook his head. "I know not the answer. Perhaps he just fears to love anything or anyone again."

"Then, perhaps, he is not so brave after all." Eleanor said the words lightly, but there was a touch of bitterness in her voice.

Raynar laughed. "You are right. That is the folly of which I spoke."

Eleanor did not join his laughter but asked him in all seriousness, "And what of you, Raynar? What do you want for yourself?"

He took her hand in his, held it as though he were weighing it, then looked directly into her eyes. "All I have ever needed is a horse beneath me, the road before me, and a story to tell at the end of the day. And it is because of Sebastian that I have these things. So there is one thing else I desire: Sebastian's happiness. Yet I fear very much that will never be. Whether he admits it or not, every time he rides away he is tearing himself in two."

"Thank you," she said. "You have eased my mind. I must go now and speak with my steward."

Raynar dropped a kiss on her brow as he stood. He started to turn away, but before he had taken a step Eleanor grasped his hand again. "Raynar. You are such a good friend."

"And so I am, but only because it is my misfortune that you are married to the one man whose wife I would never seduce. Indeed, that is why we are friends—seduction leaves little room for friendship." Raynar chuckled, then grew serious again. "Or perhaps we are friends because we are the same in our folly: We do not count the cost of our love for Sebastian." He paused as he searched for the words to express his deepest emotions. "He is a hero."

He was astonished that she suddenly laughed, a genuinely happy sound.

"Look!" She pointed over his shoulder. "Here he comes now, but it is not a very heroic look on his face."

Her words were an understatement. As Sebastian pushed his way toward them, through the ring of dancers, his scowl distorted his features into the semblance of a plum left overlong in the sun.

Still laughing, Eleanor asked, "What is the matter, Sebastian? You look like a boy who has just been told he will not be allowed a sweetmeat with his dinner."

"It is no matter for jesting, my lady. There is a woman in the yard who is embarrassing us all with her uncouth display. I was going to order her put out, but I—" He broke off and looked down for a moment, then lifted his head and continued. "I did not. I had her taken to our chamber, and I wish you to go to her there."

Raynar began to speak, but Eleanor interrupted him, a grim remnant of her smile remaining. "And do you know, my lord, what it is she desires?"

"She has with her a child." Again he hesitated. "A boy. She claims he is my son."

"And is it true?"

"It is possible he is my seed. I would not claim him as my son!"

"A son is a son; whether he is claimed or not," she said, then spun around and walked away.

Raynar grinned at his friend. "It looks as though you have just tarnished your armor somewhat."

"What are you prattling about?"

"I was just singing your praises to Eleanor. Undoubtedly, she would like to stuff my words back down my throat and make me choke on them."

"Then let that be a lesson to you. Do not sing paeans about me. They are wasted."

But folding his arms across his chest, Raynar continued to tease Sebastian. "It appears your family is growing rapidly. Frederick, Arthur, and Bran—three boys in less than two years. Judith and Bridget. This new lad, and another to be born before many weeks. Seven children!"

"And you, Raynar? Surely you will not claim to have fathered no children?"

There was a glint in Raynar's eye. "If I had a wife like Eleanor, then I would father all my sons on her."

"I see. Now it is of Eleanor you are going to sing your praises."

"Do you not think she deserves them? Not many women would take in her husband's bastards so cheerfully."

"It has been no hardship for her." Sebastian dismissed this argument with a shrug. "She has always liked Arthur."

"That is true," Raynar nodded in agreement. "She loved him from the first, but she loved him because he's your son. Admit it. She has much to put up with from you."

"I have never claimed to be an easy man. I have often wondered how you tolerate so much of my company."

Raynar smirked. "I have a great tolerance for pain."

"Come. Let us leave this matter. As always, Eleanor will do as she will." He signaled to one of his squires, indicating he wanted a stein of beer. "Tomorrow, Terlinden will be leaving and I do not wish to spoil our mood."

"You are right. These past days have been good ones." And knowing Eleanor was fully capable of dealing with the woman and her child, Raynar gave himself up to enjoying the revelry in the hall.

He did not join in either the dancing or the dicing, but used his wit to entertain a circle of admirers. Eventually, the demand for a story was raised and, laughing with pleasure, he jumped onto a trestle top and lifted his hands high above his head. His reputation for storytelling was so great that in only moments the hall was silent and Raynar began to speak.

"I will tell you a story of Jack. The very same Jack who later gained a great reputation as a giant-slayer. Jack was a poor, but good lad, who desired above all else to become a knight and join King Arthur and his Round Table. One day when he was walking through a wood he chanced upon an old lady who was carrying a bundle of sticks on her back. The load was so heavy that she was bent in two beneath the weight of it. Pity filled Jack and he said to the woman, 'Here old woman. Give me half your load and I will carry it for you whither you like.' The old woman smiled at him, a toothless smile, reeking of rot, but genuine nonetheless. She sat immediately, released her bundle, and divided it into equal parts. Jack retied the ropes and then, after hoisting one pack onto his own back, followed the old woman.

"You can imagine how surprised he was when she led him, not to a hovel beneath the trees, but to a beautiful castle which glistened in the sunlight with turrets reaching upward into the sky. She laughed at his surprise and said, 'Not everyone is as they seem, Jack.' And when he turned to look at her he saw that she had been transformed into a beautiful maiden with silken tresses that hung to her waist and a smile so sweet he could not help but laugh for joy. 'I am Grunhilda,' she said, with a voice that was as delightful as a bubbling brook. 'I am daughter to the Queen of the Fairies, and I have been watching you, Jack, for some time. I am determined that if you can prove that you are as brave as you are good, you shall have your heart's desire and become one of Arthur's companions. This is how you shall prove your bravery to me. There is a princess who is imprisoned within a castle by a fierce dragon who has burned the surrounding countryside and threatens her very life. I will set you on the path and if you can prove your bravery, you will have your reward.'

"Jack could scarcely believe his good fortune and eagerly set off in the direction which the fairy princess sent him. He walked for days, never veering from his course although he had to cross rivers and pass through swamps and thickets on his journey. At last he began to see that he was nearing his destination for the countryside became barren and parched, the result of the dragon's fire. In the distance he saw the battlements of a great castle and his heart was filled with relief that he would soon be able to complete his task and win his reward.

"Now it was necessary for Jack to pass through a town which lay in his path. He had every intention of wending his way through the labyrinth of streets and departing out the gate at the opposite end as quickly as possible. But, as he walked, a woman suddenly began to scream. Without hesitation he followed the sounds up an alley, where he found a crowd gathered outside a burning building! All were shouting in distress, but one woman was pulling her hair and sobbing, 'My baby! My baby!' Jack raised his hand and the crowd immediately quieted. Listening closely, above the sound of the crackling flames, Jack heard the wail of an infant from within.

"Forgetting all about his quest he ran toward the doorway and entered the burning house. Inside, all was smoky, and the prickling heat terrified him, but ignoring his fear he stopped and listened again, and then followed the weakening cries of the baby until he found its cradle. But as he reached his hands out to lift up the child, a burning piece of timber fell from above and landed across his outstretched arms. His own flesh had protected the infant from harm! Gritting his teeth in pain, Jack hurled the wood away, grabbed the child, and stumbled outside with the babe safe in his arms. The women of the town praised him and wrapped his arms in cool cloths and fed him and gave him a place to sleep. The following morning they sent him off on his journey, laden with food and supplies. But alas for Jack, the castle had magically disappeared. Search as he might, he could not find it again anywhere in the world of men.

"Finally, filled with despair, he returned by the path he had taken to the home of the fairy princess. Again he met the old hag in the wood. She smiled her toothless grin at him and asked, 'Did you rescue the princess, Jack? Did you prove your bravery?' 'No,' he answered sadly. 'I did not rescue her. Some magic whisked her away and I was not able to fulfill my quest.' 'Let me see your arms, Jack.' She pointed to the reddened scars which lay across his forearms. 'That babe you rescued was the princess, Jack! You were willing to forfeit your own fortune for the life of a child, and in so doing you have gained all. That was the true test of your courage. You have indeed fulfilled your quest and will receive your reward.' At her words the fairy once again took her beautiful form and Jack, looking down, saw himself attired in a suit of mail to equal that of King Arthur himself and in his hand the jeweled hilt of a—"

At this point, the cheering applause of his audience buried his final words. Grinning widely, Raynar bowed to the right and then the left. He was surprised to see that Eleanor had joined the crowd and stood looking up at him at Sebastian's side. Raynar straightened, but continued to watch her. Her face was ashen, and as her eyes met his, there was in them a silent question. He nodded in return, giving her the truth.

As Raynar watched, she reached out and took Sebastian's arm in her hands, and pulled up the hem of his sleeve to reveal the vivid scar. Angrily, Sebastian tugged his arm away, but Eleanor took it again and dropped a quick kiss on the burn, before she turned and made her way out through the crowd.

The evening was waning, and Raynar was tired. It annoyed him greatly that he no longer was able to revel until cocks-crow. The younger folk seemed ready to dance the night through, but he himself was ready for his bed. He was saying his farewells to the company when a page approached, and informed him that he had been ordered to attend the duke in his chamber.

All weariness instantly gone, he strode from the hall and ascended the stairwell which led to the upper chambers. Having received a nod of permission from the guard at the door, Raynar entered the room.

Sebastian and Eleanor were standing at opposite ends of the chamber. Sebastian, with his back to the room, was staring out the window into the dark nothingness of the night, while Eleanor was watching him in tense and frustrated silence.

"I have come as you commanded."

Sebastian turned. His face was lined with a great weariness which showed even in the flickering candlelight. "This has seemed an endless day," he said. "I want you to lend your silver tongue to my cause, and persuade Eleanor to agree to my plans."

This was curious! "I doubt I would have more influence than you, though willingly I shall make the attempt. What plans do you mean?"

"Tell him, Eleanor," Sebastian commanded as he again turned away.

"The duke and duchess of Terlinden," said Eleanor, "want Sebastian to send the boys—Frederick, Arthur, and Bran—to be fostered in their household. I will not have them sent away!"

"But Eleanor," Raynar spoke slowly, for he was trying to determine what lay behind her disapproval. "It is a good thought. The boys have not yet begun their training and it is time that they did."

"Then let them begin here!" There was a touch of hysteria in her voice. "They belong here. They should grow up attached to Westfeld—and not to Terlinden."

"But Sebastian and I fostered at Terlinden."

"A fine thing it would be, then, for Frederick to have more loyalty to Terlinden than to his own dukedom."

Sebastian interjected without looking around, "I hear well the accusation that I myself have more loyalty to Terlinden than to Westfeld."

Staring at his back, Raynar wondered whether Sebastian recognized the truth in these words.

Eleanor continued, as though Sebastian had not spoken. "Do not try to convince me there could be bad blood between Frederick and his brothers.

They are the best of friends. When Frederick is duke, Arthur and Bran should stand firmly at his side. They should not be attached to Bertha's son, Hugh, nor to Prince Stefan!"

"It is the way of the world for boys to receive their training and their spurs elsewhere," Raynar said.

She shook her head vehemently. "Sebastian should be gathering young men about himself, binding their allegiance to Westfeld with bonds of the heart, not of words alone. Certainly, there are some squires out on the tilting ground, working hard to win their spurs, but to whom will they be loyal? Not to Sebastian! They see him rarely, and have no opportunity to learn to love him. Why should I send my sons to Terlinden? They are needed here."

"There is some truth and some wisdom in what you say. But you *know* you ask of Sebastian something he cannot do." Raynar gentled his voice, hoping to avoid the eruption of an even greater quarrel.

"*Can* not! Do not mince words, Raynar. You mean *will* not!" She moved forward until she was standing an arm's length from Sebastian who still did not turn. "I have accepted all you have given me, my lord. The good and the ill. But this I will not accept. If you send the boys to Terlinden, I will be wife to you no longer. I will pack this night and withdraw to a convent, and have nothing to do with Westfeld ever again. Tonight you must choose. Will it be Terlinden, or me?"

The instant she finished, Eleanor grabbed her shawl from the bed and left the room. The door would have slammed behind her had not Raynar reached out with his foot and stopped the blow. Gently, he pulled the latch until the door shut with a soft click.

When he turned around, Sebastian was facing him, arms crossed and his lips drawn into a tight grimace. "Let her go to her convent. She cannot force me in this matter."

"But you know she is right." Raynar said, then he raised his arm to forestall Sebastian's retort. "At least, she is right that we have not taken seriously the training of Westfeld's knights."

"It is not her place to criticize."

"It is not only her place, but her duty."

Sebastian scowled. "I was honored that Gebbard wanted to take my sons, and I have already approved the plan."

"That is something else." Raynar fingered the post on the bed. "She was so adamant. I feel certain there is more. Something she has not said."

"Not said? She said all there was to say and much, much more!"

Raynar struggled to keep his breathing under control. "You would not truly let her go, would you?"

Sebastian looked down at his hands, as though counting his fingers. "She does not mean it."

"Are you that certain? If you are, then you must know Eleanor far better than I, for I think she may. When she so chooses, she is a very determined woman."

"Then if she chooses to leave, so be it."

"And your children? And Eaglesheid? What would become of them?"

Sebastian did not answer, but turned again to the window.

A shudder ran through Raynar and he pressed his fingers to his brow. He lifted his head, opened his eyes, and spoke. "I have a proposition. Swallow your pride and decline Terlinden's offer, with all deference of course. And I, myself, will stay here and see to the training of your sons and the other squires."

Sebastian spun around and looked at him, then crossed the room and gripped Raynar's arm. "Why? Why would you make such an offer? You have never desired to stay in one place. You are the most errant man I know."

"You do not know all my desires. As I love you, I also love your duchy and your family. This will be no hardship for me." He held Sebastian's arm, so that they stood face to face. "I know well that you cannot stay. But Eleanor is your duchess. You cannot let her go. And I will not. Your sons are fine boys and I will enjoy their training." He dropped his arm and moved away, but Sebastian continued to stand, drained of his anger, looking only confused. More lightly now, Raynar asked, "And why should Terlinden have them? After all, he had us, and we were the best! Let us keep your sons here."

Defeated, Sebastian sighed. "I cannot fight you both. I agree. For now. We will keep them here and you can see to their training. But only until we find another tutor."

Not showing his tremendous relief, Raynar clapped Sebastian on his back. "You know well that I have no equal. Where in Christendom would you ever find another to take my place?"

# Chapter 16

I T WAS THE KIND OF HOT SUMMER's day that Ella loved. She had been to the village, and was now wending her way home with a basket of eggs clutched within her arms. The shimmering heat of the midday sun combined with the motionless air to heighten her senses so that the world around her seemed to throb with activity. Not only could she hear the insects as they scrambled through the grasses near her feet, but she could see a family of starlings perched on a tree branch a field's-length away. A movement on the path caught her attention: A tiny brown toad, perfectly colored to blend with the earth, was hopping lazily, back and forth.

Grinning, Ella set down her basket and scooped the creature into her hands, and soon she was fully absorbed by this new interest—until a distant cry broke into her reverie.

"John!" she gasped, as she jumped to her feet. The sound brought a rush of fear; never before had she heard his voice raised in such a manner.

She began to dash forward, remembered the eggs and returned for the basket, then hurried off again. But as she came to the edge of the small clearing which sheltered her home, she stopped in confusion. Her parents were quarreling!

"I'll not do it, Kate," John was insisting. "I've done everything you've asked of me, but this I'll not do!"

Ella could not see her mother for she stood shadowed within the doorway of the cottage, but she heard her angry response. "You must! You owe this to me!"

"It is not debt we are talking about. It's my life. And my life means yours, and Ella's too."

"But I do talk of debt. Look at us! What kind of life is this? Every year we are poorer than the year before. Look at those hens. Only three left and not one worth anything. They are nothing but skin and bones. Skin and bones, just like the three of us."

"I'll work harder. Eat less. I'll do anything but sell another of your jewels. The risk is too great. What would happen to you and Ella if I didn't come back?"

"You are lying. You have done it before. Twice."

"But I was able to go to a friend. And he warned me not to return. Do you not understand how difficult it is to find a buyer for such a jewel? Do you think I can walk up to any hawker on the street and ask him to buy a valuable gem? I'd be branded as a thief in an instant."

"There was a day when you would have obeyed me without thought, without question."

"I think I've learned some wisdom."

"You're just afraid."

"Of course, I'm afraid. Not for myself, but for you. You know well that I'm all that lies between you and starvation."

There was nothing said for a moment, then John spoke in a quieter tone. "There is Ella under the trees. She has heard our quarrel."

"Good! Then she will know what a coward you are. That you count your own life of greater value than ours."

"Do you truly think that?" John asked, in disbelief.

"Ella!" her mother ordered. "Come here!"

As Ella set down her basket and ran to her mother, she tried to wipe away her tears with the back of her hand, but her mother tugged at her and spun her around so that she faced John.

"Look at her. She looks like a beggar's brat."

"Oh, Kate. Did you truly not see this years ago?" There was real agony in John's voice.

Her mother's fingers dug into her shoulders. "If you will not sell these for me, then I will do it myself."

"You wouldn't!"

"Try me and see."

John swore, and swung his fist into the wooden doorpost, hitting so hard that blood flowed from his knuckles. "All right! I'll go!" Again he slammed his fist. "After the harvest is in."

For a moment, Ella's mother clenched her even tighter, then she loosened her grip. "No. Tomorrow. The sooner you leave, then the sooner you will return."

"Ella." John lifted his hand and stroked her tangled hair, brushing it back off her face. "Go get Bridget's eggs."

"I did already," she pointed as she sobbed. "They're there in the basket."

"Then go and gather some reeds from the pond. I need to fix my belt."

Eager to obey, Ella twisted out of her mother's hands and fled across the clearing. When she reached the pond, she threw herself down on the bank and wept hot choking tears. As her fears subsided and her tears diminished, she continued to cry because the sensation was so interesting. When a duckling waddled to the water's edge and dived in head first, she paused mid-sob, and by the time she recollected that she was alone and wretched, it was too late. The tears had gone and could not be enticed back.

With a sigh, she gave up the attempt and settled down to enjoy the activity around her. Long-legged bugs skittered across the surface of the water while others, with heavier bodies, clambered over the many rocks at the pond's edge. Nearby a spider was spinning a web on some of the stockier grasses. The longer she sat, the more Ella saw—white-tailed birds pushing their way through the forest of reeds, brown-spotted frogs hopping from stone to stone, and long, slender fish swimming idly beneath the surface.

Before long, she had forgotten all about her parents' quarrel, for it was an unusual pleasure to have such an opportunity to sit and daydream. There was always work, either in the house or the fields, pressing to be done. Rarely did Mama do anything practical. Either she busied herself teaching Ella useless and embarrassing manners, or she sat idly, staring at the embers of the fire.

Years ago Ella had learned the many tasks necessary for their survival: how to coddle the last pieces of charcoal on the hearth, how to remove the foul rushes from the floor and replace them with sweet-smelling ones which she would find at the pond or the stream, and how to cook a soup or stew, carefully conserving every morsel which could be used either as substance or flavoring for another meal.

She worked hard but never felt ill-used, because her father—that was the way she thought of him though Mama forbade her to call him anything but John—worked constantly, from before first light until after the darkness had settled. Three seasons of the year he observed neither the Sabbath nor any feastday, risking the charge of impiety. Once, when frightened by some of the villagers' dour predictions, she had begged him to stop working lest God punish him for violating the Sabbath, John had answered, "Elly, I work four or more days a week for one lord. The other will just have to understand that I need to keep working." When she had continued to doubt, he had lifted her chin with his fingers and added, "Look, Elly. Which do you think is the greater sin? For a man to work when he should be resting? Or for that man to let his family starve for lack of picking up a hoe?"

So it was that Ella, herself, rarely spent an afternoon in idleness. As this day passed, she settled her feet into the still water and languished in the warmth of the sun. With silence and infinite patience, she continued to watch the pageant of nature which unfolded around her.

John had settled matters with Kate, as best as he was able, and then gone into the field where he harvested some of the early vegetables and dug out some of the weeds from the hard-baked earth. His hands worked automatically while his head swirled with visions and fears. Who would bring in the harvest? Kate was unpredictable, and Ella, although a willing worker, did not have the strength to swing the scythe nor the endurance to work in the heat. What would happen when he failed to fulfill his commitment to his liege-lord? And foremost, how would he find a buyer for the jewel without inciting the fatal accusation of thief?

His imagination answered, conjuring up vision after vision of the many possibilities. Stripped bare with his throat slit by outlaws, he would provide a feast for the carrion birds. Accused as a thief he would be exposed to public ridicule and hung on a gibbet in some distant town square. Or tossed into a stinking dungeon he would be tortured by a lawless nobleman until he died, silent until the end about the source of his fortune. Most far-fetched of all, he imagined returning triumphantly to Kate who, filled with admiration for his bravery, declared herself willing to start a new life with him in some distant town as his true wife.

With a soundless laugh he shook his head to clear it. The work was not done, nor was the sun close to disappearing for the day. Nevertheless, John set aside his tools and went to find Ella. If this was to be his last day here, then he would spend it doing what he most enjoyed.

She did not hear his approach even though the weeds rustled as he pushed his way through, and he stood, quietly watching her for several moments. She was so beautiful, his Elly. From her mother she had inherited her fine-boned body and, more noticeably, her abundant and curly hair. Yet there the similarity between the two ceased, for she was as blond and light-skinned as her grandfather, Branold, while her eyes were a startling deep brown, trimmed with thick lashes. It was part affection and part awe that led him to call her by the nickname, 'Princess.'

He used it now when he finally spoke and broke the silence of that magic moment.

"Hello, my princess. Did you find me some reeds?"

She jumped to her feet and threw herself into his arms, forcing him to lift her up even though at ten years of age she was too grown for such an action.

"Why aren't you my father?" she cried.

Taken unawares, he answered the truth. "Because I'm not worthy!"

"But you are the best father anyone could ever have!"

"I'm glad you think so, Elly. But remember that things are not always as they seem."

"Don't go away. Please don't go."

He put her down, but continued to hold her, stroking her hair, enjoying the silken feel of her curls. "I must go, Elly. Your mama is right."

"No, she is not," Ella insisted. "She's being selfish!"

John scratched his cheek. "How can I make you understand. That is her privilege. Her right. Do not think I begrudge her this. I should've offered to go long ago. And you know, Elly..." He said her name, but it was to himself he now spoke. "Perhaps it truly was cowardice which held me back. Maybe I have just been making excuses."

"But you said it was dangerous. I heard you say that."

"Elly. Elly. You make me see myself clearly." He drew her close and gave her a fierce hug, then set her at arm's length away and looked directly into her eyes. "Should I not go? Because there's danger? I hope I know better than that. Your mama is right, my princess. What kind of a man would allow his lady to live in such poverty when the means is there to bring some comfort into her life? And into yours, Elly! I would like to see you fattened up this winter. But remember that you must take care of her while I'm gone." There was no need for him to explain more. It was understood by both of them that Kate lived on the verge of madness, swinging week by week from bouts of total lethargy to undirected, frenzied activity.

"I will." Ella sniffled and wiped the back of her hands across her nose, but she did not cry.

"Come. Let's go home. We'll make a dinner big enough that I'll not want to eat for another week."

John held out his hand and Ella eagerly took it. In silence they walked together back to their cottage. At the edge of the clearing, John stopped. The scene was so peaceful, so idyllic, that he felt his chest swell with pride and pain. The house was nestled against the woods, close enough to benefit from the insulating protection of the trees but not so near as to risk igniting the overhanging branches with a stray ember from the fire. The thatch on the roof was still fresh, for he had repaired it only last summer, and the walls were sturdy and well-pitched. A bed of flowers, Ella's work, grew up around the doorway; the purple flowers of a vine climbed right up one of the posts until it nearly reached the protruding roof. As he stood, inhaling the memory, Kate appeared in the doorway. She was wiping her hands on her apron, and smiling.

"I have dinner ready," she called out. "Chicken! One less to eat our precious grain this winter."

Clapping her hands joyfully, Ella ran forward to greet her mother. John did not move; tears filled his eyes. This scene of domestic contentment was only an illusion, the sort of trick which could torture a man's soul. Reality was to be found in the wild look of despair that lay only partially hidden in the depths of Kate's eyes. A greater resolve filled him. Tomorrow he would willingly go.

The summer darkness was slow in coming. Ella, John, and Kate passed the evening in pleasant camaraderie, with none speaking of John's departure on the morrow. It was not until Ella was finally asleep on the down ticking she shared with her mother, that Kate pulled the slipper from the pouch which hung around her waist and snipped off the largest of the remaining jewels. By now the fire had burned so low that it cast more smoke than light into the cottage. Straining to see, Kate carefully stitched the jewel—it was a blood-red ruby—into the hem of John's tunic.

"I will go north," John said, at last, breaking the silence. "If I can enter one of the free towns, surely I'll find a buyer. But I'll need to travel slowly and carefully until I'm well away from the duchy. Kate, listen. If anyone asks where I am—"

"Who would ask?" she interrupted.

John shook his head, amazed at her simplicity. "Kate, I am bound to work four days every week for the duke. Surely his bailiff will begin looking for me."

"What should I tell him?" A touch of fear entered her voice. "What if he sends Ella and me away?"

"He'll not send you away. Of that I'm sure. You have value, even if you are not under oath, as I am. Plead ignorance. Tell him I was always a good-for-nothing. That I probably went and got myself murdered. Be angry at me! Make your threats louder than his own."

"But ..." She waved her hand in the air as though she were reaching for something. "You will return, won't you?"

"Within a fortnight," John said with certainty, soothing her as he would Ella. "Two at the most. And I'll bring a cow. Later we can buy more hens. I can hardly wait to surprise Elly with a new shift. One that has never been worn! And I'll bring you some spices—salt and saffron and mustard. And a goose for the Yule."

"And wine!" Kate brightened. "What a celebration we shall have."

"And bags of flour."

"And a cloth for the table."

John laughed. "Really, Kate! How would you explain linen on your table?"

"Who would see it?" she shrugged.

"All right!" Again he laughed. "I'll bring you the finest linen cloth I can find."

"In the morning I'll pack you some cheese. Would you like some of the oats? To make some cakes along the way?"

"No. That would mean carrying a pouch. I wish to take as little as possible. My only defense will be my poverty. I must look so poor there could be no gain in attacking me. I'll find my food along the way, the same as any pilgrim."

Kate was no longer listening. Staring into the embers of the fire, the tiny hut faded from her sight and was replaced by the expanse of a hall. Before her was spread a great table, almost groaning under the weight of the platters, while the room swirled with such activity that she felt her face flush with excitement. The guests all seemed large and awesome, but most magnificent of all were her parents, who sat in the center of the board on the raised dais. Eagerly, from across the room, she watched, waiting for her father to see her and beckon her forward ...

For several weeks after John's departure, Kate lived in a high state of excitement. Over and over she imagined the joys his return would bring, when they would be lifted out of the poverty she so despised; but the summer neared its end, and still he did not come. In a rush of fear, sanity returned to her. Picking up the scythe, she went to the field with Ella. From that time on she toiled every day from the first light in the morning until she could barely see to find her way home, in an attempt to harvest enough food to keep them alive over the winter. Her hands, which had grown soft, became agonizingly blistered, but she simply wrapped a cloth around them and continued to work. When the snow finally fell and she could do no more, Kate looked at the meager winter stores with trepidation. Yet with the fear came determination, the same determination that had driven her so many years before. No matter what the cost to herself, her child must survive!

Now she daily trekked, with Ella at her side, through the fields, marshes and woods, gathering firewood and mosses to provide them with the warmth they would need in the depths of the winter. Every housewifely trick she could dredge up from her memories of long ago days, she now used. There were only the two skinny chickens remaining in the coop, but each one provided pies, stews, soups, and gruels for nearly a fortnight. Every drop of fat was salvaged and reused over and over for frying and thickening, and for blending the pastries and flatcakes. A carrot could last a day, a turnip a week. As the winter deepened, Kate began surreptitiously to return her own servings to the pot, but still the broths became thinner and weaker. In the end, it was the villagers who came to their rescue, bringing the breads and the venison which kept them alive until the sun renewed the earth again.

No sooner had the snows gone than Kate headed into the field and began the exhausting task of tilling the ground in preparation for the planting. The mule had died years ago, and not having John's strength to pull the ploughshare, Kate wielded the hoe while Ella used a sharpened stick to try to loosen some of the hardened clumps. It was a pitiful patch that was eventually sown, and although neither mother nor daughter spoke of it, they both knew it could not possibly produce enough food for them to survive even half the winter. Again they would be dependent upon the charity of people who were nearly as impoverished as themselves.

Despite her despair, as the hot summer passed in waiting, Kate had watched her daughter with pride. And an unformed plan began to grow in her mind. Without a conscious reason, she hastened the pace of Ella's education.

"The steward will assign you a place to sit at the table. By your nearness to the master and the mistress you will know in what esteem you are held … You must never show an unseemly interest in your food, nor pat your stomach in satisfaction. Those are peasant manners … You must show consideration for the feelings of your host and hostess, as well as for your fellow diners. Talk only of cheerful things and never criticize the cooking or bring attention to flies on the food … Never bite bread off the loaf, but break it or cut it. Then use your bread to sop up the gravies and sauces on your trencher. Usually your trencher will be given as alms when your meal is finished, but if your host eats his then you may eat yours too … If your dress has a train on it, hold it over your left arm, like this, so that your right arm will be free … Always walk with your head erect and your shoulders straight. Your neck should be as long as you can make it. Now try. Let me see you walk. Here, put this pan on your head and walk … Always treat your inferiors with kindness and your superiors with respect. No two people are exactly equal. There is always something to differentiate between them. In that manner I always took precedence over my sister because I was the elder … You must hear your mass in the morning before you can break your fast …"

On and on the lessons went. The two, enjoying an easy companionship, were closer than ever before in their lives. Together they would stroll through the woods, searching for herbs and wildflowers to flavor their stews, or sit in the bright evening sunlight mending the worn shifts that had served them so many years. Their preoccupation with each other kept their fears at bay.

Until August. Although the month had barely turned, the killing frost had come. Death lay on the fields.

As Kate stared at her decimated harvest, a terrible calm filled her. The indecision which had been haunting her while she had waited in increasing despair for John's return, now fled. She knew at last what she must do.

Lifting her eyes, she looked past the fields to the valleys beyond, where unseen but beckoning, stood Eaglesheid. Her nemesis. The shadow which had been looming over her for her entire life.

As the minutes passed, her senses dimmed until the sights and sounds of the world faded away. She was aware of nothing except the pounding of her own blood as it coursed through her body. Louder and louder it grew—the sound of hoofbeats hitting the hardened turf—a dark rider coming for her as once she had thought Sebastian would come. Nearly fainting, she shook her head to clear it of the vision. Not yet. It was not time yet. There was still one more task she needed to complete before she could allow herself to be carried away. Drawing a deep breath she raised her eyes skyward, then without regret, she left the field.

# Chapter 17

KARL, THE STEWARD, returned his quill to the well and scattered sand over the figures he had just written. His fingertips brushed the leather binding of the ledger as he waited for the ink to dry. This set of accounts which recorded every purchase, payment or gift that came to Eaglesheid, was his second love. His first, was Lady Eleanor, who had not only recognized his talents but had understood how to use them. With his help, she had set about revitalizing the affairs of the duchy by building a walled town near the river docks. No detail was too small to escape her attention; she was as interested in the running of the mill to grind the grain as she was in the baking of the bread.

The twin disasters that had arrived one after the other this past week, would certainly challenge her ingenuity but did nothing to shake Karl's confidence in his mistress. Without any question she would find some way to turn again the tide which seemed to be pressing against Westfeld.

In the meantime, the best he could do to help was to proceed with his work. Karl lifted the quill, but set it down again at the sound of a sharp knock on the door. With a sigh, he rubbed his hand over his smooth scalp then called, "Enter!"

It was the porter. "There's another of those women here, asking for the mistress."

"Another of what women?" Karl was annoyed. He had no time for riddles.

"Ummm ..." The man glanced nervously around the room. "One of those women with a child."

Now Karl understood and he shook his head with disgust. The duke was indiscriminately careless with his seed! Arthur had been followed by James, and now here was another lad to lay as an offering at Lady Eleanor's feet. Although Karl did not doubt that his mistress would accept this lad as willingly as the others, he fervently wished she could be spared the hurt that the child's presence must surely inflict.

"I had better come and see." After carefully testing his last marks to make certain they were dry, he shut the book and stood. "Is the lad likely-looking?"

"Nay—"

"That's a pity."

"Nay, it's not a lad!"

Karl stopped mid-step and stared. "A girl?"

"Uh-huh. The mother's a drab but the child's quite comely. Beggin' your pardon, Steward. How could milady know if the child belongs t' the duke?"

"Ha! That's a good question." The steward moved to the door and began to draw it shut behind him. "She once told me she could tell by the eyes."

"Well," he scratched his head. "Is she going t' raise every brown-eyed child in the duchy?"

"Not every child," he grunted. "Only the ones with cunning mothers!"

Standing in the arched shadows of the doorway, Karl watched the woman. There was something unusual about her, for she held herself with an aloofness that was faintly disturbing. But beyond that strange stillness, there was nothing to differentiate her from the legions of other peasants. She was so thin and drawn that her clothes hung like rags from her stooped shoulders. Her grayed hair was carelessly looped into a knot, and the loose strands coiled about her face like the filthy fleece of a winter sheep.

She looked simple, and Karl breathed his relief. Perhaps, after all, there would be no need to upset his mistress. Some coins in her pocket and a threat in her ears, and he could speed this harlot and her child on their way.

"You have something you wish to discuss with me?"

She had not seen him coming and looked up in startled dismay. Then she met his eyes square on. Karl frowned. There was strength here, if only of a madness. Perhaps this woman would not be so easily frightened off.

"It is Lady Eleanor I wish to see. The duchess, and none other."

"I am steward here. You must tell me your business. If you cannot do that, then you must leave."

"I assure you it is a private matter. She will not thank you if you keep me away."

Strange speech for such a woman. And very true to the mark too, for Lady Eleanor cared more for these children than for her own pain.

"She will not know," he countered.

A flicker of fear flashed through her eyes, but they did not waver in their gaze. "Then you would be making a grave mistake."

"Are you alone?" He hoped she would hear the contempt in his voice.

"No," she pointed. "That is my daughter over there."

He did not bother to look at the child. He had already made up his mind. This one would cause trouble if she were denied. And the last thing Lady Eleanor needed now was more trouble. "I will see if the duchess wishes to speak with you. And," he added maliciously, hoping to ruffle her certitude, "see that your brat is no nuisance."

"You needn't worry. Ella knows how to behave."

"See that she does." He started to turn away.

"Wait!" she cried, clutching at his sleeve, and for the first time a touch of panic entered her voice. "Tell the duchess that she knew me well when we were children. Tell her my name is Kate ... Katrina!"

Exhaustion tugged at Eleanor's limbs and reached into the recesses of her mind. To set herself to the work which needed to be done was nearly impossible, but to sleep was more difficult still. Disaster had followed disaster in her duchy. First fire, then frost. The flames, deafeningly loud, had destroyed a portion of the new town at the river's edge, including the weavers' hall and the precious cloth which lay within. As she had watched the fruit of her dreams burn, she had thought that nothing could match her despair. But she had been wrong: Silent as a thief had come the cold, snuffing out the life of the earth. The quiet which had spread over the land had struck deeper than a widow's wail.

Would Sebastian come home now? Or was he basking in some sunny clime where early frosts were beyond all imagination? In truth, did she even want him to return? He had shown little interest in her plans to build a town in the lee of the castle, passively giving his sponsorship for the construction of a church and a market. The weavers' hall she had kept secret, planning to surprise him when next he came home, while knowing deep in her heart that he would not care. And now the gold had been spent, earning nothing in return but sodden ash.

Her chagrin had pushed her to action. Already the debris had been cleared and the cornerstone of a new building had been laid. Stone. This building would be of stone. And praise be to God, the handful of looms she had acquired over the years had not yet been moved, but were still in the women's cottages. By spring there would be cloth. And in the spring the fields would be planted.

But first would come the winter.

As she hurried toward the solar, Eleanor heard the sounds of a scuffle in the nearby stairwell. Her shoulders stiffened, for she could predict whom she would see when she rounded the corner. With all the troubles she'd had to endure this past week, it seemed unfair that Eaglesheid was also saddled with unpleasant guests—two obnoxious boys with a decided talent for riling her sons out of their usual good humor.

She prepared for the encounter by arranging her face into a look of maternal dismay, but when she rounded the corner she stopped in genuine horror. This was no small skirmish but a major battle! Four boys, including Frederick and Arthur, were swinging their fists with dreadful accuracy, while blood streamed from eyes and noses and mouths.

Dropping the linens, Eleanor shrieked—then shrieked again. In only moments, soldiers entered the passageway. Strong arms pulled apart the young offenders, and Raynar, who had arrived with the others, began to castigate the lads. But the worst was about to begin. At the sight of the blood on those beloved faces, Eleanor's control, which had been stretched almost beyond endurance, finally broke. Her sobs turned hysterical; her own cheeks started to bleed as her nails dug unfeelingly into her flesh.

Raynar hid his alarm with a terse order that the boys be taken to their chamber to be dealt with later. The faithful Karl had already taken a stand at the end of the corridor.

Grasping Eleanor's arms, Raynar held them firmly so she could harm herself no further. Desperate to calm her, he called to her, but she seemed deaf to his words. Finally, in frustration, he gathered her into his arms, sat down with her on the steps, and began to rock her back and forth. Her sobs slowly subsided and her body relaxed. With wonder, Raynar realized she was asleep.

He knew he should feel sheepish, to be sitting on a stone stair, holding a grown woman who was tousled and sleeping like a child—but he did not. He felt only gratitude for this quiet moment, and an acknowledgment of the depth of his love for the wife of his friend. With great reluctance he stood and carried her up the narrow stair and into her own chamber.

"I can bear this no longer, Eleanor. It is time to end this mummery." With the whispered words he formed a new resolve. Laying her gently on the bed, he drew the coverlet over her, then bent and kissed her cheek.

"When you awaken, we will speak." This time he spoke more loudly, and Eleanor stirred, but her slow and even breath was not disturbed. Turning, he saw her woman standing silent and expressionless in the doorway.

"I will leave her in your care, Hannah. I think sleep is what she needs most. She's had so little of it these days past. Send for me when she awakens."

"Aye, Sir Raynar. I'll do that." The woman looked directly at Raynar, and there was no sign of reproach in her eyes.

Raynar went straight to the boys' chamber where he found them waiting in subdued silence. He did not chastise them with words, for their remorse was evident, but after determining the cause of their quarrel sent them to the town with orders to use their energy helping to clear the burnt debris. Then he retreated to his own chamber where he remained, alone with his brooding thoughts until Hannah sent word that her mistress was awake and asking for him.

"Raynar!" Eleanor's face was alight as she greeted him. "Just before I awoke I had the most wonderful idea that I can scarce wait to tell you."

"An idea that still seems sane when you are truly awake?" He spoke, though without thought. He was reeling at the sight of the raw scratches on her cheeks. She looked as though she had been lashed. "That is rare indeed," he said, though without any enthusiasm.

She laughed. "You listen and tell me. We—that is Westfeld—will provide the peasants the bread they'll need to live through the winter. In return they will work, either on the weavers' hall or in one of the looming cottages. By spring, not only will the new hall be finished but we will have laid by large quantities of cloth. Everyone who works will eat. Even the children can help. We can use them to run errands, or sort, or clean. And if we allow the peasants access to the forest, for this winter alone, they can catch the rabbit and deer they need to have meat in their pots. Of course, I will need to buy more grain and more wool from the merchants, but I am certain we can do it. Do you approve my plan? I want my people to survive the winter!"

"The idea has merit," he answered, slowly. "But Eleanor, there is something else of which I wish to speak."

"The boys!" She clamped her hand to her mouth. "I had forgotten. What was the cause of their scuffle?"

"To avenge an insult. One of our delightful guests had called Arthur a bastard."

"They were fighting for that?" Her hand dropped. "He is a bastard, in truth, though it is no shame."

"For certes, both boys took it as an insult. Not to their honor, but to yours."

"Did you punish them?"

"For defending your honor? I myself would defend your honor in such a manner."

She looked down but said nothing.

"Eleanor. Listen to me. I do not wish to speak of the boys, or the weavers' hall, or the survival of the peasants. Later, perhaps, but not now."

He moved closer and touched her cheek, tracing his finger along one of the reddened lines.

"What is the matter?" she frowned. "What is it you wish?" Then with more concern, "Is it Sebastian?"

Raynar covered her mouth gently with his hand. If he did not seize this moment, he would lose all nerve to do what must be done. "Do not speak. Please! Just listen. This is not easy for me to say, but I must. You know I hold Sebastian above other men in nearly all things. As a knight, he has great valor and skill, and as a leader of men there are few to match him. Though I can make men laugh and thus ease their passing time, Sebastian can save their lives and bring them victory. Never will he ask another to do what he will not do himself. Never does he hold himself back, nor count his own life to be of more value than another's. He is strong and unyielding when he must, yet always ready to temper his strength and power with compassion, when he may. Yet with you, Eleanor, you who have deserved the best of him, he has failed. Any churl could make a better husband than he."

"No." Eleanor shook her head. "You are wrong."

"Please do not speak. I must tell you what I must. It is time for honesty between us." Raynar longed to draw her to him and hold her, but he did not. "At the time Sebastian married you, he had been freshly wounded by love. I thought time would heal him. I thought your beauty and your kindness and your intelligence would win him over. And they would have, I am certain, if Sebastian had but seen! But he had blinded himself. He refused to see what was standing right before him.

"I thought I could make him see. I thought my attention to you, my care for you, would make him wonder. Make him look again. Instead, I have become a shield, or a shade, obscuring his vision.

"Eleanor, not only do I love Sebastian, but I love you. You are my sister and my friend. But if you reached out your arms to me, I could—" He stopped mid-sentence, swallowed, then continued. "It is time to end this impasse. I will stand in the middle no longer, watching you suffer. There are two paths I may take, and you will determine which that will be."

"What are you saying?" Eleanor's eyes narrowed.

"You have never been happy with Sebastian. I offer you freedom from him. Break your bonds with him and come away with me. We can go to Aragon, or England, or Constantinople. Anywhere you desire."

Total shock blanched her face. "How dare you ask such a thing?"

"Come with me, Eleanor. Free us all."

"No!" There was no trace of indecision in her voice as she spat out her reply. "In all the years we have been wed, Sebastian has never hurt me as you do now. How can you think so little of me as to think that I would ever betray my husband? I am no Guinevere." Eleanor lifted her chin in pride. "Even if I loved you and loathed him, I would never leave. But Raynar, you have erred greatly. I love Sebastian! I have esteemed you well, and relied on you too, but it is Sebastian alone who holds my heart. You are a fool to think otherwise. You have shocked me and shamed yourself. Now leave me!" She pointed to the door. "Leave Eaglesheid! I am so angry that…I think I could be as dangerous as any man you know!"

Raynar felt heat flush his face. "In a moment. Never fear, Eleanor, I will leave. You have answered as I expected, though I'll not say as I hoped. I am not ashamed to stand here and tell you that I love you." He took a deep breath. "You have barred the first path. So, I will tread the other."

White with emotion, her hands resting on her breast as though to help her breathe, Eleanor asked, "What path? What do you mean to do?"

"That I will not say. Only, that I will no longer stand betwixt you and Sebastian." He whirled and strode to the doorway, not even glancing at Hannah who was seated wide-eyed on a stool beside the loom. But before he left, he turned again and looked back at Eleanor. His voice almost a whisper now, he spoke once more. "Good bye, my love. And fare thee well."

Then he was gone, calling for his men to prepare for an immediate departure.

⁓

The day was waning by the time Karl returned to the yard to deal with the unwanted intruder. That vile woman could not have picked a more disastrous moment to make her appearance if she had bent her efforts to that purpose. He had no time to spare today for this drab and her daughter.

They were seated side-by-each on the stair to the battlement, and as he approached they stood together. The child slipped her hand within that of her mother, and leaned her head to rest on her mother's arm. Their obvious compatibility only increased the steward's ire. Was not their shared affection enough? Why did they seek to disrupt the household of his mistress?

"The duchess cannot see you today."

The child appeared unconcerned, but the mother paled and began to tremble. "But I must see her," she insisted.

He restrained his anger. "It is impossible. The duchess is indisposed, and even telling you that is more than you have a right to know."

She drew herself erect, although it was more a position of defense than attack. "But you do not understand. It is an urgent matter."

"Then return tomorrow."

"I cannot!" She shouted the words and shivered, as though contemplating some terrifying fate. "I must do this today!"

"You do not have that choice, woman. You may sleep in the kitchens tonight and see the duchess on the morrow."

"Stay in Eaglesheid? Never!" With a gasp, she reached out her hands as though she had been suddenly blinded and was searching for a path. Her fingers touched her daughter's head, and that simple contact appeared to bring her back to her senses.

"Ella," she said. "Go to the gate." Though the girl looked reluctant, she immediately obeyed the command. When she had gone the woman turned to Karl and repeated her words. "There are things you do not understand. I cannot stay here at Eaglesheid."

"As you will." He shrugged and turned as though to leave, though he doubted she would let the matter lie.

"Wait!" She grabbed onto his sleeve in her desperation, then dropped it and clutched her hands to her breast. "Let my daughter stay. Please, sir. Permit her to see the duchess tomorrow."

Karl's exasperation was growing. "I have already told you that you may see the duchess on the morrow."

"Not me. I must go. Take my daughter in my place, I beg you." She paused, as though searching for other words to convince him of her need. Then she looked down at her hands where they lay. Her fingers moved. "She bears a token for your lady."

"A token?" His lips curled around the word with distaste, wondering what bauble the duke had paid for his pleasure. "Of what sort?"

"I cannot tell you. It is for Eleanor alone."

The desire to have this woman bundled up and dropped some distance from Eaglesheid's gate was nearly overwhelming. It was only the knowledge that such an action would of a certainty come to the duchess' ears, and cause her grief and trouble, that stayed Karl's hand.

"You weary me, woman. I have much that needs my care and have no time for you today." Remembering the look on Sir Raynar's face as he had ridden out from the gate a short while ago, Karl nearly laughed at the understatement in his words. "Your child may stay here this night, and I will see that she is taken to the duchess in the morning. All else depends on the Lady Eleanor."

She knelt and grasped the edge of his tunic. "Do you promise you will see to Ella? Do I have your word?"

He shook off her hands and took a step back. "I have said it!"

"Then it will be all right." She slipped back onto her heels, but did not rise.

Karl walked away, but turned again just before he stepped through the doorway. She was still kneeling in the dirt, head bowed low—a creature drained of pride and will.

~

"Mama? Are you all right?"

Kate felt Ella's light touch on her shoulder. "I am now. And perhaps it is better this way. What would I say to her after all these years?"

"To whom, Mama?"

"To Eleanor." Kate rose and looked around. "Tomorrow you will speak with Eleanor. But right now we must find a place where we can be alone. There is much I must tell you, and you must listen very carefully."

They found a secluded corner of the stable yard where a half-dozen bales of hay, rolled man-height, were waiting to be stored for the winter. Ella leaned against one of the golden bales and smiled. "It smells so sweet here."

Kate laughed in return. "I might have known you would find the stable yard sweet! But answer me, Ella. Do you still have the pouch I gave you? Is it under your shift?"

Ella nodded, then giggled as the hay tickled her ears.

"Now listen to me. I have told the steward that you bear a token for the duchess. When you see her tomorrow, you must take the slipper from your pouch and show it to her, and tell her that your mother was Katrina of Ravensberg, and that you were born at summer's end nearly twelve years ago. Then she will understand everything."

"But you will be there, won't you?"

Kate had to be careful. She did not want Ella to panic. "If I may, of course. But stewards are unpredictable in such matters and he may not allow me to come. Now repeat what you are going to say if I am not there."

"I will tell her that I am Ella and that my mother is … Katrina?"

"Of Ravensberg," Kate added.

"And I am almost twelve years of age … and was born at summer's end."

"Good! And what will you give her?"

"The slipper. But will she keep it? I thought it was mine."

Kate smiled and touched Ella reassuringly on the tip of her nose, then plucked a piece of hay from her hair. "She won't keep it. There are two of them. One for each of you. Oh Ella, you will be so happy! Look at those storage barns." She pointed over Ella's head. "They are filled with grain for bread and feed. No one who lives here will go hungry this winter."

"And you too, Mama. You won't be hungry either, will you?"

"No. I won't ever be hungry again. You already have my pouch and all that it holds within, but there is something else here for you." From around her neck Kate removed the key on its golden chain. As she slipped it over Ella's head she felt incredibly light, as though her spirit were already soaring, and she had to concentrate to hold her attention to Ella. "Be very careful with this key. Do not ever let anyone see it. Always wear it beneath your clothing."

Ella rubbed it between her fingers, turning it from side to side. "What is it for?"

"A chest in Castle Ravensberg. Someday you will open that chest and find wonderful treasures. Eleanor will know. Tuck it away out of sight now, and remember it is your secret. I will leave this bundle, with the bedroll and your clothes, right here behind this hay. Soon you will have much better, but the cloth is still good and should not be wasted."

Looking around at the walls which loomed above them, Kate shuddered slightly. "You will need warm clothes here in the castle. There is no place on earth as chilly as a castle in midwinter. That is one thing I certainly remember." Her eyes began to glaze over. "The only warm place is right beside the fire ... but you would always need to push aside the dogs first."

"Did you really live in a castle, Mama?" Ella interrupted.

Her eyes snapping back into focus, Kate stared at Ella. "Of course I did! Do you not understand?"

"I don't understand at all!"

"I was once ..." Kate started to answer, then shook her head as she dismissed the thought. "Never mind. It matters not. It is much too late for me. After you see Eleanor, you will understand. I want you to go and play. You cannot come with me, yet, but please don't be afraid. You are quite safe now." Kate touched her daughter's curls, her nose, and then her rose-tinted lips. "You have been the most precious of all my possessions, Ella. Never forget that I love you."

"I love you too, Mama," Ella said, pulling away.

"Don't wait for me. We'll be together again ... in time." Ella had already skipped off, and Kate allowed her words to drift into the air.

Once Ella had disappeared from sight, all of Kate's lethargy fled. Leaving the stable yard, she headed to the rear of the castle, following the wall until she found the small postern gate. Beyond it the hill sloped abruptly downward, a descent too steep for any horse. The trees and brush had been cleared away for a distance of several yards to prevent an unseen approach, but the remainder of the hillside was covered with a tangled thicket, broken by one narrow path.

The birds perched on the parapet looked more alert than the two sentries. So engrossed were the soldiers in their own conversation that they were unaware of Kate's approach until she called out, "Hello!"

With guilty swiftness they whirled around, their hands instantly reaching for their weapons. But when they saw her, they archly turned away.

"Hello! Will you unlatch the gate for me? I need to go down to the river."

Neither responded.

"Will you please unlatch the gate? I have been sent on an important errand."

"And who has sent you?" asked one, tossing the words over his shoulder.

"I have been sent to gather some hyssop. The duchess has taken ill and needs a poultice for her head."

"Why would they send you, old hag?"

Kate felt neither anger nor hurt at the insult. Nothing was of importance to her any longer, beyond escaping the castle without being seen by Ella. "Do you," she emphasized the word, "know what hyssop looks like?"

Nothing was said for a moment, then at a nod from his companion, the younger of the two guards came down the stairs and without speaking unbolted the iron latch.

"Thank you." Almost at a run Kate crossed the clearing at the top of the incline, then plunged downward into the wood. Her heart felt light and her feet fairly flew as she followed the winding path which led to nowhere—except the river.

Karl cursed as he tripped over a child crouched in the passageway near the kitchens, but her unexpected tears and mumbled apology diverted his anger. They were standing beneath a wall-sconce and, as the girl moved, the flickering light from the torch fell on her face. Quickly, for she was already scrambling away, he reached out and gripped her shoulder.

"Aren't you the child I saw in the courtyard today?" His voice was still rough but, he hoped, not unkind.

"I was with my mother," she sobbed. "But I can't find her! Do you know where she is?"

This surprised Karl, for the woman had been adamant that she would not stay at Eaglesheid, even for one night. "Did she not tell you she was leaving?"

"She wasn't leaving. We were going to stay here."

"Hmmm." He stared down at her. There was something likable about the girl. Dirty though she was, there was a perfection to her features that seemed to prove she was no ordinary peasant child. Well, why not? After all, she was the duke's seed. "I will see you in the morning. Then we will clean you up and decide what to do with you."

"But I want my mother!"

He waved his hand and cut her off. "I know not and care not about your mother. Let me hear no more of that woman. She has gone and that is it."

Reluctant to let her be seen by others until her fate had been decided, he took her to one of the locked storerooms. Sacks were piled against the walls, and he nodded in satisfaction, knowing she would be warm and comfortable.

"I must bolt the door, otherwise the grain will be pilfered. But do not fear; I will return early in the morning to release you. And then we shall see what we shall see."

In the morning when Karl entered the storeroom, the child awakened and stretched in startled surprise. He stared. The girl was a beauty! Her eyes were bright and thickly lashed, while her hair hung in long, golden curls across her shoulders and onto her lap. Her innocence stung him, arousing within him a desire to protect her from the harshness of the world. In an instant, he changed his plans for her future.

"What is your name?" he asked, delaying the moment when he would relay the crushing tidings he bore.

"Ella."

"I have sorry news for you, Ella."

She stiffened. "Is it my mother?"

He moved forward and knelt beside her. "Ella, your mother drowned last night. One of the washerwomen found her body in the stream this morning." He did not have the heart to tell her the rest. Why should the child be burdened with the knowledge that her mother had tied rocks to the hem of her gown before wading into the river?

She bowed her head, but said nothing.

"Do you have other family, Ella?"

The poor child tried to speak, but no sound came out of her throat. Instead, she shook her head.

Karl thought quickly. Perhaps this death was a blessing. He could save his mistress the knowledge of yet another of her lord's bastards, and at the same time he could watch out for the girl. He needed to ask one more question. He needed to be certain the child would not approach Lady Eleanor on her own.

"Why did your mother bring you here to Eaglesheid, Ella?"

Again she just shook her head. Tears welled in her eyes, but they did not fall. "She...she said we were to live here."

"Many people come here to live but they all have some claim on the duke's hospitality. Did she say anything at all? Did she tell you what connection she had with the household?"

"No!" Her voice was quivering but she spoke clearly. "John did not come back, and the crops were destroyed, and so she said we would live here. You are not going to send me away, are you? I have nowhere else to go!" Like a dam which bursts under the pressure of a spring torrent, the tears finally fell.

Karl touched her shoulder. "Be reassured, Ella, that you may stay here and I will watch over you. Today, I will leave you to yourself, for I know you will wish to grieve, but tomorrow you can begin work in the—" He stopped and thought. The kitchens would be stifling for such a delicate child, but the chambers would bring her too near Lady Eleanor's scrutiny. He must find a way to keep her safe, but out of contact with the duchess and her family. "You will work in the henhouse. You will do well there."

The child looked at him through watery eyes. She could not speak, for her chest was heaving with sobs, but she nodded that she understood.

# Chapter 18

R AYNAR LED HIS MEN SOUTHWARD, toward Lombardy, where he was certain he would find Sebastian. His search was not difficult, for the duke had laid an easy trail to follow. "Aye, Westfeld has been here," they heard repeatedly, as they asked in castles and towns along the way. When Raynar reached the coastal city of Genoa, and encountered some of Westfeld's men in the narrow streets, he knew his quest was nearing its end. Directed to an ancient stone hostelry at the uphill end of a winding street, he dismissed his men, and slowly approached the inn.

The time had come to complete the task which he had begun that fateful afternoon at Eaglesheid, and he was weighted down with the knowledge of what he was about to do. Never had he felt an anguish so deep. Yet he would not turn back. Not now. For a dozen years he had stood between Eleanor and Sebastian. For a dozen years he had been the shoulder for Eleanor to lean on, and the back which bore Sebastian's responsibilities. Never had they been forced to turn to each other in their need. He had told Eleanor the truth. No longer would he stand, a shield between them. Already Eleanor looked at him with new untrusting eyes. And now, with barbarous cruelty, he was going to tear himself from Sebastian's life. Then his friends would be left with only each other. It was the only chance for happiness he could give them. He could do no more.

The tavern doorway was before him. With a great sigh, Raynar stepped over the threshold and entered. He was rapidly blinking his eyes when he heard his name, and then Sebastian was hugging him and slapping his shoulders in welcome.

"Raynar!" Sebastian shouted. "I cannot believe my eyes! What are you doing here?"

"Sebastian, I've found you at last." Raynar hugged him in return. "More than a month it took."

"You have been searching for me?" Sebastian's enthusiasm vanished. Taking hold of Raynar's arm, he drew him across the room to a small table.

Raynar grimaced. The single tankard, its rim stained with remnants of foam, trumpeted the loneliness of Sebastian's self-imposed exile. "I have indeed been searching for you. For certes, such a meeting could never happen by chance." He pulled over a second stool and sat down.

Still standing, Sebastian leaned down onto the table. "What is wrong? Has something happened at Eaglesheid?"

"Sit down, Sebastian." Raynar pointed to the chair.

For a moment it seemed that Sebastian would refuse, then he grabbed the stool, spun it around, and dropped down onto it. "Tell me," he said.

Raynar ran his fingers over the ornately carved handle on the mug. "There have been some troubles," he acknowledged. "But Eleanor will deal with them well."

Sebastian did not look reassured. "The children are fine?"

"You needn't worry on their account. I've never seen such a healthy brood of youngsters. All of them are strong and proud. There was quite a bloodletting one afternoon. Not with swords mind you, but with knuckles and nails." Hooking his feet around the legs of the stool, Raynar crossed his arms, and leaned back. Then he proceeded to describe the fight he had interrupted, leaving out all mention of Eleanor, and making it sound like nothing more than a comical misadventure.

Sebastian chuckled, though not with complete ease. "It sounds as though they are in need of better training. Have you forgotten to teach them how to fight with a sword in their hands?"

"In truth, Frederick and Arthur, young as they may be, are becoming passable swordsmen. By the time they grow another quarter-cubit they will be good squires."

"And Bran? How does his training go?"

"He does well enough. He does not yet have much stamina, but in another year or so he will begin to show some skill."

"And the others?" Sebastian leaned forward. "How are the rest of the children?"

"Judith is a little angel and James is quite the opposite. Bridget is as unruly and as delightful as her curls, and Maria, who is now walking, rules the hall with her smiles."

"So all is truly well at Eaglesheid?"

"There have been some difficulties."

"Tell me!" This time, it was the duke who ordered his liege.

But still Raynar prevaricated. "There have been some troubles, it's true. But that's not why I am here. You need not worry on that score."

Sebastian pulled his fingers through his hair. "Have you always been this exasperating? If you are not going to reveal your mystery, at least do not tease me with the news from Eaglesheid. What troubles have there been?"

"All right." He deserved that much truth, at any rate. "Two disasters befell Westfeld in August. The first was a fire in the town that destroyed a few of the streets and one of the new buildings before it was put out."

"The church?"

"Nay," Raynar paused, anticipating Sebastian's amazement. "The weavers' hall."

"What weavers' hall?" The expression on Sebastian's face measured up to Raynar's expectation.

"That was a little surprise Eleanor had planned for you. Establishing a market town was never all of her plan. She also wants Westfeld to have some goods of its own to export, so she is encouraging the weaving trade. She has always loved the making of cloth. Merchants have been engaged to purchase the wool, both raw and already carded, and, as she acquires looms she has been training many of the peasant women in their use. The weavers' hall was her way of spurring the townsfolk to become involved."

"I'm impressed," Sebastian said with sincerity. "Will it work?"

"Most assuredly. In time it will bring more wealth to your duchy than pirating ever has."

"Pirating! I can tell you have been talking to Eleanor."

"So I have. And so should you. But," he continued quickly, before Sebastian could make a retort, "it was the fire we were discussing. Unfortunately, it was not only the building that was lost but the woven cloth inside."

"That was the first disaster," Sebastian held up one finger. "What was the second?"

"The fields froze. Early in August."

"Before the harvest?"

"So you do understand the importance of harvests?"

Sebastian stiffened. "What is your meaning?"

"I would have to be witless not to see that you show little concern for Westfeld."

There was a threatening edge to Sebastian's voice when he responded. "Is this why you have sought me out?"

"In part. Come." He stood, and laid his hand on Sebastian's shoulder. "Let us be off. We cannot speak here."

Sebastian grabbed up his tankard and quaffed the last few mouthfuls before slamming it onto the table. "I'm ready. But I have the uncomfortable feeling I am not going to like what you say."

Neither spoke as they left the town and rode up into the hills, far above the bay. Picking their way around the rocks and skirting the scrub, Raynar led, while Sebastian followed at his flank.

"We will stop here," Raynar said, finally, when they reached a small clearing. "This should be private enough, since I gather privacy is what you seek."

Without answering, Raynar dismounted.

"Raynar, I have waited long enough." Sebastian's voice was taut with tension. "What is this game you are playing with me? I have not the humor for it!"

Still silent, Raynar turned his back to Sebastian. A great grief rolled over him—grief for the pain he was about to inflict on his friend and grief for the loss he knew would soon be his; but when he swung around, there was only mockery in his eyes.

"I have come to tell you that I have betrayed you, and that I plan to continue betraying you."

Sebastian stared at him. "Is it your liege-lord you have betrayed? Or your friend?"

Raynar shrugged. "Both."

"And what form has this betrayal taken?"

"I have attempted to seduce your wife."

"What?" It was disbelief which tinged Sebastian's voice.

"You heard me well."

"And?" There was a great coldness in that word.

"She refused me. This time."

"You dare to stand here before me and tell me that you … my friend … tried to make a cuckold of me?"

Raynar answered with great insolence. "I was only attempting to take what you did not seem to want."

"Wanting has nothing to do with it! She is my wife!" The cold had now been replaced by heat.

"Precisely! And when have you ever been a husband to her? When have you comforted her? Cheered her? When have you listened to her? Or admired her?"

A dread filled Raynar, for he knew he was losing control. His anger had become too real. He tried to pull back—to staunch the flow of his words—but he could not. Then he gave in to his fury. As he spoke, he advanced toward Sebastian, lashing at him with accusation. "When have you hugged your children or embraced your people? You are a failure. You do not deserve her! She lies there alone, loyal to you, while you spread your seed wherever you will. Hear me, Sebastian. I intend to return to Eaglesheid and try again—"

"Raynar!" Sebastian shouted frantically, as he tried to grip Raynar's hands. "Stop this and retract! Stop, I beg you, before it is too late!"

"And again and again!" Raynar was past hearing. He was so angry now that he no longer knew whether or not the words he spoke were true. "Until Eleanor finds she is so tired of her empty bed that she welcomes me into it! Then she will be the one doing the spreading. For me!"

In an instant Sebastian's blade was unsheathed. For the barest whisper of time he hesitated, then with fury struck a lethal blow. Moving with equal agility, Raynar parried the attack at the last moment, but his hand stung from the force of it. Sebastian gave no quarter. In his eyes was a madness, the unleashing of years of frustration and despair. Stroke after stroke, with the strength of one possessed, he pressed forward, while Raynar, continually on the defensive and unable to accomplish any maneuver other than deflection of the slashing blade, gave ground before him.

With each stroke Raynar felt himself weaken, as though the vigor was being leeched from his body. His breath came heavily, and it was only with great effort that he kept his concentration on Sebastian's every move. Then a beam of sunlight hit his eyes, blinding him, and Sebastian struck. By instinct Raynar raised his sword but only partially deflected the blow. Blood flowed from his left shoulder and a wave of nausea rolled over him, but he did not permit himself to falter. As he turned, shifting his position so that the sun would not again disarm him, he felt a rush of power, and his strength returned threefold. Euphoria made him light. He now felt that he could fight forever.

All his plans fled. And all emotion too. Before him was only an enemy who wanted his blood. He fought to the victory. He fought to the death.

Now it was Raynar's turn to press. His blade slashed to the right and to the left, over and over again, forcing Sebastian to retreat under its onslaught. Not once did he temper his blow. If Sebastian had not been swift he would have been cut asunder.

Many long minutes passed. Neither could maintain the intensity. As their energy ebbed away, their heads cleared. Now their battle became a test of skill and endurance, the most challenging and the most deadly of their lives. The clearing rang with the sound of their blows, steel on steel. They were so evenly matched that neither could gain an advantage—they knew each other's strengths and weaknesses so well. Hundreds of times they had faced one another, but never before had there been bloodlust in their eyes.

Stepping out of range of one of Raynar's strokes, Sebastian turned and slashed again at Raynar's shoulder. Anticipating the move, Raynar grasped the hilt of his sword with both hands, struck downward to parry the blow, and then, while momentum still carried Sebastian's arm away, followed through and struck Sebastian's right hip. The blade had been turned and did not cut deep. Sebastian did not even pause: His sword plunged through the mailed shirt into Raynar's side, beneath his heart. When he withdrew the sword, blood dripped from its tip.

Slowly, Raynar shrank inward. As he clutched his abdomen, his head curled to his chest and his knees crumpled to the ground.

With a shout of victory, Sebastian raised his arm to begin the death stroke.

The blow did not fall. Instead, there was silence. With great effort, Raynar raised his head. Sebastian was frowning down at him like a man who had just awakened from a dream and could not understand how his friend came to be kneeling before him, waiting to die. Then his face twisted, and Raynar knew he had remembered the reason for their quarrel.

"Sebastian, I am sorry." His parched throat felt so constricted that he could barely form the words.

"Why?" Sebastian groaned. "Why did you seek me out? Why did you tell me this thing? You do nothing without a reason. Why?"

"It seemed right ... once. But if I'd known ... this." Raynar stopped and rocked forward to ease the pain. "I'm sorry. You are my friend."

"No!" His face distorted with revulsion, Sebastian stepped back. "You ask too much if you expect me to forgive you. For the sake of the friendship we once had, I vow never to seek your destruction, but I warn you to never again let your path cross mine." Spinning around, Sebastian strode to where the horses stood. Without looking back, he threw himself into his saddle and rode away.

"Ride away, you fool," Raynar shouted after Sebastian with all his remaining strength. "Ride away. You are always riding away!"

# Chapter 19

T HE SENTRY CURSED THE LUCK which had led him to draw the short straw. The bitter wind that swirled around Eaglesheid's walls was hurling snow into his eyes, tamping ice beneath his shirt, and biting the frozen tips of his fingers. Never had a new year dawned with such ferocity. But for all his misery, the guard did not slacken in his duty. As he walked the battlement wall, awaiting the arrival of his relief, he strained his senses for any warning of danger.

The smells were as expected: fresh cold air spiced with pungent smoke and tantalizing odors from the kitchens. The sounds were equally mundane. Muffled laughter and music would suddenly burst into clarity as the great oaken doors opened, and some drunkard came out into the cold to spill the contents of his bladder, or his stomach.

The muted blast of the trumpets crackled through the air. A new course was about to be served. Would it be the suckling pigs baked in honey with apples and cinnamon? Or the capons stuffed with pork and roasted to perfection on a spit? Or the rabbit served with a sauce of almond milk and wine? Or the geese? The tortoise? The veal? The sentry sighed. How slowly his watch was passing!

As the song of the trumpet died away, an entirely different sound reached his ears. With disbelief, he leaned over the battlement wall. Sure enough, a small party of horsemen was approaching at a gallop. Although the riders were barely visible, for the swirling snow formed a moving curtain, there was no mistaking the sound of hoofbeats against the hardened turf. With a shout, the sentry turned and ran down the stairs. All was forgotten now, except his need to find his captain.

Within the castle was a scene of joyful confusion. The great hall was so filled that the servants bearing the trays of delicacies could barely wend their way through the crowd to reach the tables. No one denied that this was the most magnificent feast that had ever been served at Eaglesheid.

Eleanor glowed with satisfaction as she surveyed the riotous room before her. This celebration was progressing exactly as she had planned. There was no word to aptly describe the quantity of food and drink that had entered through the doorway from the kitchens. Abundant? Bountiful? Copious? None seemed adequate. Even the leftovers defied description. Yet it was not the quantity of food that stunned and amazed the senses but the artistry and ingenuity of its preparation, combined with the spectacular entertainments between each and every remove. Every one of the hundred guests would stand in awe of the greatness of the duke of Westfeld from this day forth. His name was heard as frequently as though he were present, and would continue to be spoken with respect and wonder when the guests had returned to their homes. All rumors that Westfeld had been dealt a deathblow this past summer were now dazzlingly and effectively squelched.

The chair to Eleanor's right, where Sebastian ought to be sitting, was not empty, for eleven-year old Frederick was acting the host. He was playing the role with such seriousness that she was tempted to tease him, but restrained herself, for she knew how it would wound him. To her left sat Arthur. In contrast to his brother, he had abandoned himself wholly to the pleasures of the moment, just as his beloved mentor, Raynar, was wont to do.

Raynar. How she missed him. He was the leavening she had always taken for granted. Without him, life was very flat. In one thing he had spoken true: If happiness were measured by laughter, she would indeed have been happier married to him.

Her musings were interrupted by the butler. With exaggerated elegance he filled her goblet, clicked his heels in salute, then turned to serve Arthur. A pucker of displeasure flitted across Arthur's face when the man brought the water pitcher to thin the wine, but catching sight of the glint in his mother's eye he grinned sheepishly.

"You can't blame me for trying."

"Nay. But if I indulged you, you would soon disappear beneath the table and miss the better part of the evening."

"Is it not marvelous, Mama? I wish every day could be like this."

Eleanor smiled. "You would quickly become bored with such feasting."

"Never!"

"Indeed you would. You would even envy the lads who had something exciting to do, like mucking the stables." Then, prudently changing the subject, she pointed toward the troupe which was performing nearby. "What do you think of those jugglers? Have you ever tried to do that?"

"That's easy."

"Is it? How many can you juggle at one time." She raised her brow and added, before he could answer, "Without dropping any, of course."

"Without dropping any? Oh ..." Arthur's forehead creased as though he were calculating great figures in his head. "I should say ... one?"

Eleanor laughed and ruffled his hair. "Just as I thought."

Again the sound of the trumpets rang out, but this time interrupting the performance. As the notes of the fanfare were recognized, a quiet spread over the hall. Now all eyes turned to stare at the row of trumpeters and the colorful banners which floated from their horns.

The fanfare finished, and as the echoing sound died away the door to the hall was thrown open. There in the archway stood their duke.

A cheer erupted almost simultaneously from all corners of the hall, and as Sebastian worked his way around the trestles, tankards, goblets and fists hammered a welcome on the tables.

Though stunned by Sebastian's sudden appearance, Eleanor was more confounded by the range of emotions she underwent in the short time it took for him to make his way across the hall: joy at the sight of him alive, apprehension as to how to behave in his presence, pride that he should see the wonders she had wrought, anger that he should have been away so long and return so casually to enjoy the fruits of her labor, and fear because he was alone, without Raynar. Finally, as he neared the dais and she saw the look of bewildered amazement on his face, a giddy amusement replaced all else.

"Welcome home, my lord," she said, grinning like a simpleton caught stealing the pudding. "A prosperous New Year to you."

Taking her outstretched hands, Sebastian kissed them formally. "And to you, my lady. And ..." He indicated the boards laden with food and the raucous company still beating their ovation upon the tables. "If appearances be any omen, then I should say that all bodes well for the future."

Many hours passed before Eleanor and Sebastian were alone in their own chamber. A fire had been lit and the room was warm. Still, Eleanor drew a shawl around her shoulders and hugged her arms to her chest.

A discomforting silence lay between them. At last Eleanor asked, "Where is Raynar?"

Sebastian scowled. "I know not."

"But you have seen him?"

"Yes!" The word was spoken with such force that she could not misunderstand its meaning.

Eleanor hardly dared to ask the next question. "Is he alive?"

Turning away from her he reached out and held the bedpost, gripping it so tightly that his knuckles turned white. "When last I saw him. Yes. He was alive."

"Oh, thank God!" She closed her eyes as she breathed her relief, but raised her head abruptly as Sebastian asked, "It matters so much?"

Disbelieving his callousness, she shouted at him, "Of course it matters!"

His face was devoid of expression as he asked again, "Why, Eleanor? Tell me why it matters."

"I was afraid you had killed him! For the past five months I have lived each day in dread that one—or both of you—was dead! When I saw you standing in that doorway, my relief was great, but no greater than my fear. One was here. The other was not."

"You still have not told me why you should fear Raynar's death so much."

"Sebastian," Eleanor said. "How can you ask such a question? If Raynar were dead, of whatever cause, the world would be diminished by his loss. But if he were dead because you had killed him, then I would have lost you both."

There was a long silence. Both stood motionless. At last Eleanor asked, "Is he coming back?"

"No!" Sebastian roared out the word. "I warned him never to stand before me again!"

Eleanor began to cry. "If you think he has harmed you, you are wrong. He has taken nothing from you."

"Not for want of trying."

"Do you really believe that?"

"They were his own words. He has convicted himself."

She shook her head. Although tears still rolled down her cheeks, she had no difficulty speaking. "His words, maybe, but what was his intent? I have never known anyone more loyal than Raynar. When he ..." She tempered her words. "When he accosted me, I was so shocked and angry that I was scarcely rational. But, Sebastian, later I remembered something he said. 'You have answered as I expected.' Those were his words! Would he have spoken as he did if he truly thought I would listen? I think not. Raynar always had a reason for everything he did!"

Her words brought his head up sharply. There was agony in his voice as he asked, "What reason?" and Eleanor knew that Sebastian wanted desperately to believe that she was right.

But she had no answer. Almost in a whisper, she replied, "I do not know."

Hardness returned to Sebastian. "Well I do. The oldest of all reasons. He wanted to steal—"

"Don't say it!" Pushing her hands against his chest, she cut him off. "Don't you say it! I do not believe it and neither should you."

"You defend him too soundly. Do you regret that you sent him away?"

She dropped her hands to her side and glared at her husband. Carefully, she enunciated each word. "I think, my lord, that I am beginning to."

Only the dogs woke in time for matins the following morning. Even the priest, who usually preferred his books to his cups, did not rise to see the dawn. Eleanor was one of the first to awaken. The fire had not yet been lit in the hearth and her breath drifted from her lips, like smoke. Even so, she decided that she would rather face the discomfort of the chilly room than continue to lie abed in uneasy intimacy with her husband. Rising softly, she drew on her leather shoes and dressed in her warmest gown. Before she left the room she wrapped herself in her heaviest shawl, enveloping herself in its warmth right down to her knees.

After leaving her chamber, Eleanor's progress was slow, for the corridors were littered with sleeping bodies. She grimaced as she lifted her skirt and stepped over the tangle of arms and legs. Accommodating a hundred guests was a challenge in itself, but each party came with squires, men-at-arms, maids, cooks and even minstrels. Only a privileged few were allotted the sleeping chambers, and most of those so honored had to double and even triple the normal capacity. The remainder slept wherever they could find a space to lay their bodies down.

Once outside, Eleanor breathed deeply of the fresh air and tried to relax. Clutching her shawl, she began to walk, aimlessly, along the inner wall, passing through the maze of outbuildings until she arrived at the postern gate. She had not intended to come here, but now as she stood looking down to the river, a longing to be alone overwhelmed her.

Quietly, she hailed the two guards. "Please open the gate for me. I wish to go down to the river."

She was surprised that there was a long hesitation. The men looked at one another, then the older one spoke. "I will go with you and attend you, my lady."

"Thank you, but I wish to go alone."

"My lady? I do not think you should."

"That is not for you to say," she said, with some frustration.

"My lady," said the other. "We mean no disrespect. A woman drowned in the river last summer."

"Drowned!" Eleanor gasped. "How? Why did I not hear of this? Was it murder?"

"Nay, my lady." The first man hurried to answer. "She drowned herself. There were rocks tied to the hem of her skirt."

Eleanor's voice was lighter now. "I see." With arched brow she pointed at each of the two men. "And you think that I may go down to the river and tie rocks to my skirt?"

"Nay, my lady! Of course not, my lady." They hurried to redeem themselves.

"Then open the gate for me. I desire only to be alone. You will be able to hear well enough if I call."

"Aye, my lady."

With as much dignity as she could muster, Eleanor scrambled down the narrow, steep path. She was glad when she entered the thicket and was thus out of her sentries' vision. There were scree and branches along the river's edge and soon she found a log to use as a stool. Idly, she watched the current as it pulled the water downstream in slow and gentle swirls.

Sebastian's words kept repeating themselves in her head. "Do you regret you sent him away?" The question continued to resonate, demanding an answer. It was not Raynar's intentions that mattered now, but her own.

She let her mind drift back over the past. When had she first realized that Raynar loved her? Had she not always known that she could count on him to humor her, flatter her, and shield her? Had he not given her all a man could give a woman, without sharing her bed? And had she not willingly received all that he had given?

Whereas Sebastian, her husband, had held himself apart, giving her little, except the children.

She tried to visualize the two men—to bring them before her to weigh one against the other. Sebastian, straight and stern. Unyielding, unthinking, and uncaring. Then Raynar, fluid as an acrobat and endlessly amusing. Sensitive, considerate, and kind.

Another image, unbidden, appeared before her. Arthur. He could have brought her more bitterness than she could bear, but had instead brought laughter and joy. And why? Because she had chosen that it should be so! Was that not in truth the essence of love—choice?

The two men continued to stand before her. One beckoned, laughing. But the other, weighed down with the weariness of life, turned away.

Did she regret the answer she had given Raynar?

She was certain now of her answer. Sebastian was her husband. And he was her choice.

She reached out and grasped a large stick which lay at her feet and tossed it into the water. For a moment it was caught on a piece of ice at the river's edge, then aided by the current, it tugged itself loose and was carried downstream. She wondered briefly where it would go. Would it be tossed up onto the mud of the shore? Or would it, perhaps, travel all the way to the sea?

Suddenly, and unexpectedly, Eleanor was filled with an eagerness. All her doubts were gone. She was ready to return to the castle and face Sebastian again. Jumping to her feet, she shook out her skirt and brushed her fingers across her hair. Loosening her grip on her shawl, she turned her back on the river and began the difficult ascent to her home.

# Chapter 20

T HE CIRCULAR SOLAR in Eaglesheid's southwestern tower was the warmest room during these harsh weeks of winter; it was here that Eleanor gathered with her ladies to wile away the hours. Today, however, her pleasure was all pretense: Barely a week had passed since Sebastian's unexpected arrival, yet she could sense that he was already preparing to leave. For her own sake she did not much mind; she had long since become reconciled to his peripatetic habits. For the children, it was another matter altogether. So disturbed did she feel on their account that she lapsed in her attention to her needlework, and pricked her finger. The drop of blood on her finger annoyed her far less than the exclamations of sympathy from her ladies.

"It's nothing," she said, but as she tasted the sweet blood on her tongue, a perverseness welled up within her. "I wish this were finished." She shoved aside her work. "I am tired of this banner. By the time we are done, I shan't ever want to set eyes on it again."

Arthur, who had been patiently waiting for Freddy to make his next move on the chessboard, looked up and grinned. "Then hang it in our chamber!" He nudged his brother with his foot. "Isn't that a good idea?"

"I think it is a far better idea than Arthur usually has," Freddy agreed, earning himself a second kick.

"Those lazy boys don't need banners or anything," snorted Judith, causing her mother to laugh aloud, for the child was lying half-asleep on the tiled hearth with her arms wrapped around a contented dog.

"We're not lazy!" Bran jumped to the quarrel. "I should think—" He stopped mid-sentence for the solar door abruptly opened. "Papa!" he cried, as his father strode in.

"My lord," Eleanor acknowledged her husband's presence, but with less enthusiasm than her son.

Sebastian crossed to the window and closed the shutter, blocking out both the sunlight and the fresh air. Turning, he folded his arms across his chest as he faced his family. "Tomorrow I go. I have already ordered my men to prepare for our departure."

Eleanor kept silent, but picked up her discarded work and plunged the needle into the cloth. The children did not have her reticence. "Oh no, Papa!" they shouted, almost as one. "Not so soon!"

Sebastian's lips tightened. "Tomorrow!" he repeated, then ignoring them said to Eleanor, "This afternoon I intend to go into the town and see your weavers' hall. I hear that the foundation is—What did you say, Frederick?" Sebastian swung around to his eldest son.

Frederick had muttered beneath his breath, but now clamped his mouth shut as he picked up his rook and carelessly completed the move over which he had pondered so long.

Sebastian glowered at him for a moment, then with a shrug, dismissed him. Turning back to Eleanor, he continued, "If what I hear is true, the masons are making remarkable progress."

"I think," Eleanor said, poking the green thread into the midst of a patch of blue, "that your son is upset because you had promised to spend some time with them in the tiltyard."

"It's no longer possible. There is no time."

She did not even try to withhold her scorn. "The boys have made much progress and I am certain you would be pleased—especially considering it has been a while since someone has overseen their training. Five months to be exact. Many of the men have been working with them, but they need a master."

Perceiving that his mother was standing his cause, Frederick's face brightened. "Please, my lord, stay one day more. Sir Raynar said you would be proud of us. We want to show you what we can do!"

"When is Sir Raynar coming back, Papa? We miss him." Judith piped up, in her high, sweet voice, but when her father cast her a thunderous look, she ducked her head into the dog's fur and stifled a sob.

"Sir Raynar has gone away for a long time, Judith." Eleanor intercepted, speaking with a firmness which forbade her husband to say aught. "We know not where he is. Do not be watching the road for him; he will not be coming soon." She turned her steel-bright eyes to Sebastian. "Assuredly, you could stay one day more! Is your business so pressing that you cannot spend one hour with your sons in the yard?"

For a moment all was silence. The four children raised hopeful faces while Eleanor stared down into her lap and the women assiduously continued their stitching.

"All right." Sebastian's entire stance slackened. "I will stay one day more. In truth, I would like to see what you have learned." He smiled at his sons. "Today I will go to the town and tomorrow we will go together to the yard. Perhaps . . ." he hesitated. "Perhaps, you boys would like to come into the town with me today?"

The game was forgotten and the three boys jumped up and hooted with elation, but a cry rang out from Judith. "Can't I come too? I'm big enough!"

Having capitulated, Sebastian held back nothing. He bent toward his daughter who was staring at him with round and serious eyes.

"I think," he said, "that I can only take children who are older than—" There was a pause as he ran some calculations through his mind. "Than seven."

"But I'm eight!" she shouted gleefully, as though she had managed to catch him in a trap.

"You are?" He cocked his head. "Is this possible?"

"Yes! Yes!"

"Then," Sebastian sighed, as though she had just outwitted him. "I guess you will have to come with me, Judi."

"Hurrah! Oh, thank you, Papa!" Judith threw her arms around his waist and hugged him hard. "Now it doesn't matter that Sir Raynar isn't here!"

A look of surprise flickered in Sebastian's eyes, then he reached down and gave her a kiss. "Now all of you, go dress warmly. It is cold today and will be even colder by the river's side. Meet me at the gate as soon as you can."

In the end, the expedition did not go forth as planned, and the children were bitterly disappointed. "It's not fair!" they shouted, but stopped when their mother turned toward them with a fierce eye.

"For shame!" she chastised them as she glanced toward Sebastian, who was supporting a man, heaving and gasping in exhaustion. The stalwart peasant had run nearly a league to beg for help in rescuing a young girl who had fallen into a disused well. "I will not tolerate a word more of such selfishness from any of you. Go inside to the chapel and pray that the child may be saved."

"Get horses and be quick!" Sebastian shouted to his men. "We will ride out immediately to see if rescue is possible. And rope! We'll need rope!"

"And food and wine and blankets," called out Eleanor.

Servants ran in all direction to gather the needed items while grooms rushed to the stable for horses. The food and wine were stuffed into saddlebags and the woolen coverlets thrown over the horses' necks. The messenger, still struggling for his breath, was slung up onto one of the horses and firmly held in place by the knight who shared his seat. Eleanor, also, prepared to mount. Sebastian touched her shoulder, but before he could deny her, she insisted, "I might be needed."

She had feared he would refuse her. Instead, he nodded his understanding then placed his hands around her waist and lifted her into the saddle. Moments later, they rode, together, out of the castle gates.

There was a crowd in the open field, huddled in mournful silence under the branches of an old elm. The only sound came from the child's mother who was rocking back and forth as she wept. A chalk-faced man stood behind her, rubbing his fingers across her back in a forlorn attempt to comfort. Nearby, like a pock-hole marring the skin, was an opening in the earth.

Almost before his horse came to a stop, Sebastian dismounted and walked closer. He said nothing as he approached the small gap, but there was a sheen on his skin. As he neared the hole, he flattened himself to the ground and inched his way closer, then stretched out his hand and tugged at some of the nearly-frozen clumps of grass.

"This well has been totally overgrown." he called over his shoulder. "I can see the stones which lined the top, but it has lain completely hidden for some time. It must have been built centuries ago." Easing himself upright, he brushed away the traces of snow.

Eleanor had not yet dismounted. She had been holding her breath and clutching the reins while Sebastian had lain near the precipice. Now she looked over to the villagers, and asked, "How long has she been down there?"

A large and ruddy man stepped forward and pointed to a girl who was sitting nearby on the ground, clutching her knees to her chin. "The fraulein's sister she be runnin' home when she fell. Then we be runnin' here and we called and tried ter think. Then Toby says he'd be runnin' ter the castle fer help and so he did and we be waitin' and you be here now."

"You say you called into the well," Sebastian ignored the obliqueness of this reply. "Did she answer?"

The man bowed. "Nay, lord."

"She must have broken her neck in the fall."

"But Sebastian," Eleanor had slipped off her horse, and now clutched at his sleeve. "If she is still alive, then—" Interrupting herself, she turned to the peasant and demanded, "How old is the child?"

"She be eight, milady."

"Eight!" Her hands flew to her mouth in horror. "Oh, Sebastian! Just imagine if that were Judi down there. She would be terror-stricken and nearly out of her wits! She'd be cold and hungry..." The horror of the image overwhelmed her.

"Eleanor, there is no need to convince me to make an effort to rescue her. I would not wish anyone—man, woman, or child—to die such a lingering death. We will do our best to get her out."

Controlling her panic, Eleanor attempted to give Sebastian a smile, though the result was little more than a grimace.

The smile he gave in return was just as grim. "I wish your father's master mason were here. With all the fancy machinery he draws on his parchments, surely he could think of some means of reaching her."

Sebastian then turned and called to his men, and Eleanor began to gather the blankets into her arms. Moving amongst the villagers and offering words of encouragement, she handed them to those who looked coldest, until she came at last to the bereaved mother. She started to drape one of the warmest coverlets around the woman's shoulders, but, instead, handed it to the husband. With a slight nod of thanks, he wrapped it around his wife, enveloping her in his arms.

Eleanor walked away with tears in her eyes, then returned her attention to Sebastian and his men.

They were standing in a circle, talking, and though she could not hear their words, she could tell by their movements that they were slowly working out a plan. It was obvious they intended to use rope, wrapped well around someone's body, to lower him into the well. There did not seem to be any excitement until one of the knights pointed at the old elm. After that, their hands gestured wildly, and she sensed the men were gaining some enthusiasm for their plan.

Sebastian had said very little. Now, with curt directions he dispersed his men. Three immediately mounted their horses and looked at the duke for final directions. "Bring axes!" he called. "And search for the longest coil of rope you can find. We have no idea how deep the ancients dug this well."

In less time than she had expected, one of the knights returned with a pair of long-handled axes slung over his saddle. It was then a welcome diversion to watch the men attack the giant elm with the obvious skill of experience. When it finally crashed to the ground, with a thud which jolted the breath from Eleanor's throat, the children squealed with delight and scampered to play in the branches which had been so far out of their reach only moments before.

As though the vanquishing of the tree had been a signal, more men arrived from the castle. They were leading a wagon which bore, in addition to the needed items, one of the joiners who had been working on the construction in the town.

Eleanor watched, curious to see whether it was the trunk or the stump they intended to use. She was surprised to see a wagon wheel rolled forward, but as it was lifted onto the stump and the joiner began to firmly nail it into place, she understood. They intended to use the stump in the same manner she used a spool for her thread. The rope could be carefully unwrapped, one coil at a time, and the wheel would serve as a cap to prevent the rope from slipping and unwinding without control.

The rope was brought, and as it was being secured to the stump, Eleanor approached Sebastian and drew him aside.

"My lady?"

"You are almost ready?" she asked.

"As you see."

She pointed around at his men. "Which one is the brave soul who will descend into the well."

"Which of my men would choose to go? There is no honor in the deed."

"No honor in saving the life of a child?" she gasped in disbelief.

Sebastian placed his hands on her shoulders. "I do not argue with you. But do you not see how carefully each one avoids my eyes? If I were to ask for a volunteer to carry a banner alone into the midst of a horde of dog-headed heathen, into certain death, then every man here would beg for the honor."

"And if you asked for a volunteer to do this deed today? Would they not also respond?"

He shook his head. "Not one. Certainly, after a few moments Sir Goran or Sir Humphrey, embarrassed for my honor, would offer. But their hearts would not be in the deed."

"Then whom will you send?"

"No one. I will go myself."

A wave of nausea nearly swamped her and she clutched his arm. "Not you, Sebastian! What if the rope slips?"

He frowned down at her. "Eleanor, do you not think that everyone else here is pondering that same question? I will not send one of my men to do something which I, for fear, will not do myself. Besides, there is little danger here. I have confidence in this contraption of ours." His voice softened as he continued, "But hear me in this: I have little confidence that the child will be brought out alive."

She squeezed her eyes to pinch back her tears, and in that odd moment remembered the scars which crossed his forearms, permanent reminders of a babe rescued from a fire. How many other times, unbeknownst to her, had he risked his life to save another? Shame flooded her that she would try to stop him now, here at home, with these people who dwelt in his care. "Sebastian, I'm so sorry. Forgive me. I should I have known that you would willingly do this deed; else, you would not be the man I love."

A flicker of surprise flashed across Sebastian's face but he quickly looked down and frowned. When he lifted his head, his eyes were filled only with concern. "Perhaps you should return to Eaglesheid and await us there. You need not stand here and watch."

"No." She straightened her shoulders. "If you can be brave enough to descend into the bowels of the earth, surely I can dare to stand here and watch, and pray. God go with you, Sebastian."

There was considerable surprise when the duke stripped his tunic and called for the rope to be secured around his waist. Greatly abashed, several of his knights insisted that they be the one to make the rescue; but Sebastian's will held firm.

Eleanor said nothing. As she watched the preparations, those around her seemed but shadows; and when Sebastian disappeared from sight, she felt that she would never draw breath again. She wanted to move, to go sit with the women, or with the child's mother, or with the men who were carefully extending the length of rope; but she could not move her eyes from the gaping hole for even a moment.

A shout of excitement, "Pull up! He's given the signal. Pull up, slowly!" floated into her consciousness, but still she did not move.

As eager hands reached out to help, the white wings of a dove seemed to fly up out of the well. Then Eleanor fell into a pit of darkness, without even noticing the small arms tightly entwined around Sebastian's neck.

There was feasting that night, with as much abandonment to joy as though an enemy had been turned away at the gate, and the following day Sebastian kept his promises to his children by accompanying them to both the town and the tiltyard.

Once again Sebastian strode into the solar. "My lady, I would speak with you alone."

Eleanor nodded to her women, who set aside their spindles and left the room.

"I watched the boys in the yard today." He began to pace. "They are coming along, but they are so … vulnerable." As he spoke that word, he stopped and stared at her with agony. "So many times I could have swept their swords away with a flick of my wrist."

"They are still young," she said in their defense.

"Eleanor, I want you to understand what I am telling you. Yesterday, when I descended into that well, my mind felt numb—not only to that moment but to all the moments in my life which had gone before. I scarcely cared whether or not the rope should break."

Eleanor stared hard at the pile of carded wool at her feet, but did not interrupt.

"Then I heard a child sobbing, a totally hopeless cry. I tell you the truth that I started to cry myself. I wanted that child to live! And what was more, I knew that I wanted to live too. I wanted to truly live." There were tears in his eyes, even now. "And when I saw daylight again and felt the earth beneath me and inhaled the cold scent of the air, I thanked God for another chance at life. I saw then, with absolute clarity, that although I had wandered far, on paths of my own choosing, I had never been walking alone.

"So—" He broke off and brushed his fingers through his hair. "What I am saying is this. I shall stay. The children are mine. Westfeld is mine. And you are my wife. These things which I should have cherished most, I have treated with contempt. It is you who must forgive me, Eleanor. I've been so foolish. If it's not too late, I wish to learn of love."

Eleanor had not looked at him during this speech. Even now, she had not the courage to raise her head and meet his eyes. Hands clenched around the spindle, she sat in stillness, struggling to hold back the deluge of tears that she knew would soon be released. It would be a wild and violent storm, but in its passing would leave her cleansed of bitterness and doubt.

When she thought she could stand, she set aside the wool. "You must excuse me, my lord," she said, as she stood and swiftly crossed the room. "I will go and tell the children that you do not intend to leave. They will be very happy."

But with her hand on the latch, she paused and whispered, "I, too, am glad, my husband. I am so very glad."

# Chapter 21

ELLA LOVED TO CODDLE and care for her hens. If the coops had lain beyond the castle enclosure, perhaps she would have been completely content. Instead, the towering battlements of Eaglesheid cast a constant shadow on her joy. Every day she anticipated the moment when she would finish her chores and could slip through the gates into the freedom of the world beyond.

On some occasions her curiosity led her to the market square where the foundations to the new weavers' hall were steadily rising alongside the wooden walls of the church. At other times she would go to the docks to watch the barges, laden with an amazing assortment of goods, being poled through the shallows by men in outlandish attire. Most often, however, she would leave the bustle of the town behind and wander to a sheltered inlet on the river, a place where she could absorb the sights and sounds and smells of the earth.

On this hot summer's day, the cool water of the river beckoned to her. Following the winding riverside trail through tangled shrubs and grasses, Ella meandered along the water's edge until she came to the shallow pool which she had come to consider as her own. Tugging off her tunic, she laid it atop her leather pouch. Then, wearing only the key around her neck, she waded into the river—which she loved and feared with equal measure.

For a time she abandoned herself to play, splashing and frolicking in the shallows, imagining she was a frog, snake or fish; but at last she tired of the sport and set herself to work. As her mother had taught, she scooped up handfuls of the rich river-loam, lathered it over her body and hair, and scrubbed and rinsed until her skin felt smooth and her curls as soft as down.

Once out of the water, she made haste to retie the pouch around her waist—its constant weight had become so familiar that she felt awkward and vulnerable in its absence—then she shook out her tunic and slipped it back over her head. The cloth clung to her still-damp skin, which tingled with pleasure. Was there anything so delicious as such a summer's day? Humming to herself, Ella settled down onto the riverbank, first sitting, then lying full-length as she gazed upward. The tips of the tree-boughs fringed the sky. What would it be like, she wondered, to perch aloft where you could reach out and touch that endless blue?

The sudden crack of a branch startled her out of her reverie. Without moving, she focused her attention on the sounds in the surrounding wood. For the moment she heard nothing more, but then the burring snort of a horse on the leftward path warned her that a rider approached. As she scrambled to her feet, Ella touched the key at her neck to make certain it still lay hidden beneath her shift.

It was a boy-man who rode into sight, a fair-haired youth, slightly older than herself; but it was his attire which drew Ella's eyes. His tunic, though sleeveless, was trimmed with scarlet and embroidered with color-ful scrolls, and his neck was clasped by a golden torque. For the first time it occurred to Ella that her use of this pool might be considered trespass, and she was seized by a sudden fear. What forfeit might she pay for such an offense? Might she be even forced from her home? She knew little of the lords and ladies who dwelt here at Eaglesheid, and nothing at all of this boy.

To her relief, he seemed more amused than vexed. Halting his horse, he stared at her in silence, with his head cocked sideways. "Are you a mer-maid?" he asked, at last.

The question, so unexpected, made no sense whatever to Ella. "I don't think so," she answered. "What is a mermaid?"

"A being, half maid, half fish."

"Half fish!" Startled at such a suggestion, she peered down. Had her imaginings somehow turned into reality? No. She saw nothing unusual in her appearance, beyond the slight curves of her breast. But she knew enough to know the cause of *that* had nothing to do with fish. "Do I have scales, sir?" she asked, as she looked back up at him.

"Nay!" he laughed, a pleasing sound that removed the last remnants of her fear. "Definitely not. But do you have legs, or fins, beneath your shift?"

"Legs, I assure you." Ella whirled around to prove her point, and as she spun, her golden hair swirled around her face and across her bare shoulders. She was grinning when she stopped and steadied herself, and she saw with approval that the boy was grinning too, although he was a trifle flushed.

"What are you called?" he asked, after a pause.

"Ella. And you?"

"He ... Harry." With a wave, he indicated the rider who had just appeared on the path behind him. "And this is my groom, Pepin."

"What have you found here, my lord?" The man's words were simple enough, but Ella sensed they held greater meaning than she could understand. For the first time ever, she felt uncomfortable with her changing body, though she did not understand why.

"I am not certain. She insists she is not a mermaid, and she even has the legs to prove it."

"But surely you know, my lord, that mermaids only have fins when they are in the water."

Just hearing Harry speak gave Ella reassurance, yet still this conversation confused her. Why did they think she was a fish? How could she convince them that she was a normal child? "I cannot be a mermaid. I'm afraid of the water. I will wade no deeper than my waist."

"Ah, my lord, this is intriguing. A mermaid who fears the water. Perhaps we should throw her in, to see what happens." As he spoke, the groom leaned forward as though he intended to dismount.

"No!" Ella threw up her hands as a shield, and took a step back. "I'm not a mermaid! I tell you, I'm not!"

"Hold, Pepin!" Harry's command held authority. Turning again to Ella, he spoke with great calm, as though he were gentling a horse. "You need not fear us. We shan't throw you in."

"I'm not afraid of you." She lifted her chin and glared at him in defiance.

Harry looked long at Ella and then asked, very politely, "May I stay with you awhile?"

"I am only watching the river flow by."

"Never in my life have I sat solely to watch a river flow by. May I stay?"

She nodded. And then she smiled. She liked this boy!

Harry dismounted and gave the reins of his horse to his groom. "Lead the horses some distance away, Pepin. I wish to be alone awhile with the mermaid."

The groom scanned the surrounding trees carefully before he answered. "Aye, my lord, but I'll not be far."

All apprehension gone, Ella watched with interest as he rode away. "Does your man always follow you around? And obey your bidding?"

"It is his duty," Henry said, with a shrug.

"It must not be much fun for him."

"I've never thought about it. I only complain when he gets in my way."

"Then why not send him away?"

"I cannot do that."

"Why not? Would he not obey you?"

"If I gave the command, he would go. But if something happened to me, it would cost him his life. I like Pepin," he said, "and would not be responsible for his death."

"You make me grateful I may do as I please—when I finish my work, that is."

Harry sat down against a tree and stretched out his legs. "And what is your work? What do you do here at Eaglesheid?"

Taking a seat beside him, she picked up a stick and traced it over the ground. "Whenever you eat an omelet you can think of me."

"You cook omelets?"

"I take care of the hens and bring the eggs to the kitchens. And what of you? What do you do?"

"Eaglesheid is not my home. I am only a guest here. My younger brother and I have been sent to train with your duke's sons for a few months. We have a master at home, of course, but our father wanted us to see more of the kingdom. Already we have been to Bestilden. Next we go to Terlinden—where my cousin fosters—then on to Gildren, Reinholdt, and Marre. Six in all."

"It sounds so exciting," she exclaimed, then frowned a little as she added with a sigh, "I know so little of the world beyond. Are those places castles too?"

"They are duchies, but I will be staying in castles there, of course. Do you understand?" When she did not answer, but puckered her brow, he tried to explain further. "This place here . . ." He pointed through the trees, "is Eaglesheid. But Eaglesheid is only the name of the castle. It is the center of the duchy of Westfeld. When I go to the duchy of Terlinden, I will stay at Castle Badenar, which is where the duke and his family reside most of the time."

"But what is a duchy? I've heard the word but I don't understand."

Harry answered her in all seriousness. "The king rules a vast territory of land. He owns it all but he could not hold it alone against his enemies so he grants large portions to men he trusts. Those are called duchies; each is ruled by a duke. So your Westfeld, Duke Sebastian, holds his land by the king's hand and in turn owes the king certain obligations. Perchance, the king may need to raise an army, so he will send to his dukes and they must raise the men. Do you understand thus far?"

"I think so. But doesn't the duke inherit his duchy from his father?"

"By tradition it does pass from father to son, but by law the king formally grants the land and the new duke pays homage to the king."

"Does the king ever refuse to give the land to the son?"

"Only in the case of open rebellion."

"Sometimes I pretend that the chicken coop is my kingdom and the hens are my subjects."

He laughed aloud at that. "So, I am having the honor of speaking to the queen of the chickens, am I?"

"You are." She waved her hand in mock regality. "So you had better watch your manners."

Standing, Harry bowed and pretended to sweep off a hat. "My queen, I am at your service."

"You're so silly," she said, to hide her pleasure.

"And you are so charming. I have not had such pleasure in a long time." He flopped again to the ground. "Not that I am complaining, mind you. I love working in the tiltyard, and dream of the day when I win my spurs. But this is different."

Feeling suddenly shy, Ella looked at him with awe. "Then you are to be a knight someday? I have never spoken to one before. I stay out of their way as much as possible for they always look so fierce."

"And I've never spoken to a queen of the chickens before. Tell me, where are the coops?"

"On the side of the castle farthest from the smithies. The hens need the quiet."

"And may I come and see your kingdom there?"

"Oh, yes! I am always there in the mornings, but then in the afternoons I am usually here."

Now Harry plucked up a twig and spun it around in his fingers. "I should like our friendship to be a secret. Would you mind? My brother can be quite a nuisance sometimes. If you pass me elsewhere, would you mind pretending not to know me?"

"It would seem strange, but I don't mind." This was another riddle to unravel.

"Mayhap we won't meet anyway. Do you take your meals in the hall?"

"No." She shook her head. "I have rarely been in the hall. The steward doesn't like me to go there. And worse, he wants me to begin working in the kitchens this winter. I'll miss my chickens. I have been looking after them since I came here last summer. And I won't be able to come to the river anymore—at least not very often."

"Perhaps, if you asked, he would let you stay in the coops."

"I did already." Her voice took on the singsong quality of recitation. "He said I was growing up and soon would not be a child and he could not be responsible for letting me roam around the countryside and I had to learn a trade anyway."

"Ahh." Harry smirked in a frustratingly grown-up manner. "So he is thinking of your own welfare."

"How so?" She resented his defense of the steward.

"Ella," Harry sounded very serious now. "You are growing up, and you are going to be a very beautiful woman. This man obviously cares about you and does not want anyone to take advantage of you. I think I must agree with him."

"But I thought you were my friend," she pouted.

"I am. And so, I would guess, is he."

"Well, if that's what growing up means, I don't want to grow up."

He was laughing again. "Wanting has nothing to do with it. If we are alive, it happens."

Their conversation was interrupted by a discreet cough. It was the groom, waiting patiently with the horses. "My lord, we need to continue our ride."

"You are right." Harry stood and brushed the dirt from his tunic. "Good-bye, Ella. I will come and visit you soon."

"Good-bye." Hearing the petulance in her own voice, and afraid he might change his mind about wanting to see her again, she added quickly and cheerfully, "It was a pleasure to meet you, Harry."

Thus began a summer of surreptitious meetings. Sometimes Harry would join her at the pool, and they would wade barefoot in the shallows, splashing each other until they were both dripping wet. Or they would race twigs in the downstream current, urging their own on to victory. More frequently, Harry would come to the henhouse. He taught her how to play the game of chessmen, marveling at how quickly she learned to anticipate his strategies. She taught him how to plait the straw into comical little figures.

They were content to be children, she twelve and he sixteen. He would crow like a rooster to announce his coming and she would answer with the clucking of a mother hen. He taught her of the greater world—of hunts and tourneys, of fashion and foreign policy. She taught him to open his eyes and see the world around him—the bees in their hives, the soft down under the chicks' wings and the acorn as it fell to the ground.

Finally the day came when Harry spoke the words Ella had been dreading to hear. "I am leaving tomorrow and I shall have no other chance to bid you farewell."

"Oh, Harry, I shall miss you." Her eyes brimming with tears, she struggled to resist the temptation to beg him to stay.

He stood awkwardly for a moment, looking younger and more vulnerable than usual. "I have brought something for you. You have been my friend and I want you to have this." He thrust out his hand and opened his palm to reveal a golden ring.

Ella's eyes widened at the sight of it. "For me?" She started to shake her head.

"Here..." He now grabbed her hand and placed the ring in the center of her palm, then with great gentleness folded her fingers into a fist. "It is called a token, and I want you to have it. Not only will the gifting give me much pleasure, but reassurance as well. If ever you are in danger, or need help, take this to someone in authority and say, 'I beg a boon in the name of Henry, who gave this to me.'"

"Henry?"

"That is my name, but my mother calls me Harry. Now repeat what I just said."

"I beg a...?"

"Boon."

"I beg a boon in the name of...Henry...who gave this to me." She unclenched her fingers and stared down at the ring. It bore a device, such as those on the shields of the knights. "Are you someone very important?"

"My father is," was all he said.

"Then you are too, are you not?"

"Perhaps," he shrugged. "There is much about me you do not know." He stood taller, and Ella had to blink her eyes for it seemed that the boy had disappeared and a man now stood before her.

"I know everything about you that I ought. You are kind and brave and strong and gentle."

"That is not how I would describe myself." He frowned. "If it is true, then perhaps it is you who have made me so. Ella, I doubt we shall ever meet again."

"I know." Tears again stung her eyes.

"I want to go quickly. It is too hard to say good-bye. Fare thee well, my mermaid." He lifted her hand and brushed it with his lips.

"Fare thee well, Harry. I shall miss you." As an afterthought she added, "And the chickens will miss you too."

This seemed to strike him as particularly funny, and as he gave her a formal salute and walked away, he was laughing.

# Chapter 22

ISABEL KNEW THE TIME had come to reap the harvest she had been nurturing so long. Her castle of Newravenstein, though not fully complete, had, after more than a decade of construction, attained a degree of breathtaking splendor which would impress any monarch. Likewise, her eldest daughter, Mariel, fulfilling the promise of her childhood, had, at fifteen years of age, attained a degree of heart-stopping beauty which would impress any monarch's son.

She had little doubt that she would be able to persuade her husband to acquiesce in her plans, for Branold was always content to humor her, but she determined not to give chance any opportunity to intervene. Accordingly, she had invited the duke, her husband, to attend a very elegant and very private dinner in their own chamber.

The footman carried away the last tray, leaving only a decanter of wine and a platter of figs. Branold leaned across the table and traced his finger up the length of her arm, to hover beneath her chin.

"That, my lady, was a feast to satisfy even the fussiest of men. I thank you most heartily." A smile lifted the corner of his lips, and his brows followed. "If I did not know you better, I might think you desired a favor of me."

A flame warmed Isabel's eyes. Branold, gray-haired now, was still a handsome man and a passionate lover, and her body responded immediately to his touch. With a slight shake of her head, she cleared her thoughts and continued as she had intended. "Let us say, Branold, that this seems like a good opportunity to chat."

"All right, then." Grinning, he leaned back in his chair, folded his arms across his chest, and said, "You begin."

"Do you not think Newravenstein has been a wonderful success?"

"I do indeed," he agreed. "I think you and Master Antonelli are both geniuses."

"And our eldest daughter ...?"

"Mariel?"

"Yes, Mariel. Is she not an unsurpassed beauty?"

"More beautiful than any man could wish his daughter to be."

Isabel picked up a fig, took a small bite and chewed it slowly. "I hear that the king intends to give Prince Henry his spurs this summer."

"He is twenty years old. It is time."

"We have never held a tourney here. Would it not be appropriate for you, as the foremost duke in the kingdom, to plead the honor of holding a tournament and grand feast at Newravenstein on the prince's behalf?"

Abruptly, Branold pushed back his chair and stood, nearly spilling his wine. In silence, he strode across the room to the hearth.

Isabel was shocked by this unexpected response. "What is it, Branold? What objection could you possibly have to marrying your daughter to the future king?"

"I do not object to aligning myself with the king." Branold returned to the table and stood with his hands firmly on the back of his chair. "But, Isabel, are you so certain that Henry will be the next king?"

"What do you mean? I do not understand you."

"You are not the only schemer in this kingdom, Isabel. Your schemes are innocent enough, but others—" There was a fierceness is his eyes which Isabel had rarely seen. "Others play more sinister games! Do not look at me thus. Why do you persist in believing that I have no head upon my shoulders? I have eyes to see and ears to hear!"

"I'm sorry. Please tell me of what you speak."

"I am speaking of rebellion. I am saying that if you wish so greatly for your daughter to be queen, then perhaps it is not Henry but his cousin Stefan you should be wooing."

"Stefan?" Isabel asked in amazement. "Why Stefan?" When Branold did not answer but tilted his head to one side as though to indicate that she could solve this riddle for herself, she nodded. "You are telling me that…" She paused as her mind raced to fit all the pieces in place. "…Terlinden… is planning to usurp Henry, when his time comes, and place Stefan on the throne?"

"That's it. But I believe the traitor may plan to move even sooner than that. I do not think he intends to wait until Lothar's death."

"But with what excuse? No one has ever challenged Lothar's right to the throne. He has been king these past fifteen years or more."

"I fancy Terlinden sees himself as a kingmaker. Indeed, I think the duke has been plotting for a very long time. You remember, do you not, all you told me of the attempted murder of the old king, Stefan?"

Isabel nodded.

"It was Terlinden's son, Derick, who brought the news and roused the kingdom in the king's defense, was it not? And it was Terlinden's son who sat at board with the king the very night the poison nearly claimed his life. It is in my mind, Isabel, that Terlinden had hoped that in the confusion following the death of the king, he—as brother to the queen—could seize the power if not the very throne itself. When he failed in that attempt, he brazenly called foul and stood champion to the king. But now these many years hence he makes young Stefan his pawn." Branold shook his head and moved to stand beside Isabel. Placing his hand under her elbow he raised her to her feet. As he spoke he loosened the wooden pins which held her hair in place. "I may be wrong, Isabel. By all that is holy, I hope that I am. But if I am not, then Terlinden must soon make his move. Soon the three princes—Henry and his brothers—will all be men grown. And when they are, Terlinden will have more enemies than he could ever hope to deal with."

Isabel stopped his hand as he stroked her shoulder. Holding it tightly, she looked into his eyes. "And you, Branold? Whom will you support?"

"I am the king's man!" he answered proudly, without hesitation.

"And the others?"

"Reinholdt would support Terlinden, no matter the cause. Bestilden would stand aside until the last moment and then throw in his hand with the victor. My nephew of Marre would remain loyal to Lothar, of that I am certain."

"And Westfeld?" Isabel asked, quietly.

Branold dropped his hand to his side. "Ah, Westfeld."

He shook his head. "That is the difficulty, Isabel, for without Westfeld, the rebellion would have little chance of success. Terlinden must count on Sebastian's support."

"But does he have it? Would Sebastian stand against the king? Knowing that it would also mean fighting you?"

Branold's shoulders sagged. "I would hope not. But I cannot be certain, for his ties to Terlinden are strong. It is possible that he already is a willing party to the rebellion."

"But if he is not," Isabel suggested, again pressing her plan, "then it may be that we can have some influence. If Mariel were to wed Henry, would Sebastian then dare to raise a sword against him? Prince Henry would be his brother-by-law, and he would have more to lose than to gain by such an action."

Lifting his head, Branold stared into the corner of the room. His brows were lowered and he bit his cheek as he concentrated on his thoughts. Then relaxing, he traced his fingers across her hair. "Go ahead, Isabel. Plan your tourney. If Henry will have Mariel, he may take her with my blessing."

"Don't worry about the 'having.' What man in his right mind would be able to resist Mariel?"

Branold laughed. "There is a great deal of truth in that." But as he trailed his lips down her neck, he added—one kiss at a time, "You may be in for a surprise, my love. Young Henry is nobody's fool."

# Chapter 23

ERALDS, RESPLENDENT IN THE COBALT and crimson livery of Lothemia, were sent throughout the kingdom bearing an announcement.

*In accordance with the wishes of Lothar, the king, I, Branold, duke of Gildren and my lady, Isabel, duchess of Gildren, do hereby issue the following invitation.*

*To all the knights within the realm, being of noble lineage and true intent, to gather at the castle called Newravenstein to participate in a tournament to be held in honor of the knighthood of Prince Henry, heir to the throne, to be held three weeks hence on the second day of the month of Augustus. A purse of fifty gold francs will be given as prize to the knight who is judged to have achieved the greatest honor.*

*To all the ladies within the realm, being of noble lineage and true intent, to gather at the castle called Newravenstein to participate in a grand feast to be held in honor of the knighthood of Prince Henry, heir to the throne, to be held on the eve of the tournament on the first day of the month of Augustus. A circlet of gold will be awarded to the maiden who is deemed to be the fairest in the realm.*

The excitement at Eaglesheid was no less than elsewhere. The echoes of the fanfare concluding the herald's proclamation barely had time to die away before the women were scrambling to prepare their wardrobes for departure. None had serious expectation of winning the circlet for herself—though out of politeness twelve-year old Judith was suggested as a possible contender—but it became a matter of pride that the ladies of Westfeld would outshine all others. A delightful feeling of camaraderie flowed. Those who could, loaned hairpieces, gowns, and even jewels, with the expressed intent that everyone was to look her very best. Needles flew as seams were taken in or let out, hems raised or lowered, bodices tightened or loosened.

Eleanor could scarcely contain her own excitement as she set about supervising the selection of the household goods needed for their journey. The pleasure of seeing again both her father and her aged grandmother, and of reacquainting herself with her half-sisters, Mariel, Ailsa, and Aidrana, was cause enough for her joy, but the bubbling happiness she felt exceeded all expectation. Whatever the reason for her elation, her children were among the first to benefit. Unwilling to disappoint even the youngest, she decided that all eight of them, from Frederick right down to three-year-old Gisle, would make the journey to their grandfather's home.

As she busied herself packing some of the pewterware into crates lined with straw, Eleanor could not but marvel at Isabel's ingenuity and audacity. Would it not be obvious to everyone that the duchess wished to win a royal coronet for her daughter? Eleanor smiled. She remembered Mariel as she had last seen her, an auburn-haired child with a strong will and a keen intelligence. If Mariel had retained even half of the beauty she had possessed as a young girl, she must be stunning now at fifteen. Perhaps, in truth, she would be able to bewitch the prince.

With a laugh, Eleanor raised aloft the empty chalice she had been preparing to pack, then said aloud, "To Ambition!"

"My lady?" In the doorway of the storage chamber stood a page.

"Yes?" Her voice still reflected her mirth.

"A party bearing the banner of Terlinden is nearing the gates."

No reaction showed on her face, but within her, all elation crumbled. "Thank you. Please inform the duke. Do not bother the steward today; I will see to their refreshment myself."

"Aye, my lady."

Eleanor looked down ruefully at the goblet. The words of the toast she had spoken in jest, mocked her. There was only one reason she could think of to explain the arrival of a party from Terlinden. Duke Gebbard, having heard of the royal festivities, had decided it was time to set afoot his plans and grasp the power he desired. Ever since that long ago day when she had learned that Terlinden intended to use the young princeling as a pawn in his own game, Eleanor had remained alert, for she was determined not to be left in ignorance. Now, if her conjectures were true, Terlinden was at last planning his move.

She closed her eyes, fighting back her fear. Was Sebastian a party to the rebellion? Had he courted the king while plotting his downfall? Now that the moment had come, would he stand for, or against, his foster-father, Gebbard of Terlinden?

There was no denying that Terlinden was a powerful man with a powerful personality. She herself had liked him well from the first moment she had met him. She could understand why it was that Sebastian very nearly worshipped him. In a time when the world was rapidly changing, the aging duke of Terlinden stood like a rock, embodying all the best of the time when chivalry had been at its height. The men of Sebastian's generation listened with proud hearts to the tales of the knights who had lived and died within the span of memory, yet had already passed into the realm of legend. Henry, King of England, who had been for a time the most powerful man in Christendom. Richard Coeur de Lion, well-sung hero of the crusades. Frederick Barbarossa, Holy Roman Emperor, rumored to lie sleeping beneath the Alps until the empire's day of need. And mingled with tales of these glorious warriors, the songs of Arthur and his knights grew and took on the aspect of reality.

Could the king, a pleasant but ineffectual man, ever compete against the intense loyalty a man like Terlinden could command?

She sighed. This was not the time to sit and ruminate. It was her duty to provide refreshment for her guests, regardless of their politics. As she turned to leave the storeroom, Eleanor realized she still held the goblet. Once more she held it aloft. This time her toast was quite different. "To Peace!"

Perhaps Eleanor had anticipated the message borne by Terlinden's son, Dagor, but Sebastian had not. The news that the duke was planning to use the occasion of Prince Henry's knighting to overthrow the monarch and his heirs, in favor of young Prince Stefan, stunned him; but what astonished Sebastian most was the assumption that he already knew of, and supported, this rebellion.

"Sebastian, I must return to Badenar with all haste," Dagor had said, after outlining the plan for the removal of Lothar and his sons. Though his dark eyes were grave, they held no doubt when he asked, "Shall I tell my father he can depend upon your support?"

Clenching his fingers around the stem of his goblet, Sebastian took a deep breath. When he spoke, his voice betrayed none of the tumult of his thoughts. "I cannot give you my reply. Not yet. This is a weighty matter and it needs much consideration."

Some of Sir Dagor's courtesy was withdrawn. "Has my father erred, perhaps, in considering you to be his friend?"

"I am his friend and much more besides. He must not ever doubt it. Nevertheless, Dagor, you must remain here as my honored guest until I am ready give an answer."

"I cannot wait even until the morn. My father has commanded that I return immediately. Surely you understand that to spend a night here could betray all. I must have your answer! In justice, my father did not expect such hesitation. He considers you to be an adherent to this plan."

"What have I done that he would suppose such a thing?"

"My father says you spoke of this together, at length. And that you were both in agreement."

"He said thus?" Sebastian quickly set down his cup on the small table beside his chair. "That we had spoken of this matter? Then I can only conclude that our words, and our meanings, were not one. If you must leave today, you will have to go without an answer." Standing now, he strode to the door and placed his hand on the latch, though he kept his eyes upon Dagor. "When the time is right, Terlinden shall know my decision. In the meantime, you have my word that I will keep your confidence, and will say nothing which may bring harm to your father."

Dagor leapt up and crossed the room to confront Sebastian. "It would appear you have forgotten the debt you owe to Terlinden."

"Of what debt do you speak?" Sebastian dropped his hand to his side.

"When you desired to woo a bride and win ease for your bleeding soul, it was to Terlinden you turned for aid. It is time to repay that debt! I speak for my father when I say that the proof of your friendship will be in your action. If you do not move with him, you may consider all ties between you severed. When Stefan takes his rightful place on the throne, you will be judged as his enemy."

It took great effort for Sebastian to keep his own anger from his voice. "Then so be it."

"My father will not be pleased to have to wait upon your answer."

"If he has not yet learned patience, he had better begin." He ended the conversation by flinging open the door.

Bristling with anger, Dagor brushed past him and stormed down the corridor.

Sebastian stood in the threshold until all sound of Dagor's departure had ebbed away, then he closed the door and shot the bolt into place. Crossing to the window, he stared out into the sunlight, his mind a whirl of dark despair. For the first time in his life he felt old. So many years had passed, and so little accomplished. During the past four years he had fought to regain all he had lost during the thrice-times-four when he had been so immersed in the folly of his grief that he had neglected all that was his. When first he had returned to his responsibilities, he had drawn his family around him as one would a mantle, savoring the warmth and the comfort. Then empowered and renewed, he had thrown that mantle outward across his duchy, reaching his people wherever they were—in the abbeys, the villages, or in their isolated cots—covering them with his protection and concern. He had learned to feel and to care again. He had learned to love.

But now a devastating choice lay before him. On the one side stood the man who had been his master, teacher, and friend, who had trained him to knighthood and given him his sword: the man who had been more a father to him than his own. On the other side stood his monarch and liege-lord. And in the middle—Sebastian closed his eyes in anguish—lay Westfeld!

Rousing himself, he strode through the hall and out onto the battlements. All lethargy gone, Sebastian climbed to the highest point of the southernmost turret. Below him spread a breathtaking view of his land.

The sky was clear, with not even a haze to cut his vision. To his right lay the river, a shimmering silver band, stretching off so far into the distance that he could not be certain exactly where it disappeared from sight. To his left lay the hills, cloaked in their foliage of green and yellow. And between the two rested the fertile plain.

The harvest would be bountiful this year, for the weather had been that perfect combination of rain and sunshine which allowed the crops to thrive. He could almost see the fields of grain ripening under the warm sun. A few days more and the harvesting would begin, that wonderful frenzy of cutting, stacking, carting, and threshing which left everyone exhausted but exhilarated.

Sebastian could not explain why he had been so slow in coming to love this land, but now that he did, it was with a burning intensity. He tried to imagine what it would be like to see Eaglesheid under siege. The woods stripped. The fields churned. The crops decimated. The peasants starved. The town razed. Even if the castle walls held and the enemy were repelled, his land would be left a ruin. What perverse loyalty could demand that of him?

Yet could he fail Terlinden as he had Katrina? Could he sever another part of himself and still survive?

Light footsteps climbed the stairs at his back; a quick glance reassured him it was Eleanor. Still, he was annoyed, for he desired no company.

"My lord. I wish words with you."

"This is not a good time to—"

"But it is important," she interrupted. "At least, it is to me."

He acquiesced, but with a heavy sigh. "I will listen, Eleanor. What is it you wish?"

"To know with whom you are going to stand—Terlinden or the king?"

"How did you know of this?" he demanded in astonishment. "Did Dagor tell you of their plans?"

"Of course not. He would have no call to do that. I have known for years that Duke Gebbard intended to put his young and very royal protégé on the throne."

Lifting his hand to his brow, Sebastian asked, "Have I received some blow to my head which has caused me to forget? I fail to understand how you have known of this; and why Dagor presumed that I had such knowledge. He even told me that Duke Gebbard and I had conversed at length and were in agreement!"

Her shoulders relaxed and the furrows on her brow lessened, as though he had removed from her a weight. "Had he spoken to you of Stefan?"

"Frequently. His praise for the prince has always been high, perhaps even excessive."

"And once he had wanted our boys to be fostered at Badenar, to be companion-in-arms with the prince?"

"And from this you understood his plans?"

"I confess I am not that astute. It was Lady Bertha who left me no doubt that they expected Stefan to hold the throne someday. I thought you knew all, and approved! When you were so determined to send the boys to Terlinden, I thought it was because you agreed with his plans and wanted to use our sons in support of it."

He shook his head as he pointed out over the fields. "Just before your arrival, I was pondering with shame the black folly which led me to neglect all that should have been in my care, for so many years. I can only presume I was lacking *all* of my wits in those days. From the confident manner of Dagor's approach, his father must also have thought I understood the game." He said nothing for a moment, then added, "So that is why you fought like a she-wolf to keep the boys here for their training?"

"Yes," she admitted. "But what will you do in this matter?"

"How can I choose between Terlinden and the king?" he spoke with anger. "I owe them both my loyalty and there is justice in both their claims! But in truth, Eleanor, I would see young Henry take the throne after his father. I have great admiration for him. He is a man born to lead and for others to follow. He is a man born to be king."

"Whereas Stefan would be easily led?"

"Doubtless it is so. For the few years Terlinden has remaining to him, he would be king in all but name."

"What of my father? Where stands he in this?"

"Your father is the king's man, through and through. As I would be! Damn Terlinden for his ambition! But Eleanor, how can I betray him to the scaffold—he who brought me to my manhood? Yet how can I betray the king to whom I swore oaths?" He groaned and pressed his head. "But most of all, how can I betray Westfeld?" His hand swept an arc, drawing her eyes to the spectacular panorama below them. "Look out there. That is my land. I have had Westfeld from my forefathers and I intend that my sons shall have it from me. They may take my head in this matter, as long as they leave me my land."

"Then which one will you support?"

He stared into the distant hills. "I know not. This is a heavy choice and I do not yet see my path. I have not even part of the wisdom of Solomon. I am torn completely in two."

"Sebastian." Eleanor placed her hand lightly on his arm. "You know I will be sorely grieved if you raise your hand against the king, especially if it also means that you raise it against my father. But I want you to know that whichever course you choose, I will support you with all my strength. And even, if necessary, with my blood." She turned to leave but he forestalled her, grasping her shoulders gently and bringing her to face him again.

"I would not desire one drop of your blood to be spilled, Eleanor. The man who would do that would need to kill me first." And as he saw her standing there before him, erect and strong, with a smile of pleasure lighting her eyes and illuminating her face, he knew he had spoken the truth.

Straining to hide their tensions, Sebastian and Eleanor stood by each other's side in the paneled alcove at the head of the hall. As their retainers and guests wandered in and took their places at the trestles, the duke and duchess chatted of inconsequential matters to those gathered on the dais. A peculiar blast from a trumpet drew their attention to the entranceway, for it was a disconnected series of notes. There stood a knight, holding aloft the instrument pilfered from the hands of the chagrined musician at his side. As the knight swept a deep bow, the trumpet nearly touched the floor, then it came to rest in heroic honor across his chest.

"Sir Raynar the Unfriended at your service," was all he said.

Eleanor reached up to touch Sebastian's shoulder, but he pulled away and began walking, slowly, across the hall. His face held no expression. Ten feet from Raynar, Sebastian's fingers began to caress the tip of the dagger which rested on his hip, and every one of his men silently reached for his own weapon.

Raynar had not moved. He had no defense save the trumpet.

One arm's span separated them when Sebastian stopped. For several seconds he stood completely still. Then, he allowed the grin which he had been suppressing with a supreme effort of will, to spread across his face. "Raynar, my friend! Welcome!"

As the tension in the room broke and cheers rose up to the vaults in the roof, Sebastian placed his arm around Raynar's shoulder, raised his dagger aloft and roared, "Blow the trumpets! Bring the wine! Tonight we celebrate!"

# Chapter 24

OR TEN STRAIGHT DAYS Ella had been jostled mercilessly in the back of a wagon and for nine straight nights she had lain restlessly on the stony, unforgiving ground. She was sore. She was tired. She was hungry. And she was deliriously happy!

Beyond all expectation the steward had chosen her to be included in the company traveling with the duke and duchess to Newravenstein. When Ella had ridden out of the gates, more than a week before, she had been filled with an eagerness to see and learn all that she could; and the discomforts of travel had done nothing to diminish her enthusiasm.

Now, at last, Newravenstein was in sight, and Ella was not the only person who caught her breath in wonder. Nestled on a hillside, with a golden plain before and the majestic Alps behind, the castle glistened like a jewel catching the gleaming sunlight.

Noticing the defensive hand movement of the woman beside her, Ella chuckled. "Now why did you do that?" she asked her companion.

"Must be sorcery's work, Elly. How else could them turrets stick up in points like that? Devil's work!"

Ella laughed and shook her head. "It couldn't be. It's too beautiful. I think that if a prayer could be offered in stone, then it would look like that. Are those towers not like fingers reaching up to heaven?"

The woman stared at her. "Where do ye get such ideas? A stone prayer?" She looked back at the glimmering castle. "Still an' all, you could be right. There is something nice 'bout it."

"Nice? It's magnificent. It's like ..." She paused, thinking.

"Like what?" Now a smile curved the corners of her friend's mouth.

"It's like a roundelay, perfectly performed. But not one alone. Many. All sung at once, intertwining with one another."

"You may as well say it's like the cackling of geese."

"Do you think so? And why not like a forest of songbirds?"

"Elly, what be we talking about? Birds or castles?"

"Birds. And castles. This castle! Oh, I can scarcely wait to see what it is like within!"

When Ella stepped over the threshold and into the kitchen she was so amazed that for a moment she stood holding her breath, unable to move. Behind her the scullery boy, Ralph, nudged her forward. "Don't jes' stand there gawkin', Elly. Move on. You're blockin' the doorway."

"Sorry." She spoke the word without awareness and stepped further into the room, her eyes sparkling as she gazed at the magnificence of the kitchen.

It was huge! Twenty people could move in here without the danger of colliding while carrying heavy pans of sauces or soups. And it was light! High up in the walls, above the level of the fireplaces, were rows of windows on three sides. Most had wooden shutters that could be closed against the elements, but two on each side were covered with bubbles of glass.

In each of the four corners stood a hearth, built on the diagonals of the room, and each had its own bricked chimney which directed the smoke from the blazing fire out a hole vented in the roof. It was ingenious. Never before had Ella seen a fireplace where the smoke did not struggle to find its own path upward to an open hole in the ceiling.

Near the door there was a trough. Before she even had time to consider its purpose, a man entered the kitchen bearing a bucket of water. With the muscles in his arms straining under the weight, he set it down and tipped the contents into the trough. The water rushed through the tiled chute and into an extra large holding sink. But something in one of the smaller sinks caught her attention. Stepping closer, she caressed the piece of metal which sat in the bottom. It was a curious thing, heavy and smooth and filled with tiny holes.

A youth about her own age, who was standing nearby scraping a stack of carrots, responded to her unasked question. "It be a grate."

"A grate?" Ella looked at him with wide eyes.

"Aye."

"What's it for?"

"Don't you know nothin'? Where you bin livin'? With the Franks?" He paused to see her reaction as his words hit their mark, but she was oblivious to the sting. Almost, he turned away to punctuate his contempt, but realizing it would be a wasted gesture he answered her question instead. "It's fer the bones and skins. It keeps 'em from pluggin' up the drain."

"Amazing! It's so simple, yet must save an awful amount of trouble." Her eyes, alight with wonder, met his.

He was pierced! Swallowing hard, the lad loosed one last defensive shaft. "What be a wench like you doin' here anyways? You be too small. You don't look half strong 'nough t' carry the pots."

"I'm sixteen," Ella protested, but said no more because she was interrupted by a voice at her back.

"Carry pots?" Ralph thrust himself between Ella and the stranger. "Do you think Elly be wastin' her time carryin' pots? There ain't nobody can coddle a sauce till it's as smooth and thick as Elly can."

"Her?" The boy rolled his eyes.

Ralph folded his arms. "It's true. And if you bring me a slice of bread I'll tell you what her secret be. Not that it'd help you any."

"Secret? Huh! She won't be havin' no secrets here. I'll jest watch her and see."

"Sure," Ralph shrugged in feigned disinterest. "But then you won't be the first to know."

Ella laughed. "But I will tell you, myself. I sing to them."

The two boys reacted simultaneously.

"Sing to 'em?" scoffed the one in disbelief, while the other shouted in dismay, "Elly! He was going to give me a slice of bread, and I'm sore hungry. The carts'll be here soon, and then when do you think we'll next eat?"

"Well," Ella turned to the lad. "You will still get us some bread, will you not...ummm...what is your name?"

"Bart. An' I won't. Singin' never coddled a sauce."

"Then you don't know Elly," Ralph said, with a grin. "Look to yourself, Bart, for if she sings to you, you'll coddle too. Ain't that right, Elly? Don't all the boys coddle?"

Ella cut him off with a groan of disgust. "Don't be ridiculous, Ralph."

"Ridiculous? Why look at her, Bart, and tell me if you think I be talkin' ridiculous."

Bart, who had not taken his eyes off Ella since she entered the kitchen said nothing for a moment, then reluctantly agreed. "Boys, maybe. But sauces?"

"It is true that I do always sing to them, and my sauces do always coddle." She shrugged. "Who knows? I will let you watch me if you like, but we are awfully hungry you know, and we'll soon be busier than squirrels gathering nuts, and we would appreciate it if you brought us some bread." She flashed him a smile. "We are going to be friends, are we not?"

He capitulated. "All right. We'll each be havin' one." Within moments Bart had returned with three thick slices of almost-warm bread, each spread with a layer of butter in the new Flemish fashion. The joy on Ella's face as she unselfconsciously licked the surface, gleaning every delicious crumb, would have prompted Bart to pilfer another, but the sounds from the yard outside announced the approach of several carts.

"They're here," Ralph moaned.

But Ella had already danced back out into the sunlight.

For those working in the kitchens, the following week disappeared into a blur of chopping, grinding, pounding, stirring, basting, washing, scrubbing, carrying, and—the list was endless. Everyone labored from the breaking of dawn until there was no longer light to see at night. No time was taken out for meals. Everyone ate what he could as he worked, pausing only occasionally to drink a dipperful of tepid water.

Day followed day and meal followed meal. The quantities of food which disappeared into the bowels of the lords and the ladies, the monks and the mice, was a marvel. Nothing in the kitchen was wasted. The drippings from the roasts were caught in large flat pans and used as the basis for tasty soups flavored with exotic herbs and spices. Leftover bread was made into pudding, and fruits which were no longer at the height of freshness were fried in oil and coated with sugar.

Ella's ability was recognized and appreciated. Before much time had passed, she was concentrating hard, trying to remember every culinary lesson she had received. With feigned confidence, she directed others in the clearing away of the cinders from the stove and then relighting it with the proper mixture of oak, ash and beech, to attain the correct heat to avoid scalding the sauces. Mustard, cinnamon, pepper, and sage. The flavors must be perfect. Honey to sweeten, vinegar to sour. Keep the sauces warm and fluid. Let the puddings set. Dip the tip of a goose-feather into the white of an egg and trace a heraldic emblem onto the jellies. Gild it with egg yolk or saffron. Garnish the platter. The work both exhilarated and exhausted her.

Tired as she was, Ella knew she was fortunate, for twice each day she had a reprieve from the heat of the kitchen.

During the first evening, as she had been rolling balls of meat in parsley and placing them on a tray, her attention had been caught by a woman filling a cloth-covered platter with delicacies. "Who is that for?" she had asked. "It must be someone important."

"That be none of yer business, tho' I could be tellin' ye stories. But ye're a foreigner. Why should I be tellin' ye anything?" Nose in the air, the woman had turned away without giving any further information.

Too tired to press, Ella had shrugged and continued her work, but the following day she had learned more. A footman, fully arrayed in the tri-colored livery of Gildren, entered the kitchen at midday. After cursing the heat which assailed him, the man bellowed into the steaming air, "Pox on that Dora. Fool of a woman that she is, broke her leg. Now I need to find someone else to take the old lady her dinner. You!" His eyes alighted on Ella, who was standing near the sink looking at him with amazement. "You can take her ladyship her dinner. Put some food on a tray and then get the butler to give you a flask of his wine. Tell him it's for the royal witch in the tower."

Ella turned and looked at the cook, who was watching this distraction with obvious annoyance. With a nod of his head he indicated she was to do as she was bid.

"But I don't know where the tower is!"

"God's wounds, you're a fool then. I'll send a page to show you." Beads of perspiration were slipping down the footman's neck and under the collar of his tunic. "Better get your own arse moving." He was gone as suddenly as he had appeared.

"Move along, Ella," the cook said, tersely. "The chargers are in the pantry. Find someone in the buttery to dispense the wine. I expect you back immediately. And Ella—follow the page but pay no mind to tales he might tell you."

Ella was grateful she had received that last instruction. As the boy led her across the courtyard, he gleefully regaled her with tales of the witch in the tower and the terrible spells she spun. When he pointed to a small door, then fled into the crowd, Ella heartily wished she could follow.

It was a difficult climb, especially with a platter to balance. The staircase was narrow and the steps were unusually steep. After she had climbed more steps than she could count, Ella realized that she had seen no other passageways or doors. Puzzling over the strange construction of the tower, she made her way slowly upward, but it was not until she reached the top that she realized the answer to the mystery. This was a hidden set of rooms! The narrow stairwell was built behind the main rooms of the tower. If the doorway at the bottom were to be hidden by a tapestry or board, who would even know that this apartment existed?

So intrigued was she, by her discovery, that she forgot about the presence of the witch. When a voice called to her through the open doorway, "Don't just stand there dreaming, child, bring me my dinner," she was so startled that the tray fell out of her hands and crashed to the floor.

With horror, she looked at the fragments of the wine flask at her feet, and the food which lay like pigs' mush all around. Trembling, she knelt and began to pick up the pieces of the pottery, but had so little control over her shaking hands that she cut her finger on a sharp edge and cried aloud.

"Child. Don't be so frightened. 'Tis only broken pottery." The voice sounded strange, as though great efforts were required to bring forth the words, yet there was no hint of anger or condemnation.

Slowly, Ella raised her head and looked at the woman who stood in the doorway above her.

The woman—Ella only knew she was such by the clothes she wore—was small and shriveled with age. Her gray hair, which hung right down to her waist, was so thin that there were patches on her head where her scalp showed through. But it was her face, a monstrous parody of a human visage, which brought the bile up into Ella's throat, forcing her to swallow fiercely. But the bitterness she tasted shamed her and was followed by a rush of sympathy. What could have caused such gross disfigurement? Flesh and bone had been replaced with a hideous mass of pitted and knotted tissue, streaked vividly with white and red, and so distorting the face that even a portion of the nose was missing.

Ella's inherent kindness now prompted her to meet the eyes of this woman without flinching. "I am sorry, my lady. I did not mean to drop your food. I was busy thinking and your voice startled me. I will clean up this mess and then bring you a new platter."

There was a long pause. Ella knew that the old woman was fighting to control some emotion, but what it was she could not tell for the face held no clue.

"Stay a moment. There is no hurry. Food comes every day but new faces are a rarity for me. Tell me what you were thinking, child. What distracted you so?"

"I was wondering how this stairway was hidden in the tower. And why."

"You have a head on your shoulders, I see."

Unsure of how she should answer, Ella only nodded.

"What is your name, child?"

"Ella."

"Ella," she repeated. "A simple name, yet beautiful. It suits you. Now tell me, Ella, why do you not shrink away from me in horror? Many brave men—men who would not even flinch at the sight of their own entrails—have taken one look at my face and blanched as white as their bones."

"I know not, my lady. Truly, I feel grief that you should suffer so."

"Have you seen others such as I?"

"Nay, my lady." Ella paused, thoughtfully, then added, "But I have wondered that men will trample the caterpillar beneath their feet, yet praise the butterfly. Are they not the same creature? Does not the caterpillar carry his wings within him?"

Again there was silence. "Come sit with me, Ella. I would share my meal with you but it appears we shall both go hungry."

"I shall bring another trencher, my lady."

"Nay! I forbid you to leave. Not yet. Come in and sit with me awhile." As the old woman turned and moved toward her chair she indicated that Ella was to sit on the lone wooden stool that held her distaff and spindle.

"My lady, I have work to do in the kitchens. I am expected to return with all speed."

"As you wish then, you may go. But I will send word that you alone are to bring me my meals, and that I will require your time. You need not fear. My orders will not be gainsaid."

"Shall I bring you another tray, my lady?"

"Sophie. Lady Sophie. Dowager-duchess of Bestilden. Though I have seen neither the duchy nor my son, the duke, these past twenty years—and hope another twenty years pass ere I see them again. But, I am also mother-by-law to Branold, duke of Gildren."

"Lady Sophie. I shall bring you your dinner."

"Nay, child. I am too excited to eat now. Come to me again with my food, tonight, and we shall speak more. You may go now."

"Thank you, my lady." Ella dipped a curtsey then bent and began to pick up the pieces of broken pottery, but dropped them again at a sharp command from Lady Sophie.

"Leave them! I will send for one of the boys to clean that away. Off with you now, but come back at eventide. I shall be waiting for you."

As Lady Sophie had said, orders were given that she was to carry the tray to the tower. Each time she left the kitchen, with its cauldron-like temperatures, she breathed a prayer of gratitude that the footman's eye had fallen on her. Not only was she thankful for the reprieve from her labors, but she had quickly learned to enjoy Lady Sophie's company.

The day on which the feasting was to begin in earnest, Ella stepped out of the tower doorway into a surging crowd. Curious to see what had drawn so many people to the gate, she did not push her way to the kitchens, against the flow, but allowed herself to be carried forward like a piece of flotsam on the tide. But when rough stone grazed her arm, she cried out with alarm.

"Ella!" called out Ralph from above. "Climb up here onto the wall. You'll be able to see better."

Grasping hold of his outstretched hand, she scrambled up the steps onto the edge of the battlement. "What is happening?" she asked, as she clung to his arm.

"The king is coming."

The king! Ella stood up on her toes and looked out over the wall. A sea of people filled the courtyard below, excepting one narrow channel held clear by a line of guards. The gates in the curtain wall stood open, and as a fanfare blew, the first of the escort appeared. Horses and riders, alike, were bedecked in the royal colors. The crimson and blue caparisons, draped over the haunches of the horses, echoed the brilliantly embroidered surcoats of the knights; and the gilded hooves reflected the golden plumes. Held aloft on lances of bronze, a score of pennons pointed their lambent fingers to the king.

Trumpets blared from the top of the curtain wall, and as the salute rang through the courtyard the king and queen rode in beneath the gate. The crowd applauded and cheered, but soon their attention was diverted. A new figure rode beneath the portal. As he raised his fist and greeted the throng, the chant changed and soon became a roar, "Henry! Henry!"

"Look, Ella, there's the prince. And Roden and Gilmar too. How magnificent they look!" Ralph leaned forward and called out, "Henry!"

"Henry!" Ella began to shout. But as the sun glinted golden off his bared head, her eyes widened and she gasped. Softly, to herself, she whispered, "Harry."

For an instant she felt anger, and then it was gone. What a good jest that had been—and what fun they'd had together. In truth, had she known who he was, she would never have called him friend. "Henry! Prince Henry!" Laughing now, with pure joyous delight, she joined her voice to the throng.

# Chapter 25

THE ARRIVAL OF THE ROYAL PARTY served to increase the enthusiasm of those working in the kitchens, for everyone wanted to have a hand in preparing the dishes which might be set before the king. Ella's skills were in much demand, yet the harder she worked, the more her heart sang. Not even the blistering heat could stifle the joy which seemed to swell within.

"It be hotter'n Hades in here!"

Ella laughed at Bart who was carefully adding small logs of ash to the fire beneath her pot. "If you think it's hot now, you should've been here last night when the pigs were on the spit. I truly thought I was being roasted alive. I swear that if you had pricked me then, it would have been gravy flowing from my veins."

"Ye're so funny," Bart chuckled, then asked, "What did ye think of th' swan?"

"I didn't see it. I was searching for the spicier. Was it wonderful?"

"Oh, Elly, I wished ye'd seen it. It was sittin' on the platter, like as if it be still alive. Ev'ry feather was just where it ought t' be. 'Ceptin' two. And those two be—now ye're not gonna be believin' me, Elly. I just know ye're not."

"I certainly shall. If you ever tell me."

"Two of the feathers be ..." He lowered his voice in awe. "Gold. Pure gold."

"You *are* teasing me." Ella stopped stirring for a moment and arched her brow in disbelief.

"It be true. They be gifts from Gildren t' the king n' queen."

"Why not for the prince? After all, he's the one who's being knighted tomorrow. Seems to me he should get the gold."

"How should I be knowin' that?"

"Perhaps, they will give him an egg. A golden egg. Do you not think, Bart, that a swan with golden feathers should be able to lay a golden egg?"

"That be good thinkin' Elly. And after all," he gave her a smug look, "I hear they be wantin' a little gold in return."

"What do you mean?"

He edged closer. "A golden ring. I hear'd it myself. One of th' pages told me and he works right in the hall."

"A ring?" Ella's thoughts leapt to her hidden pouch. "I don't understand."

"A ring, ye know. A weddin' ring. Gildren wants Prince Henry t' marry his daughter. And since Mistress Mariel be very beautiful, and her father be very powerful, what more could a prince be wantin'?"

Frowning, Ella thought of Henry as she had seen him four summers before, laughing at the river's edge. "Nothing, I suppose. If it would make him happy. Surely, even a prince should be happy."

"Ye be a ninny. Princes be always happy. Besides, anyman would be happy t'ave a beautiful wife." Boldly he leaned even closer. "You be beautiful too, Elly. Anyman would be happy if ye'd be his wife."

Ella cut him off abruptly before he could say more. "Then *anyman* would be a fool. Now leave me to my work. As soon as this custard thickens I need to take a tray with dinner to the old lady." She paused, and added gleefully, knowing how much Lady Sophie would enjoy the jest if she could hear it. "And I dare not be late or she may put a curse on me. Perhaps she would turn me into a toad. Then no one would want to marry me ... especially not you."

"Yuch! Ye be right."

Half an hour later, relieved at having a break from the heat and the din of the kitchens, Ella climbed the narrow stairway to Sophie's room. The fear she had felt on her first excursion here had long since been replaced by anticipation, for she thoroughly enjoyed the dowager's company.

"Here you are, child. Set the tray down." Sophie continued to spin the wool through her fingers as she spoke. "Come, sit at my feet and tell me of the preparations for tonight's banquet. Have you seen the prince since his arrival yesterday? No? Well tonight you must go into the hall and look for him there. You can tell me tomorrow how he is clothed. Or, even better, you can come to me tonight at midnight, after he begins his vigil of prayer, and tell me all you have seen."

"My lady, what are you thinking?" Ella stared at the duchess in consternation. "I cannot go into the hall!"

"Of course you can." Sophie waved her hand as though Ella's words meant nothing. "Just slip in on your way back to the kitchens. It will be so crowded you will not even be noticed. But what I would really like you to do is to wait until the feasting has finished and the dancing has begun. I would dearly love to hear you tell me of the dancing." She closed her eyes. "I could almost wish I were brave enough to go myself. How I used to love dancing; I was light on my feet and graceful. From the moment the musicians would start until they finished, I would dance. Everyone wanted to dance with me."

Sophie was quickly caught up in the memory of days long since gone. Her hand reached out, as though a suitor were standing before her now, and she began to sway to the sound of phantom musicians. "The music intoxicates me. How I love to dance!" Then her eyes focused again on Ella, and her hand fell into her lap and grasped her spindle.

"You are kind not to laugh at me for I know you might." Sophie leaned forward and fixed her gaze on Ella. "I have a secret to tell. It was my beauty which won me my Bestilden. He saw me in the streets of Marseilles and was determined to have me. I wonder what Eleanor would say if she knew." A grin pulled at Sophie's distorted lips. "My father was only a sailor, but my Bestilden made it worth his while to forget he had ever known me. And a certain herald found it worth his while to trace my parentage back to Charlemagne."

"Do you mean that the scrolls lie?" Ella asked, amazed.

Sophie laughed. "Of course! And no one would ever dare to question the heralds, for who would like to have the truth of his own ancestry revealed? Child, if all the scrolls were to be believed, then it would be proof that the great Charles had dozens of children. And that would have been a far greater feat for his wife than all the kingdoms he ever conquered!"

Ella sat in silence for a few moments more, watching the dowager's fingers fly as they deftly twisted the wool. Finally, she pointed at the tray. "Are you not going to eat, my lady? I must return to the kitchens."

"You need not return yet. In fact, you may not go until I give you leave. Which I do not. I want you to stay longer." She leaned forward and peered at Ella. "You don't object, do you?"

"How could I? My arm is so tired from stirring that I sometimes think it will fall right off and land in the sauce."

"Which would be a rare treat for His Majesty."

Ella laughed and Sophie paused again in her work. "You are beautiful, too, child. More than beautiful. Extraordinary."

"Oh my lady, I—"

"Do not be bashful," Sophie interrupted. "Your beauty is a gift for you to enjoy while you have it. The good Lord knows how soon it will be gone. How it galls me that you return to that hot kitchen to work. If you had a gown worthy of your face, I am certain even princes would beg for the honor of dancing with you."

Looking down at her bare feet and shabby dress, Ella grinned. "That is something I will have to live without knowing, my lady. I am happy enough that this shift finally fits me after years of tying it high on my waist so that it would not drag on the ground."

Sophie rubbed the material between her fingertips. "This used to be your mother's?"

Ella nodded.

"This is fine linen. Did your mother weave her own?"

"No." Ella shook her head. "I never saw her weave. In truth, my lady, I rarely saw her do anything that was useful. She was unlike other women."

"How so? Tell me about her, child."

"Well...She didn't like to go outside. The villagers would gather together in the sunshine as much as possible, but Mama said she hated the sun, so she would spend hours sitting on a stool in the corner of the hut, plaiting and unplaiting her hair. It was as long as mine is now, and just as curly—but wild and tangled when it was free."

"Your hair is truly beautiful," Sophie murmured. "That is one thing you and I have in common; though you have not my vanity. To tell the truth, my pride in my curls has been so overweening that I could never abide the idea of cutting them, nor even hiding them under a wimple. Not even after all these years. I know it's ridiculous. They are just a mockery of what they once were, but I suppose that matches the rest of me now. You know," Sophie gently looped a tress of Ella's hair around her finger. "I have never seen anyone else with hair quite this texture—excepting my daughter, Judith, and then her daughter, Katrina. Mine was dark, and rich with colors that gleamed in the sunlight. Judith's was slightly fairer. And Katrina's the fairest of all, though not nearly as light as yours."

"Mama's hair was the color of dirt," Ella said. "That was another strange thing about her. She was the one who taught me to wash and comb my hair, and she insisted that I do it every week; but as for herself, days and even weeks would go by when she would do nothing. She would not wash, or sweep, or cook. Sometimes not even talk."

"It sounds to me like she was a little mad."

Ella nodded in agreement. "It was John, my stepfather, who would do all the work. Until I was old enough to help, that is. There was very little to eat anyway. Soup and bread, mostly. But then there would be times when Mama would rouse herself and in a flurry of activity clean out the house, washing every speck of dirt away from even the tiniest corner. On those days, when John came home his face would light up with such happiness. He would come in the doorway and take off his hat and look at her and say, 'Kate.'" Ella's eyes sparkled at the memory. "I guess that sounds pretty silly to you."

"Of course not, child."

"And when Mama was in such a mood she would fuss over me all day long. When I ate, she would insist that I learn the proper manners for being served at a great table. As if I would ever eat at a great table! And she would teach me to curtsey, like this." Ella stood and executed a graceful curtsey. "See, even after five years I have not forgotten. We had such fun when she was teaching me that. And she would make me walk erect, holding my back straight and my neck high. Sometimes she would place something in my hand like ... like a leaf ... and say 'here is your fan, my lady,' or she would take my hands and teach me how to dance while she hummed a tune. And my speech! 'Do not slur your words together. Look me in the eye when you are speaking.' The children in the village used to tease me for the way I talked, but Mama was happy.

"John adored her." A frown crossed Ella's face and she sat down with a sigh. "To him nothing she ever did was wrong. Once, when I complained that she did not treat him fairly he turned to me and said quite sharply, 'You know nothing about it! Your mother is a lady. Say nothing against her again.'

"I knew not what he meant. I had seen ladies once, riding along the road. They had furs and fancy hats and were wondrously fair. My mother was nothing like that. She was not even pretty, nor had she pretty clothes. But she did have an ivory comb and a few other baubles ... and this key."

Ella reached down under the neck of her shift and pulled out the old brass key. Leaning forward, the dowager-duchess took the key into her hand—but it was the chain which claimed her attention.

"Child. Was that chain your mother's too?"

"She gave it to me with the key the day she died."

"It is gold; and very valuable. Where would your mother have got such a thing? And an ivory comb, you said? This is very strange." Sophie's eyes were alert with excitement.

"Is it? I have never even thought about it. It was the key which seemed of import to my mother." Tears clouded Ella's eyes. "The day she gave these things to me, she drowned. They told me it was an accident but—" Leaving the sentence unfinished, Ella drooped her head as she blinked away her tears. "She gave me everything she had, and then she drowned."

"I am sorry. You need not tell me more."

"She said we were going to live at Eaglesheid." Freed by the deluge of her memories, Ella's words poured forth. "She said we belonged there, and she waited in the sun all afternoon and then she gave me everything. Her comb and the other things in a pocket to tie around my waist, and this key. She told me to go play and then she went and drowned herself." Catching her breath with a deep inhalation, Ella paused before she continued in a low, flat voice. "I have never said those words, not even to myself, but I think it is true." She sat up and held the key in her palm like a talisman. "I have never taken this off, because that was her command."

"What is it for?"

"She said that … it was for a chest in Castle Falcon-something." Ella sniffled and rubbed her hand across her eyes. "No, that's not right. Not a falcon. A raven."

"A raven?" Sophie's voice turned sharp. "Did she say Ravensberg?"

Ella nodded. "I think so. I remember wondering whether all castles were named for birds."

"But Ravensberg is here! Not even a league away. I lived there myself for twenty years or more. I would have stayed there if Branold had let me, but he insisted I come here and I am glad he did. These rooms are much more pleasant. But I am wandering. The point is, you have a key—on a golden chain—which you say opens a chest in Ravensberg. And Ravensberg is hard by."

"My lady, perhaps I'm mistaken." Ella now regretted that she had spoken so freely. "It was fully five years ago."

"Perhaps you are, and perhaps you are not. Do you not feel excited? Somewhere lies a chest which has been unopened for many years, for lack of a key. And fate has brought you here, wearing the key around your neck. Perhaps," she repeated after a slight pause, "fate has even brought you more than your key." Sophie stood up, flushed and energized. "Most of the valuables were brought here to Newravenstein years ago. We must find your chest."

Ella remained crouched on the floor. "I think I must return to the kitchens."

"Oh, posh! Are you fearful of fate?"

"I cannot go around the castle searching for chests!"

Sophie stared at Ella for a moment, then acquiesced. "You are right, child. We must give the errand to someone else. And I know the perfect person—my grandson, Arthur. He would never turn away from an adventure. If the lock which fits your key is anywhere in this castle, Arthur will find it, and what is more, he can also search at Ravensberg. I will send for him now." The dowager reached toward the tasseled pull-cord which would ring a bell in the guardroom below.

"But the feast!"

She pulled her hand back just in time. "You are quite right. We will have to wait. There are too many people around. Ella—" Sophie's voice took on a greater note of seriousness. "There is something I would say to you."

"My lady?"

"I desire that you remain here after the tournament…with me. I've had more happiness these past few days than in all the days in the past score of years put together. Could you bear to stay here with me? As my companion? No longer will you work in the kitchens; and you could take your meals in the hall, then come back and tell me all that you see and hear. Will you stay? I need you, Ella."

"This is hard, my lady. Eaglesheid is my home."

"But you have no family there, do you?" she persisted.

Ella shook her head.

"Then will you consider this?"

"Of course, my lady. When I'm alone, I shall—"

"And, I have another idea!" Sophie cut her off. "I swear by the saints that my head has not had so many thoughts in it for many a year. We need not wait for Arthur to begin our search, for there are many coffers of various sizes right here in my chambers. Not that I would expect your key to fit any of these. They are all mine after all, but why should Arthur have all the fun? Hand me that key, child, and we will begin our hunt now."

Ignoring the knot of apprehension in her stomach, Ella slipped the chain over her head. "Do you not wish to eat first?"

"How could I? I am too excited by this … this quest we are on. Here. It will be better if you take the key. We will begin by trying all the chests in this room no matter how impossible they may seem. First, that large one in the corner," she pointed to a chest so aged that its wood was nearly black.

Ella knelt before the chest, slowly inserted the key into the lock and tried to turn it, but it was far too small to engage the mechanism.

"I knew it could not open that one. I have the key to it right here, and I used it just the other day." Sophie patted the ring which hung at her side. "But we will leave no stone unturned. Rather, I should say 'we'll leave no lock unturned.' Now try that little one under the window."

Ella tried the key in every lock in the room but not one fit. She was amazed at the number of chests, and finally asked the duchess if every lady had so many.

"No, of course not. But when my husband was alive, Bestilden was one of the wealthiest dukes in all of Christendom, for he was far better with a tally than a sword. Indeed, many a king envied my Bestilden his riches—and not kings alone." For a moment, her hand fisted over her mouth as though to restrain some dreaded memory, then she dropped it to her lap and gave Ella a contorted grin. "But never mind that. Look around you now. Most of these chests contain gowns, for my dear Besti loved to indulge my love of finery. When I die, they all will go to Eleanor. Branold will see to that. Isabel is not to have my belongings!"

"My name is Eleanor, too," Ella said, then blushed, suddenly aware that she might seem presumptuous in pointing out that her name was the same as such an illustrious noblewoman, but the duchess did not seem the least bit perturbed.

"Is it?"

"But I have rarely been called anything except Ella," she hastened to add.

Not really paying attention, Lady Sophie stood slowly and reached out to take Ella's arm. "Let us try the solar. There are two more there and—" She interrupted herself. "Wait one moment! Those two were brought to me by my granddaughter just after she was married. And one of the coffers has no key! I have always intended to have Branold send a joiner to break it open but have never bothered. Oh, I feel all fluttery."

The solar was the same size as the other chamber, for the round tower had been simply divided in halves. Ella was surprised to see that it contained only the two chests, and a small bed, yet it was such a cheerfully sunny room. "Why do you not use this chamber?" she asked, amazed. "I would choose to sit here in the sun all the time."

The old lady shrugged her thin shoulders. "The sunshine is enticing, but there is no fire here. I got tired of moving back and forth between the seasons so have settled myself in the other chamber. But I am glad you like it. You may have it for your own. Now don't look at me like that, for, of course, I will use every weapon I can to convince you to stay. There." She pointed to the larger of the two chests. "That one has no key. I do hope yours fits, for I am suddenly very curious to see what is inside."

Ella knelt before the old chest. With a quick movement, she slipped the key into the lock, and then turned to look at Sophie in amazement.

"It fits!"

Sophie crossed the room with surprising agility and stood, her fists clenched and her breaths coming in rapid sequence. "Turn it."

"It won't turn. It doesn't seem to work. It must be for a—it's turning! This is the right chest!" The key turned in the lock a full circle and the two heard the catch released within.

Filled with a sudden excitement, Ella turned to look at the duchess. "Shall I open it?"

"Wait a moment." The dowager lowered herself to her knees. It took great effort but if she felt any pain she did not show it. "Now!"

Shutting her eyes, Ella counted to three inside her head then jerked the lid up, opening her eyes at the same time. Then she blinked in surprise. After the excitement of the hunt, she was anticipating that the coffer would be laden with a wealth of jewels. Instead, it seemed to be filled with gowns. Ella touched the one which lay on the top, a ruby-colored gown of brushed velvet which shimmered, even though it had been hidden out-of-sight for years. Hearing a noise from the dowager, she turned and saw that there were tears streaming down the old lady's face.

"My lady! What ails you?"

"I never thought to see this gown again. I had no idea it was here all this time. Help me up!" Scrambling to her feet, Ella helped the duchess to stand.

It took a few moments, for her spindly legs were not used to such abuse. "Hand me that gown!" she then ordered, when she was steady.

Ella placed it in Sophie's gnarled hands.

"This one …" she choked and started again. "This one was not mine. This was Judith's. I can still remember the last time she wore it. There was a feast at Ravensberg. It was autumn, but chilly, and the hall was ablaze with light. Everyone was very merry for there was plenty of food and wine, and the hall was warm and sheltered from the weather. People were drinking and singing and calling out jests to one another. A juggler was performing at the foot of the table and I even remember two dogs were quarreling over a bone. And then Judith entered the room. She received the greatest compliment a woman can ever receive—silence.

"She had never looked so beautiful. Her hair was loose and it shone in the dancing light. For once, she looked more beautiful than I ever had done, and my heart swelled with pride. Branold moved possessively to her side. He was not going to allow another man to get near her all evening." As Sophie spoke she was gazing off into the distance, seeing again the hall as it had been that night.

"A legend was born. The tale of Judith of Ravensberg was spread from lip to lip. Every move she made, every word, the sound of her laughter and the gleam in her eye, all were put into songs that were sung across the land that winter."

When Sophie turned to look at Ella, the spell was broken. "But that glow had been unnatural. That night was her farewell to the world. Soon she lay caught in the fever of the dreaded pox. I sent Branold away, with their two daughters. He was loathe to go but I would not listen to him. A week later Judith died. When Branold returned it was to an empty hearth—and I looked like this." She raised her hand to point to her own pitted face. "I was glad that Judith had been spared the agony of this, but Branold was not. He swore his love for her would have survived even that shock. And who knows? Perhaps it would. Not once did he shudder when he looked upon me." Her gaze held Ella's. "As neither did you, child."

"But, my lady, I don't understand. How could I have the key to your chest?" Ella's fear tainted her voice.

"Bring me the stool from the other room. I am suddenly weak."

"Aye, my lady." She was back in a moment and helped Sophie to seat herself. Neither spoke. Ella stood, her eyes focused on the floor and her hands
clasped behind her back to hide their trembling. Her mother had been a
thief! That could be the only explanation. She must have fled from
Ravensberg with her mistress' treasures ... and ... and then gone mad with
guilt and remorse.

"I want to see what else is in that chest. Show me, Ella," the duchess
commanded.

"Aye, my lady." Afraid to see the look of condemnation on the old lady's
face, Ella did not look up, but swiftly knelt again. The lid which she had
opened so eagerly a few minutes before now seemed heavy and weighted
against her. Gently, she lifted out the contents and laid them down on the
wooden floor. A linen shift. Another gown, this one the color of bluebells.
Two girdles, one woven and the other embroidered silk. And there, nestled
near the bottom, a slipper.

In horror she stared at it. There was no controlling the trembling in her
body now. She felt so cold and frightened that her senses dimmed, as
though the stone lid of a casket had just been shut upon her.

"Ella! Ella!" Sophie was kneeling at her side. "What is the matter, child?"
She tried to speak, but no sound would come.

"Ella!" Sophie shook her. "Are you all right, Ella?"
She nodded.

"Why are you so frightened? You have nothing to fear from me. Tell me
what is wrong!"

With great effort, Ella swallowed, moistening her throat. "That slipper."
Still, she spoke so quietly that Sophie could not hear.

"What did you say?"

Again, more loudly, "The slipper. Look at that slipper."

Agile in her concern, Sophie pulled out the slipper and cradled it in her
hand. "I remember this well. Branold gave these to Judith after he had inherited the duchy against all odds. But why should this grieve you so?"

"Because ..." Ella whispered. "I have the other."

"Impossible! I am certain the partner is here, under the linens." Sophie pulled out the few remaining items, carelessly tossing them aside. "It isn't here!"

"No. It's here." Ella stood, then slipped her hand beneath her skirting and untied the oilskin pocket from her waist.

One hand on the chest, the old lady pushed herself up, then took the pouch and loosened its cord. There, inside, lay the matching satin slipper, embroidered and beaded with precious gems.

"Your mother gave this to you?" There was astonishment in Lady Sophie's voice.

"Yes." It was impossible to deny the truth.

"Did you know it was valuable?"

"I only thought it to be precious because it had been my mother's."

"What did she tell you about it?"

"Only that her sister had the matching one." The memory of that moment, when her mother had bid her farewell, was suddenly painfully vivid.

"Eleanor. You said your name is Eleanor," the duchess gasped. "Please help me to that stool now. I must sit."

Ella was surprised to see that Lady Sophie's eyes were flashing—not with anger—but with anticipation.

"Your mother's name was?"

"Kate."

"Kate." She rolled the word over her tongue, as though tasting the way it sounded in her mouth. "No, not Kate. Katrina."

"I never heard her called that." Ella shook her head to refute the words, but as she did, a distant memory seemed to reach out to her.

"Come close, child. Let me touch your hair." Bewildered now, more than she was afraid, Ella did as she was bid.

"You may never have heard her called that, but I know it was so. I do not understand, but I thank God for this moment. Katrina's child. Eleanor."

Lady Sophie stooped, picked up the crimson gown once again, and after giving it a quick shake, held it aloft with an appraising eye. "Ella," she said, pronouncing each word with the care of an oracle. "Tonight, you are going to Isabel's feast!"

# Chapter 26

T HE FEASTING WOULD BEGIN ere long, but Eleanor felt no joy: each passing moment served only to bring the morrow's hour of doom nearer. Her limbs, weighted down by the burden of her fear, were so heavy that even the ordinary task of dressing herself seemed nigh well impossible. She had managed the gown, and the girdle, and the beads at her neck, but as she struggled to arrange her hair, her patience ebbed. With mounting frustration she pressed the jeweled cap to her scalp and ruthlessly jabbed at it with a pin. It was no use. First one pin landed on the floor, and then another, and then the cap slipped over her brow. With a cry of disgust she threw the lot across the room and flung herself onto the bed.

As Eleanor drifted into sleep, the pins continued to poke at her; no, not pins; tiny swords, held by soldiers who ran from pavilion to pavilion, pricking them into the arms of screaming women and children. Stuck full of pins herself, she searched in growing panic for her own children. Finding one, she would thrust him beneath her skirt; and then another; and then another. How many were there? How could she possible hide them all? Now the swords were no longer small and innocuous, but huge double-edged blades with deep runnels streaming with blood; and the soldiers all wore Sebastian's face. Frantic, Eleanor continued to stuff children beneath her billowing skirt; they climbed her like a pole till that she felt like a bloated spider about to burst with dozens of progeny; even so she knew she had not yet—

"Eleanor."

Startled, her eyes flew open. Seated on the edge of the bed, was Sebastian, who now drew her hand into his own. "Forgive me for waking you."

The nightmarish dream still clouded her thoughts. Terrified at the sight of his face so near to her own, she flung up her free hand as protection, but the motion cleared away the remnants of the dream. Inhaling deeply, she forced herself to relax.

"I'm sorry to disturb you," he repeated, "but we must talk."

Reaching up, she trailed a finger across the corner of his eye, caressing the tiny folds which had always stirred her heart. "You are tired," she said, though in truth he looked more than tired. He appeared as a man who would never again know the peace of dreamless sleep.

"We both have reason to be weary," he said. "To laugh and hunt and eat and dance, all the while knowing that treachery is at hand—knowing the traitor and the betrayed—"

He stopped, though still he enfolded Eleanor's hand within his own. "I have come to tell you that I have at last chosen my course. I doubt I tread wisely. Indeed, I think I choose the coward's way."

"Which?" Eleanor clutched his shoulders and drew herself up. "With which one will you stand tomorrow? Terlinden or the king?"

"With neither," he answered. "I will have naught of this rebellion which Terlinden plans, but neither will I raise my sword against him. Tomorrow morn, just before the sun rises, we will leave in secrecy. We will take the children, your maids, and less than a score of men-at-arms." He bent forward and gripped his own head. "I have agonized over this, but neither my conscience nor my honor gives me aid. So this I will do. But be warned, Eleanor, it will not be the end of the affair. By breaking faith with neither, I am in truth breaking faith with both. And the consequences will be bitter. At the best, Westfeld's name will be besmirched. At the worst, we may yet see siege-machines against Eaglesheid's walls. Whoever wins the victory tomorrow—whether it be the king or the duke—will look at me and cry foul.

What will happen then I cannot say. But know well, Eleanor, that though I choose now to hold my arms and leave the field, I will fight to defend Westfeld if matters should go thus far. I will defend my children, my people, my land."

She had scarcely heard his latter words. "Why would Eaglesheid be put to siege?"

"I am sworn to protect the king, my liege. It will matter little that I spurn to wield my sword against him, if I do not lift it in his defense. A vassal who refuses to fulfill his pledge is of little value. Please understand that this decision is the hardest I have ever come to in my life. Already I feel my head bowed with grief, yet I can raise my sword against neither my king nor my foster-father—save only in defense. So, instead, I will bring this shame upon myself." He brushed his finger against her cheek. "And upon you."

"There is no shame!" Eleanor cried. "The shame all belongs to Duke Gebbard who seeks that which is not his!" Then calming herself, she added, "I have already told you that I will follow wherever you lead. I will have the children ready to leave in the morn."

Sebastian rose and strode across the chamber to stand before the open casement. Where he stood, the mid-afternoon sun streamed through the window and bathed his face, restoring to him the look of his youth. Eleanor's throat closed around her breath at the sight of him. Never had he looked so magnificent. Rarely did he wear ceremonial robes, but today he was dressed with as much splendor as the peacock which strutted in the courtyard. His shoes, his hose, and his thigh-length tunic were set off to perfection by a spectacular silken mantle, trimmed with ermine and boldly embroidered with the twin-headed eagle.

He turned toward her, frowning. Now, the streaks of gray were apparent in his hair, the lines of worry on his face. Though he had made his decision, it had brought him no peace.

"There is one thing which grieves me above all others," he said. "Young Henry's fate is a millstone on my soul. It seems a cruel jest that on the very day he receives his sword and his spurs, he shall lose his life; for it is his death which will be the sign that the insurrection has begun."

"Can nothing be done to save him?" Eleanor flew across the room and grasped his arm. "How can we let him go to his death ignorant of the danger which threatens him?"

"But that is the agony, Eleanor." He rubbed his fingers over his temple. "By leaving Newravenstein tomorrow, I also leave Henry to his fate. I refuse to raise my sword against him yet neither can I raise my voice to save him without betraying Terlinden. And, to my regret, that is something I have promised not to do. When I bent my knees and swore my oaths of loyalty, little did I know that they would return as a blade to cleave my heart."

Eleanor could think of no response, so she reached up to brush the hair from his brow. At her touch, Sebastian wrapped her within his arms, completely enfolding her, pulling him to her with the urgent need of his pain. "What am I to do?" he groaned. "Eleanor, what am I to do?"

She held him for a few moments, drawing strength from his heat, then stepped back far enough that she could look up into his face. His eyes, darker than ever, held fathomless despair. "It is not you who brings tomorrow's battle," she said, firmly. "Nor is it you who bears the blame. It does not lie within your hand, Sebastian, to right every wrong in this world. If you cannot betray your oaths, then we must prepare to defend our home. We will leave at first light tomorrow; but not completely without hope. Perhaps, even yet, God will raise up a champion for the king."

"I no longer believe it possible. The hour is much too late—but I thank you for your words." He bent and kissed her brow. "You look very beautiful tonight."

Certain her pleasure shone from her face, she pointed to the floor. "Will you help me with my headpiece? I sent Hannah to the children, but my arms felt so leaden that I could not manage alone."

"I am at your service, my lady. Now and forever." Retrieving the cap from where it lay on the floor, Sebastian looked at it, turning it thoughtfully in his hand as though he were puzzled. "But where does it go? Here?" He held it to her knee. "Or here, on your elbow? Or here? No. Then you would need a matching one!"

Though her heart was too heavy for laughter, the joy which flooded her brought a smile to her lips. "Oh, Sebastian," she said, "how I do enjoy you. Shall I call my woman?"

"No." He bent to pick up the scattered pins. "I am not yet willing to admit defeat. Not in this matter, at least. Come now, stand before me, and I shall try."

# Chapter 27

FROM WHERE ELEANOR SAT at the high table, the complete pageantry of the feast was played out before her, wildly extravagant, colorfully fanciful and highly ritualized. The servitors, all pages and squires of noble lineage, were outfitted in the azure and white livery of Gildren. With great pride they displayed the excellence of their training. Deftly wielding their knives, they arranged platters of delicacies to tempt the palates of their lords—left wing of sparrow minced with wine sauce, stuffed entrails of suckling pig, upper crust of bread warm from the oven, kidney of fawn—all appropriately spiced and garnished. The trumpeters, standing on a gaily decorated balcony overlooking the hall, announced the arrival of each new remove with a bright flourish. The jesters used their wit to amuse, the jugglers their skill to awe.

In the interludes between the courses, the entertainment was even more fantastic. A troupe of mummers used dumbshow to indicate that they wished to play dice with the prince and the other guests on the dais, and quickly forfeited several golden rings and chalices. Thirty-two squires, wearing visors either black or white, performed a living game of chessmen, and then presented the queen with a marble board and pieces intricately formed from sugared sweetmeats.

Although undeniably entertained, Eleanor was unable to relax and enjoy the revelry, for try as she might, she could not relinquish her foreknowledge of the dire events the morrow would bring.

The brilliance of the warm summer night was giving way to duskiness before the servants began to clear the room. Empty trenchers and goblets, decorative sotelties, rose-water-filled finger bowls, and splattered linens were all speedily removed and borne away to the sculleries. The boards were lifted from the trestles and, with the chairs and benches, were carried off. The torches on the walls were already alight, but now massive chandeliers were lowered from the rafters and their candles also set aflame. In the minstrel's gallery a new set of musicians, with lute, rebec, vielle, and harp, replaced the trumpeters. Dancing began. And dicing. Chess and backgammon boards appeared.

Eleanor sighed. There were hours still to endure until midnight, when the prince and his companions would be led to the chapel, there to be stripped and bathed in the purification ceremony which was a vivid allegory of their coming baptism into the knighthood. Hours yet, of pretense of pleasure. Again Eleanor sighed. This night was going to seem an endless trial.

Arthur tamped down his impatience as he ran up the steps to Lady Sophie's chamber. Why had his grandmother sent for him, tonight of all nights? Surely she knew just how much he would resent the summons, for she understood well the lure of such magnificent festivities.

Using his knuckles he banged on the door. "Grandmama!" he shouted. "It's Arthur. May I come in?"

"If you dare."

His frustration disappeared at her curious words. What scheme had the old lady hatched tonight? Undoubtedly, it would not be dull. Perhaps, even, she had at last decided to end her self-imposed imprisonment, and wished him to escort her into the hall!

He pushed open the door then stopped stock-still in amazement. Before him stood a beautiful maiden, swimming in a golden ocean of curls.

"Grandmama?" His voice was a dry whisper. "Have you been bewitched?"

"Nay, my boy," Sophie chuckled, and Arthur turned quickly to where she sat by the hearth, then swung his gaze back to the other.

He could see now what he had not first noticed. The girl was trembling and her eyes were clouded with fear, though it did nothing to diminish the beauty of their dark depths. Hoping to reassure her, he swept into a deep and reverent bow. "Arthur of Westfeld at your service, mistress."

Her eyes widened slightly and her rosy lips quivered, but she did not speak.

"Do you recognize her?" Sophie asked. "Even the slightest bit?"

"Should I?" He continued to stare, pleased to have an excuse. "I have never seen her before in my life. Of that I have no doubt."

Sophie laughed again. "Well then, let me introduce you. Arthur, this is my ward, Ella. Of Bestilden. She has but recently come into my care. Though the feasting is already past, I wish you to escort her down to the hall for the remainder of the celebration." The lilt in Sophie's voice proved that she understood how much he had chafed at her summons. "I trust that will not tax your patience too far?"

"I would be honored to escort Fraulein Ella." As Arthur answered his grandmother, his eyes did not leave the maiden's face, though she had dropped her own eyes to the floor. Not hearing Sophie rise and cross the room, he was startled by the touch of her fingers on his arm.

"Will you be her protector? Can I trust Ella to your care?"

"Yes, of course. But what am I to protect Ella from?"

"Ah, that is a good question." Sophie wrapped her arm around Ella's waist. The contrast between their features should have been grotesque, but strangely, it was not. "From her own fear. You will make her laugh and put her at her ease."

"But of what is she afraid?"

"I see I must tell you more," Sophie sighed, as she lightly stroked Ella's hair. "The child is dear to me. Very dear! By a twist of fate, the poor child has lived a life sheltered from the courts of the mighty and is now dread afraid to enter the hall and into such grand company. But I could not bear that she miss such a celebration. So I depend on you, Arthur. You must not leave Ella's side until she is returned here, to me. Not for one moment. Will you do as I ask?"

Arthur nodded. "Willingly." That command would not be difficult to follow. Only a simpleton would choose to disobey such orders.

"And to all who question who she is, you must answer that she is Fraulein Ella of Bestilden, a ward of the dowager-duchess."

Arthur nodded as he listened to Lady Sophie's instructions.

"But most importantly, you must not let her be seen by your grandfather, Branold. Not tonight! There will be time enough for explanations on the morrow. And do not risk an encounter with him by staying overlong. Return here with Ella before the bell rings and the midnight vigil begins."

This time Arthur did not agree quite so readily. Branold of Gildren, his grandfather in name only, was a powerful man whom he did not wish to cross. "Does the duke know Ella?"

"It is not Ella he would recognize. It is—" Sophie's eyes shifted to the ruby-colored gown Ella was wearing, but she shrugged her shoulders and did not complete her sentence. "Never mind about that. Branold shall learn all, and soon enough. But not tonight. I want nothing to spoil this night."

Sophie lowered herself into her chair then reached to the decanter on her tray. "And now to send you off with Godspeed, you must share a cup of wine." Filling two goblets, she handed them to her guests. But to Ella she commanded, "You must speak, child, lest Arthur think you a mute."

Ella took a sip of her wine, stifled a cough, and dipped her head. "Thank you, my lady."

"You call that speech, child?" Sophie teased. "Lift your chin and look at Arthur. He is no ogre. In truth he is the handsomest of Westfeld's brood, for he has his father's face—if not his favor."

But Arthur was no longer listening. He was mesmerized by the hand which was wrapped around the goblet.

"Fraulein," he said in wonder. "Surely your ring bears the royal arms!"

Ella quickly shifted her cup and hid her hand in the folds of her gown but immediately seemed to think better of it. Raising her eyes to meet his, she took out her hand again and held it out for him to see. When she spoke, her voice was steady with confidence.

"It was given to me by a friend."

"Where did this come from, Ella?" Sophie demanded as she leaned forward and stretched out her bony finger.

"I have kept it in my mother's pouch, my lady, for I have never dared to wear it since the day that Harry gave it to me. But when I put on this gown, it suddenly seemed right to wear. In truth, my lady, it gives me great comfort."

"Harry?" Two voices sounded together.

"We were friends one summer. On the day he left, he gave me this, and bid me if ever I was in trouble to show it and request a boon in the name of Henry."

"Henry!" Again the unison voices.

"Yes." A smile lit Ella's face and all trace of timidity fled. "Can you imagine that? We played together and never once did he let me know who he truly was. Then two days ago, who should ride through the gates but my Harry. Prince Henry! If ever I meet him again, I shall tell him just what I think."

Though Sophie was still so stunned that she could not speak, Arthur laughed and held out his hand. "And that you shall. Come, Ella. You can pay him back for his deception threefold, this very evening. Come. We are going to have such fun!"

———

Ella's giddiness fled long before they set foot on the smooth flagstone at the bottom of the staircase, replaced once more with silent fear. After passing through the outer door of the tower, Arthur summoned his courage and drew her aside.

"Fraulein Ella, I know little of women's ways, but I am not such a dullard that I cannot see that some great dread weighs upon you. Of what are you afraid?"

She raised her hand to her brow and shut her eyes, but did not answer.

Feeling terribly inept, he tried again. "Are you afraid your manners will not be acceptable? If so, I can assure you—"

"Do you truly not know me?" she asked. "Have you never seen me anywhere before?"

He peered at her in confusion. "Never. Of that I have no doubt."

"But I have seen you, here and there, walking the cobbles of Eaglesheid, sometimes alone, sometimes with the other lads. And then just last week I saw you many times, riding ahead of the carts on the road to Newravenstein. Can you not understand what is wrong?"

More confused than ever, Arthur could only stammer a response. Was she some sort of fairy who could pass along streets unseen? But her eyes were filled with such desperate appeal that he set his own questions aside. "I'm sorry, but I do not."

"Lady Sophie has set me to play a part, like a mummer, but I do not wish it! Look at me," she cried, holding out her arms. "Everyone will know I don't belong!"

"But you look wonderful. You look like a princess." Arthur intended to reassure her, but he did not.

"A princess!" she exclaimed in horror. "I, who have never worn anything but an ancient linen shift, am now gowned in a garment made for a duchess! And look—" She lifted the hem of the gown and raised one foot, shaking it angrily. "I am wearing slippers crested with jewels. And this trinket, as Lady Sophie calls it, in my hair is something I could have saved every penny I would ever earn in my life and never have enough to make the purchase of it." Tears welled in her eyes. "Do you have any idea what it is like to suddenly not know your place in the world?"

Arthur nodded gravely, remembering the moment Lady Eleanor had first taken his hand into hers. "I assure you, Ella, that I do."

"This very evening Lady Sophie has swept away all my past, telling me that I am not who I thought I was."

"Then who are you?"

Sniffling, Ella used the back of her hand to wipe her face. "A maid from the kitchen."

"Do you jest?"

"No."

"You work in the kitchens?"

"Yes."

"Well..." he paused as his thoughts raced. "That is fine mummery."

Ella scowled at him, but Arthur chuckled. "What do you think the cook would say if he could see you now?"

"He'd probably drop the pudding right at his own feet."

"Well? There you are. Is that not a good jest?"

"Not if you were the one who made the pudding. Which," she added, unable to resist the touch of mirth, "I was."

"Oh, Ella, have you never wished to attend such festivities?"

"Of course I have."

"Well, tonight you shall. You'll see the minstrels and the musicians and the mummers. And the king, and the queen, and ..." He stretched out the sentence, raising his brows as he spoke. "The prince! Everyone will be wondering who you are. But it will be a secret. No one shall know. What greater adventure could you desire?"

"But surely anyone looking at my face would know that I am an impostor."

"Your face?" he echoed in disbelief. "Anyone looking at your face would see only a lovely maiden. Do you not wish to go? Tell me truly."

"Certainly I have wished for such a thing. But only as one wishes for the impossible. I wish that I could fly, to touch the tops of the trees or even the stars. I wish that I was not fearful of the water and could float away. Or I wish that I could be a horse and feel the earth pounding beneath my hooves as I gallop faster and faster, feeling the wind whistling in my ears. I wish that I could read, to understand the words written on a page. There are so many things that I wish for, but they are only dreams. One does not encounter them in one's waking. In such a way, I would wish that I were not a kitchen maid and could go to the feasting. Only now, it is not a dream. And I feel that I am walking in a nightmare."

"You dream of much and make me feel the lack. But why does such a dream become reality need to be so frightening? You may never fly, Ella. But tonight you may dance."

She did not answer, but stood looking at him as though asking him to convince her. Encouraged, he continued, "Ella, if you had the chance to touch the tops of the trees, would you refuse?"

"No," she relaxed a little. "I would not."

"And now you have the chance to dress like a princess and walk into that hall." He gestured toward the building which was alive with light and laughter.

She said nothing, but stood fidgeting with her hands.

Arthur waited, patiently, uncertain what he would do if she refused to accompany him. He could hardly drag Ella into the hall against her will, yet the alternative of returning her to the tower, having thwarted his grandmother's plans seemed just as undesirable.

This thought gave Arthur pause. Why had the dowager-duchess plucked a girl from the kitchens, dressed her in such a fashion and then given her the protection of Bestilden's name? Was it just a game? Or, perhaps, some small revenge for the years she herself had lain hidden, slighted by the Fates? One thing was certain, he had sworn to protect Ella and protect her he would—even if it be from Lady Sophie herself.

Straightening her shoulders, Ella lifted her head and faced him again. Her large eyes were no longer filled with fear. "You are right. Why should I be afraid of mere knights and their ladies when a prince has been my friend?"

Placing her hand on Arthur's arm, she followed as he led her to the great double doors; and as they stepped into the hall, she gazed around with wonder.

It was Arthur who quailed.

Nothing, short of nudity, could have attracted more attention to Ella than the crimson gown she was wearing. A quarter-century before, when it had been in fashion, it had been sensational. Now, it set her apart, casting an air of otherworldliness over her extraordinary beauty. Unadorned by the popular kirtle, it appeared both plainer and more fascinating than the other gowns. The velvet was light, flowing, shimmering. It caught every curve of her body as it brushed across her breast, tapered inward at her waist and then cascaded over her hips to kiss her ankles just above her slippers. Around the collar, and again reflected on the hem of the sleeves, was a simple embellishment, an ordinary embroidered scroll, but the thread was spun gold which caught the flickering light of the many torches. In contrast to the dress, the girdle which loosely encircled her waist held no pretense of simplicity. Strands of gold were braided into ringlets, linked to form an intricate chain, and firmly clasped with a buckle fashioned into the likeness of the rampant lion, emblem of royalty.

And, as though she were royalty, the crowd parted before her as she walked on Arthur's arm into the room. Many bowed their heads, or dipped their knees, but none took their eyes from her.

Arthur had expected to cause a stir, a ripple of interest, but was overwhelmed by this tide of astonishment. Seeking a familiar face, Arthur moved Ella forward until they neared the center of the room.

Exhausted, Eleanor determined to leave the hall and return to her chamber, there to await the arrival of the dawn. Preoccupied by her efforts to push through the press and reach the nearest doorway, she was unaware of the stir about her until she stepped between two people and found herself face-to-face with Arthur; an unknown girl on his arm. It was immediately obvious that his companion was garnering a great deal of attention. And small wonder. The girl was the loveliest Eleanor had seen all evening, not excepting her younger sister, Mariel.

Trust Arthur, not yet fully grown himself, to find a partner who would be the envy of many a man.

"I see I need have no concern for your well-being this evening, Arthur. Nothing could make you happier than to be the center of all this attention."

"Usually that would be true, my lady mother, but not tonight." He drew the girl forward, holding her protectively within the circle of his arm. "Allow me to introduce you. Mama, this is Fraulein Ella, of Bestilden. Ella, this is my mother, Lady Eleanor, duchess of Westfeld."

Eleanor greeted the girl, then tilted her head in bewilderment. "Have we met before? There is something very familiar about you."

"No, Mama," Arthur answered before the girl could speak. "I am afraid that is impossible. Ella has just this day arrived from Bestilden."

"From Bestilden ...?"

"Duke Baldwin, our uncle, sent her to Grandmama Sophie."

"I see." She frowned as she concentrated her thoughts. "Still, there is some—"

"Harlot!" Branold's deep voice roared beside them and Eleanor turned in amazement. Her father, face flushed with fury, had thrust his way through the crowd and was reaching out to grab hold of the girl.

But Arthur forestalled him. Boldly stepping between Ella and his grandfather, he demanded, "By what right do you speak so to a guest, my lord?"

Branold pointed past him to Ella. "That … slut … is wearing my Judith's gown!"

Eleanor gasped. That was what had seemed so familiar! It was not the girl—it was the gown! In a twinkling she was whisked back twenty-five years to the last time she had seen her mother, a vision of glowing happiness. Surely, there could be no other gown like the one Judith had worn that night.

Shaking aside her own distress, Eleanor reached out to calm her father. "Papa. This is not the place. We will find the answers, but not here."

Branold pushed her away. "You thief, I will tear that gown right off of you!"

"No, Papa!" Eleanor cried out, and again grabbed at his arm. "Don't destroy Mama's gown! Please!"

"Better to be in shreds than on filth such as this," Branold snarled, as he darted forward and swiped out at Ella with his powerful hand.

Arthur sprang forward and caught his grandfather's descending arm. "No, my lord!"

Maddened, Branold reached for his sword but it was not there. All the knights were weaponless this night.

"My lord," Arthur repeated, meeting Gildren eye to eye. "To touch Ella, you will have to kill me first. I have sworn to protect her and that I will do."

"Then prepare to die, changeling."

Eleanor screamed at her father but Arthur waved her to silence.

"Kill me if you will. But know first that Ella bears a royal token." He grasped the girl's arm and stretched out her hand, showing plainly a golden ring on her finger.

Branold stared at it a moment, then brushed aside its importance. "Doubtless another object of her theft."

"I can assure you, it is not."

This new challenge came from behind and Branold spun around. Prince Henry, rigid with anger, was glowering at him. "Be careful, Gildren. Be very careful. It is me you accuse, for I gave that ring to the fraulein myself."

Branold's eyes smoked, then were doused with ice as he struggled to control his rage. When finally he spoke, it was with proper respect, though his voice was tight with the effort. "My prince!"

But Henry ignored him. Stepping forward, he held out his hand to the girl. "Ella," he said, with great formality. "I am well pleased to see you. I did not think that we would ever meet again, especially in such circumstances as these. Would you honor me with a dance?"

If he had waited for her answer, he would have waited long; for she seemed frozen in her shock. But Henry moved to her side, tucked her hand beneath his arm, and began to lead her away. Before they had gone far, he turned back to Arthur.

"For your service, Arthur of Westfeld, you have earned my gratitude. I always thought you had a stout heart and now you have proven it. Consider me your debtor. I will return Fraulein Ella to you after this round."

The moment they had disappeared into the swirling crowd, Eleanor swung around to face her son, barely resisting her desire to slap him. "Who is that girl? Where did she come from? Certainly not from Bestilden! And what is she doing with my mother's gown?"

"I know not—" He started to speak but Branold interrupted, fiercely.

"Your life is still in my hands! If this is one of your jests, you will have great cause to regret it."

Arthur crumbled. The man disappeared, leaving the boy behind. "I'm sorry. I know little of her, truly. It was Grandmama Sophie who dressed her in that gown and ordered me to bring her here tonight."

"Only an infant attempts to lay the blame on another." Branold's voice was scathing. "Your base blood shows well."

"I'm sorry, my lord of Gildren." Though he tried to mask his feelings, Arthur could not hide his misery. "I cannot deny my birth."

No matter her anger, Eleanor could bear Arthur's pain no longer. Laying one hand on her son's arm, she confronted her father. "Your accusation is unjust. Always has Arthur behaved with honor, if not with wisdom. If he claims that he brought the girl here at Lady Sophie's bidding, then that I will believe. We must go to her. She is the one who holds the answer to this mystery."

Branold stood motionless, his face hard. "That we will do, as soon as the prince returns the girl to us. And you, Arthur, had better pray that the duchess absolves you of all responsibility for this folly."

# Chapter 28

WITH AS MUCH ENTHUSIASM as he was able to muster for a trivial game, Sebastian shouted out, "Dark!" But at the very moment he was about to throw his pebble onto the chequered board, a sleepy young voice at his shoulder croaked out, "My lord of Westfeld?"

Cradling the pebble in the palm of his hand, Sebastian turned and beckoned the lad forward. "I am Westfeld," he said with a smile, knowing that the poor fellow had likely been wrested from some snug corner where he slept, and ordered to deliver his message. That was a well-remembered peril of serving as a page!

"The duke, my master, begs you to come to the Duchess Sophie's tower."

Sebastian flicked the pebble with his thumb, and watched as it skidded across the squares and landed on—light. "Know you the reason, lad?"

"Nay, lord. But your lady wife also bids you come with all speed."

"Now there is a command I cannot refuse." To mask his apprehension, Sebastian shrugged at the board and saluted his companions as he stood. "It would seem I am saved from losing a king's ransom tonight. Wait here, Raynar, if you will."

"I'll be here. This night holds no other claim." Raynar stretched his arms in lazy unconcern, but his eyes passed a warning to his friend.

Certain that Branold had learned of the insurrection, Sebastian hastened to Sophie's tower. Though the coming confrontation would be more than difficult, there was no denying it would be a tremendous relief to share the perilous burden of his knowledge with Branold.

Eleanor was there, waiting for him in the open doorway at the top of the circular stair. At the sight of her, Sebastian's spirits soared with a thrill of pleasure. All exhaustion had been lifted from her face. In the shadowed light, her fair skin glowed with youth and health, and her eyes danced with the warmth of invitation.

"What has happened, Eleanor? I've not seen you so free of care for a fortnight."

She drew him up and into the room, which was ablaze with light from a multitude of candles. Lady Sophie was seated in her usual chair, though with an ebullience which made her appear to float, and Branold was balanced in the center of the room like a jongleur about to spring from the earth.

Sebastian stared at them all in wonder. "What has happened?" he repeated, though he nearly sang the words. The air was bubbling with an excitement which filled his lungs and made him want to shout.

They all spoke at once, then ceased, then all began to laugh, together.

"The most miraculous event has happened," said Eleanor, clinging to his arm as though to hold herself to the earth. "We have learned tonight of the existence of a child—a daughter of my elder sister!"

"But you have no older sister." Save one. Sudden pain shot through his bowels, as though a large stone had settled there.

Eleanor shook her head. "We thought she had died, but we were mistaken. She lived to have a child."

"Her name—" He forced the words through his throat, scraping their edges, and speaking them all unformed. It could not be Katrina. It could not! "What is her name?"

"Ella," she answered, but just as relief began rolling over Sebastian and he lifted his hand to wipe away the beads of sweat which were already dampening his brow, she added, in a voice filled with pride, "She named her Eleanor."

Sebastian clutched at her. "Who did? Who is this girl?"

She laughed in joy at his surprise. "The daughter of my sister, Katrina! You can well understand how difficult it was for us to believe; but nonetheless it's true. The girl is here, and the proofs she bears cannot be denied."

Though the room began to spin, Sebastian remained motionless. "Is Katrin—" He stopped, then started again. "Is your sister not dead?"

She sobered, but only a trifle. "She is; but she died not sixteen years ago as once we thought, but only five years past."

"Then how ... how ...?"

Branold, who had been listening in ill-contained excitement, now clapped his hand on Sebastian's shoulder. "I can see your bewilderment. It is hard to fathom, is it not? Indeed, my dear Sophie labored long and hard to convince me of the truth. There is no doubting it's a strange tale."

Without meeting his eyes, Sebastian pulled away and staggered to the window, where he gripped the sill and stared out into the bleakness of the night. He yearned to howl and keen his agony. Katrina had not died. Katrina had not died. Katrina had not—Stopping himself with an exertion of will beyond all he had ever thought possible, Sebastian locked his anguish within.

"Tell me," he said. "I wish to hear all."

And so they spoke. Retelling all they had learned this night. Each word cutting as deep as a well-honed knife. They told him of Katrina, pregnant, and maddened by despair, fleeing into the forest to await the birth of her child. They told of the mystery of her pretense of death, followed by her flight across the kingdom to Westfeld. They told of her bringing her child to Eaglesheid itself, and of ending her life in the river which flowed past its gates. They told of the girl working in the kitchens, earning her keep while earning respect. And then they told of the strange reunion with Sophie and the revelation of Ella's identity after all these long years.

Sebastian did not move until they had finished and silence wavered in the flickering light.

"And so," he said, though fearing the very act of speech would rend the armor of his self-control. "I have acquired a ... niece. And you, Branold, are you pleased? This is hard news about your daughter."

"I mourn deeply for Katrina and the years of hardship she suffered. Even so, I cannot but rejoice at this reunion with her daughter—my granddaughter!" He added the word in a voice alive with wonder.

"Then let us raise a cup." Concentrating his effort on the movement of his feet, Sebastian crossed to the decanter, poured the wine, then raised his hand aloft. "To the Fates," he said. "Those ever-victorious spinsters of woe."

Though all three looked decidedly confused, they lifted their cups. "To the Fates."

Draining his own goblet, he asked, "Is she here?"

Eleanor nodded and pointed to the adjoining room. "She's asleep. The poor child was exhausted and bewildered by our questions. Strange to say, Ella is the only one not yet convinced that her mother was Katrina of Gildren. She can no more imagine her mother growing up a lady in a castle than we can comprehend her living as a drab in a cot! But there is no doubting the truth. The proofs are not only in the tokens she bears, but in her very likeness. Do you wish to see her, Sebastian?"

"I would." He coughed, to hide the gruffness in his voice, then followed his wife, who was not his wife, to see his niece, who was his daughter.

Lifting a candle from the bracket on the wall just outside the second chamber, Sebastian crossed to the bed and held the light high—then immediately blew out the flame lest Eleanor see his reaction.

"Why did you do that?" she whispered.

Heat blazed across Sebastian's face. That one brief glimpse had seared his daughter's image into his mind: long lashes resting on smooth and creamy skin; high-arched brows; rose-tinted lips; hair as rich and lustrous as fine-spun gold—The hard stone of his pain now was marbled with wondrous joy. She was so impossibly beautiful. She was so like…so like…Eleanor.

"Sebastian? Are you all right?" Eleanor brushed her fingers across his shoulder.

Though he longed to gather Eleanor into his arms, and weep, he merely bent low and spoke into her ear. "When I saw the candle shining on her face, I was afraid…to wake her. The child needs her sleep."

"But did you see her?"

"I saw her."

"Is she not a marvel?"

He paused. "To behold her is to love her as one's own."

In the distance, rising above the sounds of revelry in the hall, a bell rang out, tolling the midnight hour. Sebastian drew Eleanor to the door.

"Do you hear the bell?" he asked, relieved to have good reason to quit the dowager's rooms. "The prince begins his vigil now, and I am expected to attend his purification ceremony."

Eleanor's shoulders drooped, and Sebastian knew she had just remembered the trials this new day would bring.

"Go, then, and do what you must, but I will stay awhile."

He gave no farewell, for as he turned to leave he was overwhelmed by his urgent need to escape this room before his grief broke the bindings of his self-control. Stepping onto the small landing, Sebastian steadied himself with his right hand while his left pulled the door shut at his back. The near-silent click of the latch—all but inaudible beneath the riotous din from the hall—resounded within his mind. And as though a key had released a lock, his agony would no longer be restrained.

Sebastian's stomach heaved, and a great rending sob tore at his chest. Plunging down the stairway with reckless speed, he fled Sophie's tower into the yard where he gulped one deep breath then curled up against the wall and wept.

He knew not how much time had passed as he crouched there in the shadows, but when he at last arose, the moon was resting high. Nearby sprawled a squire whose livery reeked of vomit and ale. Sebastian began to draw back, then with a wry laugh looked down at his own finery. His magnificent tunic was so smeared with filth that one could be forgiven for supposing he had fallen into the cesspit.

Feeling as weak as a dysentery-ravaged pikeman, he slowly made his way through the maze of gardens and outbuildings to the troughs by the stable door. He was not alone in the yard, not by any means: only a small portion of those who came to the tournament could partake of the official festivities, and the stable yard was abandoned to merriment.

With as much indifference to his audience as he could muster, Sebastian stripped off his tunic and thrust it, along with his aching head, into the water. He was still dripping when he reentered Newravenstein's great hall.

True to his word, Raynar had not left his seat, though he was comfortably ensconced with a flagon on his right and a damsel on his left; but when Sebastian approached and signaled to him, Raynar released both and followed him outside.

"We must talk." Sebastian's throat felt so raw that he had no difficulty conveying the earnestness of his need. "Where can we go to be alone?"

"The chapel?"

"The prince and his companions will be there, keeping their vigil of prayer."

"Then let us ride out. There is moon enough to light our way."

For Duke Sebastian, husband to a daughter of the house, there was no difficulty persuading a guard to let them pass the gate. With great care, they rode down the hill and through the encampment at its base, picking their way around fire pits and tent pegs. When they reached the open field, they set spur to their horses and galloped to the edge of the plain.

Here, Sebastian dismounted and sank onto a fallen log. Then he told Raynar all. After years of silence, he admitted how he had not only loved Katrina but had married and lain with her. How he had then, knowingly, married his wife's sister and, unknowingly, committed bigamy.

Sebastian stood and began to pace. "It is strange, Raynar, but though my head throbs, my mind has cleared. Katrina's tragedy did not begin and end sixteen years ago but continued, unbeknownst to me, for another decade! She died only five years past. Our child was raised in poverty. And this sorrow was caused by my hand. If I'd abided in patience to marry her, then she would have been awaiting me when I arrived at Ravensberg. It is because she carried my child that she fled her home. I, alone, am responsible for all this pain."

Raynar let out an exaggerated sigh, and shook his head. "I know you are trying to spare me, Sebastian, but I will fully acknowledge that the blame is mine. If I had not slept so soundly on that long-ago night, then I would not have been taken by your father's men as ransom for your behavior; you, then, would never have abducted Branold and could have married Katrina at will."

Sebastian swung around to stare at his friend. What in the world was Raynar prattling about?

"But, sad to say," Raynar continued, as he leaned against the oak at his back and twirled a blade of grass, "I am not as noble as you and will readily point out that there are others who share my blame. There's Isabel, who frightened the girl. Gregory, who killed Wolfram. Eleanor, who told no one of the child. Sophie, who stayed hidden in her tower. Branold, who kidnapped another man's bride. And, of course, Judith, who was so wondrously beautiful that Branold had to have her for his own."

"Did you not forget someone?" Sebastian asked, with a shadow of a grin.

"Ahh, indeed I did. There's that black-bearded Ogre of Westfeld who devoured brides for his dinner." Raynar sobered. "But now I speak in all earnestness. Who can untangle the many threads which led to Katrina's sad fate; yet all of those skeins were woven in innocence, save one. There was only one man who acted with deliberate intent of causing harm—your father."

Sebastian rubbed his head against the pain that still lingered there. "You are right. But I have been more like my father than I care to acknowledge."

"How so?" Raynar asked, with some surprise.

Sebastian frowned down at the ground as he sought to order his thoughts. "My father spent his life trying to avenge all wrongs. He was never content to let the past be forgotten. Have I been so different? I have not sought revenge, but atonement. And the result has been that I have spent my life either chasing the past or being stalked by it."

There was growing resolve in Sebastian's voice. "Thank you, for your words, Raynar. It is time to begin anew. Eleanor is my wife. Though I sinned in the marrying of her, she did not."

"She is strong." Raynar now rose and placed his hand on Sebastian's arm. "Tell her these things and let her share your burden."

"Do not tempt me!" Sebastian knocked Raynar's hand away and stepped back a pace. "After all her years of loyalty she deserves better of me. Am I to send her now to that nunnery to which she was prepared to flee so many years ago, simply to ease my conscience? Am I to tell her that the children she bore are not heirs, but bastards? You know well the ways of this world; though the sins were mine, she would be the one to pay the price. I tell you, Raynar, that since learning the truth of Katrina's life I am wracked with grief for all that she endured. But it is nothing to the fear I feel for Eleanor and her future. The suffering must cease! I cannot allow that tragedy to breed its endless progeny of pain. I must choose the straight way before me, walking one step at a time in what I know is right. And one thing I know to be right, is not to lay the burden of this child on Eleanor."

"Then you will not claim the girl?"

"I cannot. Nevertheless, I have no fear for Ella's happiness. She will be well-served by her grandfather, for she will have everything Branold can give her, barring a name." He had been pacing as he spoke, but now he stopped and shook his head with amusement. "Yet even that they seemed to have already considered. When I left, Lady Sophie was chattering away about grafting another name to the Bestilden tree."

He resumed walking, then once again stopped short. "You know, Raynar, that since I learned of Terlinden's plans I have been praying for a sign to direct me in my choice. Much to my amazement, it would seem these prayers have been answered, for now my path is clear."

"I would not see it thus!" answered Raynar, unable to follow Sebastian's logic.

"A loyalty greater than all others presses me now. A loyalty to my daughter. Though I cannot claim her, I must protect her. From this day forward I may only serve her grandfather, Gildren. And Gildren serves only the king."

He paused and gave his head a single, swift shake. "It is passing strange, but now that I have chosen, I wonder that I wrestled so. How could I ever have considered Duke Gebbard's plan? Is Lothar not our truly anointed king? Did he not receive the crown in full accordance with the law and the will of the barons? Did the archbishop himself not crown Lothar, and the pope send his blessing? For what reason, save for the purpose of his own gain, would Terlinden put young Stefan on the throne by violence?"

"That has been reason enough for many men."

"Not for me. No longer." Sebastian spoke with the spirit and determination of a man who at last knew his own mind. "Are you with me on this?"

Raynar's broad grin warned Sebastian that he was about to be pilloried by his wit. "As always. And, I think you are right about the child. Truly she will be better served to have no father than to learn that the one she has, has committed nearly every mortal sin."

"There is that," Sebastian admitted. "But we must dwell on this no longer for there are more urgent matters at hand. Somehow, we must forestall Terlinden in his treason."

"That is simple enough. Go to the king tonight."

"It would not stop the bloodshed."

"But it would not be your blood."

"You are wrong. We do not bleed only when we are pricked. Before this night is over, we must seek a way to prevent this folly without alerting the king. I have no desire to feed the executioner."

"But Terlinden is guilty. He deserves to die."

"And which of us is not? If we all received true justice, there would be none left living in this world."

As Sebastian spoke he looked up at the waxing moon. His tensions eased as he gazed at the glorious array of stars. Their very existence seemed such a miracle. How could it be that in the daylight, when the sun blazes in its brightness, men walk the earth in full confidence that they see all that is to be seen? It is only when the light is withdrawn that the vast depths of the heavens are revealed. What else lies hidden to the eyes of men?

What else indeed? His thoughts swung back to Terlinden. It would seem that for many years he had known the man only in the daylight. Sebastian turned to Raynar.

"We cannot know all of Terlinden's plans, but he has revealed to us more than he ought. He intends to slay Henry during the tournament and then in the ensuing confusion—before his traitorous intentions are understood—to murder the king in the royal pavilion. Of course, the others will die soon after. There must be a way to stop him! But how? If I confront him, he may simply act in greater stealth, yet we have not enough men of Westfeld here at Newravenstein to stand against him in battle."

"Do you seek battle tomorrow, then?"

"No! I seek to prevent it. If we must have war then let us have it in the open fields, with the women and children safe in their homes."

Raynar stood quiet for a moment, then asked, "How well do you trust Gildren's nephew, Gregory?"

"Not with my life, if that's what you are asking."

"But with Eleanor's? And Henry's?"

Sebastian thought of all he knew of his wife's cousin, duke of Marre by inheritance and lord of Tourant by marriage. "Yes. Of that I am certain."

"Could you trust him with the task of guarding Eleanor and the children?"

"I could. Have you a plan?"

"Perhaps. Come, Sebastian, we will walk and talk. By morning, God willing, we will be ready."

It was nearly cocks-crow before Sebastian returned to his chamber. Barely had he closed the door behind him when the maid entered to waken her mistress as she had been commanded. With a motion of his hand, Sebastian dismissed her. "It will not be necessary, Hannah. We are not leaving this morning." He kept his voice low. "Return to your own bed and take your rest while you may."

When she had gone, he moved to the window where, alone, he stood and watched the arrival of the dawn.

# Chapter 29

I T'S AN AMBUSH." Sebastian indicated yet another pair of
Terlinden's soldiers, lounging near the royal pavilion. "Without
a doubt, they have weapons hidden beneath their cloaks."

Raynar agreed. "If those others in the dun tunics are also in the game, the
king will quickly be overtaken."

"Do not speak thus! If we hold fast, we can win this day. We will place our
men with care, but unlike Terlinden, will not disguise their presence. They
will wear my colors openly and stand to arms. Let Gebbard understand that
he has not yet been betrayed but that I will fight him if he pushes the match
too far. The fool thinks himself a kingmaker; but I swear to you, Raynar, that
Stefan will never sit on Lothemia's throne." Sebastian spoke with more assurance than he felt. He was beginning to question whether it was forbear-
ance which led him to attempt a bloodless defeat of Terlinden, or arrogance.
Would it not be better, even now, to go to the king with his knowledge and
let justice take its inevitable course?

But he could not do it. Once before, when faced with a perilous choice,
he had betrayed a man. If he had not so readily buckled beneath his father's
threats, perhaps the misery of the following years would have been averted.
Perhaps, even, Katrina would yet be alive. Though he had been fortunate to
find happiness with Eleanor, he would not willingly tread that path again.

The procession leading Prince Henry and his companions from the chapel to the jousting field, had finished winding its way down the hill. The trumpets now sounded their fanfare, and the crowd slowly melted its way back behind the wooden rails. Before long, the dubbing ceremony would begin.

Still alert to the movements of Terlinden's men, Sebastian and Raynar made their way to the pavilion which sported the eagles of Westfeld on its banners. The tenting, woven of cloth dyed black and red and gold, covered a wooden platform, luxuriously appointed. Servitors, attired in Westfeld's livery, awaited with platters heaped with food kept chilled by mountain ice. Guards, with daggers in their belts and swords in their sheaths, paced back and forth—but these men wore the badge of Gregory of Marre. Eleanor also was there, seated with her ladies and surrounded by her five youngest children.

At their approach, she raised her brows in inquiry. Sebastian nodded in return to reassure her that all was in readiness and then he pointed to the vacant stool at her side. "Who sits here, my lady? You know I intend to ride in the tourney today."

Her look of worry lifted. "It's for Ella. The child will join us soon. Since Grandmama has openly declared her a scion of the house of Bestilden, I am her nearest relative of the blood. She is officially under our protection." She smiled as she met his eyes with confidence. "I trust this meets your approval?"

"Of course it does." More than she would ever know. Though he'd only had one glimpse of the girl who was his daughter, he already loved her well. And that in itself was cause for wonder—neither Arthur nor James had ever truly touched his heart. Was it Ella's beauty? He thought not. After all, Mariel's blazing beauty left him cold while his little Maria's quirked-up nose brought him nothing but delight.

"Where is she?" he asked, hoping that his interest was not too keenly written on his face.

"I believe that may be easily answered." Raynar grinned and pointed to Branold, who was approaching their pavilion with a young woman at his side.

Until that moment Sebastian thought he had plumbed all the varied depths of pain, but he learned now that he was wrong. At the sight of Ella, a new grief assailed him with the realization of all that he had missed in not knowing this most beloved daughter. Already she was a woman grown. The deep green bodice of her gown, tightly tied over a flowing yellow kirtle, subtly emphasized her curves; while beams of sunlight, catching the waves of her hair, turned her tresses into molten gold. She was alight with life and happiness. What joys had he missed by not knowing this child? And even more, what joys would he yet miss because he could not claim her as his own?

Raynar jabbed his elbow into Sebastian' side. "Can that radiant beauty be the child of which you speak?"

"Close your mouth, Raynar," Eleanor teased, as she stood up to greet Ella. "And stop staring."

Once more the fanfare rang out. "That call is for me," said Branold. "I must attend to my duties as host of these events. It would not do to keep the king waiting." Cupping his fingers around Ella's palm, he handed her up the step to Eleanor, though he was hampered by his youngest granddaughter who had grabbed hold of his leg. Beaming down at the infant, he tousled her curls while he continued to speak to Eleanor. "I have just presented Ella to Isabel and the girls, now you must do the honors for the rest, including these little imps. But if you value my advice at all, Eleanor, then do not yet acquaint her with Sir Raynar. The poor fellow's eyes are bulging so wide, she may think he has swallowed a frog."

Raynar grinned; but then as Branold left, he tipped his head towards the pavilion of Gildren. "Though we jest of Ella's beauty, I cannot but wonder what the haughty Mariel thinks of her new relative. It comes to my mind that Branold will soon see his kitten with her claws unsheathed."

"Doubtless he will meet the challenge and come away with the victory." Sebastian's eyes did not leave Ella.

"Think you so?" asked Raynar, with some surprise. "He has never clipped Isabel's wings!"

"And why should he? Surely you know, Raynar, that there is more than one way to tame a falcon; and it is most beautiful when it is flying free. If Isabel could fly only at her lord's command, I doubt she would long retain either his affection or his interest."

Eleanor drew Ella close to her side. "My lord husband, may I present to you, Ella, of Bestilden." Her eyes, brilliantly lit, moved from Sebastian to Ella—and back to Sebastian once more. And then she paled and dropped her hand.

"I am pleased to make your acquaintance, Fraulein Ella." For a moment Sebastian was distracted by Eleanor's ashen face, but he was too beguiled by his daughter's glowing presence to think on it more. "Are you enjoying the festivities which Lord Branold has provided for us all?"

Ella nodded, though only briefly met his gaze. "It is more wonderful than ever I imagined, my lord."

"That is enough speech," Eleanor said, with surprising gruffness as she grabbed Ella's arm and pulled her away from Sebastian.

Amazed, he opened his mouth to protest her ungentle behavior but a long and intricate fanfare from a dozen trumpets now blared out in a thrilling call. As the crowd stilled, Prince Henry and his twelve companions stepped forward. Dressed in tunics of purest white overlaid with purple cloaks, they knelt before the king and spoke their vows of submission; pledging their swords to the protection of widows and orphans, to the defense of the Church, and to the fight against evildoers wherever they might be found.

Flushed with the pride of parenthood, King Lothar now completed the ceremony which had begun the night before. He buckled the mailed cuirass across Henry's breast, clasped the jeweled bawdrick around his waist, attached the gilded spurs to his heels, and placed the finely-tempered sword into his hands. Then, having ordered his son to kneel before him, Lothar touched Henry on the neck with his own sword, and called out, "Henry, I dub thee knight!"

A roar of approval rose up from the spectators, continuing louder as the prince stood, tall and proud and beautiful. With perfect timing, Henry raised his own arm high and opened his fingers wide, demanding silence from the crowd—though the ringing cheers continued to echo off the surrounding mountains for some time. When all was at last still, he approached the pavilion of Gildren.

"My lord and lady," he hailed Branold and Isabel and bowed to their three daughters. "I recall that I am to have the honor of choosing a maiden to wear a circlet of gold and to sit as an honored guest in the royal pavilion."

"You are correct, my prince," Lord Branold answered as he pointed to the coronet lying on a tasseled cushion. "I have here at the ready, the crown. Now, Sir Henry, name the fortunate fraulein."

"I name Ella, of Bestilden."

Lady Isabel's hand flew to her face, but Branold beamed his pleasure.

Fearing that his own pride must shine too clearly, Sebastian turned aside and stared into the crowd. And then he froze, for there stood Terlinden's men, shouting their cheers as loudly as their fellows, raising their traitorous voices in praises of their prince. But soon they would throw aside their smiles and draw their blades—and Ella would be in the very midst of their attack! Even now, Prince Henry was taking her by the hand and leading her to the royal pavilion. With all of Terlinden's soldiers ready to attack at their lord's behest, his daughter was now an innocent hostage to this day's events.

The crowd roared and the trumpeter blew a fanfare which echoed off the castle walls and across the hills, and as though the call were a challenge, Sebastian's will strengthened. He would fight today for the right and just cause of the king, for the honor of Westfeld and the security of his people, for Eleanor, and for the children. He would fight for all these—and much more. Today, as he answered Terlinden's summons to combat, he would fight for Katrina. For Ella. For love.

The ceremonies complete, it was time at last for the tournament to begin. As the herald called the roll, the knights from each household paraded before the throng then announced for which side their menage would fight: for the chevrons of Terlinden or the ravens of Gildren.

Gregory of Marre, resplendently attired and bearing high his banner with the quartered raven and cock, removed his helmet as he marched past his uncle of Gildren and tossed him an impish grin. The reason for his mirth soon was made clear, for much to everyone's amazement, Gregory announced that Marre would fight with Terlinden. "Victory would be far too easy, were we to stand together, Uncle," he called out. "Of what worth is success if not gained with difficulty?"

Then Sebastian stepped forward with his men, a proud troop in red, black, and gold. It was time to cross the Rubicon and he did not hesitate. Holding himself tall, he called out in a voice that would carry far in the wind, "Westfeld stands with Prince Henry." He paused, but only long enough to be certain that his words had been heard. "Excuse my faltering tongue. Westfeld will stand and fight with Gildren."

Although Sebastian could not fully see Terlinden's face, the duke's reaction was plain enough; tearing a gauntlet off his hand, Terlinden cast it to the ground.

The two armies now gathered on either end of the field. The tension in the air was caused by anticipation, not fear, for in this game of war the enemy was vanquished and ransom was won without the deliberate shedding of blood. While the knights eyed one another across the expanse, marking their intended conquests, Sebastian scanned the perimeter to make certain that all his defenses were in readiness. Men of Westfeld were placed, two by two, at intervals around the wooden barrier, while Gregory's men were positioned near Eleanor and the children. Meeting Gregory's eyes, he gave a slight nod. All was in readiness. Now the true battle would begin.

The silence was broken by the shrill notes of a trumpet. Battle cries were raised and the horses charged across the meadow. The first clash in the center of the field was more for the amusement of the spectators than for any serious intent. Only one knight fell from his horse and, as no one attempted his capture, the man remounted and joined his companions. With shouts and cheers, the knights raced through the lists and out onto the open plain. Here, the melee began in earnest.

As the battle ranged across the fields, Sebastian and Raynar made no attempt to take any captives. Instead, they persisted on either side of Prince Henry while other knights from Westfeld held positions close-at-hand, forming a phalanx through which all attackers needed to force their way. And even though many of those attackers were men of Marre, who fought with little energy, guarding Henry was no easy task. The young knight was eager to prove his worth and achieve acclaim, and as the afternoon progressed made continuous forays into the depths of the enemy's lines. His frustration at the security which hemmed him in, grew steadily greater, and his temper began to flare.

Though Sebastian dared not let up on his defense, he worried that the prince might turn his anger against his companions-in-arms. Using the broad side of his sword, Sebastian continued to battle fiercely, especially against those who bore Terlinden's badge. Sweat poured down his face, stinging his eyes and scalding his vision. Nearly demented in his determination to prevent Henry from being cut down, he ignored his discomfort. He was certain that as long as the prince lived, those in the pavilion were safe: It was with Henry's death that the bloodshed would begin. Twisted though Terlinden was in his desire for power, he was too canny a general to risk leaving his rear uncovered. Henry must be the first to die. It was the only way that Terlinden could hope for success. No son—and definitely not this one—would allow the murder of his family to go unrevenged.

"Sebastian!"

Responding immediately to the warning in Raynar's voice, Sebastian turned and saw a knight, sporting the chevrons of Terlinden, break through the guard and raise his sword to Henry. With a cry of rage, Sebastian spurred his horse forward and struck out with a mortal blow. Lifeless now, the man fell from his horse, landing in an undignified heap on the ground.

Around them the battle momentarily ceased; Prince Henry glared at Sebastian in accusation. "Your sword was not blunted, my lord duke."

"You speak true." While Gregory edged near, Sebastian dismounted and went to the fallen knight. Carefully releasing the sword from the dead man's hand, he held it out to the prince. "But look—neither was his."

Prince Henry paled. "How did you know?"

"I am an old knight. I have lived long because I have learned to be observant. I know when to turn my weapon and I know when to thrust it without mercy. May I suggest, prince, that it is time you leave the field? You have acquitted yourself well, and I would not like more blood to be shed on this day." As he spoke, Sebastian pointed to the sharpened tip of the sword.

Henry frowned as he tried to read the meaning behind Sebastian's words. "I will leave the field," he finally answered, as he yielded his sword to Gregory. "Though I will forfeit the chance to win the prize."

"My prince..." Sebastian measured his words in a slow, deliberate pace. "That depends which prize it is you seek."

While Prince Henry was led away to Gregory's tent to arrange the details of his ransom—and to be guarded by the men of Marre—the body of the dead knight was carried from the field and laid out of the sun under an awning. Like many of the children, fifteen-year old Prince Stefan came to see the body, but unlike the others he did not gape and tease but stood apart with a frown creasing his brow.

Sebastian's relief that the rebellion had been thwarted, made his anger the more potent. He was appalled by the blood which had very nearly been spilt, and was determined to call both Duke Gebbard and his protégé to account for their intended treason. As the afternoon passed and the knights returned one by one leading their captives, Sebastian watched as Stefan continued to stand aloof. Once, Eleanor's young sister, Ailsa, approached the prince as though to entice him to come sit under the pavilion, but Stefan only shook his head and waved her away. Not until the tourney was all but over did he move. With purpose in his stride he walked along the wooden lists toward Terlinden—and Sebastian followed.

"My lord of Terlinden," Stefan called out to his foster-father. "And my lord of Westfeld. I desire words with you both, if you would come to me."

Terlinden hesitated to come forward but Sebastian had no reluctance at all. Feet apart in challenge, he faced the young prince. And when Stefan held out his hand in greeting, Sebastian only scowled in reply.

"I wish to thank you for saving my cousin's life," Stefan said, ignoring Sebastian's rudeness. "I climbed a hillock some distance away and watched the tourney closely. I saw how tenaciously you held by my cousin's side and how quickly you responded to the threat against him. Indeed, your actions gave me pause. Is it possible, my lord, that you knew of some plot against his life?"

Duke Gebbard paled and laid his hand on Stefan's arm, but Stefan ignored his foster-father's silent plea. "You need not answer," he continued speaking to Sebastian. "When the slain man was laid out, I chanced to see the arms on his sleeve. They looked very familiar but I could not quite place them, being no expert on heraldry myself." As he said this, Stefan turned to Gebbard with feigned innocence, for it was certain that he would recognize the badge of his foster-father as easily as his own. "Suspecting I had witnessed an attempted assassination, I pondered the purpose and concluded that someone was plotting to kill the king, my own uncle, and crown me instead. But could I ..." Stefan held Terlinden in his gaze. Though he spoke gently, his underlying threat was plain. "Could I then, as king, condone regicide? Impossible! My first act would surely have been to execute the perpetrators." Stefan bowed to Sebastian. "So, I thank you for your timely intervention, my lord. I thank you for my cousin's life, and I consider myself in your debt." Giving no time for further comment, Prince Stefan spun around on his heels and walked away.

An elation filled Sebastian. The insurrection was not only over but need never be feared again, for Stefan had never been a party to the intrigue! Though Henry must surely have his suspicions—and would perhaps in time learn all—the king would never know of the true battle which had been waged here today.

Smiling broadly, he thumped Terlinden on his shoulder and exclaimed, "So that is the end. Let this be a lesson to us both that age does not always bring wisdom. That prince, young as he is, is a better man than either of us have ever been." Then he left, without lingering to see or hear Terlinden's response.

Sebastian could scarcely wait to share the news with Eleanor. He knew her relief would be even greater than his own, for she had been forced to sit and await events while he at least had been able to direct his fear into action. After a quick circuit of the pavilions assured him that she was not here on the field, he made his way back up the hill to the castle, with a lightness of spirit he had not felt for many a long day.

Raynar was lounging outside Eleanor's door, and Sebastian smiled in greeting. "Is she within? I have the best of news!"

"Did you accost Terlinden as planned?" Raynar asked, though he did not move from where he leaned against the wall.

"I did. He is utterly defeated in his purposes. Never again will he be able to raise his banner against the king—at least not on Stefan's behalf. The boy has made it very clear that he will never support any treason against his uncle, the king."

"I don't understand. Was he not part of the plot?"

"It would seem he was not. Terlinden must have assumed that he could easily bend the will of his ward once the insurrection was an accomplished fact. I wonder if it ever occurred to him that Stefan—or anyone—would refuse the throne? We have achieved our bloodless victory, Raynar. The king is safe, and so is Westfeld."

Raynar tilted his head and raised one brow. "You do care about Westfeld."

"Is that so hard to believe?"

"You have not always felt thus. Indeed, there was a time when you would have gladly abandoned Westfeld and all the responsibility it encompasses."

Though it stung to hear such words, Sebastian could not deny their truth. "Then let me leave you in no doubt on this matter. I love Westfeld with all the passion within me—my wife, my children, my people, my land— my heart's blood beats for them all. I can only pray that you, too, will someday be as fortunate as I, and receive all you desire."

"I already have, my friend. I already have. And to that end I have been waiting here, so that I may bid you farewell."

Sebastian stepped back in astonishment. "Surely, you jest!" But Raynar's eyes blazed with such rare intensity that Sebastian knew he did not. "You cannot mean to go now. We have been together so little, after so long."

"You speak the truth, and I shall miss you," Raynar said, yet with nary a trace of regret in his voice. "Nevertheless, I am determined."

Although it was evident that he spoke in earnest, Sebastian could scarce believe him. This made no sense at all. "What has happened, Raynar? Tell me why you go!"

"You will understand soon enough, I promise you that. Though I may tell you nothing more just yet, you must believe that the path I now take, I take willingly, with full knowledge of what I do. And speaking of promises," he added. "I beg one from you."

"You know you need not ask."

"Ah, but I do."

"Then ask."

"I want you to promise to be a husband to Eleanor."

Sebastian raised his brows, then smiled. "You know my thoughts on that matter, and you need no promise from me. I choose to be bound to Eleanor in all the ways of husband and wife. Never again will I stray from her side."

"Nevertheless, I want you to swear by the walls of Eaglesheid and by the blood of your sons."

"That I will be a husband to Eleanor?" Sebastian was astounded that Raynar should be so insistent.

"No matter what the future brings."

"To please you, I swear by every stone in the walls of Eaglesheid and by the blood of my sons—all of them—that I will be a husband to Eleanor, now and in the future. The best that I am able."

Raynar beamed. "Good! Now, fare thee well, Sebastian. Go in and see to your wife. She is waiting for you."

He started to move away but Sebastian clasped his forearm. "You truly mean to leave? Just like that?"

"It is time."

For a brief moment, Raynar met Sebastian's eyes. Then he repeated, "Fare thee well, my friend."

"Come back soon, Raynar. You are needed here."

Raynar did not answer but strode away, whistling.

After this puzzling encounter, Sebastian was not surprised to find Eleanor distraught. Standing by the window, in silence, her face was wet with tears. He crossed the room in swift strides and drew her into his arms. For many minutes he stood, holding her while she sobbed, quiet no longer. Then he whispered in reassurance, "Doubtless he will return soon."

"Who?"

"Raynar, of course."

"Return soon?" She pushed him away and vehemently cried, "I pray not! You mistake my tears. I sent Raynar away! And I commanded him never to stand before me again."

"Eleanor! Why?"

"He is a wolf in a sheepskin! A demon with a halo! Do you have any idea what he has done?"

"None." He did not hide his bewilderment. "He said only that he has chosen his path."

"And I hope that path leads so far away that he never finds his way back."

"Eleanor," Sebastian tried to soothe her as he hid his shock. "Please tell me what he has done."

She tucked her head to her chin and looked to the floor. "First, I ask your forgiveness. I have wronged you greatly."

"How so?" Sebastian asked with more reluctance, for he was suddenly assailed by the memory of that long-ago day in Genoa when Raynar's confession had torn their friendship apart. Had his trust in Raynar once more been betrayed? Remembering his oath, he swallowed back the fury which began to rise within.

Still avoiding his eyes, she turned again to the window and gripped the sill. "Today, for a time, I thought you were Ella's father."

"What?" he gasped, in horror. A horror she completely misunderstood.

"I am truly sorry for the offense. It is just that ... well ... when you were standing at Ella's side ..." She stopped, as though confused. "I suppose it was her eyes which made me think it. I cannot say she is as like you as Arthur, but her eyes brought back memories and suddenly it all seemed so clear; from Katrina's fear for the life of her baby to your reaction to the news of her death. When I married you, Sebastian, you were but a wraith compared to the man who had ridden into Ravensberg bearing the treaty to free my father. I am sorry for my doubts. This afternoon, I truly despised you.

"Raynar saw the change in me." Her voice dripped with bitterness. "I suppose he thought that if I had turned against you, then he would now have a chance. At any rate, he wasted no time. He came to me after your victory on the field, and as usual I told him my fears. And do you know what he did? He laughed! He said that unless Katrina had been very abandoned in her favors, you could not be Ella's father. 'Is Sebastian the only man with brown eyes?' he said. 'Look at mine. Are they not brown also? Could I not be the child's father?' Then he laughed again and said that not only *could* he be, but that he presumed he *was*."

Fortunately, Eleanor's back was still turned and she could not see Sebastian's face, for he was unable to hide his dawning realization of what Raynar had done.

"He laughed aloud at the innocence of her trust." Eleanor's voice broke as she spun around and faced him with her misery. "Raynar used my sister like a cheap camp follower, then cast her aside and left her to her fate. How can it be that for all these years he has seemed so honorable? I despise him with all that I am."

Sebastian wrapped Eleanor within his arms and stroked her hair until she relaxed against him with a sigh. Then tightening his grasp, he shared with her his strength. From where he stood, looking out the window, he could see the gate with the portcullis raised in welcome. Soon Raynar would be riding out. He would be gone.

"Be a husband to Eleanor," he had said, binding Sebastian with a terrible oath.

Tears filled Sebastian's eyes. Silently, he murmured, "I will, my friend. I will." Then tenderly, gratefully, he turned her face to his, and kissed her.

# Epilogue

THE BITING WIND of a winter storm had forced Sir Raynar to seek shelter in this cheerless refuge. The air was heavy with the taste and smell of three hundred years of dampness, mitigated only by the acrid sting of smoke.

Beside him on the hearth sat a man, old like himself, shivering with ague, who claimed lordship of this pile of rocks. The poor fellow had provided such comforts as he could to his unexpected guest, but could not give what he did not have.

"My lord," Raynar spoke, hoping to allay some of the brooding oppression of this place. "I wish to repay your hospitality. Perhaps you would like a song? Or a story? I have some renown amongst the minnesingers."

"You owe nothing for the little I have given you, Sir Raynar," his host replied, abashed at his poverty.

"On the contrary. I would have perished tonight had you not given me succor."

"Sir Raynar." There was a tug on his sleeve and, turning, he smiled at the child.

"Yes, pretty one?"

"Would you tell a story? It is all right, Grandpapa, is it not, if he tells a story?"

The old man shrugged, as he futilely tried to pull his cloak tighter. "If he wishes, Anna."

"Then gather around and I will tell you a tale." Raynar stood, stamped his feet to warm them, and asked, "What kind of story would you like, Anna? A story of dragons? Or questing?"

"Tell us about a beautiful princess!" The child asked, more bravely now.

"A beautiful princess?" A faraway look came into Raynar's eyes and he beheld in his mind's eye Ella, as she had stood in the sunbeams that first time he had seen her. "If I am to tell you the tale of a princess, then I will need to start at the very beginning, even before she was born."

"Oh please, start at the beginning. Please tell us the whole story!"

Raynar smiled, then began to speak. "Once, not so long ago, lived two beautiful sisters with a vile and selfish stepmother. This evil woman despised them so much that she made them work, very hard, though there were servants enough in their home. They washed the dishes, scrubbed the stairways and swept away the rushes in the hall. Even this was not enough for their stepmother. She refused to allow them fine garments to wear, and soon their clothes were in tatters.

"Now these two daughters were both very beautiful—the most beautiful in all the world—and the king of the eagles, looking down from high, took pity on their plight. After soaring across the forests and fields, he swooped down early one morning and gently clasped them up into his mighty claws. Placing them on his great wings he bore them away to the safety of his mountain top. One loved him dearly, and lived with him happily all the days of her life, but the other became frightened and fled his home, returning to her own hearth. There she had a child. A daughter—"

"The princess?" Anna interrupted, clutching at Raynar's fist in her excitement.

"Yes, little one. She was the princess. And her name was Ella. The most beautiful child you have ever seen, with hair so golden that it was worth more than all the kingdoms in the world, and a voice so sweet that the birds would flock to her every morning, just to hear her sing. But poor Ella grew up an orphan in her own home, and like her mother, cleaned the cinders from the hearth—

—and so, wearing the jeweled slippers, Ella married the prince, whom she loved well."

A snore from the host punctuated the end of the tale. Quietly, Raynar sent away his listeners, then curled up beside the fire where, warmed by his memories, he slept.